Samuel Butler

The Life and Letters of Dr. Samuel Butler

Headmaster of Shrewsbury School 1798-1836

Samuel Butler

The Life and Letters of Dr. Samuel Butler
Headmaster of Shrewsbury School 1798-1836

ISBN/EAN: 9783744688789

Printed in Europe, USA, Canada, Australia, Japan

Cover: Foto ©Raphael Reischuk / pixelio.de

More available books at **www.hansebooks.com**

Dr. Samuel Butler

THE

LIFE AND LETTERS OF

DR. SAMUEL BUTLER,

HEAD-MASTER OF SHREWSBURY SCHOOL 1798—1836,
AND AFTERWARDS BISHOP OF LICHFIELD

IN SO FAR AS THEY ILLUSTRATE

THE SCHOLASTIC, RELIGIOUS, AND SOCIAL

LIFE OF ENGLAND, 1790—1840.

BY HIS GRANDSON,

SAMUEL BUTLER,

AUTHOR OF "EREWHON," "THE TRAPANESE ORIGIN OF THE ODYSSEY," ETC.

VOL. I.

JAN. 30, 1774—MARCH 1, 1831.

LONDON:

JOHN MURRAY, ALBEMARLE STREET.

1896.

PREFACE.

THE following work was begun in 1889, and was completed in its original form by the summer of 1894. I was then so generally advised that it was too long that in the summer and autumn of 1895 I reduced it by about a third, and left it with Mr. Murray in November 1895.

The length of time during which the work has been in progress must be accounted for firstly by the great bulk of the correspondence that came into my hands, and the difficulty of finding the due dates of many undated letters. Moreover I was deflected from it by the pressure put upon me to write my book *Ex Voto*, on the Sacro Monte of Varallo, and by some researches into the topography and authorship of the *Odyssey*, the fascination of which I found it impossible to resist. To these delightful studies—hardly, however, to myself more delightful than those which I am now leaving—I hope immediately to return.

When my sisters, Mrs. G. L. Bridges and Miss Butler, presented me with almost all Dr. Butler's papers, I did not at first realise the importance of keeping the collection as far as possible together, and gave away some few to

friends as autographs. Some of the drafts, again, I found
so much cancelled and rewritten that I thought it better
to copy the final state of the draft and destroy the
original. I also destroyed, with the approval of the
authorities of the British Museum (but never without
this), any letters the preservation of which might cause
pain without serving any useful purpose, or again, which
were deemed not worth the acceptance of the Museum.
The rest I gave to the British Museum, and left those
in charge of the National Collection to decide what
letters should be made accessible to the public, and
what should be, at any rate for the present, kept
back.

I may say here, therefore, that all letters or documents
given in my book are in the British Museum, unless it
is stated otherwise at the head of the letter. It may
save readers the trouble of hunting in the index if I
give the numbers of the volumes for which they should
write if they desire to see the original of any given
letter, or to search for any letters they may hope to
find. The volumes are numbered as follows :—

Vol.	Additional MSS.
I., 1764—1813 .	34583
II., 1814—1819 .	34584
III., 1820—March 1825	34585
IV., April 1825—end of 1827	34586
V., 1828—1830 .	34587
VI., 1831—1833 .	34588
VII., 1834—1835 .	34589
VIII., 1836 .	34590
IX., 1837—June 30th, 1838	34591

N.B.—In every case "Additional MSS." must be on the ticket.

Very few letters reached me from other sources than the one I have indicated above. I should, however, thank Bishop Barry (as representing the family of the Rev. T. S. Hughes), the Rev. Walter Scott, son of the late Dean of Rochester, the Rev. J. Irvine of Colchester, and J. Willis Clark, Esq., for the loan of letters, some of which will follow in due order of date.

The reader is requested to bear in mind that this work is intended to show the scholarship and the philology of the time, so far as they have come before me in Dr. Butler's papers. I am aware that much of the philology will be held to be of no present interest; its interest, however, as showing the state of this science at the beginning of the century, seems, at any rate to myself, considerable. As regards letters connected neither with scholarship nor education, I have selected them almost exclusively on the ground of their livingness and the interest attaching to the personality of the writer. If the personality has attracted me, as in the case of Dr.

James, Mr. Tillbrook, Baron Merian, and half a score of men and women whose names are now utterly unknown, I have given letters, though they contained little or nothing about either scholarship or education.

I have to express my thanks to Professor J. E. B. Mayor for much assistance given me in the course of my work. The account of Dr. Butler given in the second volume of his invaluable edition of Baker's *History of St. John's* is so full as regards quotations from Dr. Butler's works, that I have been left free to pass these over much more briefly than I should otherwise have done, and to devote my space principally to MS. documents, the existence of which was probably as unknown to Professor Mayor as it was to myself until they fell into my hands. I have also to thank Mr. Prebendary Moss, the present Head-Master of Shrewsbury School, for the warm interest he has shown in the work and its progress, though I should perhaps state that he has only actually seen a small part of it.

I would also express my sense of deep obligation to Mr. John Murray, who has read the sheets with great care, and called my attention to many slips, omissions, and inadvertencies, besides supplying me with information which I could not otherwise have obtained.

As regards the accentuation of Greek words, I believe I may say that when the reader finds the accents omitted or wrong, if he will be good enough to turn to the original MS., he will find that I have followed it faithfully. At first I found it irresistible occasionally to add an accent, or to correct one ; but before long I was advised that it would be a sounder course in a work that aims at being historical to let the accents, for better or worse, stand as I found them. I could not bring myself, however, to take out those I had put in, or to vitiate the few that I had corrected ; Dr. Butler in his drafts has generally omitted them, but when he gives them he always does so correctly.

Lastly, I would caution the reader against confusing the three Dr. Butlers who have all been eminent as school-masters. They are :—

1. Dr. Samuel Butler, Head-Master of Shrewsbury, 1798—1836.

2. Dr. George Butler, Head-Master of Harrow, 1805—1829.

3. Dr. H. Montagu Butler, Head-Master of Harrow, Christmas 1859—1885, and present Master of Trinity College, Cambridge.

The two Dr. Butlers of Harrow were father and son, but there was no relationship between them and Dr. Samuel Butler.

SAMUEL BUTLER.

February 25th, 1896.

P.S.—Since writing the foregoing I have heard with very great regret of the death of my cousin Archdeacon Lloyd, more than once referred to in the following pages as though he were still living.

March 3rd, 1896.

CONTENTS OF VOL. I.

LIST OF ILLUSTRATIONS.

VOL. I.

INTRODUCTION.

SOME few years ago I was asked to write a memoir of my grandfather, Dr. Butler of Shrewsbury, for the Transactions of the Shropshire Archæological and Natural History Society, of which Dr. Butler was the first president ; and shortly afterwards I was placed in possession of the very voluminous correspondence which Dr. Butler had left behind him. On going through this I found so much that threw light upon public school education at the end of the last and in the earlier years of the present century, that I abandoned my original design for the work I now venture to lay before the public.

Having been led to inquire into the facts of Dr. Butler's life, I turned to Professor J. E. B. Mayor's well-known edition of Baker's *History of St. John's*,* in which the fullest account of Dr. Butler heretofore published is to be found, and was arrested by the following paragraph ascribed by Professor Mayor to Dr. Robert Scott, formerly Master of Balliol, and afterwards Dean of Rochester :—

" Bishop Butler has gone to his rest, after such severe and protracted suffering as would have paralysed a less energetic mind. He has gone full of labours and honours though not of years. And yet it is to be feared that he has gone with much of his merit unappreciated. If, however, it be reasonable to suppose that the education of the higher classes, and especially of the clergy, is at least as important as that of the poor, and if the silent but most practical reformation which has been at work in our public schools

* Cambridge, 1869.

[1]

for many years ever attracts the notice it deserves, then the time will come when men will take an interest in tracing the steps of the improvement; and they will hardly fail to give honour due to that scholar who first set the example in remodelling our public education, and gave a stimulus which is now acting on almost all the public schools in the country." (*Quarterly Review*, September 1842.)

I had not known that Dr. Butler's influence was so wide or so important, and, on going through the letters addressed to him, was a good deal surprised at finding how completely the facts bore out what Dr. Scott had written. Dr. Monk, Bishop of Gloucester, for example, on hearing of Dr. Butler's intended resignation, wrote :—

"There is nothing in scholastic history which can be fairly compared with your career except that of Busby, and he did not, like you, find a school with only a single scholar. I am sorry that it has never happened to me to have an opportunity of expressing publicly how much in my opinion the cause of good education owes to you." (December 12th, 1835.)

It is possible that many a head-master since Dr. Butler's time has wished that he too could have "found his school with only a single scholar."

Mr. Drury of Harrow wrote :—

"In common with all who have the slightest love for, or pretence to, literature, your secession from Shrewsbury is the cause of my regret. The advance of learning among the young has decidedly, at all English schools of any note, generally taken its impulse from you, and where it has not, as at Westminster, the decadence has been doleful. Whatever Eton and Harrow may be, I can safely say they would not have reached even any moderate excellence if you had not been the agitator." (December 29th, 1835.)

Dr. Longley, afterwards Archbishop of Canterbury, and at that time just resigning the head-mastership of Harrow on his appointment to the See of Ripon, wrote :—

"We may mutually felicitate each other on approaching relief from our arduous duties; but I will not presume to compare my

own feelings on the occasion with those of one whose long and
most honourable career has been distinguished by a degree of
splendour and success unrivalled in the history of public schools."
(March 14th, 1836.)

Dr. Longley, on his appointment to Harrow, had come
to Shrewsbury in company with Mr. Drury, and had
attended a lesson to hear Dr. Butler's manner with the
boys. Dr. Butler alluded casually to this circumstance
in a first draft of the letter to the Master and Fellows of
St. John's announcing his intended resignation, but he put
his pen through the passage, and in the second draft of the
same letter there is no reference to an incident pleasing in
itself, and honourable both to Dr. Longley and Dr. Butler.

That Dr. Butler did sometimes let distinguished aliens
attend his lessons appears from the letter to the Master and
Fellows of St. John's just referred to, but he is careful to
explain that he never permitted this except in the case of
first-rate scholars.

Dr. Parr, indeed, if I may rely upon an excellent article
that appeared in *Blackwood* for April 1866, was allowed
not only to assist in rehearsing the boy's speeches, but,
horresco referens, to smoke his pipe while doing so. The
writer does not say where he found this story, but his work
is so well done, and the story is so intrinsically probable,
that I accept it as far as the fact of Dr. Parr's smoking is
concerned; whether, however, it was Dr. Butler who
invited Dr. Parr to come and to smoke, or whether it
was Dr. Parr who would come and would smoke, is a point
which I would not presume to decide. According, indeed,
to the writer in *Blackwood*, it was not at a rehearsal of the
speeches, but at the speeches themselves, that Dr. Parr
smoked, and this is hardly possible. The words of the
article run :—

"On more than one speech-day, Dr. Parr, for whom Dr. Butler

had an intense respect, was present, sitting in the seat of honour next the Doctor, with his pipe in his mouth and his spittoon before him—an arrangement which, together with his buzz-wig (probably the last surviving specimen), attracted considerable attention from the boys. He was good enough to signify a gracious approval of some of the speakers by the quiet tapping of two fore-fingers of one hand on the palm of the other—an amount of applause which, as Butler assured the young performers, meant a great deal from so great a man."

Returning to the letters of Bishop Monk, Mr. Drury, and Dr. Longley, even after making allowance for the partiality of personal friendship, there is more in the extracts quoted than can be explained as mere politeness. In spite, however, of the unbounded respect with which Dr. Butler's character has inspired me, I should not have gone beyond my original intention but for the consideration mentioned by Dr. Scott—I mean the importance and interest of tracing the path of public school development during a time that has been left, comparatively speaking, unchronicled.   I found so many letters that threw light upon the public school life of the half-century between the years 1790 and 1835, that I resolved to bring together as much of Dr. Butler's correspondence as might be useful to a future and more exhaustive historian of the religious, scholastic, and social life of England between the years 1790 and 1840.

As regards the extract above given from Mr. Drury's letter, not knowing what reforms could be intended I consulted the late Professor Kennedy, and Dr. Welldon, formerly of Tunbridge, then, as I believed, the last survivors of those who had been masters under Dr. Butler. They told me Mr. Drury was referring to the introduction of half-yearly examinations into public schools, and to the moving of the boys in the sixth form according to the results of their examination. I have since seen the following extract from a letter by Dr. Kennedy, of which I was unaware till the Rev. George Sandford kindly called my attention to it :—

"Dr. Butler was, of course, an excellent scholar, and no ordinary teacher; but his crowning merit was the establishment of an emulative system, in which talent and industry always gained their just recognition in good examinations. This it was that made his school so successful and so great." (April 30th, 1887. Printed in *Shrewsbury Shreds and Patches*, February 1889.)

Given examinations at the universities, and examinations at the public schools that lead up to them seem now to follow as a matter of course, but the inference had not been drawn and acted upon till Dr. Butler drew it, and in the doing so, changed the face of public education all through the public schools of England, and hence throughout the world.

I am told that the examinations of a hundred years ago did not originate with the masters of any given school, and were not conducted by them, but by the patrons and visitors, with the object of examining not so much the boys as the masters, and finding out whether these last taught the boys or not. If, then, the boys failed in their examination, it was not they who were punished, but the masters—a practice the revival of which would be hailed with pleasure by not a few of our schoolboys. I gather that some of our foremost head-masters consider examinations to be at the present day overdone ; even they, however, would hardly wish to return to the system, or no system, universal in English schools before Dr. Butler's time, and dispense with examinations altogether. From Dr. Welldon I learned that it was the custom in public schools at the beginning of this century to let the boys in the sixth form move up by seniority, so that when once he was in the sixth a boy was stimulated neither by fear of falling nor hope of rising. Dr. Butler was the first to put a stop to this, and to make even his head boy stand or fall by the result of the half-yearly examinations. These, in his hands, served to formulate and articulate a spirit of emulation among boys as regards their school-work, which had hitherto been at best chaotic ; he thus produced an effect that will survive all changes in detail in the subjects taught.

I find him throughout his long career insisting to the under-masters, in letters of which he carefully preserved the drafts, that they should mark every lesson of every boy, and thus furnish him with a bird's-eye view of each boy's industry or idleness. When, as not infrequently happened, he saw what his practised eye told him were signs of careless marking, he remonstrated in a way that shows him to have made frequent reference to the mark-record of each individual boy. The following extract from one of these drafts may illustrate his method :—

To an Assistant Master.

"*October* 10*th*, 1818.

" Dear Sir,—The extraordinary pressure of business this morning between the trustee meeting and the merit money, left me not an instant from half-past seven till three to attend to the subject of your complaint about the boys who did not say Greek grammar. Their statement to me is that they had to learn the whole rules comprised between the paradigm of the active voice and the verb εἰμί, in which I cannot suppose they are correct, for it contains the most difficult eleven pages in the Greek grammar ; they add that they were not accustomed to say the whole of these rules at a lesson, but only certain marked parts of them. The latter is a very proper single lesson ; the former is as much as I should think of setting them at two lessons. The circumstances of their statement appearing to me in a very questionable light, I have made them known to you that I may get at the facts.

" I feel myself also under the necessity of requesting that you will be more particular with regard to your marks. I lay great stress upon them, being the only clue I have to understand the merits of the different boys, except what I can pick up from the monthly examinations, and I observe your marks are greatly at variance with mine on these occasions. I find you give almost always the same unvarying *w*, and keep the order of the names unaltered, when it would appear from my examinations that very different marks and different order should be given ; and on sending up to you a whole class which you had forgotten to mark this morning, I find the marks were put in by you at once, without hesitation and without reference to papers, which is an effort of discrimination I should by no means be equal to myself. On the contrary I weigh a boy's merit very cautiously before I put his mark, and often write out the list on merit-money days four times before I can decide on the comparative merits of boys. Whoever undertakes to teach a school properly will find it no sinecure. It requires patience, activity, and assiduity ; it must be paramount to all other engagements of pleasure or business : it always is so with me, and must be so with those gentlemen who assist me. By looking at the enclosed paper you will see the sort of remarks that are useful to me at all times, and especially on merit-money days.

"I told the boys of whom you complained this morning that I had not then time to enter into the complaint (which was the fact), and that I should notice it at a future opportunity ; but between ourselves I think the lesson was too long, as also was a punishment which you set the lower remove of the same form about a fortnight ago of nineteen pages of Greek grammar to write out, and then did not call for it. If so long a punishment is necessary it is better that the boy should be flogged at once."

*   *   *   *   *

There were two sets of marks, one for *vivâ-voce* lessons, and the other for exercises—the object being to show at a glance which class of work the marks referred to. For lessons the marks were *V* (very good), *W* (well), *w* (pretty well), *t* (tolerable), *i* (idle), and *b* (bad). For exercises the marks were an upright line and a cross on the right hand near the top, a plain upright line without cross, a short upright line ; these were the three degrees of goodness. The bad marks were an *i* with one dot, an *i* with two dots and very little body, and three dots one above the other with no body or part of an *i* beneath them.

A few days later than the letter last quoted, Dr. Butler wrote to the same master :—

"October 14th, 1818.

"DEAR SIR,—I had no complaint to make with regard to the

arrangement of the names in the shell, and I was always aware of the improbability that our marks should coincide. My remarks went to show that as a variety of marks was always the result of my examination of boys, so I should have expected that some variety of marks would be found in your weekly reports. I still think the lessons and the punishments too long, and must beg you to shorten them. Supposing a Greek grammar lesson to consist of four or five pages, which is as much as seems to me proper for a lesson, if well and correctly said, that quantity, or, if circumstances require it, the same in Latin and English, is in my opinion sufficient punishment. If longer are necessary the boy should be sent to be flogged."

*   *   *   *   *

I do not know whether boys used to be marked for every lesson of every day in other public schools, nor indeed whether they are so now. There is no reference either to marks or to examinations in the description of Rugby written by Dr. James to Mr. Butler when the latter went to Shrewsbury, and it is unlikely that in so detailed an account there should be no reference to them if they had been customary. Dr. Butler may, indeed, have over-estimated the uses of marks, as showing in tabular form whether a boy is working or not. This is generally apparent without them, and they can do nothing towards making his work interest him more profoundly. I imagine that the solicitude which made him insist much on marks had more to do with Dr. Butler's success than the marks themselves had, but I speak with great diffidence inasmuch as¹ it is plain Dr. Butler laid much stress upon them— perhaps as some kind of check on his under-masters.

As for the monthly merit money which again Dr. Butler evidently thought a useful incentive, I find Dr. James writing, " Have no merit money yet. Query if ever ? " from which, and from there being no reference to it in Dr. James's long letters about Rugby, I rather conclude this to have been an invention of Dr. Butler's own, and to have been looked upon by Dr. James as somewhat of a fad. My own experience was that it was small but seasonable.

Another important cause of Dr. Butler's success lay in the fact of his keeping himself in constant touch with the universities. The present Dean of Llandaff has told me he remembers hearing Dr. Wordsworth, then Master of Trinity, say (I gathered disparagingly): "Dr. Butler comes here year after year, just as a first-rate London milliner makes a yearly visit to Paris to get the fashions." I shall have occasion to show how much Dr. Butler distrusted those fashions, and how warily he exerted himself to make them more serviceable to his pupils; but the fashions being as they were, it was his duty to study them, and I have no doubt his pupils gained greatly by the persistence with which he visited both universities, and the vigilance with which he observed the set of academic opinion. And it should be remembered that a Christmas journey from Shrewsbury to Cambridge was not so easy in those days as it has now become.

But perhaps the main secret of his success lay in his unfailing good sense and admirable command of temper. It is too generally believed that the schoolmaster at the beginning of this century was even at best passionate, overbearing, three parts pedant and the fourth part bully; it seems to be accepted almost as a truism that no schoolmaster till comparatively modern times knew either how to treat boys like gentlemen or to be more than half a gentleman himself. I have seen articles about Dr. Butler (as the one in *Blackwood* already referred to) in which, in spite of manifest good-will towards him, it is taken as a matter of course that having been a schoolmaster he must have been choleric. I have had before me so many letters from so many eminent schoolmasters of the time, that I could easily show the general impression to have very little foundation. The head-master of a public school a hundred years ago was far more like the head-master of to-day than the Squire Western of Fielding was to a modern country gentleman. I shall give some minor letters from Dr. James that will nevertheless show the relations between a head-master and his upper boys to have been much what they now are. As for Dr. Butler himself, I had gathered from his letters that he was a man of singularly forbearing and equable temper, but to make certain I have particularly asked many of his old pupils whether his manner was choleric or not, and the almost unanimous answer has been that it was very difficult to put him out of temper. The late Professor Kennedy was surprised at my even asking such a question, and replied, " I never once saw Dr. Butler in a passion ; I never saw him lose his temper with a boy." Any head-master must always be formidable to a normal boy ; perfect love, we know, casteth out fear, but it must be more perfect than it is ever likely to be between a schoolboy and his master before it can do this, and a very imperfect amount of fear will cast out love ; I have satisfied myself, however, that Dr. Butler's manner with his boys was in general singularly genial, and free from anything that could flurry them.

As regards general supervision, the following extract will show that the view of his duties taken by a school-master seventy years ago was much what it is at present :—

To an Assistant Master and Former Pupil.

August (?), 1821.

*   *   *   *   *

" I avail myself also of this opportunity of mentioning to you what you must take in friendly part, as I certainly design it to be, but what I think essential to the welfare of the school, and the continuance of that good understanding which should subsist among us. I allude partly to what you said about your private pupils, as if a boy was to be left very much to himself, unless he chose to be attentive to his tutors. This is precisely defeating the object of private tuition, which is quite as much to bring backward boys on, as to encourage and promote the progress of the studious; and when such boys do not attend properly or are grossly idle and remiss in what they do, or when you happen to know they are getting into bad habits and bad society, they should not be suffered to do as they like, but they should be reported to me, either for such punishment as I may think the case requires, or by way of enabling me to counteract without punishment such propensities as require correction.

"You must allow me to say you have disappointed me in this respect. It is an object of essential importance that I should have from my assistants free and confidential communications respecting the conduct of the boys, not only at their lessons, but out of school. It is not necessary that the boys should know I have such communications, nor is it necessary that I should always or even frequently punish when such communications are made to me, and indeed I very seldom do visit with punishment what I can prevent by precaution; but it is of the greatest consequence to one who, like myself, has the charge of their morals as well as their learning, to have all possible light upon their habits, tempers, and dispositions, their haunts and propensities, that by an unseen yet watchful control I may prevent evil habits, or at least separate the good from the society of those who would corrupt them (a thing I often do by communication with the parents), and guard against their forming bad connections in the town. I never betray this confidence, and I hope I never make an unfair use of it: I earnestly press it upon you as a duty not to be so close and reserved as you have been with me. Do not imagine that I suppose you are either so negligent as to be indifferent what becomes of your pupils provided you receive the money for them, or so ill-disposed to me as to seek a little miserable popularity among the boys, at my expense. In either of these cases I should hold a very different kind of language; all I wish is that you would show the interest which I am persuaded you take, in the improvement of the boys and of the welfare of this establishment, by being more unreserved in communicating to me the observations on them which may enable me to see a little better into their characters, and to take measures accordingly.

"I remain yours ever faithfully,
"S. BUTLER."

I sent the foregoing pages to one of Dr. Butler's old pupils, Mr. Boyce, Head-Master of the Leman School, Beccles, with a request that he would kindly tell me whether they gave a faithful rendering of Dr. Butler's character and method. He replied :—

" You may speak in the highest possible terms of your grand-father, and feel sure that all his pupils will endorse your encomiums, however extravagant they may appear to the outer world. Such a man

> "'Might be a copy to these younger times;
> Which, followed well, would demonstrate them now,
> But goers backward.'

" I remember well on one occasion, just as the dear old Doctor was entering the schoolroom, a writing by some boy in the lower school caught his eye ; I was close behind him, and hoped he might not see it—' Butler is an old Fool.' ' Ah,' said the dear old Doctor (*more suo*), ' the melancholy truth stares me in the face.' If the author had been caught, he, no doubt, would have been lynched."

I may confirm the impression conveyed above by Mr. Boyce with a sketch of Dr. Butler drawn by another of his pupils, the late Rev. C. Clarke, Rector of Esher. It is found near the beginning of a novel called *The Beauclercs, Father and Son*, published in 1867, some twenty-eight years after the death of Dr. Butler. The passage runs :—

" Dr. Armstrong was one of those admirable schoolmasters that must necessarily be rare articles in any age. Time and space are not wasted in giving a few words to himself and his system. He was in himself a grand and noble gentleman, fitted to fill with respect, affection, or awe the rising generation of the upper middle classes of a country like this. A liberal, but no pedantic admirer of classical literature, of accurate but very extensive reading among the ancients, and making this know-ledge subservient to the other purposes of a practical life : interesting his pupils by the varied stories of apt illustration which he brought to bear upon their immediate pursuits. Withal a Christian gentleman of generous sentiments, conscious of his own powers, and not intolerant of the mistakes of other men. Need I say, after this, that he was large of frame, hand-some of person, and clean-shorn ?

" Of the upper boys he made friends. His whole dependence was upon them for example and influence ; and he expected that, like the Barons of old, they should be the transmitters (the μεσίται) of all that was good in the governing body. Of the little boys he made pets. He liked to see them hearty in play, and energetic in and out of school.

" But there was another class of schoolboy, usually at a discount with schoolmasters. I mean those boys whom physical courage and a sort of natural restlessness make impatient learners, but very excellent playmates. He regarded these as a sort of connecting link between the aristocracy of learning and the democratic mixture of talent, dirt, simplicity, idleness, and genuine boyhood. He tried to bring the playfulness of the schoolroom into his sixth form, and to carry down some of their dignity below. Some of them were idle ; he knew that they wanted rousing. Some were stupid ; they wanted enlightening. 'The sixth may be trusted to go alone,' said he, 'and the little ones will have plenty of friends among the big ones ; but who is to take care of the fellows who can only run and jump, and play football and cricket ? That won't get them through such a world of scrambling and competition. I must look after them myself.' So Reginald Carloss became a prime favourite with the Doctor, being remarkably sharp, but with no capability for reading."

Not only is Dr. Butler portrayed in the above extract, but the whole of the two opening chapters are drawn from Shrewsbury School some time between 1828 and 1833—and I should say drawn with very sufficient accuracy. It was the author's daughter who told me of the existence of the passage I have quoted, and of its being intended for a portrait of Dr. Butler.

I should perhaps say one word more about what is surely a marked characteristic of the life which I am about to deal with—I mean the foresight displayed by Dr. Butler in preserving so many, not only of the letters he received, but of the drafts of those he wrote to other people. We have seen Bishop Monk say, I believe with perfect truth, that there had been no career like Dr. Butler's since Busby's. What would we not give for such a record of Busby and of his school as Dr. Butler has left us ? What again would we not give for a like record preserved by Ashton, Meighen, Chaloner, or Leonard

Hotchkis? A graphic portrait of Dr. James has been saved to us, yet so as by fire, and what Rugby man will not be grateful to Dr. Butler for having saved it? As in my selection of letters I have been mainly guided by the livingness of the writers, so in my selection of school details I propose to ask myself whether we should value them if they had been recorded to us by any of the men whom I have named above. This book is written fully as much in the hope of interesting Shrewsbury men two hundred years hence, as for those of the present generation, and if I think that a detail will age well, I shall not care about its being a little trivial or uninteresting at present.

THE LIFE AND LETTERS

OF

DR. SAMUEL BUTLER.

CHAPTER I.

FAMILY HISTORY.

D R. BUTLER was born at Kenilworth on January 30th, 1774, and was an only child. He came of an old yeoman family that was settled at Cawston, and Thurlaston, near Dunchurch in Warwickshire, and may be traced in the Dunchurch register to a Henry Butler of Cawston who was married, April 12th, 1580, to Alice West of Toft, also close to Dunchurch. Earlier than about this date the Dunchurch registers do not go, but from that time onward to 1693 members of the Thurlaston Butler family are frequently entered as being born, married, or dying, several of them by the Plague. Examination of the earlier entries convinces me that the connection, if any, between Dr. Butler's family and that of his great namesake the author of *Hudibras* must be so remote as not to be worth considering ; nor, again, was Dr. Butler of Shrewsbury related to the author of the *Analogy*, nor indeed to any other family of his own name.

On September 17th, 1693, William Butler of Thurlaston

and Alice his wife baptised a daughter Alice, and on
October 14th of the same year a son William, born in 1690,
whose baptism appears to have been neglected. I may
say in passing that the granddaughter, that is to say, the
grandson's widow of this child born in the reign of William
and Mary, was still living at Kenilworth as lately as 1891
in the house bought by her husband's grandfather on his
reaching man's estate in 1711. On December 26th, 1695,
William Butler the elder was chosen one of the surveyors
of the highways of Kenilworth ; the removal of the family,
therefore, from Dunchurch must have taken place between
1693 and 1695. He was elected overseer of the poor
April 6th, 1697, and churchwarden April 22nd, 1701, being
re-elected in two subsequent years. His signature also
appears in the Kenilworth Parish Book in the month of
April preceding his decease ; he was buried June 1st,
1709, and is described in the register as " Yeoman." His
widow Alice was buried at Kenilworth March 7th, 1733 ;
the daughter Alice baptised at Dunchurch was buried,
also at Kenilworth, June 9th, 1711 ; the son William
baptised at Dunchurch died, as appears from his epitaph
now in Kenilworth Church, on February 14th, 1760, " in
the seventieth year of his age."

From a few notes concerning his family written in 1837
by Dr. Butler I take the following :—

" My grandfather [the William Butler last mentioned—Ed.]
appears to have been the principal person among the yeomanry
of Kenilworth, and to have had the best farm, the Hundred Oaks.
He was many years agent to Lords Leigh and Hyde. His
picture is not in the dress of a yeoman, but of a gentleman of
the time of George I. or II.—a blue velvet coat and handsome
powdered periwig—whence I should conclude he was of gentleman's family, but I never thought of making these inquiries
till it was too late to get an answer to them. His first wife was
Ann Radburne of Granborough, on the borders of Northampton-
shire and Warwickshire. She died in the first year of her
marriage, 1719. There is an account of her family in Thomas's

Dugdale, Vol. I., p. 314 [Granborough], and the inscription on her monument, which I am told is very handsome, is also given.

    *   *   *   *   *

" My grandfather's second wife was daughter of Samuel Tayler, Esq., of Stretton-on-Dunsmore. He married one of the Weldons who lived at Naseby House at the time of the battle of Naseby."

I have heard my father say that an old great-aunt, Deborah Butler, used to tell him when he was a boy that, all night long before the battle, the young men of the house were busy burying the plate and linen, and going about with dark lanterns. Then, next day, the wounded were brought into the hall. My sisters still possess some of the plate and linen then buried.

I return to my grandfather's notes :—

" By his second wife my grandfather had several children, of whom my father, William, born 1727, was the eldest son; he became entitled under his father's marriage settlements to the Manor of Stretton, but sold his interest before coming into possession.

" My grandfather's other children were James, a surgeon, baptised March 11th, 1729, who died in the East Indies ; Samuel, baptised July 12th, 1733, who succeeded to the greater part of his father's property; and Charles, who died in infancy; the daughters were six in number and all died unmarried. My father, William Butler, was a tradesman at Kenilworth, and married Lucy, youngest daughter of Mr. Nathaniel Broxsell, a builder at Shepton Mallet. My mother's mother's name was Stone. She came of a respectable family at Doulting, near Shepton Mallet, and was connected with the family of whom Abbot Whiting, hanged at Glastonbury by Henry VIII., was a barren but truly honourable branch."

From my old cousins, William Henry Butler of the Stone House, Kenilworth, and his sister, Mrs. Freer, I have heard that their great-grandfather, Samuel Tayler of Stretton, was the first gentleman in Warwickshire to shoot partridges flying. He left his sword and his spurs to their father, Samuel Butler, who I presume was named after him, and after whom, in his turn, my grandfather was named.

Of my grandfather's uncle, Samuel Butler, I was told by his son, William Henry Butler above mentioned, that he was at the play with his father, while still a boy, on the night when the Duke of Cumberland's sword was stolen, and that a saying went round the house, "The butcher's lost his cleaver," the Duke being still unpopular on account of supposed undue severity after the rising of 1745. He succeeded my great-great-grandfather as steward to Lords Leigh and Clarendon, and died in 1806.

James Butler, also uncle to my grandfather, was something of an artist. I remember a very pretty figure modelled in clay by him that used to stand in the drawing-room of the Stone House, Kenilworth; the oak cupboard in the dining-room was also made by him. He was an engineer as well as surgeon.

I have given to the British Museum many letters written by him during his voyage to the East Indies in charge of troops in the East India Company's service. They bear dates 1764, 1765, and are those of an amiable and observant writer. The ship touched at the island of Joanna, of which a curious and Defoe-like account is given, but my space will not allow me to do more than quote the following few lines, in which he takes leave of the hospitable islanders :—

"When I was coming away they took a special care to remind me of their hospitality; and to show them that I was not unmindful of it, I gave to my host, Purser Jack, a pair of check shirts and a handkerchief for his wife. To the king's son I gave a pair of scissors, and to the prince's son I gave, at his request —indeed I was almost ashamed at the gift—a pair of old shoes and a quire of gilt-edged writing-paper."

"Almost" was a word which appears to have given my Uncle James some trouble. He writes on one occasion of an escape from drowning which was "almost" providential. His letters ceased soon after he reached Calcutta, and it is believed he died about that date, but it was never known when nor how.

Of my great-grandfather's six sisters only two, Mary and Deborah, lived to old age. I have been told by those who knew them well that they were the first to introduce an umbrella and a tea-urn into Kenilworth. My sisters still have my Aunt Mary's snuff-box, but more than this I do not know concerning them.

My great-grandfather, Dr. Butler's father, appears to have been an amiable, easy-going man, who let money slip through his fingers from sheer good-nature. He sold his interest in the Manor of Stretton in 1754, when he was twenty-seven years old, and it is probable that his having done so was the reason of his exclusion from his father's will in favour of his younger brother. In a few short notes written by Dr. Butler in 1838, I find him saying that he was himself "originally intended for trade," but that his "father's misfortunes most strangely led" to his being sent to Rugby, and afterwards to college. He went to Rugby in 1783 ; the misfortunes, therefore, should belong to about that date, but I have never heard what they were nor where they occurred, and first know of my great-grand-father as a small linen-draper at Kenilworth in a house now called Sion House, next to the Two Virgins Inn. He married about the year of his father's death, and for four-teen years had no family. When at last a son was born to them, I find he was baptised on the day of his birth, and presume, therefore, that he was not expected to live.

One of his godfathers was a certain Dr. Wilmot, a man notorious enough in his day, and then curate at Kenilworth. This gentleman affected to be author of the *Letters of Junius*, and his claims were put forward some half-dozen

years after his death by his niece, Mrs. Olivia Wilmot
Serres, who no doubt forged the little evidence she adduced.
She called herself the Princess Olive of Cumberland, and
pretended to be daughter of " Henry, Duke of Cumberland,
and Olive, his first wife." The claims of her daughter, Mrs.
Ryves, to the throne of England were only disposed of
in a court of law as recently as 1866.   In reference to this
lady I will add that on the morning of her marriage to the
most unhappy Mr. Serres, her uncle, Dr. Wilmot, who had
just performed the marriage ceremony, said to the bride-
groom, " Serres, she is now your wife, but mind me—keep
her employed, or she will be plotting mischief." *

Of Dr. Wilmot himself, Dr. Butler, writing to Mr. George
Woodfall, August 5th, 1813, says :—

"He was a Fellow of Trinity College, Oxford—intimately
acquainted with the late Lord, and much more so, if the scandal-
ous chronicle is to be believed, with the late notorious Lady
Archer—a tavern companion, a retailer of good stories and
steward's-room anecdotes of great people, which he embellished
after his own fashion.   He lived for many years in close intimacy
with my family ; my father, now in his eighty-seventh year, and
my mother, still alive, together with all the other surviving
branches of my family, knew him well."

The portrait of her uncle drawn by Mrs. Serres corresponds well with the foregoing, but I should not think it
worth referring to if her book were not such a literary
curiosity that some of my more idle readers may be glad
to have their attention called to it.

I know nothing of Dr. Butler's childhood, except that
he used occasionally to visit a certain General Webb, then
very old, but commonly called " Young General Webb," to

---

* *Memoir of John Thomas Serres, late Marine Painter to his Majesty,*
by a Friend (London : Hunt & Clarke, 1826), p. 16.   Indexed in the
British Museum library under " Friend."

distinguish him from his father, the General Webb of Thackeray's *Esmond*. I have been told by my old cousins that some Golden Rennet apple-trees for planting out were once sent down to him from London, and were labelled G. R. "What!" he exclaimed, " send me Georgius Rex apple-trees?" and he returned them.

CHAPTER II.

SCHOOL AND COLLEGE.

Captain Don.—School Life at Rugby.—Career at St. John's College, Cambridge. — Letters from Dr. James, December 10th, 1793, September 7th, 1794.—Engagement to Miss Harriet Apthorp.— Letters from Dr. James, December 27th, 1796, January 23rd, 1797. —Letter from S. T. Coleridge. — First Published Work. — Mr. Butler commissioned by the University to edit Æschylus.

THERE lodged with old Mr. and Mrs. Butler a certain Captain Patrick Don, a retired army captain.

This old gentleman laid a trap for himself in a somewhat unusual way. He invested what little money he had in an annuity which was to terminate in 1804, by which date he would be eighty-nine years old, for he was born in 1715, the year of the Jacobite rebellion. It did not occur to him that it might be as presumptuous to settle it that he should be dead as that he should be alive in 1804, and as a matter of fact he lived to the age of ninety-six. Not to harrow the reader, I would say that his relative, Sir Alexander Don, supported him till he died.

I have been told, by those who knew my great-grandfather and great-grandmother well, that it was Captain Don who urged young Butler's being sent to Rugby. His opinion was confirmed by that of the Vicar, Mr. Sumner, father to the brothers who became Archbishop of Canterbury and Bishop of Winchester. At Rugby, therefore, the boy was entered, March 31st, 1783, he being then a little over nine years old.

Dr. James was then head-master, and it is not too much

to say that no later master has done so much for the school as he did between 1780—1794. He was the first to give it that importance which since his day it has never lost. No subsequent head-master so completely re-created the school as Dr. James did during his fourteen years' tenure of office. Dr. Arnold unquestionably made a deep impression on those boys who were brought into close communication with himself, but I cannot find that his influence over the school survived longer than that of any subsequent head-master, while upon other schools, so far as I have been able to ascertain, he produced—I believe it is not too much to say—no effect whatever.

The widely spread opinion that he introduced the monitorial system into English public school life, and that he made use of his head boys as links between himself and the rank and file of the school more than had been long customary, will not stand examination. The monitorial system existed in Dr. James's time at Rugby, and in a letter dated November 30th, 1798, which I cannot give in full, he says: "We will talk over the politics of the Charterhouse when we meet—but I heartily thank you. . . . At the Charterhouse the monitors restrain the boys from going out of bounds by imposing tasks themselves." As for Shrewsbury, from the commencement of Dr. Butler's head-mastership, I find the præpostors entrusted with the reins of power to the full as much as they were in my own time under Dr. Kennedy, or as I imagine they are in any school at present.

Among Dr. Butler's contemporaries was Walter Savage Landor, his junior by a year to the day, who was entered January 1783, and appears in Bloxam's *Rugby Register* as Walter Landor. William Hill, afterwards Lord Berwick, was entered February 19th, 1783. He and Butler formed a close intimacy that was only ended by death. Henry

Francis Cary, the translator of Dante, was entered March 27th, 1783. Among Shropshire names I find that of Rowland Wingfield, of the Whitehall, Shrewsbury ; Thomas Eyton, eldest son of T. Eyton, Esq., of Wellington, entered January 23rd, 1787 ; and Rowland Hill, third son of the Rev. Rowland Hill, of Hough, near Nantwich, entered on the same day. Walter Birch, of whose scholarship Landor speaks so highly, was entered April 3rd, 1786.

In Forster's Life of Landor I read :—

"Among his schoolfellows was Butler, afterwards Head-Master of Shrewsbury and Bishop of Lichfield, but Landor had the reputation in the school of being the best classic" (p. 12).

*   *   *   *   *

"'I have forgotten my Greek,' wrote Landor, when he was eighty-four, 'of which I had formerly as much as boys of fifteen have now. Butler, afterwards Bishop of Lichfield, and myself were the first in Rugby, or I believe in any other school, who attempted a Greek verse.'"—*Ibid.*

The following sketch of Butler as he appeared to a schoolfellow is given in *The Shropshire and North Wales Standard* for July 1839 (the only number published). It is by Mr. Apperley, who used to write as "Nimrod" in the *Sporting Magazine,* and so signs himself here.

"But how happened it that Dr. Butler is a scholar? I remember asking myself the question when I read the Greek inscription on the fine arch at the entrance to his late school : εαν ης φιλομαθης, εση πολυμαθης—by which is implied that a great love of learning is necessary to make a man a scholar. But when was Dr. Butler φιλομαθης? Not during the many years in which I slept in the same room with him at Rugby—fishing and novel- and play-reading at that period employing by far the greater portion of his time. Then how did he get through the business of his class, or 'form,' as we called it at Rugby? How were his exercises composed? How were his lessons construed and parsed? I will tell you how all this was performed. 'Fetch me half a sheet of paper,' he would say to myself, or to any other boy much lower in the school than himself, at the hour of awaking in the morning ; when, taking some novel or play-book from under his pillow, which he had been reading over-night, and using it as a desk, he would write off the best exercise of the day, and '*play* (*i.e.* a holiday) *for Butler*' would be often heard throughout the schools.   Then his lessons :—'Where is the place?' he would say to his neighbour, on joining his form ten minutes before a Greek play was to be read.   Perhaps half a dozen words might be looked out in his lexicon, when the Greek book would be shut and one more to his mind brought forth from his pocket.   If 'called up,' however, there was *no mistake.* Now how this was done is quite beyond my comprehension.   I have once or twice seen a hound distinguish himself greatly the first day he entered the field; I have observed the intuitive knowledge some persons have displayed of what is called the run of a fox—Tom Smith of the Craven and the Cheltenham tailor for examples—but never before or since have I heard of this *Butlerian* road to knowledge, if such an expression may be allowed me. . . . That Dr. Butler (having perfected by study what he may be said to have attained by inspiration) has arrived at the honours he enjoys, must be grateful to every one who wishes to see talent and merit rewarded ; and I am happy to hear that his health is restored, so as to afford the prospect of lengthened years ; but were his lordship not quite so liberal in his opinions on some points, he would be more valuable as a bishop in my eyes."

The substance of the foregoing is repeated without alteration in an article by the same writer which appeared in *Fraser's Magazine* for August 1842 ; but Dr. Butler being now dead he continued :—

" Alas, there are no pictures without shades.   Butler was most unpopular in the school.   In fact, partly because he was the son of a small shopkeeper in the small but beautiful village of Kenilworth, and at Rugby as a foundation boy, and partly on account of his churlish temper, we in the same boarding-house voted him nothing better than a snob, and the meanness of his personal appearance gave a colour to our proceedings. Never would he offer to do us a verse or two, or construe us over ; but he would sit with his elbow on his knee, and his face resting on one hand and a book in the other, and never open his mouth.   My brother was near him in school, but I seldom heard them exchange a word ; and it will be remembered a good deal of the boy appeared in the man.   When he first commenced schoolmaster he thrashed his boys so much as to injure the school, and nothing but his high literary reputation would have re-established its good name.   He, however, wisely profited by the hint given him by parents that their children were not to be made the victims of his spleen. The *quem Jupiter odit pedagogum fecit* was at this time verified ; for the Master of Shrewsbury was then hated as much as he was afterwards liked by the generality of his pupils, his conduct towards them having undergone a great change."

The evil that men do does not live after them more surely than a good deal of evil which they never either did or wanted to do.

I see that Mr. Apperley has wisely printed φιλομαθὴς ἐὰν ᾖς ἔσῃ πολυμαθής, without breathings, accents, or iota subscripts. He who had the inscription set up (I suppose in 1630) might perhaps have done wisely to have taken the same course. The words ἐὰν ᾖς ἔσῃ are written ΕΑΝ ΗΣ ΕΣΗ, and it is creditable to the good taste of the three head-masters who between them have ruled Shrewsbury for ninety-seven years that they should have all of them refrained from correction.

To return to Dr. Butler. Though he may have written his exercises in bed, he copied them out into books which he preserved, and one or more of which may be seen in the British Museum. Good as the exercises are, considering the age of the writer and the little trouble he seems to have taken with them, the handwriting—running, but uncompromisingly distinct, as the specimen given opposite will show—is even more remarkable, and may serve in some measure to explain how the writer came to be worn out before his time.

About the year 1788, while he was still at school, a Mr. Broxsell, a brother of his mother's, died, leaving him a reversionary interest on the deaths of an aunt and of his mother in two or three small properties at Shepton Mallet, from which place his mother came. These properties were worth in all between four and five thousand pounds, and his uncle of the Stone House, Kenilworth, advanced him small sums against his interest in them during the

30 all respects to answer the character of a man
as to act in a becoming manner. Whether it is consistent with virtue is consistent with the decorum,
and what is incompatible with decorum is not
agreeable to virtue. What then is more to be
cultivated, what more to be desired, than to

35 behave with propriety and decorum, as in
that along all our duties, both moral & re-
-ligious, are involved.

Wednesday Morn.
April 8th 1700.

earlier part of his college career, so that he was saved from being seriously pinched by want of money. From the few notes already referred to as written in 1838, I find he was elected to the only Rugby exhibition vacant in 1791, and was thus enabled to enter himself at Oxford. " By accidental introduction to Dr. Parr," he continues, " I was removed from Christ Church, Oxford, where a day had been fixed by my intended tutor (Mr. Smith, afterwards Dean) for my admission, to St. John's College, Cambridge—a circumstance which I then thought very hard."

He entered as a sizar, but in January 1792, at the commencement of his second term, changed his gown. From Professor Mayor's well-known edition of Baker's *History of St. John's,* I find Mr. Butler was Browne Medallist, Latin Ode 1792-3, and Greek Ode 1794. He was Craven Scholar 1793, defeating S. T. Coleridge, Keate, afterwards Head-Master of Eton, and Bethel, afterwards Bishop of Bangor. He graduated as fourth senior optime in 1796, and took the first Chancellor's medal in the same year. He was first Members' Prizeman 1797 and 1798, and was elected Platt Fellow of St. John's, April 3rd, 1797.

I can find space for only two from among the several letters written by Dr. James while Mr. Butler was still an undergraduate :—

(Original in Rugby School Library.)

"RUGBY, *December* 10th, 1793.

"DEAR BUTLER,—I told you I had bought one hundred pounds in the 5 per cents stock, such part of which I should make over for ever to Rugby parish, for the support of this organ—that is, such part of a hundred pounds as the overplus of the subscription I might raise should amount to. Now I expect something handsome from Abraham Caldecott in the East Indies, from whom I cannot yet hear—perhaps may not hear these nine months to come—therefore, as I wish to increase this organ fund as much as I can (finding expenses of singing books, music books for organist, teaching the charity boys, etc., to be now necessary attendants of the organ), I wish to continue to receive the half-guinea subscription of any new Rugby boy that may come to the University before next summer. I never proposed anything to them before ; this is not heavy. I have now no Library subscription, and you know we have here no farewell presents ; whereas the Master of Eton, you will find, by the custom of the place, receives a present of three, five, ten, twenty, etc., guineas (according to circumstances) from every boy that leaves his school in the upper part and not being on the foundation. I have nothing, nor wish anything more than to leave this little memorial of my mastership. You now see my views. Any overgrown rich man, as Hopwood, etc., may give a guinea. I suppose you settled with Mr. W. Hill."

*   *   *   *   *

(Original in Rugby School Library.)

"Rugby, *September 7th,* 1794.

"My dear Butler,—I received your friendly and satisfactory letter yesterday, on the 6th, though yours was dated on the 3rd. However, Mr. Ingles was fixed on by the trustees last Thursday at a previous meeting, and he will be elected master next Tuesday, the 9th.   He is an excellent scholar—of my own standing in King's nearly—a very good man indeed, and very fit for the office. He saved very little at Macclesfield, and seems to me still to pant after glory.

"I received also yesterday your very elegant address to me, which is as good Latin as can be penned. I am very proud of it, and I went to dine immediately with Mr. Grimes, and we both love you exceedingly for the benevolent and kind motive that led you to collect so many subjects for me in such exact order; and we both agree that you deserved just as much for the good heart that conducted you to this work, as for the good head that produced it.

"Have you chanced to stumble on any *verse* subjects ?

"Nothing will make me more happy than to see you on the 18th, and we shall have a delightful time together as long as you can stay.

"I am, my dear Butler, your obliged and affectionate friend,

"T. James.

"Mrs. James's situation will make no difference, nor cause us inconvenience, in respect of your visit. I thank you."

On January 30th, 1795, Mr. Butler came of age, and on

the same day proposed to his mother that he should sell his reversion and buy an annuity for his parents. Old Mrs. Butler, however, would not hear of this, and remained so firm that the reversion was not sold. From letters dated about this time I find that, during the long vacation, Mr. Butler acted as tutor in the family of T. Eyton, Esq., of Wellington, and I have been told by my cousin Archdeacon Lloyd that it was Mr. Eyton who first suggested his trying for the Mastership of Shrewsbury School, he having been one of the most active promoters of the Act of Parliament by which the school was remodelled in 1798.

In the following year, when Mr. Butler took the Senior Chancellor's medal, Dr. James, then residing at Upton-on-Severn, advised him how far it might be proper for him to write and inform Mr. Ingles, then Head-Master of Rugby. Having drafted what he considered to be "a short and simple letter" for his pupil to send, he continued :—

"When I write these things you may be sure I am addressing you as a son. I wish I may ever have such a son.

"You have afforded me so many and such repeated occasions of exultation, as to make me feel a pride and a pleasure whenever I think of you. It is now time that you should think of your health, and if you feel an inclination to be perfectly quiet I shall be extremely glad to see you to stay at Upton, where the longer you stay the more welcome you will be, and where you will find me busily employed with two of my children and three pupils, and Upton Church on Sundays only, for I employ a gentleman on weekdays. I could not receive more than a fourth pupil, and that was offered last week, but I have deferred all decision upon it for a month to come.

"You do right to unfold to me the little use you had of a lexicon, but do not talk too much of that to others. How little you wanted it is demonstrated by success.

*   *   *   *   *

"Whenever you come I shall be glad to see you. A coach goes from Birmingham to Worcester every day (price 8s.), and a mail (price 2s. 6d.)—that is, a diligence conveying three persons —goes from Worcester, from the Crown Inn, to Upton, on the afternoons of Monday, Thursday, and Saturday, and you might come from Birmingham on the morning of any of those days. Wherever you are, give me notice, and the sooner the better. Mrs. James desires to be most kindly remembered to you.

" I am, dear Butler, your affectionate friend and faithful servant,

" T. JAMES."

For the next year and a half Mr. Butler continued to reside at Cambridge, and it was during this time that he formed the acquaintance of Andreas (commonly, but incorrectly, called Andreas Adolf) Merian, son of the Swiss Landamann Merian, and afterwards Baron Merian, Ambassador from the Court of St. Petersburg to that of Paris, of whom a fuller account will be given later. Towards the end of 1796, Mr. Butler became engaged to Harriet, fifth daughter of Dr. East Apthorp, who then lived in the tall gaunt house in St. Botolph's Lane, Cambridge, not long since occupied by Dr. Apthorp's grandson, the late Professor F. A. Paley.

Dr. James was up in arms when he heard of the engagement, and wrote a letter with parenthesis pullulating out of parenthesis, in a way that nothing but the original MS. can display. The following extracts from his letter, which is dated Upton-on-Severn, December 27th, 1796, are as much as my space will permit :—

" MY DEAR BUTLER,—. . . You talk of pupils, and perhaps you might get one or two ; for I think you will not find it possible to keep up a stock, as it were, of five or six. Look at Dr. Parr, that paragon of human abilities—how few pupils has he ever had at any one time, though he built the rooms over his study at Hatton with a view to accommodate them. I remember he once had six, but how short a time did that number continue ! . . . Pupils are not easily got, let a man's character and abilities be ever so superlative, whatever you may think to the contrary ; and when got their stay is very uncertain. Further, there is much anxiety attending them. I have had occasion within these three months to beg the parent to take one young man home from my house whose conduct I justly disapproved, and you have known my forbearance in such matters. Now if you were married and in my situation what a serious evil it would be to you to part with one hundred a year out of three or four hundred—and yet if this were not done you would maintain no order in respect of regular hours of an evening particularly, and no government in your family."

Dr. James then suggests that the marriage should be deferred at any rate till Mr. Butler had become established as master of some endowed school.

" In this you might easily succeed in any part of the kingdom, No such amazing amount of bodily strength (which by the way you have not—*valeat illud quoque quantum valere possit*) is requisite in a school, for it will fall to the lot of few men to have their strength so tried to the utmost as my powers were by such an extraordinary influx of members ; and that with me was all chance and luck, and it would be better for you to proceed quietly than encounter such an armed host.

" Still, perhaps you will prefer (and the lady too) the idea of private tuition, and keep the idea of a school as a desperate and last resource, if necessity should urge you by hard circumstances. Consider, then, the enormous increase in the price of every article, even these two years past since I left the school. Pork is here 8*d.* a pound, and all other meat 6*d.* a pound, bought what are called good and indifferent pieces together. Bread and malt are also very heavy articles, and beyond all former times. Taxes, and consequently the prices of every ordinary article, are daily increasing, nay, *and must increase*, while your income will be limited at best, and uncertain at all times. You may perhaps think the item of subscriptions to the poor—to accidental distress, whether of fire or other casualty—subscriptions to the support of decayed clergy and their helpless children—to the hospital of your county (now in every county established) —to the solicitations of your friends for books, to be all nothing, and yet you would find them to make a serious amount in a limited and probably a narrow income. For what is a hundred pounds a quarter (though it be undeniably certain) to enable you to provide house-rent, pay your rates, highway rates, church rates (a horse is totally out of the question—which by the bye a single man may easily keep), and to buy all the provisions for at least two maids and a boy-servant, which must be had for yourself, and wife, and four pupils.

" Four pupils, three servants, man and wife (no children), are nine times £25, or £225—but a pupil (with one glass of wine a day) is £30—exclusive of your own and wife's clothes, etc. Then, if a family succeed, a nursemaid must be had instantly—

one or two nursemaids, according to the number of children. Each servant costs now at least £25 out of your pocket, even without wages, for it is not with servants as with boys at a school. Boys are absent at least twice six weeks, or a quarter of a year, and here arises the profit of the master. Servants are for ever eating between meals, boys at regular meals; nor will servants live on cheese at night, like boys: consider also, the more servants the more waste of all the things which they use or handle in the house.

"Then where is your furniture, of beds especially, to come from? Bed furniture for decent private pupils will cost for cotton —sixty yards at 2s. 6d. is £7 10s., without making up or lining (not necessary), without sheets and bedding, and one window curtain each. Then each bedstead and its hangings will be £11, and then for each bed and blankets, two pairs of sheets and bedding, £20, which makes the price of your private pupils' beds to be £100. Then your servants' beds may be of wool, but still they will cost much money; you must also have decent furniture and real comforts, or your imagined paradise will soon become less a source of tranquillity than you expect.

" Lastly, if you had the abilities of an angel, and spake as never man spake, you would still find that the world is content with moderate acquisitions, and that young people are narrow-necked vessels, into which you cannot pour much at a time without waste and running over. As to Mathematics, remember your own aversion to them when you were younger. Familiarity and the example of students about you soon led you to conquer your dislike. Academical or college distinctions were an unceasing stimulus. Now in private education not one of these incitements exists. There is therefore a sort of *ne plus ultra* to those pursuits in private education, and you would find Newton and Biquadratics utterly unattainable by a young man. I believe I may say the same thing with perfect truth about the four branches fundamentally and scientifically taught. Nay, I may aver the same truth of Euclid himself, if it be too far urged with a very young mind in a solitary situation, without other incitement than the very love of knowledge. A very little of Mathematics (whatever you may fondly dream of, and very naturally in the bosom of the University) will suffice for young persons.

"History and philology are to be your points? Talk not to other people (say what you will to me) of all ancient and modern history. Even a tolerable sketch of it to any useful purpose is beyond the comprehension and span of a youthful education. 'Tis well done if you inform the youthful mind of Greece and Rome and England. Leave logic for the University. I had once all the fond ideas you cherish of a never-ceasing and ever-growing swelling education. I attended Dr. Symonds through two courses with vast private advantage, but I found by experience

that such extensive plans of knowledge (even though ever so well
attained) are not so soon communicable as you may suppose.
You can do no more than thousands have done before you.   The
greatest abilities in the Law (go to Westminster and see it) and in
Physic are in great numbers in want, and are often sadly straitened.
You cannot be better off than one of these, adventuring into the
great ocean of the world, without the possession of your future
estate, or anything but academical fame, which will indeed give
you a good chance for pupils, but after all nothing is certain.
Then if you are ill, if you die, what is to be done? What is to
become of your offspring, of your wife? I dare not say, Marry,
unless you can get a firm ground to stand on.
            " Your true and faithful friend, T. JAMES."

"P.S.—The Cheltenham waters last summer, thank God, restored
my spirits most effectually by removing corrupted bile, etc.
    "I shall gladly purchase your Propertius. That is good.
Pray dispose of my *Parkinson on Mechanics* and bring me the
cash when you come to see me."

One cannot help suspecting that there must have been
still a little bile remaining.   The foregoing letter produced
as much effect as such letters generally do, and the
engagement of course proceeded.   Dr. James resigned
himself to the inevitable, and began at once to look out
for something that might enable the young couple to
marry without gross imprudence.   Within a month he
wrote the following letter in respect of Shrewsbury, about
which it is plain his pupil had already consulted him.
I note that " My dear Butler " has become " My dear Sir,"
from which it would seem that he was still brooding over
the price of pork, and of " bed furniture for decent private
pupils, costing for cotton—sixty yards at 2s. 6d. is £7 10s.,
without making up or lining (not necessary)."
    His letter runs :—

            (Original in Rugby School Library.)
                " UPTON-ON-SEVERN, *January* 23rd, 1797.

    " MY DEAR SIR,—I have been perpetually changing my place
of abode since I received the favour of your last.   Among other
places I have been at Shrewsbury, where (from what you wrote in

your letter, that your strength lay there) I kept you principally in view; and on the whole I am of opinion that your fortune might very possibly be made in that city. There is a school there, having from £1,300 to £1,500 a year, of which the head-master has not above £100 a year, but he has allowances for assistants, and an excellent house and school built in a superior style. Within the memory of many, a head-master has had there (I think) not less than sixty boarders. This school was once the Eton or the Westminster of Wales, and of all Shropshire, etc. Now the present master does nothing, and there are not above three or four boys belonging to this noble foundation, although there are many exhibitions belonging to the school. The gentlemen of Shrewsbury, therefore, have an idea of pensioning off the old masters now there and in possession, and of appointing new ones. I further learned also that they have an idea that an Act of Parliament can be procured to appoint new governors to the school—for at the present moment I fear the appointment of a master is in the gift of some college. Histories there are of Shrewsbury or Shropshire, and from these (no doubt in the Public Library or of some antiquarian, at least at Cambridge) you might learn the particulars of this school. If you find by inquiry that anything here should be worth your notice, it would be a theatre worthy of your abilities, and you would play a game in which you would be sure to be a wonderful winner. The trouble of a school and of many private pupils in different classes are not widely asunder; but the school is great and certain, the private tuition humble and precarious. A lady, I assure you, has no great share of labour, and none but what serves to display her abilities, and to command the respect and esteem of her neighbourhood. If you were to embark on such a scheme as this I could give you many a hint, and Mrs. James could suggest useful and wise methods; and the world would greatly patronise you, and you would be sure of accumulating a great fortune—provided only that you avoid the rocks on which I was dashed, and these I could easily direct you to avoid. Such a plan is by far the best that can be proposed. Public speeches have never been thought of there, and the common business of classics and exercises is all that is required, for I advise you to shun Mathematics (in such a line) as a dangerous rock. Leave this to the Master of Arithmetic. Rugby would not support a married assistant with a growing family. An assistantship there is very well for an unmarried man, but believe me it is not enough for a family; and then at Rugby you could not lay up one halfpenny for the support of your offspring, if anything should befall yourself, and your prospect would be closed, for Mr. Birch is your senior. I make the same observation on the line of private tutorship, as affording no prospect of making a fortune, be it ever so successful, unless indeed you should have the good fortune to get a church living by that connection. That too and much more might befall you, but this is uncertain. Let a man be ever so great at the University, yet when once he has left it and has been melted down into the great mass of the world, he loses a very considerable share indeed of that consequence and attention which the particular interests of individuals caused to be paid him in a seat of literature. You cannot, I am sure, name or recollect a man who has sailed into the great ocean of the world from his college labour, in whose fortune the observation I have made has not been verified."

  • • • • •

I may best here introduce the little that I know about Dr. Butler's predecessor—the Rev. James Atcherley. I have heard from my aunt, Mrs. Bather, that he and the second master used to amuse themselves by trying which could kick highest at a flitch of bacon that was hung for them in the kitchen to practise at. The late Rev. W. A. Leighton told me that Atcherley used to make presents to the boys of books belonging to the school library, and that he was more or less intemperate in his habits. He was, however, a man of good natural abilities, and in 1773 published a pamphlet entitled *A Drapier's Address to the Good People of England*, which is not ill-written, and shows the writer to have been an advocate of free trade, when free-traders were still scarce. I find no other work by him in the library of the British Museum.

The only other letter that belongs to the period of Dr. Butler's life at Cambridge is one from S. T. Coleridge, which I print by the kind permission of Ernest Hartley Coleridge, Esq., who informs me that it should be dated about June 8th, 1794. The reference is to the poet's return to Cambridge after his enlisting in the army. In a letter dated September 22nd, 1834, which will be given in due course, Dr. Butler speaks warmly of his youthful friendship with Coleridge and vindicates his claim to academic distinction.

(Original in possession of Mrs. G. L. Bridges and Miss Butler.)

"My dear Sir,—I assure you I received pleasure almost to tears from your letter. There are hours in which I am inclined to think very meanly of myself, but when I call to memory the number and character of those who have honoured me with their esteem, I am almost reconciled to my follies and again listen to the whispers of self-adulation.

"That I felt pain on my return to Cambridge from the circumstance of your not having called upon me, it would be vain to deny. Misfortune is a 'Jealous God.' I attribute it, however, to the sickly peevishness of a mind sore with recent calamity.

"To-morrow morning, early, I set out on a pedestrian scheme for Oxford—from whence, after a stay of three or four days, I proceed to Wales—make a tour of the northern part, and return to Cambridge. The whole of my peregrination will take about six weeks.

"If you are disengaged, will you take your bread and cheese with me this evening?

"Believe me, with great esteem, your sincere
"S. T. Coleridge.

"P.S.—Permit me to thank you for having noticed my literary efforts."

In 1797 Butler published his first work, entitled :—

"*M. Musuri Carmen in Platonem. Isaaci Casauboni in Josephum Scaligerum Ode. Accedunt poemata et exercitationes utriusque linguæ. Auctore S. Butler. Appendicis loco subjiciuntur hymnus Cleanthis Stoici, Clementis Alexandrini hymni duo, Henrici Stephani Adhortatio ad lectionem Novi Fœderis. Conscripsit atque edidit Samuel Butler, A.B. Coll. Div. Joann. apud Cantabr. Soc.* Cantabrigiæ : excudebat J. Burges academiæ typographus. Veneunt apud J. Deighton, Cantabrigiæ, et Londini apud T. Payne. 1797.*" 8vo, pp. xiv. and 115.

What little need be said in respect to this production may be seen in Professor J. E. B. Mayor's edition of Baker's *History of St. John's*, Part II., p. 903, etc.

About this time, or perhaps before the end of 1796, Mr. Butler was entrusted by the Syndics of the University Press with the bringing out of an edition of Æschylus, under restrictions so severe that Professor Porson, to whom the task had been offered, declined to undertake it. All Mr. Butler's leisure for many years was devoted to this, as the event proved, somewhat ungrateful labour. From Professor Mayor's very full account of the work I take the following :—

> "Butler himself collated the two Cambridge MSS., and procured by means of A. Merian the collation of two Venice MSS. by Jac. Morelli. J. D. LaRoche of Basle compiled for him an index.
>
>   *   *   *   *   *
>
> "Many of Butler's notes were retained in the new edition of Schütz (Halle, 1809-22, 5 vols.), and the entire commentaries of Stanley and Abresch were reprinted (*ibid.*, 1832, 2 vols., 8vo) under the title *Apparatus Criticus et Exegeticus in Æschyli Tragœdias.* Thus that which gave the principal value to Butler's costly edition is now accessible in a more convenient form ; and the demand for it has wholly ceased."

It was a cherished wish on Dr. Butler's part to edit Æschylus *de novo*, unhampered by the conditions that rendered his earlier work so cumbrous and unmanageable ; but this, when he became Bishop of Lichfield, proving impossible, he placed his notes on some of the plays at the disposal of a very favourite pupil, Dr. Peile, afterwards of Repton, in whose Æschylus they appear with the initials S. L.

CHAPTER III.

Installation at Shrewsbury.—Dr. James's Letters of Advice detailing
the Rugby System under his Head-Mastership.

IN the course of the year 1798 the act remodelling
Shrewsbury School was passed, and his college elected
Mr. Butler to the vacant mastership. He immediately
married,* and entered on his new duties, being installed
October 1st, 1798.

Mr. Butler wrote, as in duty bound, to Dr. James, and
asked him for advice on school management—no doubt
merely as a matter of politeness. Dr. James had resigned
the head-mastership of Rugby some four years, but in his
ardour to fight his battles over again he at once replied in
three long letters, giving minute details of all that was
done at Rugby in each form, under his mastership. The
letters consist in great measure of the lessons that were
set in each form ; nevertheless they throw so much light on
the working of a public school at the close of the last
century that I should print them in full if space permitted.
I will give, however, the daily lessons of the fifth and sixth
forms, and the more interesting parts of the general
remarks. For the rest I must refer the reader to the
original letters in the British Museum, or to a MS. copy
which I have sent to the Museum of Rugby School. The
letters lose almost as much in livingness by being read in

---

* Tuesday, September 4th, 1798, at Great St. Andrew's, Cambridge
(Mayor's edition of Baker's *History of St. John's.*)

type as they gain in clearness ; and those whose leisure enables them to see the originals in the British Museum will, I think, be both interested and amused.

The first letter is undated, but must have been written October 14th, 1798. It begins without prelude of any kind.

" Fifth and Sixth Forms.

" *Monday, at* 7.—Watts' *Scripture History*, sixteen pages, or Goldsmith's *Roman History* (2 vols., 8vo), sixteen pages at a lesson at least, or twenty pages at most ; or *History of England* in a series of letters, with geography and chronology of each lesson. Ingles does geography instead of this lesson in its *turn*, as after *Roman History* finished in one volume ; then again after second volume and Watts finished.

" Perhaps twelve pages of Watts may be full enough at first.

" *At* 10.—Thirty-five lines of the *Iliad*, twice construed and parsed. The next lesson in the same book is always set after doing present lesson. Take *Selecta ex Iliade* by W. Holwell, if it can be got. But at Christmas you may come to Worcester and mark your Homer and Virgil by my books.

" *At* 3.—About fifty lines in *Scriptores Romani*, twice construed. Set Tuesday's translation.

" *At* 5.—Thirty-eight lines in Virgil, or rather *Selecta e Virgilio*. 38 × 2 = 76 construed in the week, less fifty repeated Friday, leaving twenty-six. (See Friday's lessons at seven and three.)

" *Tuesday, at* 7.—Thirty lines of Tully's *Offices* repeated. Themes looked over.

" *Note.*—I should set translation of Tully one week, the next some English to be translated into Latin (as Willymot's *Peculiars*, or my Erasmus Englished), and then translation of Tully or English theme alternately, always rendering English into Latin once a fortnight.

" *At* 10.—Thirty-five lines of *Poetæ Græci*. Verse theme set and English translation for this day.

" *Half-Holiday.*—Absence * at three and five, or half after five in summer.

" *Exercise.*—One week English theme or English translation. The next week translate English into Latin. This English was Erasmus translated by me, but Willymot's *Peculiars* will do. Lock up at . . . different times between six and eight, according to the season. The earlier Prayers are the better.

" *Wednesday, at* 7.—Translation or English theme looked over. Repeat Tuesday's *Poetæ Græci.*

---

* *I.e.* calling over the boys' names to see that they were all there.

" *At* 10.—Thirty-five lines of *Scriptores Græci.*

" *At* 3 *and* 5.—The same as Monday ; but a selection *ex Cicerone,* or his letters (at the end of the book), were construed on Monday, and *Selecta e Livio, Tacito* (you may leave out perhaps *e Paterculo*) were construed on a Wednesday.

" *Exercise Latin Verses.*—Lowest number of lowest fifth is sixteen.

" *Note.*—Tully repeated for themes and Ovid for verses is good, but sometimes Greek grammar must be said, instead of these lessons—at least the principal parts of it.

" *Thursday, at* 7.—Latin verses looked over. Thirty lines of *Selecta ex Ovidio* repeated, or Greek grammar.

" *At* 10.—Homer as on Monday.

" *Half-Holiday.*—In honour of one or even two (perhaps one of these from the fifth form) of the best præpostor's exercises.

" *Thursday's exercise.*—Lyrics of various sorts : Iambics, Sapphics, Asclep., Alc., Trochaics. Two upper præpostors make Greek.

" *Friday, at* 7.—Thirty-five lines of Homer repeated (or Thursday's Homer) ; *or* sometimes twenty-five lines of Homer and twenty-six lines of Virgil have been said, which compleats the repetition of all the Virgil of the week.

" *At* 10.—Sixty lines in Horace's *Satyrs* [*sic*] and *Epistles* and *Ars Poetica* were construed, or Juvenal, *Sat.* 1, 3, 10, 14, or Persius, *Sat.* 5.

" *N.B.*—Horace and Juvenal are thus finished in two and a half years.

" *At* 3.—Fifty lines of Monday's and Wednesday's Virgil repeated. Horace lesson of the morning construed a second time.

" *N.B.*—If twenty-six lines of Virgil be said on Friday morning, then all the Virgil construed will be said.

" *At* 5.—Thirty lines in Tully's *Offices* once construed, which are to be repeated in the following week, and also thirty lines in *Selecta ex Ovidio* once construed and once hastily read off in English, which are to be repeated *in the next following week.* Ingles's fifth form assistant teaches the fifth form the Tully and *Selecta ex Ovidio,* while he teaches *Funebres Orationes* or Pindar, or etc., for this lesson ; but these lessons are perfectly academic, and rather beyond the power of young boys, unless they be already accomplished scholars.

" *Saturday.*—Sixty lines of Friday's Horace repeated. The head-master, having no exercise, examines a lower form. Ingles takes his sixth and fifth form repetition (which is made to an assistant), etc.

" *At* 10.—Fifty lines in Greek play or fifty lines in Demosthenes twice construed ; or if time be wanted read it off hastily a second time into English. Latin theme for Monday set now.

" Third lesson of Saturday at twelve. Thirty-five lines in select parts of Milton (suppose the printed *Elegant Extracts of Poetry*, by Dr. Knox, were used). This also would be a reading book or a library of poetry to a schoolboy. Now also Mathematics were done, which was my utter ruin at the time ; or speeches rehearsed, which I advise you to avoid altogether, as being the most painful and laborious instruction that can be given. Nothing wears a man out so much.

" Saturday is a half-holiday, and of course (like other half-holidays) is for writing, dancing, French, drawing, or even fencing —as it is now taught at Rugby.

" *Sunday.*—Absence at nine, at breakfast.

" *At* 10.—Do not use Secker, which works the master, not the scholar ; but use Greek Testament and work the scholar, and throw in any supplementary explanation—even the contents of all Secker on the commandments if you will. Or, if you have any Sunday's duty to do, make the boys abridge in writing two pages of Secker.

" *N.B.*—In abridgements made at Rugby (for they now abridge Watts's *History* instead of answering orally—which is an alteration, but not an improvement), Ingles calls on this or that boy to read four or five lines of his own written abridgement, and so hears the whole of the lesson to be abridged read over by the boys in such little parts once or twice over. This saves the master, and is right if he has other duty on a Sunday.

" Call absence after church in the church, or let the senior monitor prick down absentees ; or the form præpostors may do this severally. When you come to see me (of which, however, I must have notice, as I expect some relations for some time at Christmas), I can furnish you with verses, themes, and hints, and with Latin themes—themes, etc., which you can copy if you will.

" Horace's *Odes* and *Epodes* are divided into four equal parts ; one part is construed in each half-year—being construed over regularly a first time at each lesson, and read over quickly into English for a second construing over ; and thus the whole of the *Odes* is finished in two years. You may mark twelve divisions in your Horace, when you come to see me at Christmas ; and then bring your Homer and Virgil and Milton for the same purpose.

" *Odes* are read for about four weeks and not more, or not five weeks altogether, each half-year. Four lessons are construed in them in each week—viz. sixty lines Monday at three ; sixty lines Monday at five ; sixty lines Tuesday at ten ; sixty lines Wednesday at five.

" *N.B.*—Virgil is dropped during the four weeks of Ode-time, and such other lessons as belong to the Ode school-times.

" The above four lessons (or $4 \times 60 = 240$ lines) in *Odes* are thus repeated : forty lines Tuesday at seven ; forty lines

Wednesday at seven ; forty lines Thursday at seven ; thirty lines
on Friday at seven, together with twenty-five lines in Homer or
twenty-five lines *Poetæ Graci*, as may seem best according to the
important matter contained in either lesson for the week ; sixty
lines on Friday at three; thirty lines at third morning lesson
at twelve on Saturday (dropping the Milton in Ode-time).

" In all two hundred and forty lines repeated in the week ; or
repeated three forties, two thirties, and one double of thirty, or
sixty.

"Geography, or the four quarters, with Antient Greece and
Italy—done for the second and fourth exercise of the week (on
Tuesdays and Thursdays)—is done once over in a year, and is
done for nine exercises.   For geography Cellarius in octavo, and
Guthrie's last edition by Dilly in octavo, with my geography,
will do.

" My geography may be had at Rowel's for a shilling a book
(by your application to Ingles, who has hacked and hewed my
book and reprinted it), and it will suit your purpose still.   I
have much improved it indeed, but I have not inclination now to
print it.

" Make a library for your boys, as I did—every boy giving
something at coming to school, and also on going away ; at least
a crown coming, and perhaps double going away.   Buy Knox's
*Elegant Extracts in Poetry—in Prose—*and *of Epistles* ; L'Em-
prière's *Classical and Historical Dictionary* ; Johnson's *Dictionary*
(in 2 vols., 8vo) ; with *Beauties of Pope* (in 2 vols., 12mo, 7s.) ;
Beauties of Spectators, Tatlers, and Guardians (2 vols., 12mo, 7s.) ;
Beauties of Adventurer, Connoisseur, Rambler, and Idler (2 vols.,
7s.).   These may be got immediately by a sufficient subscription
among the boys.

" Two declamations *pro* and *con* are made once in an half-
year.   Each declamation is divided into two exercises, and made
as two Latin themes : *Exordium* and *Prima Pars Probationis*,
for one theme ; and for a second theme, *Secunda Pars Probationis* and *Peroratio.*

" *Greek Plays.*—Burgess's *Pentalogia*, with a Latin translation
printed and sold by Mr. C. Dilly in the Poultry ; but the Greek
Pentalogia is out of print and not to be had for a school, wherefore the five following plays—printed separately by Mr. Pote of
Eton—are now used in schools, and may be easily had.   'Tis
laughingly called Pote's *Pentalogia.*

Euripides—	(1) *Hippolytus* ;	(2) *Medea.*
Sophocles—	(3) *Philoctetes.*	
Æschylus—	(4) *Prometheus.*	
Aristophanes—	(5) *Plutus.*	

These plays are 3s. each, and great is the advantage (to keep parents in good humour) of purchasing each half-year only what the boy uses ;—as you will find. Keep down expences.

" If no translations are printed to these (for the boys at Eton do now, I believe, depend for construing the plays on tutors), then you may get two or three old editions with Latin translations for a few shillings and lend them to the boys, as I did.

" The above plays are a good and sufficient specimen. Read also Demosthenes and Pindar, as you read Greek plays.

" If you should want more, 'tis probable more plays will be printed at Eton, by the time you will have finished the above.

" If you provide books (as Heyrick of Leicester and many masters do), then I recommend C. Dilly in the Poultry as an honest man for your bookseller—who will allow you twelve per cent on books, and perhaps more on paper, pens, pencils, etc., etc. If you do not provide books, give the profit to an assistant (it will help to pay his salary), or at least give it to your writing master, unless borough interest requires you to deal with a Shrewsbury bookseller.

" Avoid giving a whole holiday after five weeks completed as the worst of plagues, for you are sure of having a large school. The three half-holidays on Tuesday, Thursday, and Saturday are excellent things both for master and boy, leaving exercises and masters of accomplishments to fill them up. If you are obliged to give a whole holiday, suffer it not to pass without a regular exercise, by way of rider to direct it and preserve it from wild schemes and excursions.

" Candles allowed till a quarter before ten for fifth and sixth forms, and till nine for all below. A quarter clock saves much bell-ringing. Boys are locked up from a quarter after six to eight, by increases or decreases of a quarter of an hour according to the season.

" Bed-room doors are opened in the morning at half after six ; and on Sunday or a whole holiday at seven—and there is absence at breakfast at nine as well as at other meals.

" It is a cheap plan and a good one to take in the fourth form Dalzel's *Collectanea Minora*, instead of Greek Æsop and Greek Testament ; for it contains many parts of Greek Æsop—of ποικίλη ἱστορία—with various poetic selections ; so that one purchase serves for many books both in prose and poetry. It is equally good to take Dalzel's *Collectanea Majora* for the fifth form in two vols. octavo, the one volume being prose according to *Scriptores Græci*, the other volume being poetry and answering to our *Poetæ Græci*, and both contain many the same things with those our Eton books : and Dalzel's publication is of such sort as to serve even instead of the purchase of Homer's *Odyssey*, and *Poetæ Græci* too ; for there is much of the *Odyssey* at least in it—of the *Iliad*, I believe none. You may begin at least with a purchase of this in your school library. The saving expence in books is a great consideration; and the scale is easily enlarged at any time. Dalzel's notes are an excellent companion for a boy or master too, in such parts of *Scriptores Græci* and *Poetæ Græci* as are common to Dalzel and those Eton books. Dalzel has no Latin, but excellent and scholar-like notes in English; but this mode of teaching Greek without Latin is now prevalent in many places, as at the Charterhouse in London, Mr. Innes's at Warwick, and, I have heard, at Winchester. There is no objection to it, but the despair it may occasion to dull boys, who, it is answered, must rely on the brighter boys after all. You will judge, therefore, what you will do in this matter, after purchasing one set of either of the above, which will cost you but little, and nothing if bought for the boys' library. I send this to assure you that I am not forgetful of you, and will prepare you another sheet as soon as I can—in a very few days. I have just placed one son at Rugby in the upper fourth, and one son in the fourth at Charterhouse, to which I was invited by a voluntary and unsolicited offer of Lord Dartmouth, whose two sons, the two Legges, I educated. It is now an exceeding great benefit—£40 a year to the Bachelor at College, and £60 a year to the Master of Arts—being an eight years' benefit after leaving school, and the education is almost for nothing.

"I heartily give you and Mrs. Butler joy, in which Mrs. James joins with me. I thank you for your kind invitation; but I shall hope at Christmas to have all my children with me, now scattered. Mrs. James and I shall be glad to see you for three or four days, and Mrs. Butler, if you travel our way at Christmas, and indeed whenever you may come. In the meantime I will satisfy your wishes by writing; being your faithful friend,

"T. JAMES.

"I am just returned from a journey to Rugby and the Charterhouse, and I have also not been well, but am recovering. Was your lower master the Rev. H. C. Adams whom I know, or is it some other Adams that is discarded? You are right. By no means *fix* your business the first three or four weeks. Try the boys as for placing and classing, and make all easy to yourself, as I did at first, and consider your form business well before you give out a scheme. Once construing must do, and once reading off into English, as you must probably have the fifth, sixth, and fourth form too, if not some grammar boys, while your assistant takes the third and second forms and some grammar boys. Innes gets his assistants from Brazenose, Oxford—hardy working fellows—and gets them curacies. I have no doubt your Cambridge acquaintance can find out men; and bargain for their board. Entertain them not yourself."

The second letter is dated " Harvington, near Evesham,

Worcestershire, October 17th, 1798," and begins with the lessons of the upper fourth, or the two removes of the upper fourth form. I need not give the details, for which I must refer the reader to the original letters, but will confine myself to Dr. James's more suggestive comments.

" *Tuesday, at* 10.—Virgil, thirty-five lines. Lower remove, twelve verses from Horace's *Odes*—or Gay, etc., for the lower remove ; but the upper of the two removes make Latin themes this day. These exercises are made in school from eleven o'clock till one.

* * * * *

" *Wednesday, at* 10.—Willymot's *Peculiars* turned into Latin, and parse it—one and a half pages.

" *N.B.*—I think the good Latin, or master's Latin, was given out to the boys after this lesson.

* * * * *

" Throughout the school I found no proportionate improvement in Latin, until I introduced the making every exercise in Latin prose (fifth form excepted) as a lesson first. It saves blunders then, and it fully instructs the boys, because each boy hears then the faults of rendering corrected ; which is not so when exercises are looked over separately.

" *Thursday, at* 7.—Willymot's *Peculiars* looked over. In general the master's good Latin is expected, or something like it. Say Greek grammar as before.

" If the *Peculiar* exercises be many in number, then read one-third of one boy's exercise, or one-third or one-half of another's, making all stand by from the very first to hear your observations, and making all to continue to pick up your alterations, until it come to their several turns to be looked over. This same method may be extended to all Latin prose exercises whatever (except themes).

* * * * *

" *Half-Holiday.*—Upper remove have a verse theme set, twelve verses. The lower remove make ten verses as on Tuesday, *coram magistro.* Innes takes his boys into school each holiday afternoon for a time, until they have finished their exercises for the day. This secures the work and is wise ; but an assistant must be with them.

" *Friday.*

* * * * *

"You will observe how much I found it necessary, by experience, to have Ellis, Clarke, etc., done as lessons, as well as to have every Latin prose exercise (being a translation into Latin) done first lesson fashion. So very slow is the progress of some boys in making Latin, and so much do their own operations therein require to be watched.

" *Saturday.*

*   *   *   *   *

" *N.B.*—Sallust would be a better book for Latin, etc. Better also are some of the *Conciones et Orationes e Livio,* etc., but much of this last is too hard. I would not, however, drop Britain, or any interesting part of Cæsar. His sentences are long ; his expressions will not work into themes. His military descriptions are not more useful to boys than a tale of the battles of kites and crows would be.

*   *   *   *   *

" *Lower Fourth, or Second Removes.*

" *Friday,* at 3.—Thirty-six lines of Ovid's *Metamorphoses* repeated. Boys learning French repeated only thirty-six lines.

" *At* 5.

*   *   *   *   *

" *N.B.*—Boys were confined after this lesson, and made to set about as much of their making Latin for next succeeding Wednesday's *Peculiars* as could be done in an hour's time.

*   *   *   *   *

" Lower School.

" *Upper Third Form, or two Removes called Upper and Lower Greek, or two Half-Years.*

*   *   *   *   *

" *Sunday.*—Catechism said at ten.

" If you have duty on a Sunday, then your Catechism and English private prayers must be said by the lower boys on Saturday at the third morning school as often as you think right. Thus the upper third might say their private prayers once a month, and perhaps often enough. Less boys may say Catechism one week, and prayers another."

It is clear that boys were expected to, and no doubt did, say their prayers in their bed-rooms, just as they did in my time at Shrewsbury, and no doubt do in all good schools at present. The monthly repetition of the prayers was only to ensure their not being forgotten or neglected.

" *Lower Third, or two Lower Removes of the Third Form.*

" *Monday,* at 5.—Construe or explain and repeat strictly a page and a half of Latin Syntax. (Boys require much of this.)

*   *   *   *   *

"Always have, in *all* forms, at least one English exercise a week. Mind the spelling.

"*Second Form.*

*   *   *   *   *

"Confine boys to get their lessons in school (thus you are sure of it), and do not let them out to get lessons at home ; for they get them not, but get into scrapes.

*   *   *   *   *

"No rule can be laid down for first form lessons. Two lines (I have known one line) in *As in præsenti*, or three, or even four lines, may be got at a lesson, the first time over, according to the age and powers of a boy. They do nouns first, then verbs.

*   *   *   *   *

"Reading and spelling by the writing master.

"Observe that, having since I wrote last procured Dalzel, I cannot by any means, at your first setting out, recommend the changing of our Eton books for Dalzel's *Miscellanea Minora*, or his *Miscellanea Majora* (though 'tis well to have them in the school library) : and for this reason—first, because the Greek without the Latin will be only a sort of inexplicable and learned puzzle to all dull boys (and such you must have) ; next, because many boys will despair of doing without Latin, unless they can have the assistance of a tutor to prepare them.

"It is not possible to lay down any rules for provisions of meat and drink. I allowed four bushels of malt to a hogshead —that is, to about seventy gallons ; and I brewed twelve bushels together (which is very much indeed in favour of good beer). I advise you to brew no ale at all—only the above table beer. Buy your porter or ale, for your own drinking ; for if your ale be accessible it will exhaust your pocket. During all the latter years of my mastership I brewed no ale ; for it always spoiled my small beer. It may even answer to buy (at a brewhouse) your small beer, if you can get it good. I have sometimes thought—for Mrs. James had no rule—that three-quarters of a pound of meat for each boy (including bone) was rather beyond the mark, and that half a pound was certainly below it, unless it were just after the holidays, or when they had money in their pockets. Provide enough ; for yourselves and servants must also be provided for. Whatever is left (small bits on plates, etc., I gave to poor women with the pot liquor, three times a week, and with scraps of bread in it) will clearly do for a hash next day—which boys like.

"T. JAMES.

" Consult ease. Make no exertions at first going off. I was near to destroying all my hopes by it. Walk—ride—don't read after supper or just before bed-time. I shall write again, and then answer me. Dr. James's eight servants always dined after the boys, on what they had left ; and we always had a separate dinner for ourselves. Lay down, therefore, no rules in respect of provisions, lest it produce a want, and a little experience will soon direct you ; and nothing is lost, for hashes consume all that ; but Mrs. Butler must seek after the housekeeper, or you will soon probably lament it bitterly. She must oversee all provisions ; and particularly *while she can*, and until your general provisions for the week be a little settled and reduced to a system. This Mrs. Ingles does, Mrs. James always did. Even both my wives did this. —— [Name illegible—ED.] only looks after the linen and sick boys."

The third letter is dated " Harvington, near Evesham, Worcestershire, October 18th, 1798," and begins :—

" DEAR BUTLER,—I have now with this letter quite finished all you wished.

"I earnestly beseech you for your own sake not to present the Governors with any fixed, determined plan of government or school rules, just at present. By all means avoid this, at least till after Christmas, when you will have had some experience and some little time in the holidays to compose your rules with deliberation. Be assured that rules are but the offspring of experience, and therefore before any code of laws be formally presented to the Governors enable yourself at least to judge of the wisdom and expediency of your laws by the observation of a few weeks. Show by action, show by the rules communicated from hour to hour to your scholars, that you are not without laws ; but take time to do yourself a little credit, if indeed you are not yet quite sated with literary honour. But, be that as it may, you were then single ; but you have now a lady depending on your welfare, and the probability of many other dependants may be expected. Therefore, as I can do you more service in this respect than you may be aware of, I advise that you and Mrs. Butler should pay me a visit at Worcester for some days in the Christmas holidays, and we may then confer together. I will *endeavour* to get my volume of school rules, and the other volume of rules for regulating and constructing the expence of education (drawn up about the time of quitting), if Dr. Ingles will send them me by my son William, as I conclude he will.

" The Rugby time of breaking up is now the Monday before St. Thomas ; my son John will also then come from the Charterhouse, and we may chance to pick up something from him, and at any rate it is possible that, from personal conversation with me and Mrs. James, you may find it a very beneficial and gainful journey in point of saving you money in such a concern as you are to undertake. This is the best advice I can give you. The compliance with it I leave to your own decision. In the meantime I think it may be useful to present you with a general list of all the books used. Some such list must be put into the hands of your bookseller, or assistant, or writing master, who may supply the books, with the names of the boys to be supplied each half-year at the bottom of the books of each form.

"*N.B.*—It is possible that the prices of books may be increased since my time, by the new tax on paper.

"A List of Books used at Rugby School,

with the several Fines imposed for Books lost or not satis-factorily accounted for.

"*First Form.*

"*Accidence.* · Price 9*d.*; fine 2*d.* Bound in leather. *Latin Grammar.* 1*s.* 9*d.*; fine 4*d.* [Marked, or certain lines crossed out by the seller, at price 1*d.* It is also not pierced or fastened with leather thongs (which renders the price 2*d.* less), but sewed in bands or bound in leather. *No* school-book except such as was sewed in bands or bound in leather was used at Rugby; for experience had shown the folly and expensiveness of other contrivances, or of canvas binding.]

"Boys' names to be written on the leaves at the top in all books. So also names in hats, sleeves of coats, especially greatcoats, in the upper shoe-leather, etc., etc.   *   *   *   *   *

"Entick's *Latin Dictionary* was once used for lower boys, but by all means take the octavo Ainsworth, for Entick is not fit for even second form boys; look out *correptus* or any participle, and you will perceive that there is nothing to lead the child to *corripior*. Then the several meanings of words are not differently distinguished by figures as in Ainsworth, but are all huddled together. Now a master will often lead a boy's mind from the first sense of a word to the second, and so enable the boy to see the connection, which may be delicately traced in Ainsworth.   *   *   *   *   *

"*Lower Fourth Form.*

"*Schrevelii Lexicon.* Price 7*s.* 6*d.*; fine 1*s.* 6*d.* [Query whether this may not be worn out fairly before a boy reaches the fifth?]   *   *   *   *   *

"*N.B.*—If the Greek Testament be used on Sunday, it will be best to have the whole Greek Testament, I guess at about 2*s.* 6*d.*

I do not recommend it to you to have a Sunday's lesson, unless
you think it right, for I think you will soon find the comfort of
having a clear holiday on a Sunday. At any rate make such
a lesson a mere construing, short and easy. You know the
worth of Hardy's Greek Testament with Latin notes for this
purpose. Get your boys close to you and speak low. This saves
you inconceivably.

*   *   *   *   *

" *Secker's Lectures.*   3s. 6d.   [Better left out and put into the
boys' common library for Sunday reading. It will waste you to
death to lecture in it. 'Tis worse than preaching.]

    Cellarius's *Antiqu. Geog.*   6s. ; fine 1s.
    Guthrie's *Modern Geography.*   9s. ; fine 1s. 6d.

*   *   *   *   *

" Books of amusement for upper boys' library :—
    Guthrie's *Geography.*
    Beauties of Spectator, Tatler, etc.   2 vols.   7s.
    Beauties of Rambler, Adventurer, etc.   2 vols.   7s.
    Beauties of Pope's Works.   7s.
    Elegant Extracts in Prose.   Large edition, 8vo.   About
      13s. or 14s.
    Elegant Extracts in Poetry.   Large edition, 8vo.   About
      14s.
    Elegant Epistles.   About 12s. or 13s.
    Adam's *Roman Antiquities.*   About 7s. or 8s.
    L'Emprière's *Bibliotheca Classica.*   About 8s. or 9s.
    Enfield's *Speaker.*   2 vols.   About 8s.

" For little boys' library :—
    Percival's *Moral Tales.*   About 3s.
    Goldsmith's *History of England* in 1 vol.   12s.
    Tales of the Castle.
    The Old English Baron.   About 3s. 6d.
    Sandford and Merton.   (There is an abridgement of this.)
    Adelaide and Theodore.
    Marmontel's *Tales.*
    Bible epitomised (Dilly).
    Telemachus.   About 4s.
    Trusler's *Principles of Politeness,* abridged   from   Lord
      Chesterfield's Letters.   About 1s. 6d.
    Flowers of Antient History.   2 small vols.   About 7s.
    Flowers of Modern History.   2 small vols.   About 7s.
    Flowers of Modern Voyages.   2 small vols.   About 7s.
    Flowers of Modern Travels.   2 small vols.   About 7s.
    Gay's *Fables.*   Small edition.
    Robinson Crusoe.   1s.

" For writing school and little boys' reading there are :—
    Mrs. Trimmer's *Easy Introduction to the Knowledge of Nature and the Scriptures.*
    A spelling book or dictionary.   The last is very cheap.
    Ash's *Introduction to Lowthe's Grammar.*
    The *Footsteps* to Mrs. Trimmer's *Sacred History.*
    History of Little Jack—which is full of goodness for little boys."

One would have thought that Mrs. Trimmer might have been approached without footsteps. After a few passages which may be omitted, Dr. James continued :—

" Such ordinary rules given by word of mouth as you may find most immediately convenient, and, of course, most likely to be perpetual, may be, and must be, delivered to your boys from day to day. These will suffice at present—such as no article of a tradesman without a note, except from the person supplying with stationery wares. Restraint of time allowed after clock striking—at absences, at dinner, etc.—twenty minutes, or at most half-hour (suppose), without whipping, but after that always inflict it, unless detained by a parent, signified by a note, or by an assistant, etc. ; to lock up at dusk with prayers in all seasons—to whip if absent from school-house beyond the time after clock-striking (beyond such time as before mentioned). Use impositions of translations as little as possible, though they, or the more troublesome repetitions, or solitary confinement when the weather admits, must be used for all such non-attendance as above, between the quarter (for some minutes at least must be allowed after clock-striking, for difference of watches and clocks, while you always go by your own clock) and the half-hour or moment of active punishment. Nothing done at first and while your numbers are small—for they must be great, and will be great sooner than I wish for your sake,—and while every order is new, and received as a thing expected—nothing, I say, will be grievous now, but everything new afterwards will in this age stir up revolutionary principles ; for some such spirits must exist, and there is no garden without weeds. The tares must grow with the wheat, and you, like the good sun, must shine on both. Make all your rules with ten boys as strict as you mean them to be with two hundred ; and now is the time for enacting laws. You are most wise in not saying one word of what you make clearer, or what is now better or wiser than before it has been. All boasting is hideous—look at the French—and all improvements will be better evinced by the eye and by the facts than by empty words, which only expose the speaker to the charge of vanity behind his back, to dislike, etc.—and besides to numerous enemies; for they must have some friends, and these, like the mice in the fable, will hurt you. My kindest respects and Mrs. James's to Mrs. Butler. Once more we wish to see you. I cannot think of leaving my children, then assembled from school.

"Your friend,
"T. JAMES.

"For your assistant scruple not to get Clarke's translation of Ovid's *Metamorphoses* (printed for Hawes, Clarke, and Collins, Paternoster Row, 1769); Patrick's translation of Terence (printed by Dilly); Gekman's translation of Tully's *Offices*, which is excellent (printed for Rivington, 1753); Watson's translation of Horace (2 vols.); Davidson's translation of Virgil (2 vols.); some plain translation—not Melnouth's—of *De Amicitia*, as Ellis's, and *De Senectute*; and all other translations, as Rowe's Sallust, for his private use. It expedites business when many forms are to be heard, and when the mind is weary. It is the way also to have business well done, if it is done easily. God bless you.

"Before I had studies I used to let my boys study by day in their bed-rooms, but observe this will spoil all your beds, bed-quilts, bedding, and curtains. Better, therefore, to send them into school to get their lessons, with an assistant. I should think £60 a year would serve for an assistant boarding out; in time you may get him a curacy."

So end these most kind and interesting letters.

I went to the British Museum intending to get out all the books of amusement for the boys' library and look at them, so I began with Guthrie's *Geographical Grammar*, and found the preface to lead off thus :—

"To a man sincerely interested in the welfare of society and of his country, it must be particularly agreeable to reflect on the rapid progress and general diffusion of learning and civility, which within the present age have taken place in Great Britain. Whatever may be the case in some other kingdoms of Europe, we in this island may boast of our superiority to those illiberal prejudices, which not only cramp the genius, but sour the temper of man, and disturb all the agreeable intercourse of society. Among us learning is no longer confined within the schools of the philosophers, or the courts of the great, but, like all the greatest advantages which heaven has bestowed upon mankind, it is become as universal as it is useful."

*   *   *   *   *

"Asia next claims our attention ; which, however, though in

some respects the most famous quarter of the world, offers, when compared to Europe, extremely little for our entertainment and instruction. . . . The immense country of China alone, renowned for the wisdom of its laws and political constitution, equally famous for the singularity of its language, literature, and philosophy, deserves to be considered at some length.

"In Africa the human mind seems degraded below its natural state. To dwell long upon the manners of this country, a country so immersed in rudeness and barbarity, besides that it could afford little instruction, would be disgusting to every lover of mankind. . . . A gloomy sameness almost everywhere prevails ; and the trifling distinctions that are discovered among them, seem to arise rather from an excess of brutality on the one hand, than from any perceptible approaches to refinement on the other."

As regards ancient history, we find that the year 1794 B.C.—

"is a pretty remarkable æra with respect to the nations of heathen antiquity, and concludes that period of time which the Greeks considered as altogether unknown, and which they have hardly disfigured with their fabulous narrative." *

I also saw indexed under Mr. Guthrie's works *A General View of Geography*, etc.,† which I sent for. Opening it on page 10, I was somewhat startled by the following passage : " Those circular lines which run across G's world from side to side, or from east to west, are called Parallels of Latitude." But on reading further I saw that it was only Guthrie's world that was intended. On this however, I tore myself from the volume, nor did I dare to open another in Dr. James's list, lest I should be lured on till I had lost all wish to return to my original subject. For all the smaller books are bound up, in the Museum Library, with other small books, which I could see would be just as entertaining. I therefore sent the books back, and content myself with indicating this mine of wealth to others who may have more time to work it.

* Guthrie's *New Geographical, Historical, and Commercial Grammar*, etc. (London : John Knox, 1771), Vol. I., pp. 48, 49.
† Coventry, 1789.

CHAPTER IV.

FIRST YEARS AT SHREWSBURY.

Appointment of Mr. Jeudwine as Second Master.—The Relations between him and Mr. Butler.—Hostile Reception at Shrewsbury.— Candidature for the Head-Mastership of Rugby.

THE College of St. John's appointed J. Jeudwine, Esq., to the Second Mastership of Shrewsbury about a month after Mr. Butler's installation as Head-Master. I have no reason to think that there had been any disagreement between him and Mr. Butler, but the latter had evidently anticipated the appointment with misgiving. From the first the two seem to have been unable to get on together, partly no doubt from incompatibility of temper, but perhaps even more from the nature of an arrangement which seems as though designed for the purpose of setting people at variance who might otherwise have worked well with one another. The second master was irremovable, and, unless two men are exceptionally well suited, strained relations are almost sure to arise from the attempt to couple them as responsible head, and irresponsible, irremovable second.

I asked the late Professor Kennedy, who was between four and five years in Mr. Jeudwine's house, what kind of a man he was, and was told that he had no power of keeping boys in order. "They could do what they liked; they could almost pull his coat-tails and call him 'Jacky' to his face. This was his chief demerit. I suppose you know that he and Dr. Butler did not speak?"

I have been assured, on convincing authority, that Mr. Jeudwine was not only as irreproachable in character as Dr. Butler himself, but that he was in many respects highly amiable as well; but managing boys was not his vocation, and the result was that within Dr. Butler's own school there grew up another over which, during many hours of the day, there was no effectual control—a school, moreover, whose head was more or less hostile to Dr. Butler himself. Small wonder that when Mr. Welldon succeeded to the Second Mastership in 1836, he should have found his hands full.

For seven-and-thirty years the first and second masters addressed each other by letter. They generally wrote in the third person, and presented their compliments to one another. Sometimes they called each other Sir, and I have found at least one letter beginning " Dear Sir." The minutes of the trustees, throughout Dr. Butler's head-mastership, prove that he and Mr. Jeudwine pulled different ways. I have not, however, found any complaint made by Dr. Butler except in letters to Mr. Jeudwine himself. I will give the first of these, dated early in 1799, and the last, dated thirty-six years later; the intermediate ones may, with one or two exceptions, be very well spared. The two men were reconciled as Mr. Jeudwine lay on his death-bed. I have been told, but cannot vouch for it, that they took the Sacrament together—a scene than which I can imagine nothing more full of pathos. Mr. Jeudwine died, and for six months Dr. Butler had in Mr. Welldon a second master with whom he would have found it easy to co-operate, if he had not by this time been so far worn-out that nothing was to be henceforth easy.

I should have been very glad to be able to pass this story over, but without touching on it (and I do so as lightly as I can) I can convey no idea of the difficulties which Mr. Butler had to face. Without for a moment raising the question who was in the main right, or with whom the quarrel began, and assuming the faults to have been equal upon both sides, the mere fact of having a second whom he could not change but with whom he could not, in any sufficient sense of the word, co-operate, must have gone near to making success impossible. That he should have triumphed in spite of unceasing antagonism within the school ; that he should have so controlled himself during seven-and-thirty years as never once, that I have seen, to have been betrayed into angry or uncourteous language to his opponent ; that he should have avoided all public scandal save what was inseparable from Mr. Jeudwine's complaints to the trustees,—these things have filled me with an admiration which I am confident the reader will not be slow to share. Even though Dr. Butler had not changed the face of public school education from one end of England to the other, though he had never created a great school, and turned out a brilliant band of scholars, the foremost of whom no doubt in some respects surpassed their teacher—even though he had done nothing but command his temper so admirably for so many years, I should still have thought no pains I could bestow upon his memory so great as that memory deserved.

For it was not only within the school that the mischief was felt. There was soon formed a Jeudwine party within the town, who for some years pursued Mr. Butler with a hostility that must have been singularly hard to bear without loss of self-restraint. Every calumny which small-town small-talk could devise was started, as calumnies are sure to be started against those who have or are supposed to have a mind of their own. Of all offences in a pro-vincial town, this, so far as I have observed things, is the most unpardonable. A man may do pretty well what he likes, provided that he does not like anything very much, and neither knows nor cares to know how to get at his own likes more definitely ; but let him show a tendency to think for himself, and he must take the consequences ; a man of strong individuality on coming as a stranger into a small town causes apprehension, and it is felt that he should be watched closely before being allowed to have his own way.

In Dr. Butler's correspondence I scarcely ever find Mr. Jeudwine's name. It is only mentioned to tell parents that their boys are to go to Mr. Jeudwine's house, or in some other like way. Of irritation there is not so much as a trace. I had never heard from my father, nor indeed from any one else till I inquired of Professor Kennedy, that there had been any coldness between the two ; all I know is from the letters now in the British Museum which they from time to time addressed to one another, and which are fairly sampled by the first and last, which follow immediately here ; * to such a pitch, however, did matters go, that a very polite note from Mr. Iliff (another master), written on Mrs. Butler's behalf, when the school was full to overflowing, and asking how many boys Mr. Jeudwine proposed to send home on such and such a day by such and such a coach, so that she might arrange her own boys accordingly, was met by a flat refusal to give the required information, and this refusal was persisted in. Even as late as 1831 Mr. Jeudwine still considered himself aggrieved and appealed to the trustees, who, however, supported Dr. Butler so powerfully that Mr. Jeudwine does not appear to have had recourse to them again.

The two letters above referred to are as follows :—

---

* Cf. also Memorandum by the Rev. A. Willis, November 2nd, 1832.

" Mr. Butler with the greatest reluctance feels himself obliged once more to request Mr. Jeudwine's strictest attention to the manner of education and conduct of the school which was laid down in the paper sent to him after the school had opened in January last. He is compelled to observe, with great concern, how impossible it is to conduct the school, especially in its present state, without the strictest punctuality of attention in all the masters both to the hours and method of teaching laid down by the head-master, and without an account given to the head-master of the conduct of the boys. Mr. Butler expresses his sincerest and most heartfelt wish to render the situation agreeable to all with whom he is connected, though he cannot but add that he will never be led by any motives to depart from his duty so far as to forget what he owes to the school, to the parents, and to himself. Mr. Butler could not feel happy without making this frank avowal, and most earnestly hopes that Mr. Jeudwine will regard it as a mark of his extreme desire to be on the most friendly terms with him, and of his requiring nothing more from the second master than that liberal attention to the discipline of the school without which it cannot flourish or even exist."

I found no answer to the foregoing letter.

" Sir,—It is far from my wish to give you unnecessary trouble, but I observed that the boys could construe with a little occasional help, but could not parse at all, and if they were able to do the one, they should be able also to do the other. I confined myself merely to their own statement, which I do not find you contradict so far as the parsing is concerned; and if I am correct in this, I must beg you to attend to their improvement in this most essential particular. The way I would recommend this to be done, if they have not already been so practised in it, would be as follows :—

" For the next six weeks to reduce their lessons, short as they are, one-third, and to make them learn to construe and parse the whole of the lesson thus shortened; for it is bad to learn to parse a part only of a construing lesson, and it is only by construing and parsing that boys can be properly grounded.

" I would first make a boy, after construing, decline every substantive and adjective and conjugate every verb in the part which he is called up in, except perhaps where two words of the same declension or conjugation occur, when if he can do one well he need not do the other.

" I would then for the first week or fortnight parse it over to the boys by showing them the syntax rules, and their application, and making them turn to these in their grammar ; but in all cases the rule should be read to them in English, and the force of the example shown them.   They should be then called upon to parse it, at least once over, after the master.

" In a week or fortnight they should be required to prepare the parsing themselves, being allowed at first to turn to the syntax for the rules, if they cannot repeat them, which, however, they ought to be able to do.

" One of the most important lessons they can have is the construing the Latin syntax, and being made to show the force of the rules, which they may be led to at first by the little letters (*a*) and (*b*) which are usually prefixed to the governing and governed words in the syntax.   They might construe two or three pages and say by heart half or a whole page twice a week besides their first lessons, in which it might be useful sometimes to repeat a page or two of the accidence, by way of keeping it well in their memory.   A boy should never be allowed to give a Latin rule without first giving the reason, nor to construe a rule at one of the syntax construing lessons without afterwards reading it into English, and showing the force of the example.   In general, they will soon learn this.   Of course they will occasionally require explanation of some of the harder terms, as ' *redditivum*,' ' *absolutè sumptus*,' etc.

" I feel confident that by pursuing this course you will soon find a considerable improvement in the boys.   But for little boys punishment is occasionally necessary, and if you have not a convenient place in which to inflict it, I have no doubt the trustees would pay attention to an application which I mean no offence when I say I think it is your duty to make to them.
" I remain, Sir,
" Your obedient and humble servant,
" S. BUTLER.

" P.S.—If you wish I will now examine the second form, otherwise it is my intention not to examine either the third or second form for the next six weeks."

Mr. Jeudwine died October 22nd, 1835, aged sixty-one years.

I have found among Dr. Butler's voluminous papers only three, and these very brief, allusions to the hostility towards himself, which existed generally in the town for many years after his coming to Shrewsbury.   One of these is in the short sketch of the main events of his life, already referred to as made in 1838.   His words run :—

" 7. Bitter ill-treatment at Shrewsbury—a hard pill to digest, but truly a wholesome one, which brought me acquainted with mankind, and turned my thoughts from overweening vanity."

The other reference is in a letter to one of his clergy, then a young man, who had been distressed at finding himself misrepresented and misunderstood.   Dr. Butler, then Bishop of Lichfield, wrote :—

      *   *   *   *   *

" My advice to you, as a private friend, is the result of my own experience—not to make yourself too uneasy at the grumblings of dissatisfied and slanderous persons. I was hardened against them in early life, for during the first fifteen or eighteen years of my residence in Shrewsbury no man can have suffered more from vexatious and unprovoked calumny. I despised it ; it ceased to give me annoyance ; and when people found out that their kind intentions of hurting me were defeated by my contempt of them, they left off taking useless trouble. And so I say to you, do not be too much alive to every old woman's gossip. Do that which your conscience approves, and care for nothing else."

But for a very few passages, and for the anxiety that Mr. Butler evidently felt to remove a prejudice on the score of over-severity which he believed to exist against him in the minds of the trustees of Rugby, when he was standing for the head-mastership of that school in 1806, I should not have imagined that he had met with any hostility at Shrewsbury. But knowing that this was the case, and knowing also the relations existing between the two irremovable masters at the schools, and the partisanship which was sure to arise between their respective friends, I can hardly doubt that the hostility of the town should be traced mainly to this source. After about 1816 it seems to have died down, except for an occasional attack, in which the trustees and more influential townspeople invariably supported Dr. Butler.

FROM DR. JAMES.

(Original in Rugby School Library.)

."COLLEGE, WORCESTER, *October 24th*, 1800.

"DEAR BUTLER,—On the whole subject of speeches, which I have in quiet moments turned in my mind since I received yours, my advice is that you should not introduce action at all, but that you should follow altogether the mode of delivery in use in our two Universities in rehearsing public prizes, declamations, etc., which is also equally in use in the pulpit and House of Commons. Thus you will get rid of all gesticulation, in which, perhaps, you will never shine, and will bestow all pains and attention on the main thing—a delivery with propriety. For this purpose you will place your speakers (single or opposite to each other) on a sort of raised desk in the school, which need be nothing more than a board to lay the book, paper, or hand on, supported by two props on either side.

* * * * *

"Thus you would have all the advantages of a proper and sensible delivery, without the pleonasms of action. Some would like this, some perhaps would dislike it, and would prefer a delivery united with action, but you can do nothing which will meet with a general approbation, and what I recommend will please your governors and parents sufficiently, and not harass and worry you to death with what you have not naturally a taste for— imitating theatrical action—and which, by the bye, setting aside the stage, is useless. Now as to the speeches, I will send you the best collection I can when I receive the expected book from Rugby. The whole affair, according to my idea, will cost you no great trouble, and in this way of teaching every assistant master will be able of course to assist you to your heart's content; with action scarcely a soul can assist you. Another thing I recommend is to introduce the fewest speakers possible, say six, or eight, or ten, and I would not readily exceed those numbers, especially at first. Another thing will be worth attending to, namely, to have the speeches very seldom. It is a material interruption of serious business."

* * * * *

In 1801 Mr. Butler was appointed to the chapelry of Berwick, near Shrewsbury, and in 1802 Lord Clarendon presented him to the living of Kenilworth. These pieces of preferment rather detracted from than increased the somewhat narrow income that was all he could as yet look

to ; moreover, the first years of his mastership were, as I
have already shown, beset with much difficulty and discouragement. When, therefore, Dr. Ingles announced his
intention of resigning Rugby in 1806, Mr. Butler offered
himself as a candidate for that school. From the letters
that next follow it appears that he knew prejudice to exist
against him in many quarters on the score of his supposed
severity, but it does not seem that this had anything to
do with his failure to get the appointment. The following
few letters will be sufficient upon this head :—

To the Trustees of Rugby School.

"*November 22nd,* 1806.

"We the undersigned, being trustees of Shrewsbury School,
having already testified our full and unequivocal approbation of
the Rev. Mr. Butler's conduct in every respect as head-master
here, should not have conceived it necessary to have given any
further testimonial on the subject if it had not been represented
to us by Mr. Butler that a report injurious to him had been
circulated of severity on his part towards his boys. We therefore
think it our bounden duty, in justice to Mr. Butler, to certify that
we are perfectly satisfied of the malignant falsehood of such
report, and we most confidently assert the conduct of Mr. Butler
towards his boys to have been as kind, humane, and indulgent
as any reasonable parent could wish.

> W. Priffick.
> 1. Chas. Oakeley
> Tho. Eyton.
> 3. Thomas Stedman.
> Wm. Cludde.
> 1. Hugh Owen.
> 2. John Rocke.
> Edwd. Burton.
> 2. Joseph Loxdale.

"The numbers prefixed to the names of the trustees signify
the number of their sons who have been or now are under Mr.
Butler's tuition at Shrewsbury."

Draft of Letter to (?) about November 1806.

"In the year 1798 I was appointed Head-Master of Shrewsbury, which I found with scarcely a single boy. I was soon

inundated by an influx of town boys of all ages from sixteen downwards, whom as the sons of burgesses I was compelled to admit, though none of them had received any regular education. Besides these, many other boys came to me, some from various public and private schools, and some from their nurseries. No regular school, or discipline, had been established here for about twenty years. The third master, indeed, for the two last years had had six boarders, two of whom came into my house.

"In a town with fourteen thousand inhabitants, many temptations are held out to boys, and many regulations are necessary which are not required in a smaller place ; and the system which I was persuaded to adopt of not mixing at all in the society of the town, that I might attend more closely to the duties of my situation, proved mistaken. I furnished a subject for the Shrewsbury tea-tables without having any opportunity for defence. No idea of punishment had ever occurred to the good people of Shrewsbury, because no regular school had been established here for twenty years, so that whenever a boy went home (and it is to be remembered I had many day scholars as well as some town boys who boarded in my house) with a report, however true or false, that either himself or any of his schoolfellows had been punished, it furnished matter for observation and ill-natured remarks.

"An event which, though grossly misrepresented, gave colour to the prevailing gossip, took place about six years ago. Two boys whom I received into my house, apparently on good recommendation, but who I have since learnt had been previously expelled from the Charterhouse, went without leave to the races, and did not return till eleven o'clock at night, when they came home drunk. I called for them to punish them the next morning. They refused to submit, instigated the boys to support them, and ran away. They were followed by my servant and myself; the former first came up with them, when the oldest, about seventeen, drew a knife on him. I had them secured, and punished them with the ordinary school discipline, and on their contumacy I expelled them as an example which was become necessary for the preservation of my authority. From that time to this I may safely affirm that I have not punished six boys, upon an average, in the half-year, though I have never had less than from fifty to sixty boys in the school. The same general laws of punishment prevail here as in other public schools, and any one who has been educated at a public school will know what inference to draw from this declaration. I believe I have the affections of my boys as fully as any master can reasonably expect, and the indignation which every trustee of Shrewsbury School, and every parent whom I have yet spoken to, has manifested on hearing the malicious calumny that has been circulated, convinces me that I stand high in their good opinion."

According to the Act of 1777 for regulating Rugby School, Mr. Butler ought to have been elected, for it is there provided that "in the choice of such master regard shall be had to the genius of such master for teaching and instructing the children. And a preference shall be given to such as are duly qualified and have received their education at this school." No other candidate except Mr. Butler had been educated at Rugby; nevertheless Mr. Wooll was chosen, and retained the head-mastership till 1828, when he was succeeded by Mr. (as he then was) Arnold. Lord Cornwallis, then Bishop of Lichfield and Coventry, considered Mr. Butler to have been so badly used that he gave him the first prebendal stall that fell vacant after the election—that of Wolvey, worth about £60 per annum, to which Mr. Butler was appointed May 15th, 1807, and which he continued to hold till he was himself raised to the Bench.

FROM THE HONOURABLE WILLIAM HILL, M.P., AFTERWARDS LORD BERWICK.

"LONDON, *January* 21*st*, 1807.

*   *   *   *   *

"Perhaps you will not hereafter repent not publishing your Rugby business, though I think you have been hardly dealt with. One of the first persons I met on my arrival here was Lord Wentworth, and he said something civil about you, as either he was sorry, or was afraid I was sorry and disappointed, etc. I said in answer that it was what I expected from the tone of different letters I had seen, and that personally I must feel glad to keep you in Shrewsbury; *au reste*, that you had thought it a duty you owed to yourself and family to offer, and not being chosen, the matter that most affected us was, under the circumstances, a curiosity to know the reason of your being rejected, if the slander was done away.

"His reply was curious. 'Oh,' he said, 'the calumny was quite done away,' and that you must have been made perfectly easy on that score; but in answer to my first observation about my having little hopes from the beginning, he said for the matter of that he could have told me a long while ago that you had no chance.

" All this happened in the street, and he bustled away after we had engaged to call on each other. I was taken ill, and he kept his promise, but I could not see him ; however, I shall soon have an opportunity of talking to him, when I shall press him pretty home, and find out why you were so early decided against, and why I was not allowed to save you the mortification of proceeding if possible."

Mr. Butler's third child and only son, father to the present writer, was born November 28th, 1806. Dr. Parr was one of the godfathers, and his daughter Mrs. Wynne was godmother. Mrs. Wynne wrote to Mrs. Butler :—

"GARTHMERLIO, *March* 10th, 1807.

" DEAR MADAM,—After having grumbled and scolded and blushed from August to March at the repeated disappointments which so provokingly prevented me returning the contents of this parcel to you, my indignation and vexation are luckily in some degree calmed by finding that this delay has afforded me an opportunity of congratulating you on the birth of a son. I sincerely hope that you are perfectly well and in good spirits to assist at the ceremony of the christening—which I hear is to effect a sort of religious relationship between me and your little boy. And so much good-will do I bear to you that if my father neglects to teach his godson the requisite things in the vulgar tongue, I will readily make up for the omission by getting him instructed in the Welsh language, which appears to me the extreme point of vulgarity. Now I think this is behaving very well, for I know of no other probable deficiency in his education ; all the rest will be well done, but I tremble lest, in the confusion of tongues, the vulgar should unluckily be overlooked. I wish that you would all take flight from Shrewsbury to our mountains, when I promise that you shall find a most hearty welcome."

CHAPTER V.

HUGHES, PORSON, BLOMFIELD.

Thomas Smart Hughes.—Death of Porson.—Publication of First Volume of Æschylus.—Blomfield's Reviews in the *Edinburgh Review*.—Quarrel between Butler and Blomfield.—Character of Porson.—Butler's Letter to the Rev. C. J. Blomfield, B.A.

NOT a boy has been to Shrewsbury since 1806 without becoming more or less reverentially familiar with the name of Thomas Smart Hughes, who heads the long and ever growing list of Shrewsbury honours. Dr. Butler taught in the room in which he took the fifth and sixth forms (now the ground-floor room of the Shrewsbury Museum buildings on the right hand as one enters), panelled with oak, and every first-class distinction taken at Oxford or Cambridge by any of his pupils was painted upon the panels forthwith, and a half-holiday was given to the boys. When I was at school the panels were still *in situ* ; they are now of course on Kingsland in the new buildings. Hughes, some of whose letters will be given later, went to Shrewsbury in 1801, and was entered at St. John's, Cambridge, in 1803 ; he was the first to win credit for his school and teacher at either University. In those days the Classical Tripos had not been instituted, but Mr. Hughes gained the Browne Medal for the Latin Ode *Mors Nelsoni* in 1806, and for the Greek Ode *In Obitum Guglielmi Pitt* in 1807. He also took the members' prize for a Latin Essay in 1809 and 1810.

It may be added that he afterwards took a prominent place

in the University, especially in relation to the institution of the Classical Tripos, for which he frequently examined, and became well known in the literary world by his *Travels in Greece and Albania,* his continuation of Hume and Smollett's *History of England,* an edition of some of the great English Divines, and several vigorous publications in his office as Christian Advocate. He never failed to ascribe his success in life largely to his Shrewsbury train-ing, and was on terms of affectionate friendship with Dr. Butler till the day of his death. For further particulars concerning his life and numerous publications I must refer the reader to the *Dictionary of National Biography,* and to a memoir prefixed to the last edition of Mr. Hughes's continuation of Hume and Smollett's *History of England.*

At the end of September 1808 Hughes (then a master under Dr. George Butler at Harrow) wrote announcing the death of Porson, and urging Mr. Butler to stand for the Greek professorship thus vacated. Mr. Butler raised objec-tions, and Hughes wrote as follows to urge him further :—

*   *   *   *   *

"The bell is now ringing for school, and I have scarcely time to say that I have just heard that no doctor of any faculty can be a candidate for the Greek professorship ; pray, therefore, offer yourself, as your objection is removed. Monk, I hear, is the favourite, who has no more pretensions to it than myself except his M.A. degree. He was never considered at all superior to the common run of classics. I am surprised that your friends in Cambridge did not inform you of this. I see every day more and more that no one must leave the University if he expects to gain anything from it. Out of sight, out of mind."

Mr. Butler did not stand for the professorship, to which Monk was in due course appointed.

In the spring of 1809 the first volume of the Æschylus was published ; the Rev. J. J. Blakeway, writing June 14th, 1809, said :—

*   *   *   *   *

"I do not know whether I ought to congratulate or condole

with you on the termination of your Æschylean labours : the
conclusion of anything that has afforded us agreeable employment is matter of regret, rather than joy ; but I do not suppose
that the acquaintance of this old Grecian has been anything so
fascinating or hobby-horsical as to make you grievously lament
his departure. What Jews are these booksellers ! Fifty-three
shillings out of every hundred for the permission to let your book
occupy one foot of their shelves, and one yard of their ware-
houses ! This is indeed *sic vos non vobis* with a vengeance ; they
know their power, and their ability to injure the sale of most
books ; but I trust and believe this will not be the case with
yours, but that while the praises of the *clarissimus* or *doctissimus*
or *sagacissimus Butlerus* are in every *Bibliotheca Critica* or *Censura
Literaria* from St. Petersburg to Paris, from Jena to Florence,
the said learned man will reap more solid and substantial
satisfaction *pleno cum turget sacculus oro.*

" But I restrain myself, and, shocked to have detained your

reverence *longo sermone cum tot sustineas et tanta negotia solus,* I make

my retreat with all possible humility and with all obsequiousness of

prostration.

" Paternitatis vestræ servus addictissimus,

" BLAKEWAY."

I have here endeavoured to reproduce the effect of the
original MS., in which the lines grow continually farther
apart, and the letters grow smaller till the " Blakeway "
shrinks out in the minutest characters at the extreme
edge of the paper.

The only other letter of about this period that I need
give is one from Mr. Butler's mother, which refers to the
Jubilee in honour of the fiftieth year of King George the
Third's reign :—

" *October 26th,* 1809.

" My DEAR SON,—I hope you still continue to get better, and
I am very glad to hear you have no concern with Eschylus at
present ; I hope it will answer all your expectation, for the great
fatigue you have had with it.

" I must now tell you how loyall we have been at Kenilworth.

There were near thirteen hundred supplied yesterday with good beef and bread, and every one had a small portion of money besides to lay out for themselves.   Mr. Johnson gave a most excellent sermon on the occasion, and everybody was highly pleased.   I told you in my last Mr. Gresley gave an invitation to every respectable family in the village.   We sat down thirty-eight in the parlour.   There was a most excellent dinner, fish and game, and every other thing that the season could produce. Mr. and Mrs. Gresley are both so loyall.   Mrs. Gresley played ' God save the King ' three times, and we had the song to it, which was very well sung."

The words "and we had the song to it " suggest that, at any rate in country villages, the words of our national anthem were not yet familiar.

Mr. Butler's first volume, which contained the *Prometheus* and the *Eumenides*, was reviewed in the *Edinburgh Review* for October 1809 and January 1810 by C. J. Blomfield, afterwards Bishop of London, who was then on the point of bringing out his own edition of the *Prometheus*, which appeared in 1810.

Blomfield's review led to a long and very acrimonious quarrel between the two men and their respective friends, which has been dealt with at some length by Professor Mayor.   The quarrel was no doubt mainly due to the dislike which Parr and Porson felt for one another. Porson, indeed, was now dead, but any one who was known, as Butler was, to be an intimate friend of Parr's was certain to be attacked without much scruple by the Porsonian School then dominant at Trinity.

Each of the parties to the quarrel eventually regretted his several action, became friends with his opponent, and continued so for more than twenty years, until the death of Dr. Butler ; no attention, therefore, should be paid to any disparaging remarks about Blomfield that will appear in following letters, which indeed I should omit if they did not throw light upon the opinion of the time concerning

Porson himself. How far the less exalted estimate of this famous man's scholarship is justified I cannot say, but if an article signed " P," upon the Geography of Homer's *Odyssey*, which forms the opening pages of the opening number of the *British Magazine*,* is by him—and the prominence assigned to it suggests this, as also does the fact that Porson was then engaged on an edition of the *Iliad* and *Odyssey*—it is plain that he could be as reckless and as superficial as any subsequent writer on this subject has proved himself to be. It is enough to say that he places Scylla and Charybdis " certainly between Corsica and Sardinia."

The following extract from that singular book Dr. John Johnstone's *Memoirs of Parr* will help in some measure to explain the origin of a quarrel which influenced Cambridge coteries at the beginning of this century more profoundly than perhaps any other of the time :—

" Mr. Richard Porson remained at Hatton in the winter 1790-1791, collecting materials for future works, and enriching his mind with the stores of Parr's library and of his conversation. He rose late, seldom walked out, and was employed in the library till dinner reading and taking notes from books, but chiefly the latter. His notes were made in a small distinct text of the most exquisitely neat writing I have ever beheld. He was very silent, and except to Parr, whom he often consulted, and to whose opinions he seemed to defer, he seldom spoke a word. His manners in a morning, indeed, were rather sullen, and his countenance gloomy. After dinner he began to relax, but was always under restraint with Parr and the ladies.

" At night, when he could collect the young men of the family together, and especially if Parr was absent from home, he was in his glory. The charms of his society were then irresistible. Many a midnight hour did I spend with him listening with delight, while he poured out torrents of various literature, the best sentences of the best writers, and sometimes the ludicrous beyond the gay—pages of Barrow, whole letters of Richardson, whole scenes of Foote, favourite pieces from the periodical

---

* Published in 1800.

press, and among them I have heard recited 'The Orgies of Bacchus.'

"His abode in the house at last became so tiresome to Mrs. Parr, that she insulted him in a manner which I shall not record. From this time, the visits of Porson were not repeated at Hatton, and though there was no open breach of friendship on his part, there was no continuance of kindness, notwithstanding Dr. Parr's strenuous endeavours to secure his comforts and independence, by combining with other scholars, and using every effort of his interest to obtain an annuity for him."

Through the kindness of Professor J. E. B. Mayor, who had the story from the late Rev. W. H. Luard, who had it from Dyce, who had it from E. H. Barker, I have learned that the insult consisted in Mrs. Parr's setting a close stool for Porson at the dinner-table instead of a chair.

The fact of their having been worshippers of Porson throws so much light on the tone afterwards adopted by Monk and Blomfield towards Dr. Butler, that it may be well to confirm Dr. Johnstone's sketch with another by a different hand, which I venture to take from *The Correspondence of Richard Porson*, etc., edited by the late Rev. H. R. Luard.* That there was another side to Porson's character goes without saying, but that such a side as the one portrayed by Dr. Johnstone should have existed at all in the man whom Trinity held to be her greatest living ornament, explains, and even enables us to make allowance for, the somewhat autocratic spirit undoubtedly dominant in that noble foundation during the early years of this century.

The scene described in the following letter must have taken place about 1806 or 1807. The letter itself is addressed to Mr. William Upcott, by the Rev. T. S. Hughes, and is dated October 3rd, 1826.

    •   •   •   •   •

"This interview took place in the rooms of my private tutor,

---

* Cambridge Antiquarian Society. Octavo publications. 1867.

between whom and Porson a great intimacy subsisted. After about an hour spent in various subjects of conversation, during which the Professor cited a great many beautiful passages from his authors in Greek, Latin, French, and English, my tutor, foreseeing the visitation that was evidently intended for him, feigned an excuse for going into the town, and left Porson and myself together. I ought to have observed that he had already produced one bottle of sherry to moisten the Professor's throat, and that he left out another in case it should be required. Porson's spirits being at this time elevated by the juice of the grape, and being pleased with a well-timed compliment which I had had the good luck to address to him, he became very communicative, said he was glad that we had met together, desired me to take up my pen and paper, and directed me to write down, from his direction, many curious algebraical problems, with their solution, gave me several ingenious methods of summing series, and ran through a great variety of the properties of numbers. After about an hour's occupation in this manner, he said, ' Lay aside your pen, and listen to the history of a man of letters—how he became a sordid miser from a thoughtless prodigal—a . . . from a . . .—and a misanthrope from a morbid excess of sensibility.' (I forget the intermediate step in the climax.) He then commenced a narrative of his own life, from his entrance at Eton School, through all the most remarkable periods, to the day of our conversation. I was particularly amused with the account of his school anecdotes, the tricks he used to play upon his master and schoolfellows, and the little dramatic pieces he wrote for private representation. From these he passed to his academical pursuits and studies, his election to the Greek Professorship, and his ejection from his fellowship through the influence of Dr. Postlethwaite, who, though he had promised it to Porson, exerted it for a relation of his own.* ' I was then' (said the Professor) 'almost destitute in the wide world, with less than £40 a year for my support, and without a profession, for I could never bring myself to subscribe Articles of Faith. I often used to lie awake through the whole night, and wish for a large pearl.' He then gave me a history of his life in London, where he took chambers in the Temple, and read at times immoderately hard. He very much interested me by a curious interview he had with a girl of the town, who came into his chambers by mistake, and who showed so much cleverness and ability in a long conversation with him, that he declared she might with proper cultivation have become another Aspasia. He also recited to me, word for word, the speech with which he accosted Dr. Postlethwaite when he called at his chambers, and which he had long prepared against such an occurrence. At the

---

* John Heys, B.A. 1789.

end of this oration the Doctor said not a word, but burst into
tears and left the room. Porson also burst into tears when he
finished the recital of it to me. In this manner five hours passed
away, at the end of which the Professor, who had finished the
second bottle of my friend's sherry, began to clip the King's
English, to cry like a child at the close of his periods, and in
other respects to show marks of extreme debility. At length he
rose from his chair, staggered to the door, and made his way
downstairs without taking the slightest notice of his companion.
I retired to my College, and next morning was informed by my
friend that he had been out upon a search, the previous evening,
for the Greek Professor, whom he discovered near the outskirts of
the town, leaning upon the arm of a dirty bargeman and amusing
him by the most humorous and laughable anecdotes. I never
even saw Porson after this day, but I shall never cease to regret
that I did not commit his history to writing while it was fresh in
my memory."

Writing from Nuneaton, April 15th, 1810, T. S. Hughes
said :—

(Original destroyed by me.—ED.)

*   *   *   *   *

"Blomfield has been so flattered and caressed at Cambridge
that he is now quite spoiled, and is much disliked by a great
part of the University. There are some who think his attack
rude, unfair, and unscholarlike ; others think just the contrary.
Monk seemed to regard you with sentiments of great personal
kindness and respect, but was nettled when I abused the *critique*
and asked me whether at least I did not think it showed great
learning and ability. Blomfield prides himself upon it so much
that he now confidently owns himself the author. I don't know
whether he thinks he has mortified you or not, for I did not
condescend to hold much conversation with him. The review
in Cambridge is received better than it ought to be—I mean I
think they give too much credit to the author's learning ; indeed,
Cambridge has taken its opinions in classical literature entirely
from the *penetralia* of Trinity. I have heard several express an
opinion that it ought to be replied to. Mr. Wood was one who
wished me to do so, and I should have offered unless I had
known beforehand that you would either do it yourself, or not
have it done at all."

*   *   *   *   *

Mr. Butler did reply in April 1810, by means of " A

Letter to the Rev. C. J. Blomfield, A.B., etc." Of this production Professor Mayor says, I am afraid I must own with
justice, that it is written "in a tone of somewhat dreary
pleasantry." I will only make the following extract from
the synopsis given by Professor Mayor :—

" . . . ; for in this respect I differ from our lamented late
Greek Professor, whose general rule was to address his writings
and bestow a good deal of his time on the 'Juventus Academica,'
from whom he could not fail to obtain undeviating homage and
unqualified applause. . . . I need not, I am sure, bear my most
sincere testimony to the transcendent merits of that Colossus
of critical learning now no more. . . . But I cannot content
myself without entering my fearless and vigorous protest against
the narrow, jealous, dogmatising, vindictive, and invidious spirit
which both you and I well know to be prevalent among his
disciples. . . . His followers, absorbed in the contemplation of his
greatness, seem, I think, but too much inclined to indulge in
narrowness which will not listen to investigation, in jealousy
which will not admit a rival, in dogmatism which will not hear of
fallibility, in envy which will not allow of praise. I do not
recollect to have met with many passages in the writings of the
late Professor which tend to applaud his literary contemporaries ;
this could not arise from envy, because envy implies inferiority,
which that great man could certainly neither have felt nor
acknowledged. I should rather impute it in him to a fastidious-
ness of judgement, and a consciousness of the value of praise from
one so far above the generality of mankind as himself. But
whatever may have been the cause of this conduct, it certainly
has had a bad effect in its consequences among his disciples, and
has generated in them not unfrequently a certain narrowness or
niggardliness of praise not altogether becoming liberal and
candid men. But they are mostly young, and probably feel the
want of this commodity so much themselves, that they have but
little inclination to part with it to others."

Of Mr. Butler's reply the Rev. James Wood, afterwards
Master of St. John's, said in a letter dated May 27th,
1810 :—

*   *   *   *   *

"You have given Blomfield a severe, and, in the opinion
of those with whom I have conversed, a well-merited chastise-
ment. The motives which apparently induced him to make his

attack, were his observations well founded, are highly disgraceful to him.

*   *   *   *   *

" What steps the Trinitarians may take I know not ; they will feel the smart more acutely as the lash is laid on by a Johnian. I have observed the spirit of that society for nearly thirty years, and it has been their invariable and unceasing practice to abuse us. Whether in jest or earnest it matters not, the youths are brought up with a rooted aversion to St. John's, and, like bulldogs of true breed, are always ready to fall upon us at the loo of their seniors."

*   *   *   *   *

To Professor Monk, afterwards Bishop of Gloucester.

"*June 8th*, 1810.

*   *   *   *   *

" I looked upon your long silence—and I say so without any intention of sarcasm or insult—as a determined and pointed affront ; I acted on this supposition, and am perfectly satisfied with my conduct.   I do not mean my present letter to be an apology.   But having said this, let me also add that I fully accept your explanation, and have an equal claim on your belief of mine. I therefore repeat that I had no intention of making any of the dishonourable charges which you have supposed, and that, though I think my slight attack upon you was perfectly warranted, I shall not hesitate to avow both publicly and privately my belief that your neglect originated from mere inattention, and not from design.   Permit me now to add that, though I have a very extensive correspondence with many who are much occupied with public and private concerns of great importance, I never ex- perienced, but in one instance, and that was from a fellow of your own college, similar neglect, for you must remember that my letter was one that required an answer.

" Let me repeat also that both Mr. Blomfield and yourself were persons of whom I always thought well.   I could therefore have no animosity to gratify, by attacking either of you—in fact I can hardly consider what I said about you to be an attack.   As for Mr. Blomfield, I considered that, besides having made many erroneous and unfair statements, he was desirous of showing himself off at my expense ; if, therefore, to use a phrase of his own, he has 'caught a Tartar,' he must thank himself, for I was most sincerely and warmly well disposed towards him, and even now perhaps am less of his enemy than he supposes.   I detest resentment.   Towards you I feel none, being convinced that your explanation is sincere.

" If you chuse to interpret this letter as proof of my conviction that your behaviour to me originated rather from inattention than intentional neglect, you will interpret it as I mean it. If you chuse to consider it as proof that I bear you no hostility, have no kind of resentment lurking in my mind against you, and am perfectly willing to be on friendly terms with you, you will consider it in its proper light. View it as you please, but I have so much confidence in you, that I am sure you will not misconstrue or pervert it. I am, Sir, etc.,

"S. BUTLER."

No doubt in the letter actually sent the conclusion was more ceremonious, but I have only had the draft before me, and in this no more would be written than was necessary.

CHAPTER VI.

INSTALLATION SERMON—LUCIEN BUONAPARTE.

The Doctor's Degree.—Correspondence, December 16th, 1810—
February 4th, 1811.—The Installation Sermon.—Correspondence,
August 17th, 1811—December 5th, 1811.—Translation of Prince
Lucien Buonaparte's *Charlemagne.*—Correspondence, February
18th, 1812—December 28th, 1812.—Notes taken after a Visit to
Prince Lucien Buonaparte.—Difficulties about the School Chapel.

DOCTORS' degrees are not now thought so much of
as they were at the beginning of this century, but
Mr. Butler evidently believed that such a degree would
help him to establish the position of his school, and to the
end of his life regarded his having been made a Doctor by
Royal Mandate with satisfaction. Dr. Welldon told me
he heard Dr. Butler say that he had once complained to
Parr of the difficulty he had in keeping his boys under due
control. "Wear a wig, thir," said Parr; and the wig was
for a time tried. It used to hang in a small dark lobby, and
Butler would assume it on entering the schoolroom. The
boys, however, took liberties with it on every opportunity,
and the experiment proving unsuccessful, Butler again
complained to Parr, who this time said, "Wear a broader
brim, thir"—*i.e.* "Get yourself made a D.D.," whereon
Butler set about procuring the necessary Grace of the
Senate, with what success the following letter from T. S.
Hughes will serve to show. In passing I may say that
the Grace was carried in the non-regent house by 23 to 3,
and in the regent by 33 to 11.

CORRESPONDENCE, DECEMBER 16TH, 1810—FEBRUARY 4TH, 1811.

FROM T. S. HUGHES, ESQ. (AFTERWARDS REV.).

"HAIL, THOU THAT SHALT BE DOCTOR HEREAFTER!

"*December 16th,* 1810.

" MY DEAR SIR,—The thing is done, and done in grand style. We beat them off their legs and carried the Grace with a large majority. I think the Senate House was nearly as full as at an election. Hornbuckle and myself were out this morning from eight o'clock till one, flattering some, abusing others, and counteracting the Trinitarians.

" I went to King's College and made my friend Lonsdale speechify before the combination room upon the meanness of Tavel and his crew, and the effect of his eloquence was so great that the fellows of King's came in a body to vote for you and for the honour of Literature. Some of them had never trod the floor of the Senate House before. Those who pleaded their consciences for voting against you, we forced to stay away and keep their own rooms, whilst we mustered quite an army from the Stye, many who were going from College early in the morning staying for so laudable a purpose. Monk behaved very well. He neither voted himself, nor allowed any of his particular friends to vote against you. Every M.A. from Sidney and every M.A. from Emmanuel came in your favour. The people of Caius, I believe, were against you, except the Master. We should have had a stronger opposition from Trinity, but we manœuvred most skilfully, and had the Grace passed on their grand commemoration, and as the dinner was on table smoking hot, and the voting here was cold, they wisely sacrificed their spleen to their pudding."

*   *   *   *   *

FROM THE REV. P. ELMSLEY.

"ST. MARY CRAY, KENT, *February* 3*rd,* 1811.

" DEAR SIR,—I am about to send to Jeffrey a few additions to my article on the *Prometheus,* to be inserted in the next number by way of appendix. I should be very happy if you would allow me to mention, as from authority, that you think seriously of publishing at some future time a supplementary volume, containing a corrected text of Æschylus, together with your δεύτεραι φροντίδες, etc. I take for granted that you are neither quite indifferent to the sale of your edition, nor ignorant that the adherence to the text of Stanley has retarded the sale considerably. If you will let the public know that you mean to give them a better text in a thin volume by itself, I have no doubt that you will find the demand increase rapidly. Now it appears to me that the best way of letting the public know anything is to mention it in the *Edinburgh Review*, of which I am informed that thirteen thousand are now printed. You see I make no stranger of you, as the saying is. I shall wait for your answer as long as I conveniently can, before I send off my despatches to the Rhadamanthus of Literature.

*   *   *   *   *

" I have been informed that Blomfield is dissatisfied with my treatment of him. If the information is correct, I am sorry that I have not pleased him. I likewise understand that some persons think that I have not treated Porson with sufficient respect. You must have observed the strong disposition which his school feels to convert him into an idol. The natural consequence of this idolatry is to produce in the minds of the non-initiated a disposition to bring him nearer to the pitch of common men than they are justified in doing. I am not quite sure that I have not some leaning to this kind of critical Protestantism.

" I think that I have heard that you are lately become D.D. When you do me the favour of answering this letter, will you have the goodness to mention the state of your academical honours, that in future I may address you by your proper title ? "

To the Rev. P. Elmsley.

[About February 4th or 5th, 1811.]

(Original destroyed by me.—Ed.)

After saying that he would adopt Elmsley's suggestion about a supplementary volume of his Æschylus, Dr. Butler continued :—

" When Blomfield was first introduced to me I felt particularly anxious to show him marked attention, being then much pleased with his unassuming manners. Afterwards, when I heard that he was (very unjustifiably, as it seemed to me) engaged in publishing the Cambridge Odes without the consent of their authors, I wrote him an extremely kind letter, begging him if possible to publish none of mine (which I told him I considered by far my worst compositions), and most earnestly requesting him to suppress one in particular. I concluded by exhorting him to turn his brilliant talents to better account. The Porsonian spirit of his reply—in which, however, he did consent to the suppression of the one Ode in question, though he printed another against my will—much disappointed me, for I had formed better hopes of him ; but his disingenuousness in not then telling me he was about the *Prometheus* did more. I found afterwards that he was become so overbearing to all but the narrow circle of young men who had agreed to look upon him as the successor to Porson, and so elated with his review of my Æschylus, that I considered my letter as an act of kindness to him, as well as of justice.

"The mischief of the Porsonian school can only be appreciated by a residence at Trinity. Its spirit is well described in a letter which my friend Dr. Parr wrote me not long after Porson's death. He said Porson had left his disciples scraps of Greek and cart-loads of insolence. I do not deny that Porson was a very illustrious scholar, but what I read in Bentley, in Valcknaer, in Ruhnken, in Tyrrwhitt, and what I see daily in my friend Dr. Parr, would be enough to keep me from blind idolatry, were any antidote to this necessary beyond one's own spirit of independence."

* * * * *

On June 30th, 1811, Dr. Butler preached at St. Mary's, Cambridge, before H.R.H. the Duke of Gloucester and the University of Cambridge, on the occasion of the Duke's installation as Chancellor of the University. The sermon was printed at Shrewsbury in the same year under the title of *Christian Liberty*; it was directed against the gloomy views of religion taken by the Methodists, and borrowed from them by the Evangelical party then dominant in the Church. The notes are longer than the sermon, and are mainly in support of Catholic emancipation, a cause warmly espoused by Dr. Butler at a time when English churchmen generally were opposed to it.

The sermon gave great offence in many quarters, as being too broad in its theology, and too generally liberal in tone, but there is not a sentence in it which any one would now take exception to. Professor Mayor says of it :—

"This sermon is a singular instance of the bitter feeling between scholars and the Evangelical party, which cannot be set down entirely to a repugnance to zeal and religious activity ; the remarkable personal vanity of Simeon and Is. Milner, the narrowness and uncouth phraseology of their school, seem to have exasperated it to an unusual pitch at this time in Cambridge."

At present it is difficult to conceive that such a sermon in such a place was needed, and this very difficulty makes it fall within the scope indicated on my title-page. I shall therefore quote from it at greater length than I should otherwise do.

The text is from Gal. v. 1 : "*Stand fast therefore in the liberty wherewith Christ hath made us free, and be not entangled again with the yoke of bondage.*"

After describing the freedom of Christ's ordinary converse from any acts of ascetic mortification, he continues :—

"May I be permitted to remark, that an adumbration of this conduct is to be found in the life of him whom Plato describes as the most just man he ever knew, and whom we are accustomed to consider as one of the wisest philosophers of the heathen world? Increasing his usefulness without diminishing his dignity, Socrates associated with the lost sheep of the Gentile flock, even with courtesans, libertines, and sophists, and by expedients the most gentle he endeavoured to rectify their errors, and correct their irregularities ; did not our Master, for the same benevolent purpose, mingle in familiar converse with publicans and sinners? Socrates, on the most serious topics, drew his images from surrounding scenery and the objects of common life ; have not the most judicious and learned expositors observed the same beauties in the discourses of Christ? Socrates condemned the mischievous subtleties of those disclaimers who displayed their ingenuity and fondness for paradox in separating the useful from the honourable; did not our Lord in the same manner combat the doctrinal refinements of those teachers who not only tore asunder what God had joined together in the religion of Moses, but set the ritual above the weightier matters of the law, and made of little or no effect some express prohibitions in the Decalogue, especially those which are pointed against perjury and adultery? Socrates, as Cicero justly remarks, brought down philosophy from the skies to the bosoms and business of men in social life; did not our Lord, in a yet nobler strain of simplicity and sublimity, inculcate the first and second great commandments? and when revealing or enforcing the will of His Father, did He not uniformly appeal to those clear and salutary apprehensions of right and wrong which the hand of God has deeply engraven upon the tablet of the human heart?"

It was the note on the foregoing passage that gave the greatest offence. It runs :—

" In the following passage from the *Dialogues* of Erasmus, besides some masterly touches on the character of Socrates which must affect every mind endowed with taste and feeling, the sagacious and enlightened reader will find ample materials for reflection :—

    *   *   *   *   *

" ' NEPHAL. Profecto admirandus animus in eo qui Christum et sacras literas non noverat. Proinde, cum ejusmodi quædam lego de talibus viris, vix mihi tempero quin dicam, *Sancte Socrates, ora pro nobis.*
" ' CH. At ipse mihi sæpenumero non tempero, quin bene ominer sanctæ animæ Maronis ac Flacci.
" ' NE. At ego quot vidi Christianos quam frigide morientes ! Quidam fidunt in his rebus quibus non est fidendum ; quidam ob conscientiam scelerum, et scrupulos quidam obstrepunt morituro, pene desperantes exhalant animam.
" ' CH. Nec miror eos sic mori, qui per omnem vitam tantum philosophati sunt in cærimoniis. . . .'—*Erasmi Conviv. Relig.,* p. 95 (London, 1717)."

After supposing a heathen to have been informed for the first time of the Christian Redemption, and to have been struck with its general conformity with the instincts of his own conscience, Dr. Butler continues :—

" But what would he say then, if after thus far soothing his benevolence, and thus far kindling his piety, we were also to tell him that his rational enjoyment of temporal blessings will ruin his eternal happiness ? that they are scattered indeed around him with a bounteous hand, but that he must touch not, taste not, handle not ; that he may see the birds exulting in their liberty, the beasts bounding over the plains, the fish sporting in the waters, the whole face of nature smiling in grateful testimony of its Creator's love, but that he alone must grieve for his unworthiness in voluntary and mysterious gloom ; that the senses, with which his Creator has framed him, are but the instruments of his ruin in the hand of the tempter, and that his desires, which are the natural and only spurs to action, are to be subdued into supine indifference and listless insensibility. Tell him, further, that when he has done and willed to do all that man is capable of doing ; when, by a life of mortification and melancholy and entire abstraction from all worldly interest, he has wrought himself into habitual and invincible apathy ; when he has accustomed himself to look with sullen and sour disgust upon the pleasures, and with carelessness, or, it may be, with scorn, upon the employments, and, as I should call them, the duties of social life, his labour, even in the Lord, may yet have been in vain; that as to him, Christ may in vain have shed His blood upon the cross, and that the God whose mercy is over all His works may have secretly and irrevocably doomed him, even before his birth, to everlasting perdition, from which no contemplations, however serious, upon the attributes and works of the Deity, no belief, however sincere, in His revealed word, no thanksgivings for mercies already received, no prayers for protection and succour, no remorse for sins past, no resolutions or efforts for amendment in time to come, can rescue, I had almost said the hopeless, helpless, guiltless victim;—and that nothing but certain tumultuous, irresistible, inexplicable intimations can afford him any safe and well-grounded assurance of pardon or reward.

" Who is there, gifted with the faculty of reason and the feelings of humanity, that would not shrink from such doctrine when first addressed to his understanding, and from such discipline imposed upon all his instincts, appetites, and affections? Yet for the existence, and even the prevalence of such doctrine, and for the vindication and praise of such discipline, I need appeal only to the observation of those who now hear me. No man who views the daily increase of Puritanism (which in its root and branches, in its tenets and effects, resembles the Pharisaical system of the Jews), no man who compares its late and present progress with events which the history of our own nation has recorded in dark and blood-stained characters, no man who has remarked the subtlety, restlessness, and impetuosity of spiritual pride, when united by opportunities favourable for action with the inordinate and insatiable lust of temporal power, can look without alarm and dismay to consequences which not only exercise the sagacity of the philosopher in his closet, but, in truth, force themselves upon the most common observer of human nature, as unfolded in the events of daily life.

" If the great and characteristic blessing of the Reformation was the removal of needless and burthensome ceremonies, of an usurped dominion over the minds and consciences of men, of authority bearing down right, and of dogmatism putting reason to silence and setting at defiance the clearest and most salutary suggestions of common-sense, let us beware that we are not again entangled in a yoke of bondage not less galling than that from which we have been set free. Let us look well to ourselves and our posterity, and let us be careful to preserve that liberty which our ancestors obtained for us by their wisdom, and sealed to us by their blood.

" True it is that the modern fanatics profess a very sincere theological hatred for the Church of Rome, from which they differ on various points of discipline and doctrine; but they have a discipline and doctrine of their own, in many respects as burthensome, as offensive, as dogmatical, and as anti-scriptural as that from which the Reformation has delivered us.

" I do not say that they practise ascetic mortifications in a hermitage or cloister, but they bring the gloom and austerity of a cloister into domestic life.   I do not say that they believe in the miracles of St. Ignatius or St. Dominic ; but they believe in daily miracles performed among themselves, in preternatural effusions of the Spirit, in hourly and especial providences, in sudden celestial influences and impulses, in Divine visitations of favour or of vengeance.   Now when pretensions to the peculiar and exclusive approbation of God are thus set up by any sect, and when the common accidents of life are interpreted into deliverances for those who belong to that sect and judgements against those who differ from it, we surely have a decisive proof before us that the effects of superstition on mankind are in all ages nearly the same, and that, whether the subject of it be a Catholic or a Calvinist, a Pharisee or a Puritan, its tendency is equally fatal to the best interests, the highest duties, the noblest pursuits, the most generous feelings, and the most enlarged conceptions of the human mind."

I asked the late Professor Kennedy, shortly before his death, to what school of theological thought I ought to say that Dr. Butler had belonged.   The Professor paused a while, and then began to laugh with a good deal of heartiness, saying the while, " He did not like an Evangelical " ; and that was all I could get.

From Professor Mayor's remarks on the sermon from which I have made the foregoing extracts, I will take part of a letter from Elmsley to Blomfield, which I see Mr. Mayor quotes from the Rev. Alfred Blomfield's Memoir of his father.

"*May 18th*, 1818.

"There certainly must be some connection between Greek and Popery.   Besides Messrs. Blomfield and Elmsley, there are Doctors Parr, Butler, Maltby, Raine—all men conversant in .the subjunctive mood, and all supporters of the Catholic claims, as they are called.   I have just received a letter from Dr. Butler, in which you are mentioned in a way that is creditable to his good nature after the review of his *Seven against Thebes, and Agamemnon*.   It is plain to me that he wishes a reconciliation with you.

" I think it would be creditable to both of you to shake hands, if your arms are long enough to reach from Shrewsbury to Aylesbury. The doctor has lately passed through a good deal of δυσφημία, in his theological character, on account of his Commencement Sermon. A neighbour of mine, who has something of an Evangelical turn, takes in the *Christian Observer*, in which Dr. Butler ' points a moral ' almost every month."

Seven years, therefore, after its delivery, the sermon still seems to have been remembered.

CORRESPONDENCE, AUGUST 17TH, 1811—DECEMBER 5TH, 1811.

FROM THE REV. P. ELMSLEY.

"LLANGEDWIN, OSWESTRY, *August* 17*th*, 1811.

*   *   *   *   *

" Do you happen to know the name of the author of the review of Blomfield's *Prometheus* in the *Quarterly Review*? * He is evidently a Cantabrigian, a friend to Blomfield, a fierce enemy to you, rather hostile to me than otherwise, and, above all, initiated in the higher mysteries of Porsoniasm.

" Next week I shall publish a little *Œdipus Tyrannus*, a copy of which I wish to send you, if you will tell me how to do so. To send it by coach will cost you more than the value of the performance."

*   *   *   *   *

FROM THE SAME.

"*November* 14*th*, 1811.

*   *   *   *   *

" As to your Mandarins and green dragons, vain pomp and glory of the world, I hate you. To me an old book into which I am certain never to look is of more value than cartloads of useful or useless china.

" I wish you would persuade some of the *Porsonulettes* of Cambridge to review my *Œdipus Tyrannus*, which I hope you have received. Having no acquaintance with *ces gens là*, I cannot ask them to do it. I wish it because I know they are in possession of the scriptures as well as of the oral tradition of Porsoniasm. With his mantle they possess a double portion of his spirit. My best respects to Mrs. Butler."

---

* This article, I learn from Mr. Murray, was by Professor Monk.—ED.

From W. Roscoe, Esq., M.P.

"*Allerton, November 7th,* 1811.

" My dear Sir,—I have to return you my very sincere thanks for the honour you have done me in sending me your excellent Installation Sermon, the liberal sentiments and Christian-like doctrines of which have, I assure you, my full assent. Would to heaven that the final object of revelation, and the precepts and practice of Christ, had been more forcibly and more early insisted on by the friends of true religion, in opposition to the horrible doctrines of reprobation, election, and justification by faith alone, which have been revived in modern times with a degree of fanaticism that bids fair to bring on another crisis of religious commotion.

" To have opposed this in time was peculiarly incumbent on the teachers of a Church which boasts that it has separated itself from the absurdities of the Romish See, discarded its superstitious ceremonies, and appealed to reason and Scripture alone for the foundations of its creed ; but unfortunately this has not (except in a few illustrious instances) been the case, and the English clergy have in general devoted their talents and their learning too exclusively to the discussion of polemical subjects and points of faith, thereby tacitly acknowledging the pre-eminence of such inquiries, as opposed to the inculcation of positive duties, and forgetting the example of their Master, who during His whole mission appears to have lost no opportunity of contrasting the conduct of those who do the will of His Father with those who only talk about it, and giving the preference where justice and common-sense point out that the superiority lies.

" Whatever may be the result, you, my dear sir, have done your duty, as well in this respect as upon the great question of the Roman Catholics, in which I have also the pleasure to meet with a lucid statement of opinions which I have always entertained, and which I cannot but wish were more generally diffused. In the year 1807, upon Mr. Littleton's motion on the change of administration, I made some very sincere but ineffectual remarks in the House of Commons (which were scarcely noticed in the public papers), tending to show that, as the grounds on which the pains and disabilities consequent on religious professions were originally founded were now completely altered and the succession to the Crown indisputably secured, the time was now arrived when a more liberal policy might with safety be adopted.

" 'This idea I find more fully stated and illustrated by historical proofs in your note on p. 28. Undoubtedly the Roman Catholics have, as well in foreign parts as in these kingdoms, divested themselves of their ancient prejudices and animosities, and why the Protestants should retain theirs it is not easy to conceive.

The assertion and defence of truth is incumbent upon every one, and particularly on every teacher of religion, but there is one truth paramount to all the rest, which is the very basis of religious inquiry, and without which all discussion is absurd—viz. that every person in his spiritual concerns has a right to adopt such opinions as he may think proper. This being previously understood, a free and useful discussion may take place ; but until this foundation be once established nothing but confusion and dissension can ensue. You, my dear sir, would concede this liberty as readily as you would claim it, but it must be feared that these sentiments are rather those of the individual than of the body, and that neither Luther nor the Churches founded under his sanction or that of his successor Calvin tolerate, in the full and fair meaning of the word, any opinions but their own.

   *   *   *   *   *

" Believe me always, my dear Sir, most respectfully and truly yours,

                                            " W. ROSCOE."

To MAJOR J. SCOTT WARING.

(Original destroyed by me.—ED.)

                                   " December 5th, 1811.

   *   *   *   *   *

" Unless our Government act cautiously the Methodistical proselytisers by their absurd enthusiasm will bring about the loss of India. When we consider how much the Hindu and Mahometan religions are interwoven with the affairs of common life, the little disposition manifested by Oriental nations to change the habits and customs of their forefathers, their hatred of European settlers, or, as I may rather call them, conquerors, their natural love of the marvellous, their pertinacious adherence to their castes, and their aversion to the labour of research, how can we reasonably hope for the conversion of Oriental races to Christianity ? "

   *   *   *   *   *

Of Dr. Butler's share of the English version of Prince Lucien Buonaparte's poem *Charlemagne*, it will be enough to say that he drifted into it through undertaking at the end of the year 1811 to supervise a translation begun by Mr. Maunde, then his curate at Kenilworth. Mr. Maunde died shortly after undertaking the work, and the whole translation had practically to be done by Dr. Butler and the Rev. Francis Hodgson, afterwards Provost of Eton. Both translators believed *Charlemagne* to be a great poem, and thought they were covering themselves with glory by connecting their names with a work which they were confident would be immortal ; nor do I know of any excuse to make for them, except that a good many people of that time were of the same opinion— among them, notably Lord Byron, a letter from whom upon the subject will be found upon a later page.

I may be too hasty, after all, in assuming that *Charlemagne* is in reality a commonplace work, for I have never read it, and never mean to do so. Baron Merian in one of his letters to Dr. Butler said, " You are right, there have been only two great poets, Homer and Shakespeare." I am of the same opinion, except that I should prefer to say there had been only two great poets, Homer and Shakespeare, and one great poetess, authoress of the *Odyssey*. This being so, I will leave what little need be said about the translation to appear in letters that will be given in due order of date. I will only add that the main reason for the failure of the poem in England was not its dreariness—this would not have mattered—but the fact of Lucien Buonaparte's reconciliation with his brother Napoleon after his escape from Elba. This, as Dr. Butler immediately foresaw, sealed the fate of the work with English readers. Unfortunately it had been published a few weeks previously.

CORRESPONDENCE, FEBRUARY 18TH, 1812—DECEMBER 28TH, 1812.

FROM THE REV. P. ELMSLEY.

"St. Mary Cray, *February 18th*, 1812.

*   *   *   *   *

" I have just been reading fourteen pages of very small print in the *Christian Observer* for January respecting your Commencement Sermon.   All the comfort that I can give you is, that your piece has not missed fire.   The review is by one of their best hands.   You will soon be convinced that another piece of yours did not miss fire.   I know from the best authority that the continuation of the review of your Æschylus in the *Edinburgh Review* will show that the author has not forgotten the Letter to the Rev. C. J. Blomfield.

"Do you remember how you were censured in the *Quarterly* for not detecting the antistrophicity of the 'wild ravings' of Io ? You have great authority on your side.   Since I began this letter I have seen the second edition of Mr. Blomfield's *Prometheus*, in which those wild ravings are left exactly as they were in the first edition, without the slightest hint in the notes of their being antistrophical.   Throughout the whole of his second edition, he carefully avoids taking any notice of my strictures, except where he is absolutely forced to do it.   This is the consequence of flattering young men into a notion that they are phœnixes.   As he has chosen to adopt this dignified silence towards me, I rather wonder at his condescending to rail at you, after so long an interval of similar silence.

"When you are reconciled to Blomfield, as I know you will be some time or other, I must trouble you not to sacrifice me upon the altar of reconciliation.   I have a high opinion of him as a scholar, and I have no doubt, when he is as old as you or I, he will think more as we do than he does at present.   I have had three letters from him lately on critical subjects, and I shall be very glad to continue the correspondence.

*   *   *   *   *

"I do not think that Blomfield sufficiently considers the difference between the lumbering edition of Æschylus which you are forced to publish and the elegant pamphlets which he publishes. He does not consider the disadvantages under which you labour from want of assistance, want of leisure, and, I am afraid, want of health.   If he once says 'Colb 1' when he ought to say 'Colb 2,' you are fairly entitled to say so ten times.   I wish to my heart that critics never would say 'Colb 1' instead of 'Colb 2.'   These mistakes are the torment of my life.   They prevent me from sleeping.   But who is free from them?   As Dame Quickly says upon another subject, 'All vintners do the same. What's a joint of mutton or two in a whole lent?'

"I know of know (*corrige*, no, *meo periculo*) time at which literary squabbles are so delightful as at present.   I should be glad to have a Letter to the Rev. C. J. Blomfield laid upon my table every morning (although I do not say that I should advise the publication of many such letters).   They serve to take off the attention from public affairs, in which I think there is nothing to delight or instruct.

" I cannot write to Dr. Parr until I know how to address him. I find the addition of the post town to be very necessary in writing to eminent literary characters who live in the country. When you give me this information, pray let me know how your eyes are, which you omit to mention in your last letter. I hope Mrs. Butler keeps your study door fast locked ; it is the only way. You will never get another pair, so take care of those which you have got. The length of my letter puts me in mind of a letter of poor Dodd's which I saw the other day, in which he tells his friend that he has written more at length to him, as he is to be hanged on Friday, and shall not have leisure to write again.

" Truly yours,
" P. ELMSLEY."

I found only a few letters from Marmaduke Lawson, whose name will be almost as familiar to Shrewsbury men as that of Thomas Smart Hughes.

He was born in 1793 or 1794, and was sent to Shrewsbury School, but I do not know in what year. From the following letter it seems that he was a resident undergraduate at Cambridge at the beginning of 1812, but it does not appear whether he had then just left Shrewsbury, or whether he had entered at St. John's in the preceding October. He took the Browne Medal Latin Ode in 1812. He was first a pensioner of St. John's, but afterwards migrated to Magdalene. He was Pitt University Scholar in 1814, and Chancellor's Medallist (the two Medallists being bracketed) in 1816. In 1818 he published a pamphlet in answer to an attack by a writer named Maberly on the discipline and morality of the University. This pamphlet, which is about thirty-five pages in length, evinces not a little of the quaint humour which pervades his letters to Dr. Butler ; among other sallies he compares the Proctors to a two-pronged fork amid a plateful of peas. He was three times in all elected to Parliament for Boroughbridge, and died in March 1823 in the thirtieth year of his age.

From Marmaduke Lawson, Esq.

[CAMBRIDGE, *February* 27*th* or 28*th*, 1812.]

" DEAR SIR,—I am sorry to inform you that on my arrival here I found Scholefield had just been elected.

" I cannot find out with certainty who were considered second, but am afraid I was not. Dr. Jowett certainly voted for Price ; but the rest did not think him even second.

"Three causes contributed principally to my failure : first, doing two copies of Alcaics ; secondly, all my verse translations assuming an appearance of paraphrases ; and lastly, the difficulty they had in reading my compositions, and the want of stops and capital letters, which seemed a mark of culpable negligence.

" However, though defeated and disappointed, I am not disheartened, and am pursuing a course of reading for the Greek Ode, of which I hope I have some chance. Price reads eighteen hours a day, and said before the scholarship was vacant that he would with pleasure give up the health of all his life, if he could but get one of these scholarships.

" I had very fine travelling from Shrewsbury hither. Betwixt Birmingham and Coventry, I apprehended a man who had run off from a public-house leaving his score unpaid. I spied him under a holly bush, jumped off the coach, ran him over two or three large fields, and at last caught him and held him till his pursuers came up, and then returned to the coach with an honest conscience as having contributed my mite towards effecting the ends of justice.

" I staid Sunday at Leicester, where I heard the celebrated Robinson preach on the very topic I most wished—faith and works, and he said any one who thought any works or any human performances could have the least effect towards his salvation was instigated by the devil.

"'Towards the close he manifested some strong Calvinistic symptoms.

" At Leicester on Saturday night I got shaved, and when I gave the man twopence he thanked me, but as I was going out he ran after me and said, ' I think, sir, you have made a mistake ; it is only a penny.' I bade him keep the remainder, on which he broke out in a fervour of gratitude. I saw a newspaper there for nothing. The only objection was that it was in a cellar, and all the time I was shaving there were some blackguard discontented stocking-weavers abusing the ministry.

" At Birmingham I met with some French officers on *parole*, whom I found very instructive and entertaining companions ; at the same time they were atheists and profligates, possessed of very little sense of religion or virtue.

" I dined with them and played at billiards. They did nothing but crack their jokes on the waiter, and laugh at him.   They were astonished at seeing him affect the dress and manners of a gentleman.

"We are here in a turbulent state.   On Friday some men who were drunk knocked up the grass on the grass plots, making horrible outcries, and on Saturday a party at Downes's broke out drunk at three in the morning, smashed all the lamps, broke open Rushworth's door, pulled him out of bed, and fired a pistol. Another row on Sunday night.   Downes is confined to chapel and gates, but the offenders are of other colleges, chiefly Trinity.

"If you will be kind enough to look over my odes before I send them in I will send them to you, and shall be very much obliged if you will solely mark the mediocrities.

"I play moderately at whist, billiards, and ball.   Nothing can be done here without immense reading.   Give my very best respects to Mrs. Butler, the Miss Butlers, and Tom.

"I remain, dear sir, your affectionate pupil,

"M. Lawson."

To Monk, March 25th, 1812, Dr. Butler writes :—

*   *   *   *   *

"My fourth volume is dreadfully heavy upon my hands; the trouble of fragments, of revising the *scholia*, of making an *index rerum* and an *index auctorum* to all Stanley's notes, of digesting the mass of materials into a preface, with a life of Æschylus and some criticisms on his works—the weight of all this oppresses me, and though I have made and am making some progress with it, I fear it will not be finished till the year 1815.   The *Persæ* is printed, but my mind sickens under these indexes.   I have also to digest near a thousand references which I have made to passages in which Æschylus is quoted by the ancient writers, and ignorance of which was one of the many συκοφαντίαι alleged against me in the *Edinburgh Review*.   My eyes, moreover, which were very much better, have within the last six weeks become materially worse.   However, I must proceed as well as I can— before the night cometh."

*   *   *   *   *

From Colonel Leighton.

"Ludlow, *June* 1st, 1812.

"My dear Sir,—Your letter reached me here.   In reply to it I have only to say that I am as much in the dark with respect to the cause of the increased suspicion of Monsieur Lucien Bonaparte as yourself, but that I fancy from the nature of my late correspondence with the Foreign Office that representations have been made from some quarter to Government, which it is not thought prudent to disregard. Being much hurried, you will, I trust, excuse the shortness of this letter."

The following paper, in Dr. Butler's handwriting, evidently written immediately after a visit to Prince Lucien Buonaparte, belongs probably to the year 1812.

"Lucien went to meet Joseph at Florence on his road to Bayonne, and to dissuade him from accepting the kingdom of Spain. Joseph told Lucien that he was commissioned by his brother Napoleon to offer him the inheritance of Spain. 'You will not dare,' said Lucien, 'to repeat my answer truly—therefore I will write it.' 'Vous me demandez si je veux être héritier d'Espagne. Je ne veux pas être héritier d'Espagne. Je voudrois mieux me pendre.—LUCIEN BONAPARTE.'

"The kingdom of Naples, and of Portugal also, were offered to Lucien if he would divorce his wife and marry the Queen of Etruria.

"The last time Lucien sat in Council was on the death of the Duke D'Enghien. Present : Napoleon, Lucien, Joseph, Jerome, Kellermann, and one more. These three last creatures of Napoleon were so convinced by the arguments of Lucien and Joseph against the death of the Duke that the Council were *unanimous* against it. Napoleon broke up the Council in a rage, and in a very short space of time the Duke was shot, but without the order of Council.

"Lucien told Joseph he ought not to accept Spain, for that he (Lucien) having been ambassador there knew the spirit of the people and that it would not do. Struck by Lucien's arguments, Joseph wrote from Florence a wavering letter to his brother Napoleon. In consequence, when he approached Bayonne, he found the thing was done. Grandees were sent to meet him, deputations, guards, etc. Napoleon went to meet him in his carriage, entered his brother's carriage, called him his Catholic Majesty, and in all respects treated him as an equal. Lucien says that Joseph has not talents for governing Spain—might have done well at Naples.

"Lucien on coming here wrote direct to the Prince of Wales for permission to proceed to America. Six weeks after his letter was returned *unopened*, with an intimation that he must never presume in future to write direct to the Prince. Lucien fired at this, and wrote to Lord Wellesley a most dignified letter, in which he says: 'Accoutumé d'écrire *directement* à sa sainteté le Pope régnant, et à plusieurs Souverains de l'Europe (sans conter aux Princes de ma famille), j'avois cru qu'il y avoit quelque chose de sacré attaché au nom que j'ai l'honneur de porter, qui me pouvoit exempter des formes d'office.   Mieux instruit, je conformerai pour l'avenir à l'usage général.'

" Lucien says that, if our Government would but make his own and their situation comfortable, he would engage to detach all his brothers from Napoleon and get them to England.

" As the children were playing the pantomime of *Pylades and Orestes*, Lucien and I were talking of the story of Damon and Pythias.   I told it in the usual way.   He said it was Pythagoras himself and a friend who was to be roasted in the bull of Phalaris, and that Phalaris pardoned both.   ' Voilà un bel trait!' said he. But when Phalaris demanded to be admitted the third into their friendship, Pythagoras said that no tyrant could share in the friendship of the virtuous and the wise.   ' Voilà,' said he, ' un trait plus bel encore !'

" In showing me his medals, which he did with great affability, kneeling down at a cabinet on one knee and supporting a large heavy drawer on the other, and selecting the best and most rare for my inspection, he said, on returning the drawer into its place, which I observed was full of small pieces of paper, except where occupied by the case of coins, ' C'est pour les enfans.' Puzzled at this, I could not understand how this paper could amuse them, but I found it was sugar-plums wrapped up in separate papers for them.   He appears to dote on them—without spoiling them.

" Mademoiselle Bonaparte played the part of Nausicaa in the pantomimic shipwreck of Ulysses, and sang me a little Greek song."

FROM JOHN BANNISTER, ESQ. (THE COMEDIAN).

(Original in possession of Mrs. G. L. Bridges and Miss Butler.)

"65, GOWER STREET, BEDFORD SQUARE,
"*December* (?) 28*th*, 1812.

" MY DEAR SIR,—I have now been confined more than five weeks with a severe fit of the gout, and continue in so weak a state that I can scarcely, even with the assistance of crutches, convey myself from one end of the room to the other.   Allow me, therefore, to hope that you will not attribute my long silence to want of respect or gratitude, for indeed I shall ever retain a true sense of obligation for such frequent instances of your friendly conduct towards me ' while memory holds a seat in this distracted globe.'   Although I could with difficulty move in my bed on the arrival of your mutton, yet by the assistance of propping and a tolerable appetite I continued to be as well fed as the mutton itself.   I feasted for three successive days ; my palate was pleased, my stomach satisfied, and good digestion followed.   I felt as full of gratitude as of mutton, and by the flavour of the fat I swear, no mutton can with Welsh compare.

" I think, however, that you do not abound in fine oysters at Shrewsbury.   We have in London at this time of the year excellent Purfleet oysters—and I have taken the liberty of sending you two barrels, which I hope will arrive safe and good by the mail. I wish at the same time to send you something of a different kind.   I was the first subscriber to the ' Death of Nelson ' by Heath.   I am in possession of five fine impressions ; let me therefore beg you will receive from me the first which was taken from the plate as a proof of my regard.

" The subject you mention is an excellent one for a farce — throw aside the black coat and the Doctor, put on a flannel jacket, and in a running hand produce a Running Farce.   Doctor Hoadly wrote *The Suspicious Husband,* and I believe he was a bishop afterwards.   I hope there is no sin in making the public laugh ; if so, what will become of 'your humble servant to command '?   I am glad to hear that my friend Crisp is sufficiently recovered to play *solus* : in future he shall drive *solus* for me ; the next time I am under his management he shall find that I am more easily to be ' led than driven.'   *Apropos,* can you commission a friend in London to call in Gower St. and take charge of the print, as I should be sorry to have it injured by any of the coaches?   I have now only room to add a very few, but very sincere words, that I am, and shall ever remain, with best regards to Mrs. Butler, your obliged and faithful humble servant,

" JNO. BANNISTER."

During his whole head-mastership, Dr. Butler was at variance with the trustees about the school chapel.   He did not like the boys going to the parish church, and wished them to attend no other services than those within the school itself.   In 1812 he took the matter into his own hands and had special services on Sundays in the school chapel, but the trustees wrote and desired that the boys should attend church at St. Mary's, as till recently they had always done.

Dr. Butler was nettled, and argued the matter further. After saying that the seats were insufficient now, and were rapidly becoming more so as the number of boys increased, he continued :—

" Added to this, I have frequent complaints from Mr. Blakeway and Mr. Powlett of the disturbance which the boys occasion to the congregation or the minister, and which I cannot wholly prevent, though I endeavour to repress it. Every reasonable man knows the impossibility of restraining the volatility of young people, and will think it a great thing if they are tolerably quiet during a long service. Devotion from a collection of boys in church may be a very fine thing to talk of, but I must affirm that I never witnessed and never expect to witness it ; the utmost that can be hoped for is that they may be tolerably orderly, and if there is anything special to attract their attention it is hardly possible to hope for even that.

"The special objects at St. Mary's are the charity children close behind them, and the manufactory girls in front. The Sunday Schools also, close to us, attract the attention of the boys. The children are noisy, and the master and mistress, in their endeavours to keep them in order, often make tenfold confusion, much of which is unjustly set down by the congregation and officiating minister to my boys.

"Nor are the evils above mentioned counterbalanced by any advantages ; whereas, by taking the boys to chapel, I not only remove the evil, but get much good ; for as one of the upper boys officiates as clerk, and the rest read the responses aloud, they all take an actual share in the service, and are beneficially impressed by it. If any of the trustees will attend my morning or evening service, he will, I venture to think, be greatly struck by the order and attention of the boys. At the church the sermon is necessarily addressed to a mixed congregation ; at the school chapel the sermon in the morning is adapted especially for those who have to attend.

*   *   *   *   *

"There is, therefore, every security that the boys will receive the best and most suitable religious instruction from the change I have made, and I must add that from a sense of the service I might render them, and a wish to discharge my duty in giving them more religious instruction than I can otherwise give, I was first induced to make it. The benefits resulting from it are in my opinion very great, and I beg leave to observe that none can have so good an opportunity of forming an opinion about them as I have.

*   *   *   *   *

"The other business which I have to mention to you greatly concerns the improvement of some of the boys, and I should have mentioned it years ago, had I not thought it better to wait till my house was full and seemed likely to remain so. It is that you would build eight studies ; these, as every one who has been at a public school knows, are small rooms just big enough to hold a table and a few chairs, to which a boy may retire for the purpose of doing his exercises and getting his lessons without interruption. I have found a convenient place for them, and Mr. Birch has given me an estimate, which I enclose. They must be entered by a door separate from the dwelling-house, to avoid the window tax. It is necessary that the boys should be unable to get out from them at night. I may add that I believe no foundation school of respectability in England, except this, is without them. I have the honour to be," etc., etc.

It appears from a letter of Dr. James's given above that it was he who introduced studies at Rugby, and as it was necessary to explain what studies were, it seems probable that their introduction at most public schools was still comparatively recent.

The trustees promised that studies should be built as soon as funds permitted, but would not yield in the matter of the chapel. It appears that their objection to change was based on fear lest some head-master might be appointed who would instil either Popish or Methodistical doctrines into the boys' minds. As long as the boys were made to attend at St. Mary's, it would be possible there to undo any mischief that a Popish master might be doing in the school chapel on a week-day ; whereas, if the master had everything his own way, there was no knowing what might not be going on, without a chance of its being corrected.

CHAPTER VII.

GEOGRAPHY—OWEN PARFITT.

The Geography.—Correspondence, January 29th, 1813—October 20th, 1813.—The Mystery of Owen Parfitt.—Correspondence, June 18th, 1814—October 20th, 1814.

NOTWITHSTANDING the increasing numbers of his school, Dr. Butler, who was a very early riser and did much work before morning chapel, found leisure to write his sketch of *Modern and Antient Geography*, the first edition of which was published in 1813, as well as to proceed with the third volume of Æschylus and with his share of Prince Lucien Buonaparte's poem. In the preface to the first edition he claims no novelty of idea as regards his Modern Geography.

"'The second part,' he continues, 'which contains a short view of Antient Geography, has been unattempted in this manner, so far as I know, by any one but myself.'"

In a note on page 179 of the work just referred to, I find an indication of Dr. Butler's opinion on a subject that still agitates the world of scholars. After saying that Chios and Smyrna have the best claim to be considered as Homer's birthplace, he adds :—

"I am not one of those who doubt his existence. The uniformity of plan and diction convinces me that the *Iliad*, with possibly a small exception, is the work of one man. The *Odyssey* I attribute to different hands, and to a somewhat later, but very early age."

In an edition published about 1838 the note stands :—

" The *Odyssey* is perhaps attributable to a different hand, and to a somewhat later, but very early age."

The " perhaps " probably means nothing more than that Dr. Butler knew the question to be a burning one, and had not gone into it fully enough to make him feel safe in speaking positively ; but he seems to have retreated from his original view that the *Odyssey* was by more than one hand, though not feeling as confident as I could have wished to see him that it was not written by the author of the *Iliad.* A copy of the *Iliad* with Dr. Butler's MS. notes, as used by him in teaching, is to be seen in the library of St. John's College, Cambridge. The writer considers the words πέρην 'Εὐβοίης (II. 535), in reference to the habitat of the Locri, as meaning that Euboea lay between the Locri and the abode of the poet. I know that Liddell and Scott do not take this view, but in this case I think Dr. Butler right and his distinguished pupil wrong. The peculiarities of the Homeric dialect he considers to be Ionic archaisms,* and the source of the poem is held to be Asia Minor, not Greece, I do not doubt correctly. The *Odyssey* does not appear to have been read at Shrewsbury, and I question whether Dr. Butler knew it anything like so thoroughly as the *Iliad*; he does not seem to have even suspected the Sicilian origin of the poem. How can a head-master, who has to give boys a bird's-eye view of all Latin and Greek literature, afford time for the close study of a poem so fatally easy as the *Odyssey* generally is ? It is not paradoxical to say that if the *Odyssey* had been harder to understand it would have been sooner understood.

---

* See a letter in the British Museum (Additional MSS. 34583, immediately after a letter dated August 17th, 1802) in which the writer projects an edition of the *Iliad.*

CORRESPONDENCE, JANUARY 29TH, 1813—OCTOBER
20TH, 1813.

FROM MARMADUKE LAWSON, ESQ., WHO HAD LATELY MIGRATED
FROM ST. JOHN'S TO MAGDALENE.

"CAMBRIDGE, *January* 29*th*, 1813.

*   *   *   *   *

" Our year at St. John's fell to nothing. Wood* said at first
if they went on as they began he had seventeen Wranglers in his
lecture-room ; the best man, however, is in a decline. The Senior
Wrangler ran off in the morning, being disappointed in his first
examination ; this was Bond of Pembroke ; the two next fought
nearly equal to the last. Sperling, the last, and 22nd Wrangler,
is the first 22nd, and the first Wrangler from Harrow.

*   *   *   *   *

" I thought we might perhaps have seen you here to vote for
the Professor of Anatomy, which made great commotion here.
Lord Byron came for Clark, and met with some partial applause.
We have no chapel at Magdalene, there being no one in orders
in the College.

*   *   *   *   *

" The election occasioned a memorable boxing match, which
ought to be transmitted to *Boxiana*, a new work. It was between
Brass, Fellow of Trinity, and Blown, my barber at St. John's.
The night after the election, as the bells were ringing for
Haviland's election, Brass met Blown, and asked him what they
rang for ; he said, for the Johnian candidate. ' Oh,' says Brass,
' they are ringing a pig.' ' That's brassy,' said Blown. They
fought, and Brass getting the better, Blown complained to the
Vice-Chancellor. Brass compounded by paying £9, which was
at first to have been given to Addenbrook's Hospital, but the
Vice-Chancellor, fearing lest an event disgraceful to the University
should be perpetuated on their annals, recommended Blown to
pocket the affront, which he for some time refused to dirty his
hands with, but at length consented to with seeming reluctance. I
have a notion Blown will be knocked down as often as you please
at so much a head."

*   *   *   *   *

I have been assured that Lord Byron was so much
affected by the applause above referred to that he burst
into tears.

---

* Then Tutor and afterwards Master of St. John's.—ED.

To George Woodfall, Esq.

"*August* 13*th*, 1813.

    *   *   *   *   *

" It is a presumption in me to offer a suspicion to one who has so much better means of information than any other man now living, but I own, among the very small number of persons who can have any possible claims to be considered as the writers of the *Letters of Junius*, I have sometimes preponderated towards Lord Ashburton. I must own my reasons are very weak and inconclusive—yet, when Philo-Junius in one of his letters tells you that he knows nothing of Junius, you are not bound to give implicit credit to Junius when he tells you he is no lawyer by profession, while his letters everywhere evince a most profound knowledge of the laws, and his attacks on Lord Mansfield are of that triumphant sort which one can hardly attribute but to a professional man. Adopting as I do the general politics of Junius, and admiring or rather idolising him as gifted with the most uncommon powers of argument and the most consummate talents as a writer, I am not blind to his faults, and among the very worst of them I reckon his inhuman and repeated attacks upon the domestic calamity of the Duke of Bedford. If Junius was Lord Ashburton, can we not mark even a providential dispensation of retributive justice, that he who had insulted the feelings of a father should himself fall a victim to them, and while he held up the Duke of Bedford's equanimity or resignation to public abhorrence, should himself, under a similar visitation, die broken-hearted ?

"If Junius was not Lord Ashburton, still the circle of suspicion can comprehend but a very few characters. I think Junius must have been a member of one of the houses of parliament, and have been always conversant with the very first society. I will go a little further. It is impossible for Junius not to have been a public man. The talents and spirit which dictated his letters must have brought him out, and could not have suffered him to be in obscurity. The very idea that a man like Junius should have had a commonplace book—that last resource of indolence and stupidity—is fit only for Mrs. Serres to entertain."

    *   *   *   *   *

Mrs. Serres, under the pseudonyms of " Metellus " and " Phil-Atticus," was then trying to sustain her uncle's claim to the authorship of Junius in the *Gentleman's Magazine*, against Dr. Butler, who was showing that this was impossible. I cannot conceive what Dr. Butler means by abusing commonplace books. He set one up himself in 1816, but soon dropped it.

From the Rev. P. Elmsley.

"St. Mary Cray, Kent, *October*, 1813.

" My dear Sir,—I have not written to you for a great while, and the only excuse I can make for my silence is that I had not written to you for a vast while before the last vast while began. I am a very bad correspondent, and when I once omit to answer a letter in due time, I seldom write again to the same person unless I am compelled to do so.

" I consider the second edition of your Geography, which I received last night [*vide infra*—Ed.], a kind of compulsion, and so here goes. It is now two years since I sent an article to the *Edinburgh Review* (the last article which I sent was inserted several months after it was sent), and I am not likely to send another. The irreligious tone of the Review and the Jacobinism of some of its articles have compelled me to withdraw from it. When I sent my review of Blomfield's *Prometheus*, which is printed in the thirty-fourth number, I had contributed nothing to the Review since the fifth number. I was assured by the editor that he had every disposition to correct the faults of the Review, but that he could not govern one or two of his coadjutors. Lately, I think he is become worse rather than better. I am sorry for it on every account, but particularly because I should be glad occasionally to write an article. I have written one article in the *Quarterly*,* but I have private and personal reasons for not contributing again to it, at least at present. So that I cannot lend a lift to a friend.

" I am glad to perceive that you do not want such a lift. Your second edition is a real and *bonâ fide* second edition ; not the first edition with a new title-page. I wish I had known it was in the press, as I would have sent a few trifling corrections, according to the invitation given at the conclusion of the preface. They chiefly relate to the orthography of names. Experience has convinced me that in all minutiæ the author is the very worst judge of the correctness of his own work, and that he frequently makes mistakes against his own better knowledge.

" About four months ago, I saw Blomfield for the first time in my life, and had a long conversation with him about your quarrel with him. It is evident to me from your letters that you wish for a reconciliation, and I give you great credit for feeling that

---

* Mr. Murray tells me that Elmsley reviewed Grant's *History of the Mauritius* in the *Quarterly* for February 1811, Markland's *Euripidis Supplices* June 1812, and Monk's *Euripidis Hippolytus* September 1812.—Ed.

wish. Φιλοφροσύνη γὰρ ἀμείνων is the rule to be followed. I found Blomfield not indeed averse from reconciliation, but not very desirous of it. If you think proper to make any advances to him you may depend upon having them received with civility. As he tells me that your acquaintance was never more than slight, and as you are not likely to meet each other frequently, perhaps it is not worth your while to take any further steps in the business. Indeed, there is a small circumstance, which I have noticed since I began this paragraph, and which tempts me to conjecture that your sentiments are not quite the same as they were when you last mentioned this affair to me. At the end of both the editions of your Geography, you advertise your letter to Blomfield. If this is done deliberately it shows no wish to abolish the recollection of your disputes.

"You are to understand that 'last night' at the beginning of this letter means some Saturday in October : I cannot recollect which. As happens to me continually, I did not finish my letter at one sitting, and could not find it in my heart to resume it till this moment (18 Nov., 1 p.m.). What an alteration has taken place in the affairs of mankind between the two words 'disputes' and 'you'!" *

From Lord Byron.

(Original in possession of Mrs. G. L. Bridges and Miss Butler.)

"4, BENNET STREET, ST. JAMES'S, *October 20th*, 1813.

"SIR,—The honour of your letter has laid me under an additional obligation to my friend Hodgson. I am truly proud of your favourable opinion, and glad of the opportunity of adding my testimony—my most sincere suffrage—to the acknowledged merits of a man whom I have known intimately for several years. To yourself I can safely say that I never knew a being more warm in heart, more amiable and inoffensive yet independent in spirit, and where not occasionally biassed by feelings which though the kindest are the weakest in our nature, one of sounder judgement than the subject of your letter and of this reply. So much for him as a man—as a man of talents, I trust he is and ever will be far above the necessity of appealing to me or any individual of prouder pretensions in behalf of abilities already neither unknown nor unappreciated. As a translator his Juvenal has placed him in the first rank, and I know nothing wanting to his fame as an original writer, except the more frequent exertion of his own powers, and less diffidence (a rare fault) in his own capacity.

"The little that I have seen by stealth and accident of *Charlemagne* quite electrified me. It must be a stupendous

* The battle of Leipsic.—ED.

work—it seems to be of another age, and, I grieve for the certainty, of another country. Hodgson must make as much of it our own as he has done by Juvenal; and then we shall have less, and the author nothing to regret. M. Lucien will occupy the same space in the annals of poetry which his imperial brother has secured in those of history—except that with posterity the verdict must be in his favour. Once more begging you to accept my best thanks for your communication, I have the honour to be, very sincerely,

"Your obliged servant,

"Biron.

"P.S.—I have written in great haste and after a long and freezing journey from Yorkshire, which must form my apology for not having said half enough what I ought of Mr. Hodgson. But I console myself with the idea that more would be superfluous."

The approaching completion of his Æschylus left Dr. Butler leisure to attempt the elucidation of a mystery that had long fascinated him, but which, do what he might, he was obliged to leave in its original obscurity—I refer to the sudden disappearance of one Owen Parfitt, a bedridden old tailor, who was born about 1700 or a year or two earlier and lived at Western Shepton in the parish of Shepton Mallet.

Dr. Butler had written to Mr. Hyatt, the leading solicitor of Shepton Mallet, with whom he had frequent business in connection with his mother's property at that place, and had urged him to take down the depositions of those who had been neighbours of Owen Parfitt at the time of his disappearance, while so many of them were still living. Mr. Hyatt pleaded age and deafness, whereon the matter dropped till November 1813, when the discovery of a skeleton, in the garden of a man named Thomas Strode, and not more than a couple of hundred yards from the cottage in which Parfitt had been living, gave a fresh stimulus to Dr. Butler's spirit of inquiry.

Mr. Hyatt had retired, and had been succeeded by Mr.

William Maskell, whose son, the late Rev. W. Maskell, published in 1857 a short account of the story. Mr. Maskell, on being urged by Dr. Butler, had the necessary depositions taken down, and these were evidently used by the Rev. W. Maskell, but I have had before me what are obviously copies of these documents, in the handwriting of Mrs. Butler and one of her daughters. I have also had the draft of the letter from Dr. Butler which has been published by Mr. Maskell; the draft differs materially from the published version, doubtless because Dr. Butler shortened his letter in copying it. All the documents that came into my possession in connection with the matter are now in the British Museum.

From the depositions I find that Parfitt was believed to have been a soldier in his youth, but Joanna Mills—aged eighty in 1814—who was related to him and knew him well, deposed confidently, in contradiction of previous deponents, that he "never was in the army or navy, or otherwise in the King's service." She admitted nevertheless that he had been rather wild in his youth, and had been to America and to Africa. While he was in Africa he messed with a man, presumably a magician, who asked him whether he wished to have a sight of any of his friends in England, but he said that he had no such wish. It seems, however, that he was never quite able to shake off the reputation of having had dealings with the occult world, through the offer thus supposed to have been made to him.

On his return from Africa he settled at Shepton Mallet, married, and resided in a house on the Wells Road, in which Mrs. Parfitt had a life interest. Here he had one daughter, and worked at his trade as a tailor; he was now "a very careful saving man," "a quiet sober man," according to the testimony of Joanna Mills and others who remembered him.   In the course of time, first the daughter and then the wife died ; whereon he left the house on the Wells Road for a cottage at Western Shepton near Board Cross.   The losses both of his daughter and his wife seemed each to affect him so powerfully as almost to derange his intellect.   Joanna Mills had often known him come to her house in the middle of the night " with nothing more of clothes on than his shirt and shoes, alarmed, as he said, by the loud whisperings of his departed wife."

He had no annuity or property, "but might have had a little money by him."   He was looked after when he grew old and infirm by a sister, older than himself, who lived with him and was allowed a trifle by the parish for her trouble.   He worked at his trade when he could, but on becoming more infirm " was supported in great measure by the gentlemen of the town."   He had been ill some time before his disappearance, and asked one witness's father "to partake of the sacrament with him, which he did."   At the time of his disappearance, in May 1768, he was "about seventy," "grey-haired," "some five feet seven inches in height, and stout grown."   He had been "a complete cripple for six months or so before his disappearance."   Again, "he had been a cripple many years, but especially for nearly half a year before his disappearance, and could not walk during that time without a stick and the assistance of some other person."   Again, "he had been a cripple for half a year or more before his disappearance, but was still able to walk a little, not enough, however, to enable him to get away by himself."   All the foregoing is from the deposition of Joanna Mills, who is the most reliable of all the deponents.

He was generally considered "of a fair character," "neither a very good man nor a very bad man," but one witness had heard that he was "occasionally violent."

I will now make extracts from the deposition of Susanna Snook, aged eighty-one.

"An old sister, very feeble and much older than Owen Parfitt, took care of him. Deponent oftentimes helped the sister to get him into a chair, while the bed was made, and this chair was usually placed either in the passage or just outside the door, so that he might have a little air. About half-an-hour before he disappeared, the deponent had helped the sister as usual to place him in the chair, and an old great-coat was thrown over his shoulders. She then left the house, but on the alarm being given that Owen Parfitt had disappeared, which, she believes, could not be more than half-an-hour after she had left him, she returned and found the sister sorrowing bitterly for the loss of her brother, and very much agitated at not knowing what had become of him. The sister gave the following account to the deponent :—

"'After she had made the bed she was going downstairs, and, not hearing her brother, called "Owen"; no answer being made, she went directly to the spot where she had left him, and found only the chair and the great-coat.'

"The deponent said that search was immediately made in all the wells and ponds, as well as in the fields, etc., but to no purpose. She further says that the weather had been fair during the day, but after the alarm of Owen Parfitt's removal, it began to thunder and lightning, with a heavy fall of rain that continued the greater part of the night. Indeed the deponent herself was wet through in returning to her house."

The date of the disappearance was stated by a deponent who had helped to search the ponds and wells to have been about the middle of May 1768. Joanna Mills, with a picturesqueness that makes me lament that I know no more about her, said that the time of the disappearance was "in the evening between light and dark, when the mowing grass was about."

"The thunder and lightning," says Susanna Snook, "began about an hour after Owen Parfitt's disappearance, but they did not prevent the neighbours from coming to the house nor from searching for him. This dreadful weather continued the greater part of the night, but search was immediately made and continued the next day."

No trace of the missing man was ever found; nevertheless

Joanna Mills deposed to a report that a person answering
to his description called, the day after his disappearance,
at a public-house at Leighton, near Frome, about twelve
miles from Shepton Mallet, and had a pint of ale and a
halfpenny cake, but she could not vouch for it.   This
person was never traced nor identified.

Other deponents besides Susanna Snook and Joanna
Mills were Samuel Bartlett, aged (?), Jehoshaphat Stone,
aged eighty-four ; Joseph George, aged sixty-eight ; Benjamin George, aged sixty-six ; Prudence Millard, aged
seventy-two ; William Millard, aged seventy-two.   All
these people had known Parfitt well, and had either
assisted in searching for him or been otherwise closely
connected with him.   They contradict themselves and
each other in small unimportant respects capable of easy
explanation, but they are sufficiently unanimous to leave
no doubt that the facts are as I have given them above.

The general opinion was that Owen Parfitt had been
carried off by the devil, nor is this opinion even now as
extinct as might be wished.   On going down to Shepton
Mallet a year or two ago to study the topography on the
spot, I talked with an old lady who lived in the next
cottage to that from which Parfitt disappeared, and said
I supposed she knew the story.   " Yes," she answered, " but
whether it was true or whether it was a miracle, that we
shall never know."   I felt as one who has stooped to pick
up a piece of glass and has found a diamond.

Not content with the depositions, Dr. Butler had requested
that the bones found in Strode's garden might be also
sent him for examination by Dr. Darwin and Dr. Dugard.
These were sent, and in due course returned with the
following letter from Dr. Butler—which I have taken from
the Rev. W. Maskell's pamphlet, as probably the form in
which the letter was sent :—

*   *   *   *   *

" I return the bones, which I hope you will receive safe, and that they will be taken care of, and not buried or thrown away. Anything short of ocular demonstration would not have satisfied me, but I must yield to convincing proof. In the judgement of very able professional men, they are not the bones of an old man but of a young woman.

" There are still wanting : 1. The depositions of a few more living witnesses, if they can be had, lest in future time a cavil should be raised about their paucity ; 2. A copy of any records left by Dr. Purcel or Mr. Wickham [two clergymen who were contemporaries of Owen Parfitt] as to the fact of Owen Parfitt's disappearance ; 3. The distance of the house of Susanna Snook from that of Owen Parfitt ; 4. The age of Owen Parfitt at the time of his disappearance, to be stated if possible from the register.

" A very material circumstance is mentioned by Jehoshaphat Stone, unnoticed by Susanna Snook : that the sister of Owen Parfitt was induced to come downstairs by hearing a noise, and that the chair was displaced. Pray inquire of Susanna Snook as to this fact, and whether it was ever so stated by the sister to herself or to any others ; and of Stone whether he is certain he heard this from the sister, or remembers it as common report of the time.

" I think that a small annuity of £7 a year was paid to Owen Parfitt; can you ascertain if this was so, and by whom ? And particularly whether the woman Lockyer was concerned in the payment of it.

*   *   *   *   *

" Was Owen Parfitt absolutely bedridden at the time of his disappearance? It is very important to know whether he was commonly placed at the door about the same time of the day. Did the thunderstorm and rain prevent an immediate search being made after the alarm was given?

" I have heard that a person answering his description was seen wandering in the woods near Frome, on the evening of Owen's disappearance. . . . Surely in that case his body would have been found somewhere.*

" But put these questions to the old people already examined :

---

* In the draft letter I find an inquiry " whether a skeleton was not found in some woods or fields about ten miles from Shepton, thought to be his," and a request for any information available about such skeleton. It is also stated that the bones found in Strode's garden can hardly have lain in the ground less than forty or fifty years—a statement probably derived from the opinion of the medical men who examined the bones.—ED.

'Was Owen Parfitt able to walk ten miles? or half a mile? Do they recollect him as able to walk at all? Did he walk to his chair at the door on the day of his disappearance?'

" I remain, etc.,

"S. BUTLER."

In consequence of this letter Susanna Snook was re-examined. She lived about a hundred yards from Owen Parfitt's house. She repeats most positively that the sister told her she had heard no noise. The chair had not been displaced, and the great-coat was left upon it. Then comes the remarkable statement that she did not " remember that Owen Parfitt was in the habit of being placed in a chair for the purpose of air ; she never assisted him nor saw him in such a chair, for he usually sat in a lower chair within the house." This contradicts what she is reported as having said on her first examination. Probably her words were then wrongly taken down. The explanation perhaps is that for many months it had not been warm enough to allow of his sitting out of doors, but that it had been a hot day, and he was therefore able to do so.

The depositions of a few more old people were taken, but no new facts were elicited. It is to be regretted that no question was asked in regard to Owen Parfitt's stick— for he is pretty sure to have had one. I should have thought this would have been an important clue to the view we ought to take. If the stick was gone we should think the owner crawled a few yards, as far as the road, and got taken off in a passing vehicle at his own request. If the stick remained, we might be confident that he did not go away voluntarily. The probability is that he had his stick with him when he was helped into his chair, and the mention of the great-coat's remaining without the stick's being named suggests that the last (if there was one) had disappeared. It should be also noted that the old man was placed in a higher chair than that in which he generally sat—a chair from which he would be better able to rise without assistance.

To these depositions the Rev. Thomas Smith, then curate of Shepton Mallet, appended the following general remarks :—

" The exact age of Owen Parfitt cannot be ascertained by any register.

" Susanna Snook lived not more than a hundred yards from Owen Parfitt.

" Jehoshaphat Stone speaks from hearsay only of a noise being heard in the passage about the time of Owen Parfitt's disappearance.

" It appears from the assertions of several persons that Owen Parfitt was generally placed in a chair, either in the passage or out at the door, during the summer-time, for the sake of fresh air.

" No evidence can be obtained which would go to implicate Lockyer [who then occupied Strode's cottage—ED.] in the fact of Owen Parfitt's removal, nor does it appear that any acquaintance existed between Owen Parfitt's sister and Lockyer afterwards.

" None of the witnesses remember Owen Parfitt's having a pair of silver buckles.

" The skeleton discovered at Board Cross [in Strode's garden] can be tolerably accounted for, and is considered to be that of a female under twenty, in the murder of whom some persons who are since dead have been strongly suspected of having been implicated ; but another skeleton is said to have been found some years since, not far from the cottage in which Owen Parfitt lived, which was not at that time nor has been since accounted for. The bones of this skeleton cannot be obtained, and they are supposed to have been at the time thrown into the charnel house belonging to the church. No suspicion that they were the bones of Owen Parfitt occurred, and they underwent no examination."

Mr. Maskell accompanied Mr. Smith's remarks with the following letter :—

●   ●   ●   ●   ●

" The bones discovered at Board Cross are strongly suspected to be those of a young person who was murdered by a man and his wife who lived in the house now occupied by Strode. Both of them died about six years ago, within a few weeks of each other. They kept lodgings for strollers, and the person murdered was supposed to have been a stranger, as no one is remembered to have been missing in this neighbourhood. The facts from

which the conclusion of murder is drawn are that the man, who
was a gardener, never broke up the mould of that part of the
garden in which the bones were found, and his wife, though they
were poor people, constantly kept a light in the house during the
night. A person of the name of Wilmot is supposed to have
known something about it, but he is since dead. He lodged in
the house many years, and was often heard to say, when in liquor,
that he had never murdered any person, but that he knew who
had. He did not go further, and no suspicion attached to the
occupiers of Strode's house. There are other circumstances which,
I think, upon the whole leave strong ground to suspect that these
people concealed the bones.

"The skeleton said to be found some years since at West
Shepton we can get no account of; it is said to have been lying
in a garden on the west side of the field late George's. The
account given of this is very vague, and it is not described as a
skeleton, but as a quantity of bones.

"I do not find that any paper was left by Dr. Purcel, Mr.
Wickham, or any other person relative to this transaction; my
own belief is that the sister was not concerned in the disappearance of her brother, and I own that I am altogether at a loss to
account for it in any manner."

   *   *   *   *   *

The late Rev. W. Maskell gives the following " curious
example of a narrative, distorted and untrue, but apparently
resting on the most trustworthy proof," in connection with
the story which I have told above. The version to which
he refers appeared (so he tells us) in *Household Words*,
Vol. III., p. 246, and runs thus:—

"When I was a child I was sometimes permitted to accompany
a relation to drink tea with an old lady of about seventy. She had
seen and known much that was worth narrating. She was a
cousin of the Sneyds, had known Major André, and her father
had been one of the early patrons of the beautiful Miss Linley.
I name these facts to show that she was too intelligent and
cultivated by association to lend an over-easy credence to the
marvellous. One of her stories was this: Her father's estate lay
in Shropshire, and his park gates opened right on to a scattered
village, of which he was landlord. The houses formed a straggling
irregular street. Now at the end house or cottage lived a very
respectable man and his wife. They were well known in the
village, and were esteemed for the patient attention which they
paid to the husband's father, a paralytic old man. In winter his

chair was near the fire ; in summer they carried him out into the open space in front of the house to bask in the sunshine.   He could not move from his bed to his chair without help.   One hot and sultry June day the village turned out to the hay-fields ; only the very old and very young remained.

"The old father was carried out that afternoon to bask in the sun as usual, and his son and daughter-in-law went to the hay-making.   But when they came home in the early evening their paralysed father had disappeared—was gone !—and from that day forwards nothing more was ever heard of him.   The old lady who told this story said, *with the quietness that always marked the simplicity of her narration* [/], that every inquiry which her father could make was made, and that it could never be accounted for, and left a painful impression on many minds."

Mr. Maskell continues :—

"Now in the above account, guarded as it claims to be by so much of corroborative proof, almost every particular rests on imagination : whether the old lady, ' the cousin of the Sneyds, etc.,' was a myth also, no one can tell, but the scene being laid in Shropshire leads us to conclude that Dr. Butler was the original teller of the story ; right enough perhaps at first from himself, but in after-years altered not only as to the circumstances, but as to the place and county."

I have been informed, but cannot vouch for it, that the writer of the account in *Household Words* was Mrs. Gaskell.

CORRESPONDENCE, JUNE 18TH, 1814—OCTOBER 20TH, 1814.

FROM S. DICKINSON, ESQ.

"WELLINGTON, *June 18th,* 1814.

"SIR,—I have no doubt but your goodness will excuse the trouble I am giving you.   Mr. Hart of the Lion Office hath informed me by request that there was several gentlemen left your house on Thursday morning last by the Union Coach as outside passengers through this place : will you therefore be good enough to inform me their names and residence ?   You will wonder no doubt, sir, at such a request being made, but when I inform you their conduct through this town, I think you will join with me in conceiving the necessity of bringing them to their better senses, in order to prevent their so committing themselves for the future.   I understand from a variety of people who were travelling along the road that it was their pleasure to use a Coachman's whip about them most lustily, and when out of the reach of the whip to pelt them most unmercifully with stones ; and upon the arrival of the Coach at our Pheasant Inn they each of them filled their pockets with stones as a fresh supply, the use of which was the wantonly breaking every window in their power through the town and, I have heard, country. I of course do, as an individual so injured and insulted, feel most indignant, and am determined to bring them to punishment ; this is not only my case, but that of very many more in Wellington. Feeling no doubt but that you will concur with me in the justice of my determination and also its necessity, I hope to be favoured as requested by return of post."

*   *   *   *   *

To a Parent enclosing the Above.

" Dear Sir,—I have no doubt the offence complained of has been committed by your sons. Be so good as to let me know the result of your inquiry, and send it to me, together with this letter, to Barmouth, Dolgelle, N. Wales.

" Yours faithfully,
" S. Butler."

From a Draft for a Letter written, but not sent, to Mr. Jeudwine.

(Original destroyed by me.—Ed. Fuller copy in British Museum.)

[*About August 13th—15th,* 1814.]

*   *   *   *   *

" Of course I push boys on as fast as I can consistently with their improvement ; it is my duty to do so. Formerly, it is true, a boy learned the *As in præsenti* and *Propria quæ maribus* while in the first form. This took him half a year, and was so much time thrown away. I discontinued it, and since that time it has been discontinued by most head-masters in the best classical schools.

*   *   *   *   *

" If a boy of common capacity comes under you knowing nouns from verbs, and having learned his syntax twice over, I consider him fit for the second form. In the space of one year he ought to be qualified for the third form. In a year after this he ought to be ready to leave your school, and should begin Greek grammar under Mr. Griffiths. An average boy who had never learned Latin grammar will take from a year and a half to two years in passing through the first form.

*   *   *   *   *

" In general boys entering the first form are ten or over ten years old. This will bring a boy to be fourteen or upwards before he leaves your school, and sixteen or upwards before he comes under me. What can I make of him if he does not have at least three good years under me? How can I give him that learning, expansion of views, and taste in composition without which he may be a dull joiner of words, but can never become a scholar unless I have him continually under my own eye for fully three years?

* * * * *

"If, as you state, I originally required eight lines of construing to be learned by boys in the lower remove of the second form, it never can have been in my contemplation to require a boy immediately on coming from his grammar to learn eight lines of parsing and construing. I must have qualified the lesson in some way that you have omitted or forgotten.

* * * * *

"Even supposing, however, the fact to be as you state, I must beg you to recollect that the rule, if it ever was one, was laid down at the very opening of the school, while it was yet in its unformed inchoate state. Experience has taught me many improvements in the mode of teaching, and many highly useful improvements have been made by all schoolmasters in that time. I have introduced such alterations as I thought beneficial into every other department of the school, and why not into yours?"

FROM PRINCE LUCIEN BUONAPARTE.

(Original lost sight of.—ED.)

"ROME, 20 *Octobre*, 1814.

"MON CHER DOCTEUR,—Je m'empresse de vous annoncer l'heureuse arrivée de ma femme et de mes enfants, qui me chargent de vous faire leurs compliments affectueux. Je vais répondre à quelques articles de la lettre que vous avez adressée le 11 Septembre de Shrewsbury, à l'abbé Charpentier de Bâle.

"L'édition de Paris sera de deux volumes in 4to outre les éditions in octavo; à Rome il n'y en aura pas avant deux ans, parceque les presses sont trop mauvaises, ou tout au plus une édition de 200 exemplaires.

"Les gravures je les réserve toutes pour mon édition de Rome : si Longman ou l'éditeur de Londres veulent des gravures il peuvent les faire faire : c'est à eux à voir si cela convient à nos intérêts communs.

"Madame et moi nous sommes fâchés qu'on ne vous ait pas laissé de gravures de Madame, et dès que les cuivres seront venus nous vous en enverrons avec grand plaisir.

"Je vous prie d'avoir soin qu'on m'expédie de la manière la plus prompte mes exemplaires de la première édition ; ayez la bonté de me prévenir lorsque l'impression est commencée et recommandez bien à Longman d'avoir un bon probe pour corriger les épreuves.   M. Boyer a reçu de moi quelques corrections à faire au manuscrit : je désire qu'elles soient faites scrupuleusement. Ce qui était honorable à dire dans l'exil des Bourbons ne peut et *ne doit* plus se dire à présent.

"Je désire qu'il n'y ait pas d'autre titre que *Membre de l'Institut de France, etc.*

"Il me reste, mon cher docteur, à vous parler de votre voyage d'Italie.   Ne viendrez-vous pas nous voir ?   Cette terre classique vous appelle, et l'amitié vous offre son toit.   Dites-nous si dès que *Charlemagne* (français et anglais) sera publié vous ne viendrez pas nous voir : il faut faire connaissance avec Rome antique et Rome chrétienne, avec Tusculum et Tibur, avec, etc.   Madame et moi nous vous en prions bien.   Rien ne pourra nous être plus agréable que de vous revoir, et la promesse que vous nous en donnerez sera déjà pour nous un véritable plaisir.   Mille compliments de toute ma famille.   Ecrivez-moi sous l'enveloppe de M. (?) le duc de Torlonia, Banquier, Rome, et croyez à mon inaltérable amitié.

"Votre très affé

"Lucien Bonaparte.

"P.S.—Mes compliments à M. Hodgson."

CHAPTER VIII.

CORRESPONDENCE, JANUARY 29TH, 1815—MAY 28TH, 1816.

FROM MARMADUKE LAWSON, ESQ., WHO HAD MIGRATED FROM ST. JOHN'S TO MAGDALENE.

"CAMBRIDGE, January 29th, 1815.

"DEAR SIR,—I write to you again most unexpectedly. It has only just come to my ears that Dr. Craven, my late Master, died last night completely senseless and exhausted; so I just left St. John's in wrong time, otherwise I should have had a chance perhaps of succeeding him. As it is, James Wood succeeds without opposition. I have also to request that, any time at your leisure, you would send a certificate signed by yourself and Mr. Jeudwine stating that I was two years at Shrewsbury School, as that will entitle me to a scholarship at Magdalene. So with that and my University Scholarship, for which I have never yet got a farthing, and what every man ought to make annually at Newmarket, I may scrape together quite a little income. There was a singular thing happened here in the death of Gillam the banker, worth £100,000. The Cambridge paper said he died very suddenly, which, though it told nothing but the truth, was far from telling the whole truth, as he in fact hung himself. This reminds me of my late journey up here, when I greatly offended an old lady in the coach for talking of Lord French's suicide. She observed that in general women showed more fortitude than men, and certainly could bear more inconveniences. I said, 'Certainly, ma'am, for women occasionally bear children, and these are sometimes great inconveniences.' This highly offended her, as she proved to be a single lady."

FROM PRINCE LUCIEN BUONAPARTE.

"TUSCULUM, 2 Mars, 1815.

" AU D. S. BUTLER,—Je reçois, mon très cher Docteur, à Tusculum, où je désire bien vous faire promener, votre lettre du 5 Janvier. Nos postes sont si bien servies dans les états *libres* du Continent, qu'il nous faut deux mois pour recevoir de vos nouvelles.

" J'ai reçu les exemplaires de l'édition faite à Paris, et j'attends l'edition de Londres qui est en route.

" J'espère que vous n'aurez pas oublié d'adresser de ma part avec mes plus sincères respects deux exemplaires du poème aux Universités de Cambridge et d'Oxford : je vous prie de le faire, si ce n'était pas fait.

" L'article du Monthly revue est très beau et j'y reconnais facilement la plume d'un ami : je désire que vous m'envoyez la critique d'Edimbourg.

" Les critiques de nos misérables journaux français doivent vous avoir fait pitié : à Rome nous nous en moquons ainsi qu'à Londres : l'essentiel était qu'on laissat imprimer l'ouvrage en France, et du moins sous le gouvernement actuel on le laisse imprimer, quoiqu'on défende d'insérer dans les journaux les articles favorables. Il serait bon de faire insérer dans une de vos gazettes libres l'article suivant :—

" ' Le poème de *Charlemagne*, dont l'impression était défendue sous le régime impériale, a paru bien imprimé à Paris, mais les feuilles publiques de Paris refusent d'insérer la copie des journaux anglais favorables à ce poème et s'empressent de prodiguer les injures à l'ouvrage et à l'auteur. Cette conduite n'est elle pas encore plus déshonorante pour le pouvoir que le refus d'imprimer ? Heureuse Angleterre ! il n'y a de lois que chez toi. Il est remarquable que la *Henriade* a été publiée chez nous pendant la persecution de l'auteur, et que *Charlemagne*, imprimé dans les mêmes circonstances, est accueilli à Londres comme il le mérite et couvert d'injures à Paris ! . . . Mais quelques feuilles de Paris ne font pas l'opinion de la France ; et l'ouvrage et l'auteur sont au dessus de ces folliculaires esclaves.'

" Rédigez cela comme il vous paraitra convenable. Je vous embrasserai en Juin : Madame vous dit mille choses.

" Votre t. cher ami et élève,

" Lucien Bonaparte."

To M. Ch. Boyer.

[*April* 10*th ?*—20*th ?* 1815.]

" M. C.,—J'ai reçu ce matin l'exemplaire français de *Charlemagne*.

" Je ne puis pas vous exprimer comment je suis étonné de ce que vous venez de m'annoncer à la fin de votre lettre. Si cela soit vrai, nous ne devons pas compter sur une seconde édition ni de l'original ni de la traduction en Angleterre, tels seront les préventions de tout le monde contre le Prince de Canino. Pour moi je ne vois rien de déraisonable qu'il se soit reconcilié avec son frère, mais il faut vous avouer que je suis bien surpris qu'un homme d'une telle grandeur d'âme, après avoir renoncé aux affaires publiques, s'y mêle encore. Neanmoins je suis bien persuadé que ses vertus et son mérite sont beaucoup au dessus de mes louanges, et je lui conserve une amitié zelée et très fidèle. Mais il me sera impossible à dessiller les yeux des prévenus, qui seront en ce cas, je vous l'avoue, presque tout le monde ici ; sans doute je souffrirai moi-même pour la partie que j'ai pris, mais patience, je suis anglais, et je ne saurai point abandonner mes amis lorsqu'ils ne s'abandonnent eux-mêmes. Répétez donc au Prince, je vous en prie, mes assurances d'une amitié bien respectueuse et sincère, et croyez que je suis avec beaucoup d'estime

" Votre, etc.,
"S. Butler."

The foregoing of course refers to Prince Lucien Buonaparte's reconciliation with the Emperor Napoleon.

From E. Jackson, Esq. (a Former Pupil).

"Bury St. Edmunds, *April 21st*, 1815.

* * * * *

"Cambridge now is horribly stupid, not a gown to be seen. The fever still continues. The only remaining undergraduate at St. John's had it when I was there on Saturday, and was scarcely expected to survive. It is also at Trinity, where a few of the men have been rather rebellious. The other Colleges are without a tenant, save perhaps one or two port-drinking fellows. Lawson, of course you know, carries the medal to Magdalene. He probably will be a Wrangler, since he never passes a day without doing something considerable in mathematics. The Latin Ode he also professes to write for, and most probably the Greek, without he quarrels with that most unfortunate of subjects, the restoration of Louis. All this I learnt from a letter of his to Ned Hughes.

* * * * *

"The papers for the University Scholarship are not yet, I hear, looked over. Pennington, a freshman of King's, and Hare, an old opponent of Lawson's, are the two favourites. Downward professes to do nothing, but at present reads nearly as much as any one of his compeers. Irton professes to do nothing and does nothing. Matthews * is little more than a mad, infatuated politician ; he reads the papers all day long, to furnish him with matter of abuse towards the Regent and his Ministers for the evening. George Yate, an old pupil of yours, is at Queens'—the most staunch, the most devoted, the most inveterate Simeonite in the University, and S—— is as great a beast as ever. Here ends the Shrewsbury catalogue.

---

* See letter of February 19th, 1833, and later letters.—Ed.

*   *   *   *   *

" Of course you have seen the decree which prevents us from returning to Cambridge till May 20th. Not anticipating anything of this sort, Hughes and I returned on Thursday. He remained, but I was compelled to retreat immediately. I am now in Bury, and have procured very good private lodgings; if you know the town, at Winn's, a very gay toyshop in Abbeygate Street. Hughes, I expect, rejoins me to-morrow. You perceive we are becoming more and more intimate, and I sincerely hope we shall continue to do so. Do not be so long before you write to me again. I promise not to be so tardy an answer in future. I am afraid, however, Tom Hughes is too great a monopoliser of your affections. I hope I need not be jealous, but I confess I fear. Mrs. Butler, I hope, is well ; it is quite a pleasure to me even to write the name, so many kindnesses have I received from the original, and so many grateful associations arise from the remembrance of it. I have very often indeed, with an Euclid or a Wood before me, detected my truant thoughts revisiting my old haunts in the school gardens and re-enjoying their old scenes of happiness. But all the time I lose by such reveries be assured I lay to your charge. With kind remembrances to all my friends in Shrewsbury, believe me

" Yours most affectionately,

" E. Jackson."

From the Rev. Francis Hodgson.

"*April 23rd*, 1815.

*   *   *   *   *

" I was sick when I heard of Lucien's adherence, and thought of ' Je te désavoue.' Thank Heaven, *mi carissime*, foolishness of conduct is not faithlessness of, or to, principle. Oh, what a fall is here if it be true !

*   *   *   *

" As to Bonaparte and the Allies—' Three blue beans in one blue bladder, rattle rattle beans, rattle rattle bladder.' See Lord C——'s speeches."

The first of these two extracts leaves little doubt that Lucien had used the words there quoted to his brother.

From Marmaduke Lawson, Esq.

(Original destroyed by me.—Ed.)

" Yarmouth, *May 12th*, 1815.

" Dear Sir,—Although my mind at present (as you may suppose with a man far advanced in Newton) is entirely set on things above, yet I cannot neglect the less celestial duty of thanking you for your kind advice, as on other occasions, so more particularly on this last. As to Newton, I fear I shall never be under much obligation to him, for any honour I may attain, though I give him due credit for undeceiving the vanity of those men who imagined that this little earth, like a great prince, kept the sun and stars as butler and livery servants, when in fact she has only one little link-girl, the moon, to show us our way home on an evening, and she only does half duty. In fluxions, however, and algebra I have great hopes, though I cannot help smiling at J. Wood's raptures on the consummate symmetry of the hyperbola, and of impossible roots which always go, like partridges, in pairs.

"They made me pay income tax for my scholarship, and much of the money had been lying at low rate in Mortlock's hands, so I only got about forty pounds. This, as you would say, is most Pittiable. Having just received my salary I am bound to speak well of the author of it, but the name is an insurmountable obstacle.

"Cambridge will now feel her dependence on the University. Hudson received for many weeks ten shillingsworth of letters per day about the fever. Besides scarce any admissions for next year; only six in the last six weeks at Trinity, against thirty last year. Hildyard will have another chance of a Bell. Thirlwall is the first who ever migrated to a more honourable but less lucrative scholarship. This is rather singular, as Price and Owen were Bell's Scholars. Hildyard did some excellent exercises and was first of all, and some as bad.

"Yarmouth has been ruined by the peace. Shopkeepers say that no one buys anything but necessaries, and lament the depression of the farmers, who were the best customers and paid best while they had the pence. The change in affairs, however, may do good. I am astonished at reading every day the newspaper of that day last year. All seems a mockery. Kings turned out for mere sport, like bag foxes. All trades suffer, but particularly innkeepers, for no farmers stay to dine as before. The best trade now seems that of Hangman. The one at York has just retired after nine years' duty commuted from sheep-stealing; he has amassed nine hundred pounds in his professional capacity, and is to receive the fair hand of a respectable tradesman's daughter.

"I never ride here—the horses are all broken-kneed by young midshipmen who know nothing about the matter. I expect my own mare to meet me at Cambridge. I travelled here with a noted character, Amos Todd of Acton near Bury. He is the man who wrote his name and abode on a taxed cart in such a way that he was near being indicted for a libel on Parliament. He wrote 'A most odd act on a taxed cart,' hereby complying with the act which requires that every letter of the name and residence shall be inscribed on the vehicle. He was a very curious fellow, but abominably mercantile. He wanted to know what line I was in, and compared Lord Wellington exposing himself unnecessarily in battle to a grocer who, though immensely rich, will keep coming behind the counter among his apprentices. . . . I am near the church, the only one in Yarmouth, which contains twenty-five thousand souls. This is indeed for one man a pretty good cure of souls, which word ' cure ' implies that they are all diseased, and thus confirms the Church's doctrine of original sin. I see of course three or four funerals daily, and about one marriage. Opposite me is an hospital for seamen, who breakfast at seven, dine at twelve, tea and supper at seven, and yet I am shocked to say are most impious people ; and so are all sailors. To prove this, a vessel was lately wrecked here, all the crew of which would have been saved, but they, thinking it over, ran to the spirit room, and twelve were found literally dead drunk—I mean they died drunk. Yet if, as the ancients held, it is dangerous for a pious man to go on board with impious, we shall have to wait some time before we can be safe in travelling abroad. Scholefield at Simeon's offended many of his hearers by telling them this fever was a judgement on Cambridge for its wickedness.

" My exercises, I hear, were criticised in the *Antijacobin,* how I cannot tell ; I did not suppose a work privately circulated would have been noticed. After all I fear the Vice-Chancellor's bias to Eton, as he was second master there. Their style is peculiar."

From a Parent (a Lady).

"*Midsummer,* 1815.

" My dear Friend,—In consequence of my having omitted to send to the post on Thursday, I did not receive the unpleasant intelligence conveyed in your letter till yesterday (Friday evening). I am truly distressed to hear that Eliab has been concerned in such a terrible transaction. I sent for him immediately after I received your letter, and desired him to tell me the truth, which he did directly, without attempting to conceal any part of his conduct, and I found he had last week told his brother and sisters the same account, therefore I have reason to suppose he has not deceived me. This sad business took place a few weeks before the vacation. Eliab says V——, H——, and himself went to the cellar door, and he believes it was V—— who proposed taking the wine, but that he was the first who began with his knife to cut the spar of the door ; the others helped him, but finding they could not accomplish their purpose, P—— fetched a saw and finished cutting it ; the boys then scrambled in, and Eliab first got out a bottle which lay within his reach, but most of the wine was at a considerable distance from the door, so H—— invented a long stick with a hook to it to get it out. There were very few bottles that any boy could reach excepting H——, who was left-handed, and nearly all the wine was taken out by him. H—— told the other boys it never could be found out. All the boys helped to drink the wine and rum, and Eliab says they are constantly in the habit of doing things as bad as this, and therefore they did not think it worse taking wine than taking other things. He does not know that more than seven boys went to the cellar, but as he was not always with them, and they fetched it at different times, he does not know. Their names are . . . He thinks the latter did not take any wine, but only helped to saw the door. All the boys knew of the transaction; Eliab says he is sure he is not more to blame than the rest, and that when the windows were broken the bigger boys ordered the little ones to break them, and, if they refused, said they would beat them. He says no boy dare tell of another or the rest would nearly kill him. I believe I have now told you all he said on this subject, and I know you will advise me what is best to be done with him. I think his share in the transaction cannot have proceeded from a propensity to drinking, for though I offer him wine daily he never will drink it. If you do not think it right that Eliab should return to Shrewsbury you will let me know immediately, because I know a clergyman who takes a few pupils, and who would, to oblige me, take him, but I shall leave it to you to judge for me what is best for him. Accept my kind regards, and excuse a letter written in hurry and agitation."

FROM DR. DU GARD TO DR. BUTLER, WHO WAS AT BARMOUTH
FOR THE HOLIDAYS, *re* THE REJOICINGS AFTER WATERLOO.

(Original in Shrewsbury Museum.)

"*July*, 1815.

"DEAR SIR,—Your fireworks went off by coach from the Lion on Monday morning, and Burrey would send the rocket sticks. Our big days exceed all description. There could not be less than thirty thousand to forty thousand spectators to see Lord Hill enter the town. I conjecture the procession must have reached two miles foot and horse; no less than five thousand horses were in town; stalls and beds were at a great price. The dinner tickets sold for thirty shillings and upwards, or ten shillings premium, such was the enthusiasm to dine in the same room with Lord Hill.

"To drink tea in the Quarry there could not be less than twenty thousand to twenty-five thousand: immense tin canisters, capable of holding all your children, were the tea-pots; seven hundred pound weight of cake was cut up and distributed in baskets, with many barrels of ale. Near three thousand people were dined besides in the public-houses, on good roast mutton, new potatoes, etc., etc., three pints of ale each and a paper of tobacco. There were no drunken people about, and all were satisfied with the dinner. The gentlemen's dinner was good : a cold collation and hot venison ; turtle and turbot in profusion. The ball-room crammed so that you could not move till they divided, and part went below into the dinner-room at the Lion. There was then a crowded ball in each room and three long sets of dancers. Every one was delighted with Lord Hill, and his attentions were universal. In the Quarry he was near being crushed to death by the press upon him, and he literally ran away across the field up to Mr. Rocke's garden—the people hunting him like a hare to shake hands with him, or touch the skirt of his coat ; one poor woman kissed the button on his coat and went away very much satisfied. The presentation of the box took place on the terrace at Mr. Rocke's : the Mayor, Aldermen, and Corporation, with the ladies, formed a crescent, the open part towards an immense concourse of people in the Quarry below. The applause on his Lordship's entrance was beyond anything I ever heard, and his reply to Loxdale's speech on delivering the box was delivered very gentlemanly and well, but the thing which amused all was his returning thanks on the top of the wall to the Quarry assembly (which he did neatly, feelingly, and off-hand) for their support at the election.* Give my kind regards to all."

From a letter signed J. Sheepshanks, and dated June 30th, 1815, as also from Mr. Hodgson's letter here given, it is clear that Dr. Butler contemplated applying for the head-mastership of Leeds Grammar School, then vacant. I have often heard my father say that Dr. Butler had fully made up his mind to leave Shrewsbury, but that, as he was on the point of doing so, the school suddenly filled in 1816, after which date the only difficulty was that of finding accommodation.

From the Rev. Francis Hodgson.

"BRADDEN, *July 23rd,* 1815.

"MY DEAR FRIEND,—In the most rapid haste I write to ask you what this means ? Out of Herefordshire I hear that you are

---

* Lord Hill was M.P. for Shrewsbury till he was raised to the Peerage in 1814.—ED.

about to leave Shrewsbury, and for Yorkshire. Of course this means for Leeds School, of which I thought and have ever regretted not being a candidate. For heaven's sake, if so, remember me, and let me step into your shoes at Shrewsbury, or turn out that horrid what's his name, and associate me with you there. Sir, 'the Hotspur and the Douglas' (I cannot help this gross vanity; for heaven's sake again, forgive it) would be 'confident against the world in arms.'

"Never more affectionately, more seriously, more rapidly, or more foolishly,

"Yours,

"FRANCIS HODGSON.

"Pray write by return of post without fail.

"Of course I shall be secret on the Herefordshire report, which perhaps after all is most absurd. Heaven help you."

Mr. Tillbrook, many of whose letters will be given in due order of date, must have been a great letter-writer, but it is to be feared that no other series of letters from his pen has been preserved save those now in the British Museum among Dr. Butler's papers. Of all Dr. Butler's friends there was none to whom he was more cordially attached, and I can hardly doubt that, if asked who was the most fascinating companion, who, if I may say so, the most Shakespearian man whose path had ever crossed his own, he would have at once named Mr. Tillbrook. By the kindness of his son Major Philip Tillbrook, I am able to furnish the following brief outline of his life. He was born at Bury St. Edmunds, April 16th, 1784, and educated at the free school in that town. He went thence to Cambridge, where he entered at Peterhouse, of which College he became both Tutor and Bursar. In May 1829 he was presented to the College living of Freckenham ; on December 15th in the same year he married Frances, daughter of the late John Ayling, Esq., of Tillington in the county of Sussex, by whom he had two sons, Major Philip Tillbrook, Standard-Bearer of Her Majesty's Body Guard, the Rev. William John Tillbrook of Strath-Tay Parsonage,

Perthshire, and one daughter, Mrs. Frederick Inman of Bath. He died on May 20th, 1835.

The only work catalogued under his name at the British Museum is *Historical and Critical Remarks upon the Modern Hexametrists, and upon Mr. Southey's Vision of Judgement* (Cambridge, 1822). It consists of eighty-four pages, that abound with quaint and elegant scholarship. He appears to have been a universal favourite at Cambridge. " I have not yet seen old Tillbrook," says one correspondent, " but we shall ere long have a laugh together ; he is a queer old rogue ; he limps like Vulcan, and raises inextinguishable laughter among the immortals. His hair has fallen off and bared his open front, which shines like Hesperus. . . . He never sees me without uttering imprecations on my head for defrauding him of a beefsteak which he says I have long promised him."

From the Rev. S. Tillbrook.

"Peterhouse College, *February 4th*, 1816.

" My dear Doctor,—All the parties concerned in the future prospects of young A—— feel infinitely obliged to you for the very kind manner in which you have listened to our petition.

" But unless your good rules, like those of grammar, admit of occasional exceptions, our labour is poured out in vain, and our longing young *protégé* will never drink at the fountains of Helicon. Alas ! he is more than sixteen, for his birthday fell the 12th of last September; nevertheless he is less than sixteen in stature—indeed he is not equal to the common race of fourteen- or fifteen-year-olds. It is reckoned a pleasant thing to kill Time ; dare you not for once become a tempicide ? Though neither you nor I have any right to break Priscian's pate, or to transgress the laws of the land, yet for once we may crack the hour-glass of our old enemy, and transgress laws of our own enacting. If this were not so, self-lawgivers would furnish fetters and manacles for themselves, and stand in perilous similitude of certain folks alluded to by Master Ovid's speaking nut-tree.

" Let me then beseech you by all the endearing ties of *hic hæc hoc*, by ὁ ἡ τό, by *propria quæ maribus, fœmineum genus, quæ genus*, and all the other *genera* that are knit together in the bonds of pedagogical amity, leave not this poor lad masterless, schoolless, witless, hopeless—Nonsense! Presto, pass, begone!

* * * * *

" P.S.—Pray let us have your veto or *liceat* by the *tabellarium reducem.* Is that right for 'return of post'?"

FROM MISS MONEY, AFTERWARDS MRS. ST. BARBE.

[*March 1st* (Lincoln post-mark), 1816?]

* * * *

"We have had such a gay winter, our heads are nearly turned : such lots of dances, such lots of beaux, such lots of parties, and such lots of flirtations; every lady three or four deep, and all coming to nothing Oh! these are things to make the heart leap! I hear Miss H. Butler is the belle of Shrewsbury, that your house is perfectly beautiful, and that you are altogether the life and soul of the town, but I don't believe one word of it."

* * * * *

FROM R. W. ELLISTON, ESQ.

(Original in possession of Mrs. G. L. Bridges and Miss Butler.)

"WORCESTER, *March 24th,* 1816.

"MY DEAR SIR,—A letter suddenly delivered brings me news of an intention of shutting the theatre at Salop after the next week. I hear of your friendly solicitude with much gratitude, and I thank you.

"When Mr. Crisp made me renter of the theatre he spoke of no definite time beyond the 1st of May, and spoke of no restriction before that period.

"The times have been very awkward, and my exertions liberal. I have done what I always will do, made the profession as respectable as I could, and made the stage the vehicle of instruction.

"I will not disguise the truth to you that I have lost much at Shrewsbury I am not, however, discontented, though I could have wished to have closed the season with the patronage of Lord Hill.

"That you have not interfered in this effort, I am convinced has arisen from the purest motives. I have, however, written a letter to his Lordship which I send you opened, and if you think it worthy of comment, I leave it to your judgement.

"I have also written to the Mayor of Shrewsbury, for my plans were formed upon a supposed permission and I would wish to hint that the sanction of Lord Hill will give me all I wish for in this eventful period, and give me the opportunity of making my last bow to the inhabitants near the Wrekin."

* * * * *

From a circular issued to parents dated May 3rd, 1816, it appears that Dr. Butler held £2 2s. 0d., or at the most £3 3s. 0d., to be sufficient half-yearly allowance for the pocket money of the upper boys, and half or one-third that sum for the lower. This, however, was supplemented by a weekly dole of a shilling to the upper and sixpence to the lower boys. There was also the monthly merit money.

FROM THE REV. S. TILLBROOK.

"PETERHOUSE COLLEGE, *May 28th,* 1816.

"MY DEAR DOCTOR,—I have a difficult task to write two epistles to two wise men, and as you are incontestably the wiser of the two, and a D.D. into the bargain, I shall allow you the precedence. I trust you will consider this preference as a mark of the respect I feel for savants in general, excepting only for those of Greece and Rome, the majority of whom Dean Swift has proved to be mere simpletons. I suppose, however, he will allow them to have been wise by comparison, as I may be in a barber's shop, or in my own lecture-rooms among a parcel of blockheads who construe Greek and Latin as if they had been taught before the rules of grammar had been laid down—when all parts of speech were alike declined or undeclined, when language was a chaos, and Babel stuttered—before birch grew or the ferula (handmaid of Minerva) was brought forth;—miserable ages of darkness, when the sun and moon and stars were the only lights of the world; when Whitfield, Wesley, and Wildgoose, the triad constellation of the New Jerusalem, had not deigned to shed their influence upon the old and new world; when children were as blind as owls in the sun, or as anything you like better. But let us leave our fooling, or rather, perhaps, let us play the fool, as the rioters are coming and we may be murdered, like Wat Tyler's foes, because we can read.

"You have heard of the rows at Ely and Littleport? Houses gutted, and other pleasant operations performed upon the dwellings of farmers and landholders. Alma Mater threatened, etc., etc. Bute Dudley's fight with the rebels, and capture of four score villains now lodged in Ely gaol. Similar outrages in Suffolk and Norfolk—all tolerably quiet now, flying artillery and other sedatives arriving. Steel and gunpowder in the armoury—special commission of judges. Gallows and hemp have also spread a universal calm among the malcontents, who are returning to their homes hungry, penniless, and discomfited. Poor rogues, they

are to be pitied, and I do not know whether or no I should not
have joined them if Alma Mater had reduced my wages to sixpence and eightpence a day, which I am told has been the case
among the servants of the fen farmers."

The style of this last paragraph and that which we
associate with Carlyle are evidently descended from a
common source, but I am not well enough versed in the
literature of the time to know where the common source
is to be looked for.

CHAPTER IX.

WATERLOO, 1816—BARON MERIAN.

Extracts from Diary, with a Visit to the Field of Waterloo, July 1816.—
Correspondence, November 2nd, 1816—June 30th, 1817.

IN the summer holidays of 1816 Dr. Butler left England for the first time, accompanied by his wife and daughters. The following extracts from his diary are all that my space permits :—

"*July 1st*, 1816.—Left Dover at half-past one, landed at Calais at half-past seven.

  *   *   *   *   *

" Hitherto our inns have been very clean, the beds and linen excellent. The Sedan chairs at Lille are on two wheels with a shaft. A man draws before and another pushes behind.

" I have looked very carefully at Ghent and Antwerp for Greek books, and, to my surprise, have been as much stared at as though I had asked for so many books upon the black art. They do not seem even to have heard of Plantin.

" We observe the women here habited much in the Spanish dress, with long black veils which they draw over their faces at pleasure, and which cover them from the back of their head to their feet. In the street I met one or two gentlemen conducting ladies having their hats off, according to the old fashion.

  *   *   *   *   *

"*July 7th.*—Attended high mass at the Cathedral—the music very fine—about fifty performers. The processions also and the altars lighted with tapers had a fine effect, but the actual ceremonies of the officiating priests seemed a disgusting mummery.

"*July 8th.*—No Greek books to be got in Brussels.

"*July 9th.*—From Brussels through Waterloo to the field of battle, about fourteen miles, through the Forest of Soignies, almost all the way a most detestable *pavé* full of holes. Waterloo is a miserable village of about twenty houses ; its small red brick church, designed in segments of ellipses, is about twenty-five or possibly thirty feet in diameter. Here are monumental inscriptions to the memory of many of our brave country men. In about half a mile from Waterloo we quit the Forest of Soignies, and the ground becomes an elevated plain with some moderate undulations. In about two miles more we come to a place where a bye-road crosses the principal road. Here is an elm of moderate size on the right-hand side of the road, some of whose branches have been torn off by cannon balls ; this is the famous Wellington tree, where the Duke was posted during the greater part of the battle, and is somewhat nearer the left wing than the centre of the battle. Close to the cross-road opposite this runs La Haye Sainte, a broken stumpy hedge. Directly opposite this tree, on the road-side, lay the skeleton of an unburied horse, and near the tree itself I picked up a human rib. The whole field of battle is now covered with crops of wheat and rye, which grow with a rank and peculiar green over the graves of the slain and mark them readily. About one hundred and fifty yards below the Wellington tree, which itself stands on the top of Mount St. Jean, in the hollow, is the little farm of La Haye Sainte, where the dreadful slaughter of the German Legion took place ; they defended the place till they had spent all their ammunition, and were then massacred to a man, but not till they had taken a bloody revenge. The house and walls, the barn doors and gates, are full of marks from cannon and musket balls. In the barn are innumerable shot holes, and the plaster is still covered with blood, and the holes which the bayonets made through their bodies into it are still to be seen.

" In a hollow near this scene of carnage lie the bodies of two thousand French Cuirassiers in one grave, and about twenty yards farther is the spot to which Bonaparte advanced to cheer the Imperial Guard for their last charge ; it is scarcely possible but that he must have exposed himself greatly in so doing. The little valley between the undulation of Mount St. Jean, where the British were posted, and that of La Belle Alliance, which was occupied by the French, is not more than about a quarter of a mile across ; the Duke of Wellington and Bonaparte, whose general station was on this hill, cannot have been more than that distance, or a very little more, from each other. On going to the station of Bonaparte we had a fine view of the whole field, and, though quite ignorant of military affairs, could not but see the superiority of the British position. The undulation on their side being a little more abrupt than that of the French, they were themselves protected in some measure, and their force considerably concealed, while that of the French was perfectly distinguishable. The right wing of the British was at Hougoumont [rather Goumont], a *château* of great importance and of very considerable strength. Their left wing was at the end of La Haye, about a short half-mile or less from the farm of St. Jean, which was almost of the same importance for its protection as Hougoumont for that of the right. The whole line could not extend more than a mile and a quarter. The French were posted on the opposite eminence, and here in this small space three hundred cannon, independent of all other weapons, were doing the work of death all day. Our guide, a very intelligent peasant, told us that the whole ground was literally covered with carcasses, and that about five days after the stench began to be so horrid that it was hardly possible to bury them on the left of the British, and of course on the right of the French position. At less than a mile and a half is the wood from which the Prussians made their appearance. La Belle Alliance is about half a mile or a little less from Mount St. Jean; here we turned off to see the *château* of Hougoumont, which was most important to secure the British right and French left wing, and was therefore eagerly contested; four thousand British were posted here, and withstood with only the bayonet and musketry all the attacks of an immense body of French with cannon. The French were posted in a wood, now a good deal cut down, close to the wall of the garden at Hougoumont. The British had made holes in the wall to fire through, and the French aimed at these holes. The whole wall is so battered by bullets that it looks as if thousands of pickaxes had been employed to pick the bricks. The trees are torn by cannon balls, and some not above eight inches in diameter, being half shot away on one side, still flourish.

"Passing round the garden wall to the gates, the scene of devastation is yet more striking. The front gates communicate with the *château*, a plain gentleman's house, the back ones (which are directly opposite) with the farmer's residence. This was occupied three times by the French, who were thrice repulsed; but the English were never driven from the *château*. The tower, or rather dovecote, of the *château* was burnt down, but a chapel near it, about twenty feet long, was preserved in the midst of the fire; the flames had caught the crucifix and had burnt one foot of the image, and then went out. This was of course considered a great miracle. From the chapel we went into the garden. Its repose and gaiety of flowers, together with the neatness of its cultivation, formed a striking contrast with the ruined mansion, the blackened, torn, and in some parts blood-stained walls, and the charred timbers about it. In a corner of this garden is the spot where Captain Crawford and eight men were killed by one cannon ball, which entered opposite them by a hole still there and went through the house and lodged in another wall; I have seen the ball in the Waterloo Museum. Going along the green alleys of the garden, quite overarched with hornbeam, we see the different holes broken by the English to fire on their enemies, and a gap on the north-east angle of the garden is the gap made by the French, who attempted to enter there, but were repulsed. Had they gained entrance the slaughter would have been dreadful, as we had four thousand men in the garden, which from its thick hedges has many strongholds, and they were greatly more numerous. The English also lined a strong hedge opposite the wood in which the French were, which they could not force, but the trees are terribly torn by cannon. The loss of Hougoumont would probably have been fatal to us. From the gap above mentioned, looking up to the line of the British on Mount St. Jean, is one small bush ; here Major Howard was killed.

" Leaving Hougoumont, we returned to La Belle Alliance, where we once more reviewed the field of battle, and found some bullets and fragments of accoutrements among the ploughed soil. The crop is not so thriving on the French side, but it was still more richly watered with blood ; in fact the soil, which on the British position is rather a light sand, is here a stiffish clay. From La Belle Alliance we proceeded to Genappe, another post, passing by a burnt house called *la maison du roi* ; here Napoleon slept on the eventful eve of the battle. Following the course of the French in their retreat, we proceeded to another post, to Quatre Bras. Here was the famous [stand ?] made by the Highlanders against the whole French Army on the 16th. It is a field a little to the left at the turning to Namur. Hence we proceeded, having Fleurus on our right, to Sombreffe, where was the severe battle of the Prussians on the 16th, and thence to Namur, where the French continued their retreat. At Genappe, which is a straggling village, with narrow streets, dreadful slaughter was made by the Prussians on the night of the 16th ; here Bonaparte's carriage was taken, and he narrowly escaped himself. From hence to Namur the road was strewed with dead, the Prussians having killed, it is thought, not less than twenty thousand in the pursuit. Nothing can be more detestable than the paved roads, more miserable than the villages, or more uninteresting in the natural appearance of the country than the whole course from Brussels to Namur, about forty-seven miles, the scene of all these great historical events in the present and past ages.

*   *   *   *   *

"*July* 11th.—We left Givet, and passed through an army of Cossacks, Calmucks, and all the multifarious swarm of nations which compose the Russian force. They are stationed at Givet, and in its immense and apparently impregnable citadel and barracks. The fortress is on a very high and inaccessible rock. The various dresses of this motley group of nations, some of them in handsome uniforms, some in undress, and the majority in the dirtiest costume imaginable, were very striking, as was also their physiognomy—from the handsome, tall European with reddish hair, grey eyes, and aquiline nose, to the Calmuck, not five feet high, with square flat face, long eyes at a great distance

from his flat nose, and leather cap fastened by a thong under his
chin. The Cossack vest fastened by a belt round their waist,
and made of linen resembling hopsack, was very simple. These
nations were all without arms, except a few soldiers on duty and
some officers. We saw the barracks, containing an immense
number of men ; their filth and the *congeries* of carrion meat for
food, their unwashed rags, and, above all, the ugliness and filth of
their women, far exceed any spectacle of disgust I have ever yet
encountered or even imagined. Many were picking miserable
herbs, nettles, and thistles among the rocks at the foot of the
inaccessible fortress. These they put in their caps (of course
already well tenanted), and then took to their barracks to boil.
We passed multitudes more of these uncivilised beings in bodies
of dozens or scores on the roads, but were never molested by
any of them."

       *   *   *   *   *

Baron Andreas Merian, more than half of whose letters
to Dr. Butler I have been obliged reluctantly to exclude,
was born at Basle in 1774, being eldest son of Andreas
Merian, J.U.C.,* Burghermaster of Basle and Landamann
of Switzerland. The only published account of him that
I have met with is in the supplementary volumes of the
Biographie Universelle, but several of his German letters
are given in the memoirs of Karl von Nostitz.† His niece,
the late Madame Bischoff Merian, kindly furnished me
with notes of the main events of his life, from which I take
the following :—

He was christened Andreas, but generally styled himself
Andreas Adolf. He studied English while very young,
and a school prize essay on Captain Cook, written when
he was only fourteen, shows that he was already proficient
in the language. He came to England some time between
1790 and 1795, residing with his uncle, Luc Iselin, at or
near Norwich. About 1796 he became acquainted with
Mr. Butler, no doubt at Cambridge, and a warm friendship

---

* " Juris utriusque consultus."   † Leipsic and Dresden, 1848.

was formed between the two men, which, however, was interrupted between the years 1800 and 1816.

From Norwich Merian went to Vienna, where, through the interest of friends, he was soon employed by the Government, and was Secretary to the Legation at the Council of Regensburg in 1802.   In 1805 he was at Nuremburg at the headquarters of Archduke Ferdinand, and his constancy to the pre-Napoleonic governments in Germany was so conspicuous that the minister of France desired all the governments of the Rheinbund not to employ him in any diplomatic capacity at their courts.

Being now unoccupied with politics, he lived at Vienna, in the house of his friend Kormayr, studying science, and more especially Greek and Roman literature.   He knew many Asiatic as well as European languages, and through his various sojournings in many countries became acquainted with all the leading literary men in Europe.   In 1809, when the war broke out again, he went with Count Stadevin to Prague, and then as Counsellor of the Embassy with Prince Esterhazy to Dresden.   It was at this time that he was created Baron, under the name Baron Merian Falkach.

In 1812, when Austria allied herself with Napoleon against Russia, Baron Merian so strongly disapproved, that he at once closed all connection with the Austrian Government, and entered the Russian diplomatic service. Being a Russian Counsellor of State, he worked with Stein as a member of the central administration in Saxony under Prince Repnin.

In 1815 we find him in France, as a member of the commission for the liquidation at Paris, where he remained after the evacuation of the allied troops, as Ambassador from the Court of Russia, till his death (of measles) April 25th, 1828.   During these years he was repeatedly employed in political negotiations of the highest importance.

Correspondence, November 2nd, 1816—June 30th, 1817.

From Baron Andreas Merian, Russian Plenipotentiary at Paris.

(Original in possession of the heirs of the late Madame Bischoff Merian, Basle.—Ed.)

" November 2nd, 1816.

" Five whole minutes are elapsed since I read your dear letter of October 25th, and here I am taking up a milk-white pen in order to answer most studiously. Εὕρηκα. That's the *punctum puncti.* Twenty years since I saw you, fifteen since my former letters greeted you, and the world turned upside-down a few times in the meanwhile ! *Sit. Tandem bona causa triumphavit.* You may thank God in your unattackable island to be in a safe and pleasant situation, while the Continent has still a taste of new-drawn beer. *O terque quaterque beati Angli sua si bona nôrint.* But your countrymen all blazing with everlasting glory are too apt to overlook ninety-nine good things, because, forsooth, the hundredth is wanting ! Just as if they had never heard of the great maxim ' *Que le mieux est l'ennemi du bien.*'

" *Jam satis !   Ad ea redeamus quæ ubique locorum et temporum pulcra sunt atque bona, veterum divina carmina vatum.*

" *Gratulor ex animo de Tragœdo feliciter absoluto.* My impatience to see that work is not to be described—to see, read, comment, talk with you about it. But be indulgent. The little I knew twenty years ago is rather diminished than increased. Storms, camps, administrations and liquidations, are not, you know, *lectuli Musarum.* Let me confess to you that I am not sure now to write Latin elegantly, nay, correctly. 'Tis a sad story, but unavoidable in such a Caïnical life. What a pity ! I arrived in Paris at the beginning of July, and ten to one I passed a dozen times before the windows of your Hôtel de la Paix, which is right between my present and my future residence, but you would not have known me in my Russian kaftan and cap.   I am to stay here four or five years, perhaps more.   Perhaps you may come over again, or I again to England, and so we shall and must meet either near the Seine or the Severn.   Pray be so kind as to let me soon have your famous Aischylos, and other books.   I shall take good care of every piece of them, and am really hungry *fame enecor* [?].   Forget not to send your *sharp* * letter.

" There once flourished a Mr. Bloomfield a poet : I hope 'tis not he who undertook to teach you and John Müller !   I am,

* The Letter to C. J. Blomfield, Esq.

indeed, sorry that the Edinburghers shot so far beside the mark, for I esteem and love the Scots for their sound and solid learning, as well as for their brave and warlike deeds. Let me hear something of your family : you have two daughters ? Of what names ? No son ? No *parvus Iulus patrem qui referre possit?* But 'tis still time, you are younger than I. I am, alas ! not married, which is very wrong. Domestic happiness is the only true happiness. You know that Müller died not aged sixty.

" If it is not too late, I think you ought to stop a little the publication of your preface and last volume, because I shall very soon be able to inform you of an excellent little work of a professor of Leipzig *de re metrica Æsch.,* which would, I believe, give a brilliant nice finishing stroke to your learned edition. Ruminate on this.

" Yours most sincerely,
" M."

From Old Mrs. Butler.

"Kenilworth, *November 25th,* 1816.

" My dear Son,—In my last on Saturday I informed you Dr. Parr called on me Friday, but I was in bed. How great was my surprise on Saturday night after dark, I heard a carriage drive up, and such a rap before Mary could answer it, when I heard Dr. Parr inquire if Mrs. Butler was down : in he came in great spirits and told me of his marriage—had he ever mentioned his intention to you ? She is a woman that is extremely well spoken of at Coventry, and very much liked there."

* * * * *

From W. W. Currey, Esq.

"Chester, *January 4th,* 1817.

" Dear Sir,—A severe cold has detained me here for the last ten days and prevented my replying to your letter sooner.

" There were seven young gentlemen from Shrewsbury, only six of whom were to have gone on to Liverpool ; the seventh, however, left his trunk at the inn here, and returned by the coach back from Liverpool the next morning. Proceeding by the Manchester coach from hence, they all rode outside ; four of them (not the four oldest) rode in front and the rest behind. The four in front had a pistol and some gunpowder ; they fired three or four times as they passed along the streets of Chester, and afterwards several times upon the road, betwixt here and Sutton, where the coach changed horses. The coachman remonstrated with them, but conceived they were only firing gunpowder. Each of the four boys in front, he thinks, fired more or less ; those behind had no share in the fun. On coming to the village of Thornton, where I reside, they fired into the window of my bailiff's house, and broke several panes of glass, but, being a bedroom window, no one was hurt or alarmed. It was then the coachman first perceived they had more than powder ; passing on a few doors farther, they fired into the cottage of the poor woman whom I before mentioned to you. In the next village of Eastham they broke Mr. Grice's windows, and in the next village of Brombrow two small panes of glass in Mr. Hankinson's. It then grew dusk, and they desisted firing for the rest of the journey. This I believe is the utmost extent of the delinquency, and I feel now quite satisfied it was peas and not shot they fired. This in my mind very much extenuates the offence, and I trust will do so in your mind also ; I am quite certain your discretion will point out the mode of punishment most likely to mark the offence and prevent a re-occurrence of it. I certainly do think it ought to be noticed, but still not with any severity, either as to present feeling or future disgrace. I can only consider it as an act of boyish indiscretion and thoughtlessness, but cannot attach any more opprobrious epithet to it. I forgot to mention they had a flag upon the coach with them, which they waved as they passed through the different villages.

" I return you a two-pound banknote. Two gentlemen, I find, have been over and paid the poor woman a pound ; she has therefore returned me the one I gave her. They also called and paid Mr. Grice twelve shillings for the repair of his window, and he is perfectly satisfied. Mr. Hankinson says his damage is too trifling to mention, and my bailiff's I will see to the repair of, so that we have no pecuniary claim of any kind upon you. I conclude the two gentlemen were parents of the boys ; being in Chester I did not see them, but with the pound note returned me, by the poor woman, received a civil message from them."

From Old Mrs. Butler.

" Kenilworth, *January*, 1817.

" My dear Son,—I am very much obliged to you for your very kind present of salmon and the rhubarb ; the salmon lasted me till Saturday last, for I had it every day for a week. I think myself much about the same as when you was here, but the cold weather agrees with me much better than warm.

*   *   *   *   *

" I have had a visit from Dr. and Mrs. Parr ; they both looked very well and happy. The Dr. was in great good-humour and great spirits ; his dress was so much like a dignified clergyman, a very handsome velvet coat, and the handsomest wig I ever saw him in, very full of small curls ; they were going to return their visit at Stoneleigh Abbey. They both inquired in the kindest manner after you. Lady Peel is returned ; she made me a long afternoon, and inquired very kindly after you, Mrs. Butler, and all your family."

*   *   *   *   *

From the Rev. S. Tillbrook.

"**Cambridge**, *February 6th*, 1817.

" *Vir doctissime*,—Your last report of young A—— has given great pleasure to his friends, and I hope your kindness to him will excite still greater efforts on his part. Lopping, rasping, polishing are certainly necessary to rid him of all the stiffness and quaintness which, as you are pleased to say, have originated in *me*.

"But remember your own pedantry and affectation. Why must you write Latin quotations on the outside of your epistle, as if you were sending despatches to the Roman Senate? I suppose the next superscription will be in Greek, and if it be I shall not understand it. *Apropos* of Greek, what was the symbol of hospitality among the Athenians? I wish to place something of that sort over my door at Ivy Cottage, the salt box, or *Sportula*, or something not understood by the *profanum vulgus*.

"For the last week, I have seen your name and heard you speak Latin more than my pupils can understand, *e.g.* in the observations on the *Prometheus Vinctus*. It is a grand thing for me to sit with a great quarto volume before me ; to look big, and chatter like a parrot about what I do not understand ; to offer objections to the opinions of Butler, Schütz, and others ; to choose this, and damn that, and have it all my own way. This is a privilege which even you have not among your boys. My lads cannot convict me out of the words of my own mouth, for they never remember a word I say; perhaps it is better for their judgement and taste that they should not.

"Then the metres ! How delightful to scan over the *Tentamen* of that old proser Burney—the dimeter trimeter spastic minstrel of the buskin ! Pray, what did the ocean nymphs smell of? Do you incline to the godlike, mortal, or compound scent? Prometheus had a better nose for a nymph than ' Naso had for smelling out the sweet flowers of poesy.' There is great similarity in the olfactory powers of this fire-stealing thief and those of the giant Hurlothrumbo. Do you remember his exclamation? Vide *Nursery Stories*, Vol. I., p. 20: ' Fi, fo, fum, I smell the blood of an Englishman.' Now could you not as a mythologist and Grecian undertake to prove that this said giant was one of the Titans, and therefore might be Prometheus, who, according to the comparative testimony of historians, may be anybody? Again, in the exclamation ' Fi, fo, fum,' you might trace the use of the digamma. Is not this succession of syllables as pleasant as ἰα ἰα ἰα or πῦ πῦ πῦ, or any other of choric systems ? ' Heigho ! '

is certainly a corruption of ἰώ, and why should not Fi, fo, fum be something else? Accept my challenge to produce more nonsense in a page than I have done in this, and you may expect a better supply than this soon, for I am reading the Latin *Facetiæ Laus Asini, Laus Stultitiæ*, etc.

"Your most devoted friend,

"S. T."

FROM THE REV. T. S. HUGHES.

(Original in University Library, Cambridge.—ED.)

"*March* 18*th*, 1817.

*   *   *   *

"The Fellows of Trinity are all like a hive of bees when a wasp has got in among them. Old Saint Ramsden holds the living of Chesterton and requires them to present him to one of the best in their gift, without his vacating the former. This they are unwilling to do, so he has thrown them into the visitors' hands, and from certain circumstances will probably gain his point. You must know that Chesterton fell when Mansell was made Bishop, and so may, for that presentation, be considered a Crown living."

*   *   *   *   *

FROM DR. BURNEY.

"RECTORY HOUSE, DEPTFORD, *April* 15*th*, 1817.

"MY DEAR DR. BUTLER,—Do not suppose me insensible to your great and continued kindness; I was unwilling to return thanks till I had found time to look over your volume, and well and amply have I been repaid for my delay.

"Your work has been long and laborious, and I congratulate you very heartily on your arrival at its termination. When I consider, indeed, the length of your task, and the difficulties by which you were chained down, independently of your Æschylean difficulties, I cannot but think that the time you have devoted to this author has been well spent, and has been crowned with success.

"When your fourth volume arrived from Mr. Evans, I was fighting against or bearing with an attack of the gout. After its leisurely departure I was obliged to give my time and thoughts to various occupations which I had neglected during my illness. It was not till Easter approached that I could fairly buckle on my armour, and attack my friendly foe—friendly, indeed, I may term him, for never was a lance broken with so little hostility.

"As for my *Tentamen*, allow me to advise you not to waste many lines on it; it was merely an experiment to see how far the generality of choruses might be reduced to antispastics, but by no means as presenting a system for others to follow. During its printing, I must observe, I was troubled with a complaint in my eyes—which then left a variety of blunders in the printing, and particularly in the longs and shorts, on some of which the critics, *hic et illic*, have lavished a few loose shots.

"When I am to have the pleasure of seeing you I know not, but whenever fortune may be so much in good-humour as to indulge me, I shall exclaim, '*Numero meliore lapillo.*'"

From the Rev. S. Tillbrook.

"Cambridge, *April* 21*st*, 1817.

"Dear Doctor,—Do not imagine that you are to offend my sympathies and associations and to caricature Ivy Cottage by an uncouth hieroglyphical libel with impunity; *horribili sectare flagello* says one of the Greek poets, so take care of yourself, Doctor Birch! *Flumina amo sylvasque*, and alder-trees and banks and other picturesque objects, and pray don't you? As to your questions I respond as followeth.

"Black ingratitude in one pupil and desertion in three more have left me £140 poorer than I expected to be at this time last year. I am glad that better feelings have left you £300 richer. *Audaces Fortuna juvat*; but I being a meek-spirited, modest man, clothed with the sevenfold *surtout* of pride, obstinacy, and indomitable independence, am slighted, and always have been by that fickle rotatory Goddess. *Sans* interest, *sans* patron, *sans* everything that makes a man no-man, I left my cradle to swagger through the wilderness of life, gathering crab-apples by the way, and munching them on the thorn-stuffed stool of repentance. But not to depress your tender heart, which I am happy to find was only cracked, not broken (and therefore, like ice, will bear the better till it thaws), I will be silent on my own woes.

"I should like much to pass through Shrewsbury on my way to the north—I suppose you will be at home till June 20th? If I come, I will approach like Apollo, *cum cithara carminibusque*. I will be a Tibicen. Oh for the liberty of the mountain boy, the frisky mutton of the fields, the roving tyrant of the seas, or any other poetical type of freedom!

"My dog *Pepper* is as playful as a *piper*—so much so that I am inclined to think (being a disciple of Pythagoras) he formerly filled that station in some of the Roman palaces. He greets your dog, the noble Rolla to wit. He has rendered the College great service by clearing the buttery and kitchen of rats. I have thought of turning him into the House of Commons soon, where he would play the very devil. The other day he went with me to the public library in search of dog-Latin, which he found in great abundance; when the librarian entered Pepper set up a barking, and treated some of the ancient authors with great contempt. . . .

" Farewell, *amico stimatissimo* ; commend me to your good and kind household. . . .

" P.S.—Young A——'s progress is very pleasant for all the parties therein concerned.

" Two days ago I was séanced by one of the philosophers of the Spurzheim and Gall school ; what, think you, were the leading characteristics of my thick skull ? Pride and obstinacy, organs full and distinct—wit and imagination superabundant—benevolence unlimited—poverty undeserved—friendship strong and lasting—of morality and religion a smattering—of true scholarship a vacuum—of nonsense a plenty—χαῖρε."

FROM THE REV. S. TILLBROOK.

"CAMBRIDGE, *May 25th*, 1817.

" Do you know what has befallen St. Peter's old house ? Who could believe it ? An unknown person has given to the Master and Fellows of this college no less a sum than £20,000. Ah ! twenty thousand pounds sterling ! And down upon the nail. The history of this affair is veiled in as much mystery as the Eleusinian rites were ; all I know is that I began the adventure at the risk of being made a fool of and of losing my expenses to town, but I will give you an outline of the business.

" Ten days ago our Master received an anonymous letter, the contents of which appeared partly like an extract from a will and partly like a copy of instructions from a secret agent. The paper began thus : —

" 'I give and bequeath to etc., etc., and their successors the sum of £— to found scholarships and fellowships, without preference to school or county. . . . The residue of my bequest, *i.e.* the annual income from such residue, I give to the Master and Fellows for their full and entire disposal,' etc.

" On the other side of the paper was this : ' Provided the College accept this offer a handsome present will be made to it, but the name of the donor must not be inquired into, and an agent must be sent to receive the money.'

" This was treated by all except Smyth and myself as a hoax. The Master did not answer the letter. I requested him to allow me. He did so. I wrote a *rara epistola,* threatening vengeance upon the pate of any one who dared to quiz the Petersians. This brought a reply stating that there was no hoax, that if any one would take the trouble of a visit to town he would be referred to a most respectable agent, and the money would be paid if the letters were shown as credentials. No one but myself would stir, and I was called a fool for my pains, but ever obstinate as a brute, off I went—inquired for the reference offered—found parties highly respectable—agent told me that he had the money and would pay it to the College Bursar. I sent off for the Master from Cambridge, and for Veasey from Bath. Bridge was in town. In two days the regulations were drawn up to found four scholarships of £50 a year each, to be held till M.A. degree; also two fellowships of £125 a year, each to be vacated by marriage or preferment, or by any permanent income above £250 per annum—the residuary interest at the full and entire disposal of Master and Fellows for ever. Two days after this the money was paid, and now stands in bank stock in the name of the Master and Fellows of Peterhouse! Thus ended my adventure, and thus commences a new era in the prosperity of our most antient foundation. . . .

" P.S.—Hughes is as unsettled as a pauper with a pass. He knows not what to do or where to go. He ought to be shut up in your school library and flogged till he had finished his *Travels.*"

The buildings which were paid for with part of this curious bequest bear the initials of the Master, F. B., and of Mr. Tillbrook, S. T. These may yet be seen. The donor I find from Gunning's *Reminiscences* proved afterwards to be the Rev. Francis Gisborne, formerly a fellow of Peterhouse.

From the Same.

"CAMBRIDGE, *June* 5*th*, 1817.

" Mine Hostess of the Garter when she respondeth to Sir John Falstaff doth not use the saying of ' Tilley Valley, Sir John,' but she sayeth ' Filley Falley.' But you ask me for the etymology. I will endeavour to make it out, for I am not deep in letters, yet am I ingenious or inventive, wherefore I say that mine hostess lispeth and from ' Fiddle Faddle ' has arrived at ' Filley Falley.' Theobald, nor Steevens, nor Johnson, could have derived this better, and I contend that, in future editions, instead of ' Tilley Valley ' it be said ' Filley Falley,' and that a note be appended showing how easily T and F are mistaken in either Roman or Italian characters.

" Your friend Dr. Parr has been here. I met him at Emmanuel, and was introduced to him as your friend by T. Hughes. The old boy shook me by the hand, and then again for your sake, and mentioned you in such laudatory terms that you must have blushed had you been present. I smoked five pipes and played three rubbers with him, and a cheerful day we had—but I should prefer a trio of the three Sams.

"I wish you were here to-day; we have a feast, a symposium in honour of our noble friend Ignoramus. I believe his bounty will not stop at the £20,000. There is a talk now of his buying livings for his fellowships. I wish I could come within reach of him. I would try and angle out of him a few of his golden fish, to furnish Ivy Cottage with.

"What stay do you make at Barmouth? I suppose one may trace you by Greek inscriptions, mottoes, etc., on windows, the bark of trees, on the sands and elsewhere. I am reading your notes on Æschylus with more pleasure than you can imagine. 'I can construe but do not entirely see the construction of the following passage, in a chorus in the Seven Chiefs: Δράκοντας ὥς τις τέκνων ὑπερδέδοικε λεχέων δυσευνάτορας πάντρομος πελειάς. Now' [word for word, and expletive for expletive] 'what a d——d lot of genitive cases are here gotten together!' I have quoted the above from one of my pupils."

FROM BARON MERIAN.

"PARIS, *June* 10th, 1817.

"DEAR SIR,—Item, a remarkable instance of book-learning: Johnson did not know what a rake is, and had recourse to the *Edda* instead of asking his farmer! See his first note to *Coriolanus*, and his islandic dog. This puts me in mind of a celebrated professor who used to quote Aristotle in testimony of a most hazardous assertion, viz. that hens lay eggs. Not long ago I read as follows: Παππάζουσιν. Note, 'Solebant enim veterum, scias, pueruli patrem invocantes voce quadam uti quæ pappa sonum referebat.'

"There's another doctification in the notes to *Coriolanus*, about 'quarry.' Why, 'quarry' is nothing in the world but *curée*. I am surprised that your commentators titubate about such common things.

"Steevens is very often evidently in the wrong. He may be a very learned man; *non moror;* but as for judgement, he has none or little. I venture to say that he does not understand Shakespeare, whose immortal flights are at least sixty thousand stadia above Steevens' capacity. The commentator of a poet, dear sir, needs to be a bit of a poet; *atqui ergo* . . . I don't know who wrote the note on Brutus' speech 'He is grown too proud to be so valiant.' That note is wrong too; Brutus says Coriolanus's pride is excessive, on account of his being or because he feels himself so valiant. See the answer of Sicinius.

"You ought to draw your sword, my dear friend, and not suffer such inexactnesses to pass. Better no explanations than false ones. Remember the Byzantines, and let not the glorious flames of your unrivalled bard be drowned in the *sentina* of muddy commentation.

"Now I stay for your commands concerning the books; if you would give me leave I would present Æschylus to the Emperor....

"P.S.—I am now reading again Shakespeare, and shall send you, if you think it worth the while, a few remarks.

"Set some of your boys about *Slavica.* Believe me that there is no complete *linguistica* unless a man be able to compare those three large rivers, issuing most likely from one source; viz. the river *German,* comprehending English, Danish, and the river *Slavon,* comprising Russian, Bohemian, Polish, etc., and the river *Welsh (Galica pars),* comprehending Latin, French, Spanish, etc. Thousands of Indian and Persian words are German. What Englishman knows what 'bale' is (*Coriol.,* I.)? The Russian will tell you presently it is pain, suffering, evil. And so in innumerable instances.

"*Ohe, jam satis est, et plus quam satis.* It is an odd thing in me to fight with Englishmen about their language. But you will excuse me, if you consider my great veneration for, and consequently application to, your immortal poet, and that I speak not from a vain notion of understanding English better, but from a consciousness of knowing German and French perfectly, unto which then your English resembled much more than now. So you find in Ariel's song a burden which is by no means an *onus,* but a true French *bourdon.*

*   *   *   *   *

"As Cato cried 'Carthago delenda,' so I cry 'Slavica discenda'! Do select one or two of your pupils for that purpose. I am confident the event and fruit will astonish. Take a tripod, knock off one leg; there's our linguistic without Slav. We are and shall be out, and lame, and purblind, in ninety-nine thousand grammatical questions, as long as we remain ignorant of that third essence, sure indeed quite as essential as the other two. Your own opinion confirms this. I think it possible to get up to the very elements of language; general construction or articulation is evidentest in Greek: ἄω, ἔω, ἴω, ὄω, ὔω (all verbs), then βάω, βέω, βίω, βόω, βύω (all verbs), and so on."

To Baron Merian.

"*June* 30*th*, 1817.

"First to business, my dear Baron, and then to criticism. You will greatly oblige me by retaining the English books, which you can so perfectly understand and enjoy, for your own use. I should feel proud indeed if you would undertake to present the Æschylus for me to your magnanimous Emperor. Dare I venture a simple Latin inscription, without adulatory epithets and flourishing superlatives?   If so, and if you approve of it, get some *plume d'or* to write the following in the first leaf:—

ALEXANDRO

RUSSORUM IMPERATORI

MAGNANIMO INVICTO CLEMENTI

LIBERTATIS EUROPÆÆ ADSERTORI AC VINDICI

LITERARUM ATQUE ARTIUM HUMANIORUM

FAUTORI ATQUE PATRONO

REGIIS OMNIBUS VIRTUTIBUS UBERRIME ORNATO

ÆSCHYLUM POETAM NOBILEM

CIVEM BONUM MILITEM HAUD INSTRENUUM

OMNI OBSERVANTIA ATQUE OBSEQUIO COMMENDAT

SAMUEL BUTLER S.T.P.

REGIÆ SCHOLÆ SALOPIENSIS APUD BRITANNOS ARCHIDIDASCALUS.

A.S. MDCCCXVII.

You may add before the day of the year, if you like, the day of the month upon which your Emperor for the second time entered Paris.

"I am not sure whether I sent you my Installation Sermon preached at Cambridge before H.R.H. the Duke of Gloucester, our Chancellor.   If I did not, tell me in your next.

"Now for criticism.   You are, I perceive, a better English scholar than the generality of my countrymen, and your observations upon the commentators are very just; but we laugh at them here too.   Of all editions of Shakespeare, Pope's is the worst.   Theobald's, whom Pope attacks so severely in the *Dunciad*, is very superior to it, and is indeed a respectable edition.   Johnson frequently misunderstood Shakespeare.   Steevens was far better versed in the ancient lore and contemporary writers of the Elizabethan age, but you justly appreciate him.   Malone's is much the best single edition, but is now very difficult to obtain, and there are some good recent variorum editions, one of which you found in the chest.   The preface to Shakespeare by Johnson is inimitable.   About 'quarry' you are clearly right.   Your explanation of ' He's grown too proud,' etc., is certainly quite right.   It is curious that a great many Persian words are English, but they come, I suspect, through the German.   Welsh is nearly all Hebrew and Greek, but the names for all the conveniences and luxuries of life are not Welsh; they are Celtic, or English celtified.   This is curious, and at once shows the antiquity of the language and the barbarism of the people."

CHAPTER X.

THE FORTUNATE YOUTH—HUGHES'S INSCRIPTIONS.

The Fortunate Youth.—Correspondence on this Subject, October 29th, 1817—December 24th, 1817.—Correspondence, October 31st, 1817—June 9th, 1818, with Review of Porson's *Adversaria.*—Paper on some Greek Inscriptions that appear in Hughes's *Travels in Sicily*, etc.

WITH regard to the extraordinary imposture referred to in the heading of this chapter, I would say what I can in extenuation of the offender, and in explanation of the gullibility of the public.

It appears from a letter written by Mr. Cawston, senior, August 5th, 1817, that his son, the so-called Fortunate Youth, had been desperately ill for some weeks during July, and at the beginning of August he was still unable to go back to school. This illness, which I suppose we ought to accept as genuine, may have affected his brain. I have made inquiries about him from those who remember him, and have found he was generally liked, while the tenor of whatever few allusions to him I have found among the letters of Mr. Sheepshanks and other schoolfellows is kindly. The Rev. F. E. Gretton, in his *Memory's Harkback,** says of him :—

"He was a big boy when I was a little one, was among the senior lads, and held his own in point of scholarship.† He was

---

* Richard Bentley, 1889, p. 31.

† In a letter to Dr. Butler dated April 25th, 1826, Cawston gives his place in the school as third, Frank Matthews being head boy, and Andrew Lawson second.

a good-natured easy-going fellow, much given to sham out of school, that he might devour novels and romances and fruit. He called himself Augustus C——, but it oozed out that his real name was Abraham ; but woe betide us small boys if we ventured so to address him ! ”

As for the credulity of the public, it must be remembered that a very few months previously every one had believed that Mr. Tillbrook was being hoaxed—but Peterhouse got the £20,000 and the laugh had gone against the incredulous, who accordingly resolved not to be sceptical next time, hoax or no hoax. The idea, moreover, of a young man of prepossessing manners coming unexpectedly into an enormous fortune is one that appeals readily to those who lead the public on domestic matters more surely than any others can do—I mean mothers with marriageable daughters. Nine mothers out of ten will swallow with avidity any romantic story about a lad of eighteen, which they would not even listen to about an elderly married man with a wife and a family of grown-up children. Wildly improbable again as Cawston's story was, it was hardly more improbable than that a well-conducted, popular, and promising boy of eighteen should have the technical skill to fabricate, and the effrontery to propound and persist for many weeks in, such an astounding false-hood. Lastly, an uncle, by instantly accepting the boy's tale and placing £1,200 at his disposal, gave him money enough to fling about in the eyes of the public, and make it clear that he had a considerable sum actually in hand.

Cawston was no longer at Shrewsbury, and Dr. Butler had no responsibility in connection with him, but when the story reached him as a matter of common report he accepted it. No doubt he was set off his guard, by having already found Cawston in possession of more money than a boy commonly has. I find from a letter of December 21st, 1817, which will follow in order of date, that Dr.

Butler had more than once remonstrated with the boy's father about the quantity of money he appeared able to command. This is confirmed by the account of Cawston given in Gunning's *Reminiscences*, Vol. II., p. 305.*
Mr. Gunning writes :—

"When at a subsequent period Dr. Butler was writing to the young man's father, and expressing his entire satisfaction at the progress and general good conduct of his son, he also remarked that being allowed so much for pocket money might eventually be injurious to him, for that when he had asked one of his scholars a few days previously, to procure him change for a £10 note, young Cawston had offered to change it for him; besides which he had learned on inquiry that he always had abundance of money."

From the Hon. H. G. Bennet's letter of November (?), 1817, it seems that the incident above recorded occurred some time previously to Cawston's leaving school, and it was most probably the occasion that led Dr. Butler to send all parents his circular of May 3rd, 1816, in regard to the pocket money they should allow their sons. It must be remembered also that the imposture was not set on foot till after Cawston had left Dr. Butler's care. Had he gone back to Shrewsbury after his illness at Edinburgh he would (as he probably very well knew) have been cross-questioned and detected at once ; as it was Dr. Butler never saw him after June 1817.

Mr. Gunning's account of Cawston is as follows :—

"His story was that on his return to school after the previous vacation he had met with an old man in the stage coach ; that they had had much conversation, but as they had upon most points differed so much in opinion, they seemed to part with no friendly feeling for one another. He further stated that, soon after he was settled at school, he had received a note from his travelling companion (who was residing in the neighbourhood) requesting he would call upon him ; that he had found him living in very humble style, but that he had told him

---

* London, George Bell, and Cambridge, Charles Wootton, 1854.

he was possessed of enormous wealth, and had been for many years looking out for some person to make his heir; and he further added that he had been so much pleased with the spirited and independent manner in which young Cawston had maintained his opinions as to become desirous of a more intimate acquaintance with him. The old man then gave him a general invitation to his house; but he had requested their interviews should for a time remain private. When paying him a subsequent visit he found his patron very ill, and believing that he should not recover he had made him a *deed of gift* of his whole fortune, with an earnest request that it should not be divulged to any person till the following January, as in the early part of 1818, he said, there would be no further occasion for secrecy. Soon after this the old man died, he said.

"*The Fortunate Youth* (for by that title after a time he became everywhere known) expressed a desire that his good fortune should not be generally mentioned, as he had given a solemn promise that the iron chest in which the *deed of gift* had been deposited, as also many other important documents, should not be opened until the period stated, nor was he at liberty to divulge where his eccentric old patron had deposited it. He, however, expressed a desire to his father that he should lose no time in making him and his family independent; and that he wished to state his views to Mr. Weatherley, a solicitor at Newmarket, of great eminence, and who was closely connected with all the nobility and gentry resident in that neighbourhood.

"So clear did the young man's statement appear, that although the circumstances seemed very mysterious, Mr. Weatherley did not doubt the fact, and in all his intentions his client seemed to be guided by the most disinterested feelings. Mr. Weatherley took directions for his will and agreed to be his executor.

"There is no doubt but that the want of ready money would have puzzled this young impostor, had not an uncle requested him to make use of twelve hundred pounds, which he said was lying in his banker's hands at Bury.

"He entered his brother a Fellow Commoner at Emmanuel, stating at the time that his reason for deciding on that college was that the Master's wife (Mrs. Cory) was sister to Mrs. Butler of Shrewsbury, by whom he had been most kindly treated.

*   *   *   *

"I was afterwards informed by the Master of Emmanuel that young Cawston had accompanied his brother to Cambridge; that he had been extremely pleased with his manner and address, and that he seemed to have much general knowledge and was a great connoisseur in paintings. When looking at the Fitzwilliam paintings, he remarked that some of them were pretty good, but that he had a far more valuable collection at his palace in Spain. Dr. Procter also told me that when Weatherley was asked one day whether his client's rent-roll equalled that of the Duke of Rutland, his reply was that he had more than double the amount.

"Weatherley was instructed to be on the look out for a house calculated for a nobleman's residence; and his client also expressed his intention of purchasing such boroughs as offered themselves, his opinion being that the possession of parliamentary influence was the sure road to honour and distinction in this country.

"Among other statements, he said that the Empress of Russia was indebted to his benefactor one hundred thousand pounds, and that she paid annually six thousand pounds interest; that on the King of Spain he had immense claims; that his most valuable estates were in that country, but that he had also property in Germany and Italy. To give an air of truth to these incredible statements, he said that his mysterious benefactor had been a diamond merchant.

"Nothing could exceed the romance of his story, nor the ingenious stratagems he devised to keep up the delusion. Tradesmen of all classes solicited the honour of serving him. This perhaps is not so much to be wondered at, but that bankers should contend for his account is rather a startling fact.

"Mr. Weatherley suggested that the first thing requisite to be done was to make him a ward of the Court of Chancery, for which purpose two very eminent lawyers were employed; he also recommended that a treaty should be entered into for the purchase of Houghton Hall, in the County of Norfolk, which had been for some time in the market, and would be a very suitable residence for him when he came into possession of his wealth.

"Upon one occasion a draft to a large amount was picked up; when it was restored to him he affected great vexation at his carelessness, saying it was so very material that his money trans-actions should be kept as secret as possible. He was frequently heard to express a hope that he should never become so avaricious as his benefactor must have been. He further applied to Government to take and bear the arms of Devereux; and the Heralds' College was actually waiting for information as to what branch of the house of Devereux his patron belonged, when the bubble burst and he fell a sacrifice to his apparent security.

"Dining with his friends one day, he spoke of the expected arrival of some Sicilian wines from his estates at Mount Etna. When they arrived he requested a few gentlemen to dine with him, that they might give their opinion as to which quality it would be most advisable to encourage; he also talked much when they met on the advantages that would be derived from the improved cultivation of the Sicilian grape. On one of the bottles being opened a gentleman strongly suspected he saw a familiar name of a London wine-merchant on the cork, which he managed to get into his possession. He then wrote to the wine-merchant respecting his dealings with young Cawston, and received for answer that his son-in-law, who had been employed for many years in the Sicilian vintage, had written to Mr. Cawston strongly recommending a trial of his excellent Sicilian wines, and that a supply had accordingly been sent him.

"Eyes that had so long been closed now began to open. The papers teemed with suspicions, and in a few days a caution was inserted against the fortunate youth, who was spoken of as an impostor."

The *Morning Chronicle* of December 11th, 1817, seems to have given the first public expression of distrust. This was replied to in a Cambridge paper of the following day, in a manner that shows Cawston to have still had warm defenders.

"'The delusion,' continues Mr. Gunning, "lasted between two and three months, at the sacrifice of about sixteen hundred pounds. It was very evident that Cawston's object could not have been altogether for pecuniary gain, for he might have availed himself of thousands that were offered him. His repeated refusal and his expressed desire not to launch into any heavy expenditure previous to taking possession of his *countless wealth*, which, according to his statement, was on a near approach, encouraged the cheat."

Mr. Gunning concludes by saying :—

" The deceptions practised on his family were very cruel and must have been deeply felt. A gentleman conversing with a farmer who resided in Mr. Cawston's neighbourhood, asked him whether the disappointment, added to his son's misconduct, had not materially altered him ; to which he replied that to him the *only perceptible change* was, his taking his brandy and water stronger than he had before accustomed himself to."

CORRESPONDENCE ABOUT THE FORTUNATE YOUTH,
OCTOBER 29TH, 1817—DECEMBER 24TH, 1817.

FROM THE REV. T. S. HUGHES.

" CAMBRIDGE, *October 29th*, 1817.

" MY DEAR FRIEND,—Old Till talks much of the *noctes cœnæque deûm* of Shrewsbury. I hope this wonderfully fortunate boy will think of you, his old and good master, in his strange and good fortune.   What an extraordinary incident !   I never heard of that rich old man in Shrewsbury, and it seems no one else ever did. What a fool and an ass to leave such a mint of money to one boy ! Why did he not augment the revenues of Shrewsbury School with a part,—or found at least a hundred almshouses ? "

    *   .   *   *   *   *

From Mr. Abraham Cawston.

(From a copy in the handwriting of Mrs. Butler.)

" Chippenham, *October* 31*st*, 1817.

" My dear Sir,—A daily expectation of visiting Shrewsbury on business with a mortgage of mine in the neighbourhood has alone prevented my giving you the earliest intelligence of an event in which your constant kindness warrants that you would take due interest.   In fact I have some thoughts of purchasing an estate near Shrewsbury, as one has been offered on what my lawyer considers highly advantageous terms.   The newspaper reports are equally destitute of foundation, truth, and probability. The real fact has not yet transpired, beyond the lawyers, etc., and my own immediate family, the full explanation of which I leave for a personal conference.   My foreign property is immense, and my English very considerably above even that arrant jade Report, who for once is under par.   My unfunded English property amounted to more than half a million at my friend's death, besides innumerable mortgages, etc.   Perhaps my inconsiderate and volatile conduct when under your charge will admit of some palliation from the consideration that this enormous fortune has been hanging, like the fruit of Tantalus, at my very lips for upwards of two years, though compelled by interest and honour to conceal my expectations.

" Every one knows the nature of a rich man's promise.   Had I been disappointed, in case of a premature disclosure, what excuse could I possibly have offered to the public ?   How could I have indemnified my friends for raising false hopes which must have inevitably ended in their ruin.   Conceive, sir, the weight of concealment upon a young mind ardent and impetuous, and perhaps you will not be so much surprised at my having plunged myself into dissipation, as the only refuge from thought and anxiety. Hence that vacillating turn of mind, that false pride, that indecision of conduct, which I fear too much distinguished me at Shrewsbury.   I am thus anxious to palliate my conduct because I covet your esteem and regard more than that of any man breathing. This from me is no flattery or blarney, but the genuine tribute of attachment and respect.   I have laid the whole circumstances before you.   I shall leave it to your judgement whether I might or ought not to go abroad in a few months.   At the same time

I wish to consult you on two or three points upon which the direction of my future life entirely depends. With feelings of the deepest gratitude and respect, believe me ever your most sincere and attached pupil,   " ABM. CAWSTON.

"I do not mean it as a compliment when I entreat you to use my means and interest to the utmost, if anything in which I can possibly be serviceable occurs. You know me too well to be offended at my begging that in case any sum of money would be at all at any time convenient, no other person may be consulted but myself. I shall be happy to furnish you with it at a day's warning to any amount, and in fact shall by no means leave England comfortably unless you allow me to show my gratitude for my past favour in a manner adequate to my present situation. Present my respects to Mrs. and Miss Butler. May I take the liberty to request you will tell Andrew Lawson I shall, if in health, see him soon, and also Leicester.

"Dr. and Mrs. Cory, etc., were this morning in perfect health. I have a Hanoverian residing with me, who undertakes to teach me Spanish, French, and German without any other assistance. He also professes to be a correct classical scholar."

FROM THE HON. H. G. BENNET.

[Upper Grosvenor Street. Letter not dated, probably *November*, 1817.]

"MY DEAR SIR,—I thank you very much for the trouble you have taken in sending me so detailed an account of your acquaintance with young Cawston.* I fear your own kindness of heart and want of all guile has made you judge too favourably of him ; from all I can hear, and I have the best authority, the whole story is a fabrication ; there never was either gift or giver, and he never had any acquaintance with any one who either gave or bequeathed to him one penny. All he has is the money advanced to him by his dupes.

"I was the more curious to learn from you what you knew of this singular person, from the use he made of your name, and the abuse he indulged in of your school. He said that you were some time back so struck with his great command of money (as his acquaintance with the gentleman began a year and a half prior to the publication of his fortune by the testator's death), that you wrote to his father requesting him to cease supplying him with such large sums, as it would ruin the boy and his companions too.

          *   *   *   *   *

"I can explain no part of these phenomena but by one solution —is he insane? Here I learn that he could not sleep alone, and

---

* No draft of the account here referred to was found by me.—ED.

that a nurse and servant were with him all night. You know perhaps that he had a typhus fever; is it possible that his mind has never recovered its assaults?

"Of course a prevailing· fantasy would carry all before it, and all would be brought to aid in its accomplishment. Why should there be delusions strong enough to make the King forget the living and hold converse with the dead, and yet not strong enough to make another fancy himself heir to untold millions?

"I shall thank you to answer me as to the fact he has urged about his possession of money. I, as you may imagine, never fail to speak of you as you merit, which I am happy to find all the world concurs in."

To Mr. J. Cawston.

[KENILWORTH, *December* 21st or 22nd, 1817.]

"DEAR SIR,—I have received your letter on a subject too painful for me to recur to without deep concern. Any accounts that your son may have given you of his transactions with Messrs. Rock, Loxdale, & Coupland at Shrewsbury, I am sure are utterly destitute of foundation, but I am lost in amazement that on hearing such marvellous stories you never took the trouble to write to me to ascertain the truth. Messrs. Rock & Loxdale are my bankers, and from what passed between us not long before I left Shrewsbury, I am convinced in my own mind that your son never had any pecuniary transactions with them, but I have written to Mrs. Butler to make the necessary inquiries, and to send me word. I shall be at Emmanuel Lodge from January 1st to January 10th, and will in the course of that time contrive to come over to Chippenham. I shall also very much like to have half an hour's conversation with Mr. Weatherley.

"I cannot avoid feeling great surprise at your inquiring whether your son spent much money at school, because I am sure that once, and I believe twice, I thought it necessary to write to you a letter of remonstrance on this very subject, owing to the profuse supply of money which he always appeared to have. How he got it, if you did not give it him, heaven knows.

"There is no George Inn at Shrewsbury; I believe there is a very small pot-house of that name. The principal inns are the Lion, Talbot, Raven, and Raven and Bell.

"I had with great pains secured for your son an exhibition of £60 a year, and considered him as likely to make his way extremely well at College. Are you aware that, after his supposed accession to his immense property, I advised him from time to time to be on his guard against persons who might probably wish to make a prey of him, and recommended him to place himself under the care of some able and highly respectable man at the University? The last letter I wrote to him must, I suppose, now lie in the dead-letter office, and is much to the same purport as those preceding. I wrote but two or three days before his departure in consequence of a message I received from him through one of his schoolfellows. I have too much reason to think, from some facts which I have heard lately, that this unparalleled and disgraceful imposition has been in preparation a long time, and am anxious to see you that I may endeavour to develop my opinion. I shall write to you from Cambridge that I may fix a day for seeing you, and am,

"Dear Sir, your obedient and faithful servant,
"S. Butler.

"I am much surprised that so serious an engagement should have taken place between your son and a young lady at Shrewsbury with your sanction, and without the slightest inquiry or communication made to me on the subject."

From Dr. Cory, Master of Emmanuel.

"*December 24th,* 1817.

*   *   *   *   *

"I am sorry to add that all is over with Cawston. I received a letter last night from Mr. William Cawston, full of the distress in which all the family were involved by his brother's unaccountable conduct, and informing me that he left London a short time ago for Paris, where he remained two days, and thence proceeded towards Spain, leaving no address nor any means of tracing him. All the references which he had left with his solicitor were dishonoured, and there was no trace of any property whatever except what his brother-in-law had advanced him without solicitation."

I doubt whether Cawston went to Spain. If he did he must have soon left for Italy, whence he wrote to Mr. Weatherley in the early days of January 1818. Mr. Weatherley, writing on the 10th, says he had received a letter from Cawston on the preceding day, and that he was then in Italy; "he speaks," says Mr. Weatherley, "of the events of the last few months as a delirium, but still writes as impressed with the idea of his having a large property. He does not state any particulars, and leaves everything relating to him as great a mystery as ever." Cawston's father, writing April 30th, 1818, says : "He is now in Genoa, and without a farthing of money ; and I am happy to find adversity have (*sic*) brought him to his reason, as from his letter (which is full of contrition for his conduct) his eyes are open to the duplicity he has been guilty of. He can do nothing there, and knows not how to get home without assistance."

His father helped him home, and from a letter of Mr. Sheepshanks dated May 12th, 1819, it seems that Cawston was then in Cornwall "leading a very quiet regular life." In 1826 he was taking pupils at Flempton near Bury, with a fair prospect of doing well; he was afterwards ordained, and was living at the end of 1839, but I know nothing of what became of him. His name does not appear in the Clergy List for 1841, nor in that of any subsequent year; I incline therefore to think that he must have died about 1840. At all events he never became notorious again, and even though his imposture was matured with care, and executed without flinching, I would ask the reader to remember that, to quote a letter of Dr. Butler's, "boys are strange creatures," and very bad ones have often nevertheless developed into men fully as good as their neighbours.

CORRESPONDENCE, OCTOBER 31ST, 1817—JUNE 9TH, 1818.

FROM DR. PARR.

(*Re* Beloe's *The Sexagenarian*—a postscript and date only in Dr. Parr's own handwriting.)

"*October* 31*st,* 1817.

"DEAR NAMESAKE,—I scarcely ever felt such indignation at impudent falsehood and malignant calumny. You do not wonder that a man of such inordinate vanity and such a spirit of abuse should, as a boy, be odious to his schoolfellows and to his master. In volume first, page 24, he talks impudently and most falsely of an atonement. He is a liar; it was my mercy, my mere mercy, when I knew that he wished to marry, when I hoped for better things from experience and from gratitude, and when I procured for him a reputable situation, upon the strength of which he took a wife, a saucy varlet. I offered no atonement; I made no peace; I did not mean to put an end to hostility, for in my own mind there was none. He professed to accept the office as a mark of my good-will, and for a time was thankful, but his ruling passions soon made him insolent and unbearable. I could account for his writing anything, but that, when living, he should publish such falsehoods as he evidently intended, seems to me almost infatuation. The compulsory removal from Stanmore was one sore place. Now translation of *Bellenden* is another. He refers to it in p. 221 and p. 201 of Vol. I., and p. 261 of Vol. II. The case is this. I had heard of this translation without my leave; he heard that I was not pleased; he sent me the book, with a letter of compliments upon the merits of the book and an apology for translating it. I warily thanked him for the gift. I allowed the right of any one to translate the book, and I avoided all praise upon his translation, because he very often mistook the meaning, and never represented the meaning, of my words. Not one tittle then did he utter about a crabbed book, difficult to be translated, not one tittle about intemperate party praise and blame, not one tittle about Porson and the cunning shaver. The demerits of the translation tended to give ordinary readers a mean notion of the original, and this very circumstance recommended the translator to Porson. I knew at the time that Porson abused the Latin book, and Harry Homer told me that he made to a bookseller some proposals for attacking it. Porson hated me, for the fame which I might get, and at the midnight meetings of College boys and ale-house cellar sots he very often was witty upon Dr. Bellenden. It was his favourite nickname for the writer. Beloe merely wanted to turn a penny, while the public curiosity was directed towards my book. As to the pompous Author, who was to be excluded from his select company, pray observe that Beloe again and again invited that author, made parties for him, and never, never, never had the slightest reason to complain of the disputatious and browbeating qualities of which he speaks. I say never. As to the story of ' metaphysics ' and ' my metaphysics '— I forget the facts—if Porson's answer appeared to me a mere jest, I was likely to laugh only; if it had seemed to me intended for a sarcasm, I should not have been very slow nor very feeble in my reply, and this you know. I never flattered him, I never feared him, I never yielded to him. I knew that he abused me, but I continued, as Beloe owns, to speak of him with great admiration and some regard. I had him at my house for nearly three months.* I, at his request, endeavoured to get a situation in some school for his brother. I subscribed handsomely, and

---

* Cf. page 57 of this volume.—Ed.

procured subscriptions where I could for Porson. I wrote an elaborate letter to Dr. Davies, the Master of Eton, who disliked him. I received an answer not very complimentary to Porson, but I got from Davies £30. I was always cheerful with him, always just to his stupendous learning, always fearless of his opposition, and this was my sin. I told you numerous instances of my placability, my kindness, my generosity to the sexagenarian. I now have to add that I wrote for him the intended dedication to Lord Orford. He has published it, and speaks of it as a composition not his own. Pray let this be noticed. Now comes a very foul deed. It is in the article next to Henry Headley, and I believe in Vol. I. He there speaks of Tom Monroe and his disappearance from school. The fact is this : he and another lad ran away from school. They got as far as Lincoln. The companion was a cross-grained perverse lad, and continued so through life, to the annoyance of his family. Monroe was rather of a gloomy turn, and his mind was vexed by some domestic occurrences, but the cause of his disappearance was no act of rigour exercised or expected from me. From pity I received, when perhaps I ought to have expelled him. He was sensible of my mercy. He afterwards obtained my regard. His spirits were at rest. His behaviour was regular, his application was very diligent, and then began that love of learning which I cherished, and which enabled him to be very early an author. How shocking it is that his return should be described, as it is in p. 181, Vol. I., as the only incident of his life which he remembered in life with anything like self-reproach ! I not only pardoned him, but I saved him. I saw him often when he was at Magdalen College, Oxford. Once I lent him £100 to rescue him from some pecuniary embarrassments at the University. I continued my kindness to him through life. I recommended pupils to him in Essex. He has called upon me several times at Hatton. His family, putting me in the catalogue of his best friends, gave me the earliest notice of his death. Since his death I have received many grateful and respectful letters from his widow. She has consulted me about the College education of one son and the choice of a school for another."

I learn from the *Dictionary of National Biography* that Henry Headley was a pupil of Dr. Parr's at Colchester, and accompanied him to Norwich. He was born in 1765, and published a volume of fugitive verses in 1785, which were reprinted with another title in the following year. He wrote various essays that gave great promise, but died in 1788, before the expectations his friends had formed of him could be either fulfilled or disappointed.

From the Rev. P. Elmsley.

" Oswestry, *January* 1st, 1818.

*   *   *   *   *

" The death of poor Burney must have surprised you. I rate him higher as a scholar than some of my friends do. He was the Copernicus of our art; very inferior indeed to Galileo Porson, but still the first man who put us on the right scent."

*   *   *   *   *

To Professor Monk.

" *January 8th*, 1818.

" Dear Sir,—I shall be very happy to take Mr. Blomfield's hand, if he offers it, but I cannot possibly make advances, though I shall most willingly meet any. My determination was always the same, and though perhaps he thought me not serious, I was perfectly in earnest when I expressed from the first moment a similar disposition. I will not advert to past uneasiness a moment longer than to say that, if you will take the trouble of looking at the article on Porson's *Adversaria* in the *Monthly Review* for this month, you will see how I am disposed to speak and think of your, and I hope I may soon say our, friend. From the little I saw of him some years ago I felt a great prepossession in his favour, and I most truly can assure you that nothing hurt me so much in the attack as that it should come from a quarter where I felt not only no dislike but every sentiment of kindness and esteem. I must leave Cambridge to-morrow, and my schemes are so much broken by an unexpected summons to go into Kent for the purpose of being godfather to the daughter of one of my old College friends that I fear I cannot even see Nuneaton upon my return, but letters will always find me at the Prince of Wales's coffee-house, Leicester Square."

The article on Porson's *Adversaria* above referred to appeared in the *Monthly Review* for December 1817, not in the January number for 1818. There is no trace of bitterness in it either against Monk or Blomfield, and it contains some interesting criticism on Porson, which I should be glad to give if space permitted. In the January number there is an article by Dr. Butler (a draft of which I found) on Kidd's *Tracts of Professor Porson*. The following extracts may be worth reprinting, in spite of an

unfortunate passage in one of them about Gerard Dow
and Michael Angelo. At the beginning of this century
people did not appear to understand that a scholar's
opinion on sculpture or painting is no better worth having,
as a general rule, than a sculptor's or painter's on a point
of scholarship. The only excuse for Dr. Butler is that
he was writing a review, and, like Macaulay after him,
had caught the cant of the time without suspecting it.
I once asked that excellent artist the late Philip Browne
of Shrewsbury whether Dr. Butler had any taste for or
knew anything about pictures. Mr. Browne's eyes
twinkled shrewdly, and he said, " No man ever less "—
which I imagine was about the truth. The extracts above
referred to are as follows :—

" In Bentley's Horace passages are indeed sometimes happily
restored, but not seldom daringly and rashly altered. Innova-
tions are often made apparently for no other reason than the
sake of change ; and mere conjectural and unsatisfactory readings
are not unfrequently introduced into the text with all the
confidence of consentient MS. authority. Yet even in the
wildest and most presumptuous changes we discern something
that marks the great and founded scholar : a singular or conjectural reading in the text is supported by such an accumulation
of learning in the notes, that the reader must be always instructed
if not always satisfied ; and it is impossible for a student of
tolerable capacity to read these notes without rising from the
study of them a far better scholar than he sat down. His
general views of the phraseology of Horace, and his knowledge
of the idioms of the Latin language, must be widely extended,
though his inquiries on a certain passage may not be always
answered satisfactorily ; and he cannot avoid imbibing some of
that critical acumen which may direct his future studies in the
investigation of a perplexed or doubtful passage in other authors.
He may go right with Porson in the mere text of Æschylus
without becoming in any degree the better scholar, but he cannot
go wrong with Bentley without having his knowledge increased
and his mind enlarged.
            *   *   *   *   *

" From the parallel which we have attempted the reader will
draw his own conclusions ; but, for ourselves, we scruple not to
avow that of these two great men we think that Bentley was

decidedly the greater. Porson was the scholar, and a worthy one he was, of this illustrious master. Though his learning was the more accurate, that of Bentley was the more varied and profound. Where Porson would be cautious, Bentley would be daring; and where Porson brought conviction Bentley would sometimes scarcely condescend to bring probability. Such a strength and vigour of mind were displayed even in Bentley's errors—and such a magnanimity of learning, if we may venture the expression, was evinced even in his boldest flights—that in him we recognise at once the generosity of the hero, while in his celebrated successor we are content to admire the sagacity of the man. The emendations of Porson, taken altogether, approach perhaps nearer to certainty than those of any other critic; for where he could not amend with certainty he conjectured nothing; but those of Bentley, in Greek especially, which was undoubtedly his *forte*, are little inferior in certainty; and they are at the same time accompanied by such a store of learning, brought to bear on them from every branch of classical literature, that while they correct the individual author, they powerfully charm and improve the mind. The works of Porson may be considered as the cabinet pictures of a Gerard Dow, finished with the utmost minuteness of labour and the last polish of perfection; while those of Bentley are the daring efforts of a Michael Angelo, whose minor blemishes, if they occur, are lost in the general effect and sublimity of the whole.

* * * * *

"Bentley was conscious of his great powers, too proud to court applause and too manly to affect humility. Porson lived more with boys than with men in the University, and carried his professions of humility to a length which made them altogether questionable, if not disgusting. Besides his celebrated '*Lectori si quis erit*' and his '*Monendi estis lectores, si qui forte mearum ineptiarum lectores eritis*' (*Advers.*, p. 39), we find in his *Prælectio in Euripidem*, p. 4, '*Sin autem oratio mea non omnino displicuerit, si tironibus forte circumstantibus tantillum arsiserit, id equidem serio sum triumphaturus*': a hundred other instances might be adduced. Now though we by no means approve of arrogance, we are still less pleased with an excess of humility, because we would rather see an open and avowed bad quality than a specious and assumed good one."

If, as I can hardly doubt, Porson wrote the article on Homeric geography referred to on p. 56, he seems to have been able to conjecture with some freedom when he was in the vein for it.

Mrs Butler.

From a pastel drawing made in 1810

Walker & Cockerell Ph.

Correspondence, January 19th, 1818—June 9th, 1818.

From Mrs. Butler.

"*Monday, January 19th,* 1818.

"Dearest B——,—I have received your letter by Mr. Smith, and one about the carpets. I have written to Mr. Tomlinson to order the smallest carpet of the two, as I think the largest would be too wide for the room, and we may quite as well have it too short, as too wide, which would be a worse evil, but I think the shortest will be long enough—four feet longer than the present one, which is a good deal. I have received the teapot, which I think very beautiful indeed; the French wine is come, and it is taken into the cellar—I have paid £1 5s. for the carriage of it. I shall certainly leave the purchasing of the lustre till the room is finished, as by that time you may see some one you will like. I have at last succeeded in getting a cook, and who should it be but Mrs. Parr's cook at last. I had met with one from Mrs. R. Hill's near Chester, which I should have taken had not the former applied, whose time is not up till the 6th of February, but Mrs. Parr has been very civil and promised to release her by the 26th of this month, if she can suit herself. I have sent her two or three cooks, and shall hunt up all I can find who are out of place; therefore I am in great hopes I shall get hers in time. I was much pleased with the woman from Mrs. R. Hill's, who gave her an excellent character; but I was fearful she would be too mighty for me: she did not like the thoughts of sleeping with any one, neither did she like the cleaning her kitchen; the latter I could perhaps have dispensed with, but I was afraid there might be many things she would object to, and therefore gave her up, though she would have taken the place without any alterations in my plan. The red cow has calved against the boys come, and another is shortly expected to accommodate me. I have been in a grand fright about our old favourite Durham : a coach and four was driving furiously down by the coach-house and drove over the poor cow; it is surprising to say that she is none the worse, as the application of a little bay salt and vinegar has quite cured it of its bruises."

    ●   ●   ●   ●   ●

From Marmaduke Lawson, Esq.

"Borobridge, *June 9th,* 1818.

"Dear Sir,—I am just returned from my ten days' campaign, covered with dust rather than glory. For the impossibility of acquiring a practical knowledge of the various manœuvres before the time of trial necessarily exposed a new officer to many errors.

" We had most severe duty—what with the labours and what with the dissipations of a military life. We were at the field at seven in a morning, of course up at six, and from the late hours, balls, etc., etc., it was impossible to get to bed sometimes much before. Of course to me who require eight hours' sleep every day this defalcation was of no little moment. A week or ten days was as much as I could endure it. However, I have kept a regular time bill, and, like coaches which make up in one stage the ground they have lost in the preceding one, I am determined to lie in bed day by day till I have got back my eight hours per day.

" Another grievance with me was the absence of whiskers, without which the face finds a greater degree of friction from the scales of the helmet than is conducive either to comeliness or comfort. By the scales I mean those dependencies of brass which are tied under your chin, just as the mob caps worn by old ladies. However, next year we are ordered to be all provided not only with whiskers, but moustaches, and it was probably for this reason that my mother, who pays my cavalry expenses, refused to allow an item of 5*s.* for shaving, alleging that a soldier had no business with the razor—a beard was as much a part of his armour as his helmet or his shield. Accordingly I must have recourse to some of those many devices advertised so frequently for supplying the defects of nature—the Russian or the Macassar oil. Clarey water won't do this excessively hot weather, as it would attract the wasps, whose familiarities, particularly at church, are extremely coarse, to say the least of them.

" It is a great bore to have to put one's face, like one's portrait, in a kind of circular black frame. And then, after all one's trouble and expense, to be told by a surly democrat that soldiers in peace are chimneys in summer—yet who would pull down his chimney in the dog-days, for which he must needs have occasion in the approaching winter ? The occurrence of war, some time or other, is, I apprehend, as morally certain as that of rain after fine weather. This we see is the law of nature by the proportion of males to females, which is twenty-one to twenty, where that odd one is meant to be killed off, that the equilibrium of the sexes may continue unimpaired. The expense, however, with us varies inversely as the danger. The uniform is a sheet of silver . . . [word torn out]. Officers are treated with a dozen of champagne instead of entrance money, and the company I command receive a gratuity of £20, besides giving a ball, expensive mess, £20 to the regimental fund, and a great variety of horse equipments—in all about £160. Others talk of risking their lives for their country ; we, however, do more than risk our money, without which what would be life ?

" I am going to Cambridge soon, where I hope to have a better account of my essay for the Bachelor's Prize than I had last year. I wish you could inform me what residence is required of me by the new decree. Andrew cannot get in at Oxford till 1820, so will probably come to Cambridge. Peacock, he says, is a good man, but very near. When he goes to Darlington market, he gets all his goods weighed a second time at the inn."

I have heard my father say that Dr. Butler on one occasion told Dr. Parr that he had an amusing letter of gossip from Marmaduke Lawson—whereon Dr. Parr rejoined that he too had received one. The letters were then produced, and were found to be identical. The two doctors on this concocted between them the best letter they could arrive at, and each on a preconcerted day sent Lawson a copy of it, without, of course, a hint in explanation—Dr. Parr sending his from Hatton and Dr. Butler writing from Shrewsbury.

I fear the letter just given may have been the one in question, for I have found no further letters from Lawson among Dr. Butler's papers.

Some two or three years ago my friend Dr. Garnett of the British Museum told me that a MS. of Dr. Butler's was advertised for sale in a catalogue of Messrs. Sotheby's. I accordingly went to see it, and found the following interesting paper, endorsed "Composition and Writing of the Rev. Dr. Butler of Shrewsbury, on some Inscriptions in Hughes's *Travels*," *i.e.* T. S. Hughes's *Travels in Sicily*, etc. I bid for it, and was pleased to find so spirited a competition that I was run up to sixteen shillings before I could acquire it. I then placed it with Dr. Butler's other papers in the British Museum. The MS., which I give in full, and with no more breathings and accents than Dr. Butler wrote (for even the best scholars of the time were very lax about these, unless when writing for publication or otherwise on their best behaviour), is as follows :—

Approximate date : August, 1818.

"The first is to be read thus :—

"Αρχοντος Διοκλεους του Σιμμιου, Μηνος Ομολωιου πεντεκαιδεκατη,[1] Δεξξιππα [2] Αθανιου,[3] παροντος αυτη του ανδρος Σαμιχου του Φιλοξενου, ανατιθησι τας ιδιας δουλας Καλλιδα και Πυθιν, και το εκ της Καλλιδος παιδαριον, ω ονομα Νικων, ιερους τω Σεραπιδι, παραμειναντας Δεξιππα Ευβουλου τη κατα φυσιν μου μαμμη[4] παντα τον της ζωης αυτης χρονον ανεγκλητως · τα δε γεννηθεντα εξ αυτων εν τω της παραμονης χρονω εστωσαν[5] δουλα Δεξιππας της Αθανιου, την αναθεσιν ποιουμενη[6] δια του συνεδριου κατα τον νομον.

"[1] We may observe that these inscriptions do not subjoin the iota to the dative.

"[2] Δεξξιππα with a double ξ in the inscription is an error of the stone-cutter.

"[3] Αθανιου in common Greek would probably be Αθηναιου Athenæus.

"[4] In the inscription one of the μ's in μαμμη is transposed.

"[5] In the inscription a σ too much is inserted in εστωσαν.

"[6] We might expect ποιουμενης, but by comparison with the subsequent inscription we see ποιουμενη is the right reading referred to Dexippa at the beginning of the inscription.

" Translation.

"In the archonship of Diocles the son of Simmias, the fifteenth day of the month Homoloius,[1] Dexippa the daughter of Athenæus, in the presence of her husband Samichus the son of Philoxenus, dedicates her own [2] slaves Callis and Pythis, and the child of Callis called Nicon, as sacred to Serapis, they having first remained [6] with my own [3] natural [5] grandmother [4] Dexippa, the daughter of Eubulus unreclaimed [7] the whole term of her life.[8] But their children [9] born during the time of their residence with her shall belong to Dexippa the daughter of Athenæus, who makes this dedication by means of the assembly according to the law.[10]

" Remarks.

"[1] The month Homoloius [Note unfinished.—Ed.]

"[2] The dedication is made in the presence of her husband ; and possibly therefore his consent may have been necessary, but the word ιδιας would seem to imply that these slaves were the property of the wife apart from the husband.

"[3] This change from the third to the first person is very common in inscriptions, and was probably used to mark the relationship more strongly.

"[4] I have translated μαμμη ' grandmother.'

"⁵ *Natural.* Probably this expression is added to show that the slaves (which, if she had a private property in them apart from her husband, probably came from her own family) are disposed of in the family from whence they came—to *her own natural grandmother*, not to the grandmother of her husband.

"⁶ The participle of the Aorist here has evidently a future signification, as the potential future of the Latins, which may be called an Aoristic future—*cum vixerint*, when they *shall have* lived, *i.e.* they having first lived. That παραμείναντας must be used here in a future sense is evident, as in the subsequent part of the inscription reference is made to the appropriation of the children to be born during their residence.

" A question hence arises, Why is the dedication made, which is only to take place at some future period? I reply that various reasons occur for these dedications. A slave thus dedicated, though not alienated from the immediate service of a master during that master's life, might go into the service of the temple on his death; and thus would not be liable to be sold with his effects. This sort of dedication might confer some privileges to the slave during the lifetime of the master. It might be a sort of half freedom, as it is evidently a superior kind of servitude at his death. Some services on certain occasions might also possibly be received by the priests from such slaves, even during the lives of their masters.

"⁷ ανεγκλητως is generally used to signify *blamelessly*, and if the dedication conferred any privilege, then the slave who was thus conditionally dedicated had an incitement to good behaviour if the dedication was to take place only in consequence of it. But I do not think such to be the meaning of the word here; I translate it *unreclaimed*, by which I understand that the priests of Serapis should have no right to claim the slave till the death of the person specified took place.

"⁸ 'The whole term of her life.' This is a periphrasis to avoid the mention of the ominous word 'death'—παραμείναντας ἕως θανάτου.

"⁹ 'But their children.' Here we see is an *exceptio* in favour of the original proprietor. The slaves Callis and Pythis, and Nicon the child of Pythis, are dedicated to the god, but their future offspring, though born after the dedication and in the house of Dexippa the elder, are to revert to the original owner.

"¹⁰ This was therefore a public act on the part of Dexippa the younger.

" 2. Αρχοντος Ευανδρου μηνος Αλαλκομενιου τριακαδι Αγαθοκλης Ευανδρου ανατιθησι τους ιδιους δουλους Ζωσιμον και Ευμονα ιερους του Σεραπιδος παραμειναντας ανεγκλητως εαντω τε και τη γυναικι μου Βουκατια· την αναθεσιν ποιουμενος δια του συνεδριου κατα τον νομον.

" Nothing occurs in this inscription that requires further remark. The month Alalcomeneus was [Note unfinished.—Ed.]

" We may observe that the pronunciation of η and ι seem to have been very similar, as the month is spelt ηου and ιου in these inscriptions.

" 3. Αρχοντος Φιλοξενου μηνος Αλαλκομενηου πεντεκαιδεκατη Αλεξων Ροδωνος ανατιθησι την ιδιαν δουλην Διονυσιαν ιεραν τω Σαραπι [*sic*] παραμεινασαν εαυτω ανεγκλητως παντα τον του ζην χρονον, την αναθεσιν ποιουμενος δια του συνεδριου κατα τον νομον.

" The Philoxenus here may possibly be the father of Samichus mentioned in the first inscription.

" 4. Αρχοντος Καφισιου μηνος Βουκατιου τριακαδι κρατων Αμινιου και Ευγιτα Νικαρετου συναρεστουντων και των υιων ανατιθεασιν το δουλικον αυτων κορασιον Σωσιχαν ιερον τω Σεραπι, παραμεινασαν Κρατωνι και Ευγιτα, εως αν ζωσιν, ανεγκλητως· την αναθεσιν ποιουμενοι δια του συνεδριου κατα τον νομον.

" Καφισιος or Cephisius is a name probably derived from the river Cephisus. Αμινιου would perhaps more properly be written Αμεινιου. By the expression συναρεστουντων και των υιων it is probable that their sons were arrived at manhood, and we may suppose their consent is here inserted in order to prevent any claim on their part as heirs, after the decease of their parents. In this and the preceding inscription we have the Ionic dative Σεραπι, and here also the Ionic form ανατιθεασιν. The adverb ανεγκλητως, which would be more naturally inserted after παραμεινασαν, here is left to the conclusion of the sentence, possibly having been forgotten either by the writer of the inscription or the stone-cutter in its proper place.

" 5. Αρχοντος Πατρωνος μηνος Ηλθιου[1] πεντεκαιδεκατη Παρθενα Αθηνοδωρου παροντος αυτη του υιου Αροπινου Μεγωνος[2] και συναρεστουντος, ανατιθησι τον ιδιον Θρεπτον[3] παραμονον[4] ιερον τω Σεραπει μη προσηκοντα μηθενι μηθεν[5] την αναθεσιν ποιουμενη, etc.

" [1] The month Elthius [Note unfinished.—Ed.]
" [2] The son's name and his father's are mentioned.
" [3] The name of the slave is omitted.
" [4] Here is a great difference in the mode of dedication. The slave is here dedicated at once to the god, without any intervening service.
" [5] 'Free from all claims of every kind.' By which I understand his absolute and immediate dedication to the god.

" 6. Μηνος Αλαλκομενιου πεντεκαιδεκατη Κηφισοδωρα Κρατωνος παροντος αυτη του πατρος Κρατωνος αφιησι[1] την ιδιαν δουλην Ευαμεριδα ιεραν του Σεραπιδος, etc.

" ¹ Here is the word ἀφίησι, by which we may understand that the slave is absolutely given up and dismissed from the service of the owner to that of the deity—which was probably a sort of free servitude, if such an expression may be used.

" 7. Αρχοντος Αντιγωνος μηνος Προστατηριου πεντεκαιδεκατη Μιλω Μιημινου¹ και Τηλεμαχις Ευβουλου ανατιθεασιν² τα ιδια δουλικα κορασια Αλεξανδρον και Θαυμασταν ιερας τω Σεραπει μηθενι μηθεν³ προσηκουσας,⁴ παραμηνασας⁵ δε Μιλωνι και Τηλεμαχιδι, εκατεραις εως αν ζωσιν ανεγκλητως την αναθεσιν ποιουμεναι,⁶ etc.

" The dedications are made either on the 15th or 30th.
" ¹ The name is corrupt.
" ² Note the Ionic form.
" ³ This expression seems inserted in a more qualified sense in this than in the preceding. Their services are contingent to the deity, after the death of their mistresses; and the words μηθενι μηθεν προσηκουσας seem inserted to bar all other claims.
" ⁴ The original has προσηκουσα.
" ⁵ Observe the usual corruption of Η for ΕΙ.
" ⁶ The original has εκατεροις and ποιουμενοι, and seems cut by a more ignorant artist than any of the preceding.

" 8. Αρχοντος Σωιλου του Ευανδρου μηνος . . . τω . . . ιος . . . ραδιον . . . υσιος . . . σιμιου και Παρθενα Αριστονικου αφιασι¹ την ιδιαν δουλαν Ερμαιαν ελευθεραν ιεραν² τω Σαραπει παραμεινασαν Παρθενᾳ εως αν ζη ανεγκλητως μη προσηκουσαν μηθενι μηθεν την αναθεσιν, etc.

" ¹ αφιασι [Note unfinished.—ED.]
" ² ελευθεραν ιεραν. The slave here seems manumitted, yet dedicated; but the priests, who were not slaves, were also dedicated to the god. But then παραμεινασαν? Can this mean that the manumission was not to take place at the death of Parthena, or that the dedication to the god was not to take place at that time ? "

CHAPTER XI.

EPIDEMIC OF TURBULENCE.

Disturbances within the School.—Dr. Butler's two Circulars to Parents.
—Correspondence, November 30th, 1818—May 17th, 1819.

IN 1818 there was an epidemic of serious turbulence in almost all the leading schools of England, with (to quote Dr. Butler's words in a letter dated April 3rd, 1819) "one real and one ostensible exception." At Shrewsbury insubordination began by the boys eating more than they wanted, and then complaining that they had not had enough ; they got up fights in the town ; they very nearly killed a farmer's pigs, in what they called a boar hunt, and intimidated the farmer himself so greatly that when brought into the school by Dr. Butler, and asked to identify the offenders, " he was either unwilling or afraid to do so " ; an insulting placard was posted up in the hall threatening Dr. Butler with personal violence ; the painted glass in the school library was broken by stones of considerable size, evidently thrown by big boys ; the glass in the Doctor's library had been also broken ; other acts of insubordination occurred which made it necessary to expel three boys and dismiss a fourth. Dr. Butler therefore sent a circular to the parents of all his boys, desiring them to examine their sons and see whether they could find any reasonable ground of complaint, in which case they were to let him know. He concluded by saying :—

"You will hear your son's account and give it what credit you think fit ; but it is my particular request that no boy may return to me who is not duly sensible of what he owes to me and to his parents, and who will not promise to them and to me a cheerful submission to such rules as I may think necessary for the general improvement and discipline of the school."

In a second circular, dated December 10th, 1818, and sent with every boy on his going home for the holidays, Dr. Butler writes :—

"I have also remarked this half-year that the boys have been in the habit of receiving baskets of game and poultry from their friends. This I consider a very pernicious indulgence. They have three plentiful meals here every day, at which they are under no limitation ; and whenever any parents are so kind as to send me a basket of game, some is always sent to their sons, and frequently part is dressed for the other boys in their turn. Under these circumstances I cannot but consider supplies of game, or hams, or any similar provisions sent to the boys them-selves, as highly prejudicial, tempting them to form junketing parties at low houses, and exciting to other irregularities. I have therefore to request that where such practices have begun they may be discontinued, and that nothing may be sent them beyond fruit or cakes.

"It has come to my knowledge that some of the upper boys, with whose turbulent conduct I have great reason to be dissatis-fied, are diligently instilling insubordination into the minds of those younger boys whom they think likely to receive their instructions. I have resolved on removing every such upper boy whom I know of from my school this Christmas, though, for obvious reasons, I have never mentioned this to them ; and I earnestly entreat every parent to whom I do not think it necessary to recommend his son's removal, to examine him most closely upon this subject, and impress him with the great im-portance of regular and orderly conduct and subordination, and of the impossibility of my showing any lenity or indulgence to a contrary behaviour."

This was much the most serious and protracted case of disaffection with which Dr. Butler had to cope during the whole term of his head-mastership, not excepting the better-known " beef row " of 1829.

CORRESPONDENCE, NOVEMBER 30TH, 1818—MAY 17TH, 1819.

FROM DR. KEATE, HEAD-MASTER OF ETON.

(Original at Eton.)

"ETON, *November 30th*, 1818.

"SIR,—I have received your letter of the 27th this morning, and am very sorry to perceive that the contagion of rebellion has reached your school also. I am sorry too to be thought to have sufficient experience to be referred to as an authority on these occasions. I beg leave, however, to assure you that I am very ready to give my opinion.

"The best answer I can return to your question, indeed the only one which I think I ought to give, is, that it has not been my practice either to rescind or to mitigate a sentence of expulsion. I was requested to do it upon one occasion some years ago, and I have been importuned in the same manner in six out of the seven late unfortunate instances, but I have uniformly resisted, thinking my public duty paramount to every consideration of private feeling."

FROM DR. GABELL, HEAD-MASTER OF WINCHESTER.

(Original at Winchester.)

"*December 1st*, 1818.

"MY DEAR SIR,—You ask me if it is usual in cases of declared expulsion to change the sentence into dismission, or even revoke it altogether : I never heard of such a practice, nor do I recollect a single instance of it.

"You ask me also if the master is not bound to be inflexible, etc. This question I would rather not answer in general terms, but I recollect no case which justified in my opinion the reversal of such a sentence, when once passed. No man could be more importuned than I was on a similar occasion, after our unfortunate disturbance last spring, but I thought it my duty to resist all importunity.

"You have heard probably of the proceedings at Eton and at the Charterhouse, but perhaps you do not know that the Military College at Sandhurst has been in rebellion. The boys drew up in battle array against the professors.

"It is not unlikely that I shall be in Warwickshire during the Christmas vacation, and I hope we shall meet."

From the Hon. Cecil Jenkinson, afterwards Lord Liverpool.

"Pitchford Hall, *December 5th*, 1818.

"My dear Sir,—I am extremely flattered by your attention to my feelings, as expressed to my friend Mr. H. Owen and others, respecting the late disagreeable occurrences in your school, and very happy that what I said to them was sufficiently noted to be repeated to you. To say the truth, but that I always fear putting myself forward, I should have troubled you with a letter as soon as I had read the statement which, as parent to one of your pupils, you sent to Mr. Corfield.

" Believe me, sir, that no one sees with more anxiety than I do the conduct of those to whom public education in this country is entrusted ; on it in a great measure depends the production of those talents which, fostered and matured in this soil of rational liberty, make England a beacon and example to every other nation of the civilised world.

" But that I fear and dislike to flatter you, I might say that your talents as head-master of a public school deserved a better field of exertion than Shrewsbury ; but you have shown, even on this comparatively unproductive soil, how much these talents could effect, and it would, I conceive, be most unjust and illiberal on the part of those who from property and residence observe this, not to render every assistance in our power, or to pay every tribute which is due to them.

" Believe me, dear Sir, with these sentiments most sincerely
"Your obedient humble servant,
"Cecil Jenkinson."

From the Rev. C. J. Blomfield, afterwards Archdeacon of Colchester, and Bishop, first of Chester, and then of London.

"Chesterford, Essex, *December 4th*, 1818.

" My dear Sir,—I have directed my publisher, Mr. Mawman, to send you a copy of my *Agamemnon*, which is just published. I trust that, although I have often been compelled to dissent from your opinions, you will not find anything offensive. At the same time I am free to confess that, had an opportunity been afforded me, I should have expressed two or three things rather differently, but I beg you to bear in mind that the text and notes were printed a twelvemonth ago. In the preface I could not avoid alluding to the question about Casaubon and Stanley. I hope you will think that I have not done so in an improper manner.

My own opinion on the subject remains the same. I beg you
will present my respects to Mrs. Butler and the young ladies,
"And believe me, my dear Sir,
"Yours very sincerely,
"C. J. Blomfield.

"P.S.—I entirely agree with you in your explanation of
Hughes's inscriptions, with one or two trifling exceptions. I
have no doubt but that in the last ΠΑΡΑΜΟΝΟΝ is the name of
the slave."

The name appears in inscription No. 5, and not in "the
last."

To the Rev. C. J. Blomfield, Chesterford.

"Shrewsbury, December 6th, 1818.

"My dear Sir,—Before I receive your kind present I cannot but wish to assure you that nothing which I may find in
it can make any alteration in those sentiments of friendship and
respect which I entertain for you. The past is past ; τὰ μὲν προτε-
τῦχθαι ἐάσομεν, but I trust that each of us can add ἀχνύμενοί περ,
in one sense only, and that a different one from the meaning of
Achilles—a sense of mutual regret that it ever took place.

"When I receive your *Agamemnon* I shall run over it as fast
as ever I can, reserving a closer study of it for a more convenient
opportunity. I have no doubt that you will often find occasion to
differ from me, and that I shall often find occasion to differ from
myself. I am glad to have the opportunity of telling you that the
whole plan of my publication was devised contrary to my most
strenuous exertions, by a literary friend now no more,* who had
great theological and more than moderate classical attainments,
but who wanted judgement and taste. Hence arose those divisions
and subdivisions which, having been adopted in the first volume,
I could never afterwards get rid of. I was wrong to yield, and
yet I can hardly blame myself. What could a young man not
two-and-twenty, and wholly unused to the press, say against a
ripe and practised scholar of nearly seventy—especially when he
had a tender interest at stake? True, I became emancipated in
the course of the work, but the first volume had given a fatal cast
to the whole, and from the first I saw no remedy but a re-publi-
cation with my own text and selected notes. Whenever I undertake that work I shall, in the preface, say of your labours what,
under any circumstances, I should have thought it justice to say.

"I have no copy of Hughes's inscriptions, and could see them
but cursorily, having been constantly interrupted while writing

---

* Dr. Apthorp, to whose daughter Dr. Butler was then engaged.

my few remarks upon them.   I have not the least recollection of
the passage, but think it highly probable you are right in the
name.   The verb παραμένω, if I recollect, occurs so frequently
in the inscriptions that I suppose in my hasty perusal of them
I was misled by it.   I cannot get at a single book till after
Christmas, my library being yet unfinished.   I have had a
stirring half-year since I wrote to you.   *Luctantes ventos tempes-*
tatesque sonoras.   I hope I chain them as well as their old
master in Virgil.   It has, however, completely put a stop to my
book on metres, which must be delayed half a year.

"If you see Hughes, that ἀλλοπρόσαλλος now at St. John's,
now at Trinity Hall, now at Emmanuel, and at present at some
Cambridge fen curacy, you may ask him to show you a sketch
of mine on Dodona.*

"Last night I had a letter from Dr. Parr, in which he says he
has heard from you again, from which I infer that you are in
correspondence with him.   I wish more that you were in his
company; you could and would appreciate him.   There are
many who cannot and many who will not understand him.   I
venerate him, and if you knew him as I do, I think you would
feel as I do.   Mrs. Butler and my daughters beg their kind
remembrances.

"Believe me, my dear Sir, yours very sincerely,
                                        "S. BUTLER."

So ended this long and bitter quarrel.   The only breeze
that ever afterwards occurred between the two men arose
out of a little affair of which my kind and illustrious old
friend the late Rev. Richard Shilleto told me as having
happened when he was a boy at Shrewsbury School.
Blomfield had then become Bishop of Chester and was
paying a visit to Dr. Butler.   He of course attended
morning chapel with the boys, and was much scandalised
at seeing Dr. Butler, towards the close of the service, begin
to cut his pencil so as to be ready for marking and correct-
ing exercises.   Dr. Butler of course promised faithfully that
he would never cut his pencil in chapel any more, and, let
us hope, kept his promise.

---

* Slip of the pen for Delphi.   See in British Museum among Dr.
Butler's papers, Additional MSS., 34584, letters to E. D. Clarke, April 4th,
April 23rd, 1816.   I know of no memo of Dr. Butler's on Dodona.—ED.

From the Rev. S. Tillbrook.

"*December 7th,* 1818.

"My dear Doctor,—I hope by this time that Heaven is quiet, and that you have expelled the Titans and all their rebellious crew. I have spoken to our youth Smith on the bursting subject. He seems very ready to accept the situation, and on comparing his strength with that of your present assistant feels no great horror at the thoughts of treading in his shoes, though he would avoid his steps.

"I have seen your honest letter which has been circulated among the parents of your pupils. It seems to me that you have been too indulgent to the appetites of the young rogues. Who could ever hope to satisfy the real or fancied cravings of a hungry schoolboy? I remember a schoolfellow of mine who after dinner drew the wick of a mould candle through his teeth, and ate the cold tallow afterwards. Upon this he piled up eight raw turnips and twelve large cooking apples. Besides these, he cracked nuts during a walk of four miles from the wood where he had gathered them, and then at night ate toasted cheese, and drank a joram of treacle, or ate it so crumbed with bread that the spoon stood erect in it. What do you think of that Master Apicius?

"I must dish up this hasty pudding."

To a Tradesman in Shrewsbury.

"Schools, *Monday, December 7th,* 1818.

"Sir,—Great pains were taken by me to appreciate the damages among the boys. I publicly declared my intention of exempting Mr. Jeudwine's boarders and the day scholars if they should be proved by their respective head boys to have no concern in the general mischief. No attempt to exculpate them was made that day. The next day the head boy of the day scholars said that only one was concerned. I then declared that only one should pay. Another was then named. I said that one, or two, or even three, should pay individually, but that as I knew many of my own boys and many of Mr. Jeudwine's were equally innocent, and yet were included in the general estimate of damage (towards which even my own son contributed, though to my knowledge perfectly innocent), if more were concerned all should pay. I left the head boy of the boarders and the head boy of the day scholars to settle it, and they agreed that more were concerned."

*   *   *   *   *

To a Parent.

"SHREWSBURY, *December 9th*, 1818.

" DEAR SIR,—When I sent you my first circular I think I told you that your son had been misled at first, but that he had subsequently behaved very well.   I wish I could confirm that opinion, but I am persuaded that he has not a proper sense of his duty to me, nor of my unwearied exertions for the moral and intellectual improvement of all the boys under my care.   As it is of great consequence that there should be a frank and cordial understanding between the master and the head boy, who is obliged on many occasions to be in official communication with him, and to possess his confidence in many things, I think it right to request that he may not return to me.

" I have the pleasure to send him to you a very elegant and accomplished scholar, and whether you send him to Trinity College at once or place him with a private tutor for the ensuing half-year it will make but little difference to him.   I might perhaps in justice to myself have sent him to you a week ago, if not earlier, but I resolved that I would keep him if possible to the end of the half-year, that he may leave me, if not with all the satisfaction I hoped to have felt, at least without any mark of disgrace to himself.   I heartily wish him well, and have little doubt that he will distinguish himself at college."

FROM THE MASTER OF ST. JOHN'S COLLEGE, CAMBRIDGE.

(Original in Cambridge University Library.)

" ST. JOHN'S, *December 18th*, 1818.

" MY DEAR DR. BUTLER,—Every member of the University interested in the support of discipline must feel thankful to you for the firmness with which you have resisted the turbulence and self-will of foolish and presumptuous boys.   Children nowadays very early imbibe most pernicious notions, if not from their parents and relations, at least from the spirit of the times.   I approve heartily of every point in your proceedings, and doubt not your school will stand as high in reputation for the due subordination and modesty of the scholars, as it does for their improvement in learning.

" I wish it may be consistent with your feelings either to give me the names of those whom you have advised to leave the school or to withhold the usual certificate of admission to St. John's.   We have a very numerous, and, I am happy to say, a most respectable and orderly set of young men.   I could not knowingly introduce any sowers of sedition among them.   They have no rights here, but are under obligation to submit to the statutes, and such regulations as the Master and seniors may see necessary."

To Dr. Robert W. Darwin.

"Shrewsbury, *February 4th*, 1819.

"My dear Sir,—I shall have great pleasure in sending my little boy to you on Sunday. I have requested Mrs. Butler to suspend the fulfilment of her promise to you made this morning. Every boy has one under and one good upper blanket, and a good quilt, which, if not new, is always double-lined. This has been the allowance ever since I have kept house, and care is always taken that, when an upper blanket becomes at all worn, it shall be removed and a new one put in its place. The same quantity of blankets, and the same quality as near as it is possible to get them, are on every bed in my own and in the adjoining house. What is the rule for one must be the rule for all, and I shall immediately get an additional blanket for every bed, if after this statement you think it necessary or even desirable. It is my anxious wish always to attend to real complaints, but not to gratify boys in foolish whims and prejudices, and I cannot help thinking that some such exist or have lately arisen among them on the subject you mention. You shall judge from what I am about to state. Immediately on Drew's arrival he put his hands on one of the beds (I think that of your son Charles *) and pronounced it 'as damp as muck.' It had in fact been certainly for two and I think for three days constantly before a large kitchen fire. When I consider that the complaint of Erasmus is the very first that I have received in twenty years upon the subject, and couple it with the other fact I have mentioned, I cannot help thinking that the boys have got some whim into their heads on the occasion. Last night indeed was a particularly cold night, and might perhaps be more felt than another, especially after boys have just returned to school from domestic indulgences, but it was not so cold as many have been in other winters when I have had no complaint. You see how much I rely on the friendly interest I know you to take in what passes here, and I must trespass on it still further while I make it my particular request that you will not answer this note till you have seen Erasmus, and questioned him a little; if you think it desirable that an addition should be made to the boys' blankets after what you hear from him, you cannot do me so great a kindness as by recommending that measure, and they will immediately be put on every bed in my two houses, if they can be procured at once in this town. Otherwise I must wait till a sufficient number can be got, as what is done for one must certainly be done for all."

---

* I need hardly say that Charles Darwin of world-wide fame as author of the *Origin of Species*, etc., etc., is here alluded to.—Ed.

From Baron Merian.

"*April 9th*, 1819.

*   *   .   *   *   *

"My feelings on your account can never be altered; a long war and a suspicious peace passed and pass away before them without leaving the smallest impression; but let them preserve their beneficent nature in its perfect purity, and may you frequently ask ' Why does he not write?' never ' Why does he write?'

"Your rooms, my dear friend, are ready. You can, on going and on returning, alight and stay nowhere (unless you wish to incur a capital forfeiture) except at my humble cottage, which is situated Chaussée d'Antin, Rue St. Lazare, No. 56. Order your postilion to drive directly thither at any time of the day or night, *et cætera linque mihi.*

"And I shall not only *cretâ* sed *minio* notare the end of June 1819.

"Yours most sincerely,

"M."

To the Overseer of the Shrewsbury Factory.

"*May 17th,* 1819.

"Sir,—I have received information of an intention of some of the boys belonging to your factory to attack my pupils on their way to the water, either this or some following evening. I think the information is correct, but in my opinion it would be better not to take public notice of it, as the plan may go by. I suppose the scheme has been suggested by the election politics, in which I take no part beyond perhaps giving my vote to Mr. Corbet, perhaps not voting at all. If you think proper to commission a couple of your workmen whom you can trust to keep a look out from six to eight, or perhaps a little after, in the evening during the election, I shall be very willing to give them a reasonable compensation when the election is over, and I shall also caution my boys not to commence provocation, but shall not state that I have heard there has been any design of attacking them, which it is better that they should not know.

"I remain, Sir,

"Your very obedient servant,

"S. Butler."

CHAPTER XII

FIRST VISIT TO ITALY.

Tour in Switzerland and North Italy.—Correspondence, August 5th, 1819—July 10th, 1820.

THE following extracts from Dr. Butler's diary of his second foreign trip are as many as my space will permit :—

"*June 23rd*, 1819.—Wednesday evening, 6 p.m. Left London from the White Bear in Piccadilly; paid £3 18s. for fare from London to Paris, including passage from Dover to Calais and 12s. for luggage. Arrived at Dover at seven on Thursday morning; not much troubled at the custom-house; embarked at half-past ten, and arrived at Calais about a quarter before one, having had a short but rough passage of about two hours and forty minutes. Hôtel Meurice; comfortable *table-d'hôte* at four, and a good bedroom. Went to bed early, slept well and comfortably, without any bugs.

* * * * *

" At ten left Calais with tolerably agreeable companions ; dined at six at Montreuil-sur-Mer upon a plentiful but not well-dressed dinner at four francs each. Tea and coffee at midnight at Abbeville (Tête de Bœuf; twenty-five sous each, and half a franc at dinner and three or four sous at supper). Breakfast at ten at Beauvais (the Écu), exceeding in dirt and filth all that I ever saw in France, except at Mezières ; reached Paris on Saturday the 26th, excessively tired. The diligence is not in itself a disagreeable conveyance, going at a regular pace of six miles an hour and being hung very easy and roomy enough for six persons—and there are no stoppages at ale-houses. But the journey from Calais to Paris in hot weather is very fatiguing.

" *Sunday, 27th.*—Dined with the Baron Merian in a private apartment *au Cadran Bleu*—rainy day, no stirring out.

* * * * *

" *June 29th.*—Weather still unfavourable. The Baron has engaged a *calèche* for me at six francs a day, and a very respectable and well-recommended servant at ten francs per day, finding himself.

"*June* 30*th*.—Passports signed at the Prefecture, where I was obliged to attend in person ; then by the British Ambassador, the French Minister for Foreign Affairs, the Austrian Ambassador, the Swiss and Sardinian Ministers.   Dined at the garden of Tivoli and went down the Montagnes Russes in a car with the Baron. The car is a kind of chair like a gig body on four low wheels— a man pushes you to the edge of the precipice and lets you loose. The car descends nearly perpendicularly some distance and acquires a great velocity, which is ultimately retarded by the gradual rise of the end of the course.   I did not find it very pleasant or very disagreeable except where the car has to pass under an artificial grotto, the roof of which when you are above it in the course of the descent seems to threaten inevitable destruction by being too low for the heads of those who are to pass under it, but on arriving it is a few inches higher than the traveller and permits him to pass with perfect safety.   The whole amusement seems very childish—much more so are the swings and what they call the *chars aériennes*, which consist of a number of little boats with sails to them, fixed to the end of revolving poles."

After saying that Paris was left at 3 and Fontainebleau reached at 8.45 (*i.e.* about eight miles an hour), the writer continues with a description of the *château*, from which I take the following :—

"In a small apartment, a kind of cabinet to the King's bed-chamber plainly fitted up, there stands a round wooden table made I believe of cherry or some very ordinary wood, and about three feet in diameter.   Its intrinsic value may be four or five francs, but at that table and in that chamber Napoleon signed his abdication of the empire of France.   It is a little notched on the edges by a penknife, whether by his own or not I could not learn."

　　　　*　　　　*　　　　*　　　　*　　　　*

Whether the table is still there or no I cannot say.   The next day the journey was made to St. Florentin, about seventy-eight miles in eleven hours, *i.e.* about seven miles an hour.   Leaving St. Florentin at four in the morning of July 3rd, Dr. Butler reached Tonnerre at seven and went on thence to Montbard.

" At Montbard the mountains begin—which are of an uninterest-ing kind, being low, tedious, and unpicturesque ; they continue for many leagues, but at length, on having climbed the summit of the mountain which overhangs the Vale of Suzon, and bears the same name, the horizon being excessively clear, what were my feelings on discovering in the W.S.W. the majestic pyramid of Mont Blanc ! This was at twenty minutes before seven in the evening. I was then six leagues from Dijon, and therefore about seventy, *i.e.* more than two hundred miles, from Mont Blanc. The horizon being excessively clear, I could see the immense extent of the Jura Mountains distinctly in a pale blue line ; above them, but at a much greater height, and so exceedingly faint as not to be distinguished by an eye unpractised in mountain scenery, ran a line which marked the Alps, and very distinctly in the W.S.W. the pyramid of Mont Blanc raised its eternal snows into the cloudless blue of the horizon. My feelings I cannot express. I gasped— yet hardly dared to breathe as I viewed for the first time this monarch of the mountains. I seemed to fancy the genius seated on his stupendous throne far above his aspiring brethren, and in his solitary might defying the universe. I was so overcome by my feelings that I was almost bereft of my faculties, and would not for worlds have spoken after my first exclamation, till I found some relief in a gush of tears. With pain I tore myself from contemplating for the first time, ' at distance dimly seen ' (though I felt as if I had sent my soul and eyes after it), this sublime spectacle.

" The descent into the Vale of Suzon is exquisitely beautiful ; the road is good, and everything that rock, wood, and mountain can contribute are here united to form this exquisitely secluded spot. It is five leagues long, from fifty to a hundred and fifty yards broad, and inhabited by a simple and contented race, who support themselves by their flocks and herds."

The journey made was a hundred and eight miles in fifteen hours, or a trifle more than seven miles an hour. On Sunday, July 4th, Poligny was reached in nine hours from Dijon.

" The country becomes less pleasing till we approach Champag-nole, where the first pine woods begin. The excessive dark and sombrous green of these trees, their formal shape and want of branches, all tend to make them unpicturesque, while at the same time the novelty of their appearance is such as to give them a kind of interest.

*   *   *   *   *

" Noirmont and Dole, along which I passed, are the highest

points of the Jura, but after I got to Avalley the scene was most
truly magnificent.   The road, as level as a bowling-green, runs
under enormous precipices of the Jura, many hundred feet in height
and quite perpendicular. 'These are for the most part covered
with pines, but where there is no fissure in the rock the naked
and perpendicular precipice above is sublimely terrific, and these
feelings are not a little enhanced by the traveller's recollecting
that he is hanging, as it were, in mid air on the very brink of a
precipice still more frightful, and without the least protection.
The road, however, is wide and very good, but the prodigious
height—at least 3,000 feet above the level of the sea—can only be
estimated by casting a look into the valley beneath.   The whole
scenery, the pine-clad rocks, the green and smiling valley, the
herds which graze it and which are scarce distinguishable by the
eye, the *châlets* of the shepherds, and, above all, the everlasting
variety of the rocks and distant mountains, are all delightful, but
how shall I express my feelings when on a sudden turn in the
road the whole panorama of the higher Alps presented itself to
my view !   I saw all their summits piercing the very heavens and
clad with everlasting snows for the distance of a hundred and
fifty miles, from Mont Cenis along St. Bernard to the Simplon.
Mont St. Gothard was wrapt in angry storms, which swept along
the rest of the Alps to the east.   Towering above them all rose
Mont Blanc in solitary majesty.   It was exactly the same hour
as when I first saw this king of mountains from Mont Suzon, then
two hundred miles distant.   I am now within seventy, and the
distance does not appear above fifteen or twenty miles, so clear
is the atmosphere.   Above the highest Alps floated an immense
mass of thick clouds, which in about half an hour began to assume
a singular colour.   As the sun declined (and it sets in these
southern regions about a quarter before eight) the clouds which
were no longer lighted by his rays assumed a very lovely sea-green
colour ; those which were partially lighted appeared of a yellowish
green, and those huge masses which still received his rays
became of a bright flame colour.   The lower Alps soon began to
be indistinct ; the snow-clad region was still visible ; soon it also
became less clear, but Mont Blanc assumed an indescribable tint,
a kind of rosy purple.   The twilight here is short.   The descent
of the Jura is no less than twelve miles, all descent, but so
easy that a carriage need not lock more than a hundred yards,
though the postilion by way of precaution locked mine through
the whole descent, and the wheel was almost red-hot when we
arrived at Gex.   I walked nine of these miles.   My mind and
heart were too full to sit still, and I found some relief by exhausting my feelings through exercise.

   " I reached Gex at nine, and was obliged to drive hard to get
from thence to Geneva before the gates were shut.   The night
was heavenly : the moon was so bright that I could plainly

distinguish all the lower Alps near Geneva, which lay absolutely under my feet ; when I first caught the panorama of the Alps from the summit of the Jura, I could even see the city with my naked eye, though more than twenty miles distant, and distinguish the houses very plainly with the telescope. It was quite dark at nine o'clock, when I arrived at Gex. From thence I drove through Ferney (Voltaire's abode) to Geneva. The night was heavenly : the full moon shone brightly on the Alps. The comet was conspicuous over the Jura, with a train of considerable length, like a falling sky-rocket. The evening star was shining with a splendour almost equal to the moon over the mountains of Voirons, and the north-west was in a continual blaze with the flashes of sheet lightning. I arrived at Geneva just as the gates were about to be shut, and though at a good hotel (the Balance) it is so full that I have been most miserably lodged this evening.

＊   ＊   ＊   ＊   ＊

"I left Geneva at half-past seven and reached Lausanne at half-past five, having been ten hours in going eleven leagues. . . . On sending to a tailor for stuff for a waistcoat, I found all his best stuffs were English. . . . In the catalogue of a circulating library kept at this place (Lausanne) by Louis Knab, which is now lying before me, I can scarcely find anything but translations of English novels."

Vevay, Clarens, Chillon, Bex, Martigny, were visited in due course.

. " *Saturday, July* 10th.—I left the inn at Martigny, which I found clean but not very comfortable (Les Cygnes), at about a quarter past five. The road to the Col de Fourclas bears, as does all the Valley of Martigny, dreadful marks of last year's inundation. This inundation arose from a glacier having fallen into the Val de Bagnes, nine hours from Martigny. It there choked up the valley at a place called Malvoisin, and formed an immense dam for the waters of the Drance. After three months these waters were so accumulated that they burst their barrier and arrived in an hour and a quarter at Martigny, the usual time by the same route being nine hours. They destroyed three hundred houses, but fortunately only thirty-five persons ; the misfortune having been long apprehended, the inhabitants had withdrawn at the first notice to the mountains. This notice was a hurricane driven before the waters in their furious descent, which caused more damage than they did. I saw trees yet standing about ten or twelve feet from the ground, whose trunks of enormous size were snapped by the hurricane like reeds, and the trunks yet remain in some places where they have been swept by the waters and carried among the rocks. The water seems not to have risen at Martigny more than twelve or fourteen feet, but as the valley is wide this is a great height, and the trees that remain have still all their trunks torn and stripped of bark by the enormous stones which were carried by the torrent and still remain on the plain.

   *   *   *   *   *

"I have seen to-day at Chamouny that rare animal the bouquetin. It was caught by the hunter who killed its dam when it was just born, and is now two years old, and very playful and lively. I have seen only one eagle soaring in the Alps, and at present no vultures, of which I am told there are many.

   *   *   *   *   *

"*Monday morning, July* 12*th.*—This morning I rose at five, intending to reach Martigny in good time, but I have been detained by my wish to see Jacques Balma, the guide so often mentioned by Saussure, and the very interesting circumstance of seeing two American travellers reach the summit of Mont Blanc. The direct distance from the summit to this place is only six miles, but the difficulties of approach are so great that the journey is no less than thirty-six. I went to Balma's house, and found the good old man not yet up (7 o'clock). He seemed much flattered by my coming to see him, and would accompany me a little way up Mont Blanc itself, that I might have the pleasure of saying I had been on it. We returned by the Glacier of Boissons, which is very magnificent. With my telescope I can very distinctly see the travellers, now within an hour of the summit. They have eight guides ; they took nine, but one seems to have failed—at least he is absent. It is very curious to see these little insects, for such they look, going in a line on the snow. They appear to proceed well and rapidly. Their names are Dr. Van Rensselaer and Mr. W. Howard from Baltimore. Half-past twelve. They have this moment reached the summit, and I proceed on my journey.

   *   *   *   *   *

"*Tuesday, July* 13*th.*—I am just about to set out for the Grand St. Bernard. . . . Among several bad wooden bridges I have had to pass, the worst was this day. A Swiss bridge is always terrific. It is composed by two fir-trees, which if they grow near the spot and are long enough are felled so as to cross the stream. These are covered with a few inch boards when at best, but in general with a few deal scantlings, round as they come from the tree, and always loose. The bridge is almost always at a cataract, because there the river is generally narrowest, but you always feel and see the planks bend under the weight of your mule and see the water through the crevices.

   *   *   *   *   *

"At a quarter past seven I reached the Hospice, involved in

clouds, and exceedingly cold and fatigued. The effect of coming to a comfortable establishment after such a journey is inconceivable. The porter rang a bell on my arrival, and a monk immediately appeared, who conducted me into the refectory. Here I found the Prior and seven brothers had just finished dinner, and there were four strangers. Wine was instantly brought me, and in half an hour a very good dinner, consisting of *potage au riz*, eggs, spinach, and roast veal, with figs, cheese, and nuts for dessert. As soon as I had done, grace was said by one of the monks, and after a few minutes' general conversation we all went to bed, about nine o'clock. I was shown into a good room with a warm fire of pine logs, a bed well covered with an eiderdown quilt, and all things suitable. The wind whistled at my window like a dreary November evening, and the snow fell fast —all this on the evening of a day the morning of which I had found intolerable for its heat. The whole of this day's journey seemed like a dream, its conclusion especially in gentlemanly society, with every comfort and accommodation amidst the rudest rocks and in the region of perpetual snow. The thought that I was sleeping in a convent, and occupied the bed of no less a person than Napoleon, that I was in the highest inhabited spot in the world, and in a place celebrated in every corner of it, at . . . feet above the sea, kept me awake for some time.

"*Wednesday, July 14th.*— . . . After breakfast I saw all their collection of natural history and mineralogy, and the coins and inscriptions which have been found in the Temple of Jupiter Pœninus (for so it is always spelt), and went to the temple itself, where are some remains of foundations. It stood at a little distance to the west of the present Hospice, at the end of the lake, than which nothing can be conceived more dreary, and which has only been thawed five days ago. But my great delight in this little excursion was the fine dogs of the Hospice, and the monk who was with me set them to work in the snow. They are in the head something like a Newfoundland, in the form like a mastiff, and most exceedingly docile and sagacious, very fond of strangers, and of great strength. When I had all the four jumping at once about me I could hardly stand. Two were remarkably fine, one called Courage, a sort of brindled colour dog, but getting old, and the other Jupiter, young and quite white. As I went to the Temple of Jupiter they all four began to dig in different places of the snow. This they do in a manner exactly different from a dog when he scratches a hole. They push away the snow with their feet instead of accumulating it behind them, and in this manner in a minute will make a hole larger than themselves. They then put their noses to the snow to see if there is any one underneath. . . . With regret I took leave of these hospitable fathers, and after ten hours' descent reached Martigny, exceedingly fatigued."

In the notebook from which I have taken the foregoing extracts there is a copy of the Latin elegiacs on the Hospice of the Great St. Bernard, inscribed by Dr. Butler in the visitors' album, and given in the *Arundines Cami*, to which I must refer the reader.

" *Thursday, July 15th.*—Rose at six. . . . About a league from Sion I hear a noise more resembling a mixture of that made by young ducks and watchman's rattles combined than anything I can express. On my inquiring, I had the delight to find that it proceeded from the cigales on the neighbouring trees.

'Et cantu querulæ rumpunt arbusta cicadæ.'

No person can enjoy this line who has not heard them. . . . I reach Bryg at half-past five o'clock, having performed eighteen country or twenty-five post leagues in less than eleven hours. Good work. . . . [On the following day, after crossing the Simplon], . . . I have reached Baveno, and shall sleep, if my feelings will allow me, for the first time on Italian soil.

*   *   *   *

" *Saturday, July 17th.*—Set out at five in the morning to see the Isola Bella. . . . On my return left Baveno at seven (where I was agreeably disappointed in not finding any bugs), and proceeded through a most cheerful and lovely country till I crossed the Ticino by a flying bridge at Sesto Calende, and entered Lombardy. Here I found the Austrian custom-house officers very exacting, and the face of things a little, or rather a good deal, changed for the worst. The first alteration that strikes one is the road, which is no longer so good, but rather like a common English turnpike road, with high hedges on both sides, and where, when you do not see the vines and Indian corn and hear the cigales, you might think yourself travelling in the flat part of England.

" I reached Milan at five, and am at a most capital hotel (De la Grande Bretagne). I have been to see the Cathedral. . . . From the first story upwards all the richest part has been rebuilt *de novo* within the last fifteen years by Napoleon. He renewed all the statues and pinnacles in the purest white marble after the antient model ; instead of the decayed and miserable roof of tiles, he had begun and had roofed more than one-third of the church with white marble. He is in great, and I think I may reasonably say in just, favour with the Milanese.

*   *   *   *   *

" *Sunday, July 18th.*—Set off at eight o'clock to see the most particular curiosities. The amphitheatre of Bonaparte, in which he exhibited a naumachia on the birth of the King of Rome, is no great matter ; but his superb triumphal arch of pure Carrara marble, adorned with sculptures worthy of the best age of the antients, is indeed a stupendous and admirable work.   It is yet unfinished, and I suppose ever will be so, to the great grief of the Milanese, who adore Bonaparte.   It was to cost ten millions of francs, of which only about six have yet been spent.   I saw a magnificent column destined for it lying by the roadside as I was passing the Simplon.   In the cornice of the amphitheatre, which is very finely painted in relief, I saw a curious thing.   The heads of Napoleon and Josephine were there in medallion.   By the addition of a beard and hood and one wrinkle Napoleon is turned into Neptune, but the features are evidently to be traced, and Josephine by the help of a helmet has been transformed into the virgin goddess Minerva.   Thence I went to the Church of St. Ambrose, and saw the cypress doors from which in antient times the archbishop repelled the Grecian emperor.   They are quite perfect, and the outside richly carved.

*   *   *   *   *

" Thence I went to the Cathedral to high mass, which was celebrated with a splendour I never before witnessed, and was certainly a most interesting and imposing spectacle.   The preacher made a very good, plain, and practical sermon of about half an hour on Jesus opening the eyes of the blind.   He divided his treatment into bodily and mental blindness, and made proper and sensible remarks applicable to the subject.   He spoke so distinctly that I was able to understand him throughout.

*   *   *   *   *

" *Monday, July* 19*th.*—Left Milan for Turin at half-past four. The road is all the way on a dead flat, cropped with rice, Indian corn, and millet, with nothing interesting but the magnificent view of the Alps when gilt by the morning sun.   It is difficult to express the glory of a sunrise under an Italian sky.   There is a blue in the heavens unknown to and inconceivable by the inhabitants of our climate.   A flood of fire is poured from the east, which gradually subsides towards the west in white, pale, and at last celestial blue.   Monte Rosa, which is only two or three hundred feet lower than Mont Blanc, and which is so called from its summits inclining towards one another like a rose, appeared at first almost blood-red on its snow-capped summits. By degrees as the light spread down its sides it assumed a fainter colour, but continued till near nine o'clock of a faint tint of blood. . . . I reached Turin, exceedingly fatigued, at about half-past six, having performed a journey of more than a hundred miles in fourteen hours.

*   *   *   *   *

" *Tuesday, July* 20*th.*—I have just made a discovery which is very characteristic of the people. I observed that all the knives are of a singular form. Instead of coming to a point, they all of a sudden expand again, and end in a singularly formed blunt button, a little like the end of a foil. This is a precaution on the part of government to diminish in some little degree the frequency of assassination, and no other knives are allowed to be sold.

"*Wednesday, July* 21*st.*—Passed the day with William Hill. Saw nothing but the magnificent view of the Alps from the ramparts, and the sugar-loaf of Monte Viso where the Po rises, directly opposite his windows. The Alps seem as if one could actually touch them at the end of each street. I witnessed two customs which I was gratified with remarking. One is the Eastern mode of clapping hands instead of ringing a bell to call servants. The other is the serenade; in returning from the ambassador's hotel about eleven I saw three lovers in different streets serenading their mistresses. The music consisted of a violoncello, violin, bassoon, and (I think) clarionet. One man sang well; the rest was very moderate.

"*Friday, July* 23*rd.*—Rose at half-past three, and found myself very unwell, and unfit for the journey. Proceeded, however, to Susa, where I was so very ill that I much doubted whether I ought not to return to Turin. . . . I am now by a comfortable fire of pine logs, at the Hôtel Royal at Lanslebourg, which is kept by an Englishwoman, and I found myself better than at Susa. About two-thirds of the way down Mont Cenis I saw a sight that illustrated a passage of Virgil. He makes Discord mount upon the roof of the shepherd's cottage, where, he says, ' Pastorale canit signum.' In the very same situation on the ridge of the roof of a *châlet* did I see a peasant girl stand blowing the *cor des Alpes.*

" I may also note the general custom in Italy and here of spinning in the antient classical mode, by the distaff stuck in the bosom, and the spindle hanging from it.*

" *Saturday, July* 24*th.*—Left Lanslebourg, where I found everything but my bedroom as uncomfortable as possible, at a quarter before six. . . . After travelling a considerable distance on this noble road, I came to the fortress of Echellons, now building by the King of Sardinia to command the road. . . . I arrived at the Hôtel de la Poste at Chambery at half-past seven, having accomplished about a hundred miles in thirteen hours. I have been much better since I have been among the mountains.

" *Sunday, July* 25*th.*—Left Chambery, which is a most miserable

---

* When I first remember Italy, in 1843—and I remember it exceedingly well—one hardly met a woman on a country road but she was spinning as she went along. Now it is rare to see a spindle and distaff at all. —ED.

town (but the Hôtel de la Poste is not bad), at half-past five.
. . . Having left Beauvoisin, I met a large and jovial group with a
violin before them, leading an old man on an ass with his face
turned to the tail, and a woman following him holding a large
distaff over his head filled with flax. This I found is the rustic
mode of marking contempt for a man who suffers his wife to beat
him. . . . At one of the post-houses I saw a girl carrying what I
thought at first was the top of a round oak table on her head,
but it turned out to be a loaf of rye bread: the diameter could
not possibly be less than five feet, and I found it was intended
to last a numerous family six days. It is baked of this size
because it keeps moister, and the longer it is kept the further a
little of it goes. The road to Lyons is broad, but was rather
rough. I reached this superb city, by far the finest I have seen
in France after Paris, at half-past six, having performed fourteen
and a half posts, or between eighty and ninety miles, in thirteen
hours. I am at the Hôtel de Provence, a very grand house, which
looks out into the grand Place. My apartment, which is about
twenty-four feet square by eighteen feet high, is sumptuously furnished. *Dieu me garde de punaises.* Two looking-glasses, each
above six feet high ; magnificent bed, with curtains and coverlet
of crimson satin, with green and gold frieze ; fine carpet of real
Lyons tapestry ; calico curtains, with broad striped muslin frieze.
The Rhine here, after its junction with the Saone, is a truly noble
river, wider than the Seine at Paris, but not quite so wide as the
Thames at London—about equal to it at Fulham.

"*Monday, July* 26*th.*— . . . The want of cleanliness in the streets
of Lyons is striking, and the stench of them is almost poisonous.
I left at two, and having bad postilions and excessive heat did
not arrive at Macon till near ten—eight and a half posts, or about
fifty miles, in eight hours. . . . I also now see the use of shepherds,
cowherds, and swineherds ; for the fields being all unenclosed,
even a single cow requires its keeper, and one sees women and
children tending their little flocks and herds everywhere along the
road, the poor animals having nothing to eat but the grass and
weeds of the ditches.

"*Tuesday, July* 27*th.*—I was up at four, but owing to the
inattention of the post I could not get off till a quarter before
five, and this has in fact been a day of vexations. I soon after
had the misfortune to overtake a *calèche*, which by the laws of
the post being a carriage of the same description as my own, and
drawn by the same number of horses, I might not pass. At last
I contrived to pass it while the owners were at breakfast, but I
had then the misfortune to overtake the mail, which no carriage
may pass, and was obliged to follow in its train for forty miles,
by which I lost a good hour. I got past this plague at Autun,
where the mail stopped to dinner, but broke a spring on the
road between that place and Saulieu, where I arrived at eight

o'clock, having performed nineteen and a half posts, or about a hundred and sixteen miles, in fifteen and a quarter hours. At the entrance of Autun there is a very large and handsome college. I met about two hundred of the boys walking two and two, attended by eight or ten teachers—the youngest boys first, who seemed to be from nine years and upwards. The last seventy or eighty seemed quite adults, from eighteen or nineteen to twenty-four. Some of the younger and middle-sized boys had a gentle-manly appearance; the adults were evidently of low rank and shabbily dressed. . . . The air is indeed sensibly cold, and the sky different in colour and transparency from that of Italy. My dessert this evening at Saulieu has been not according to its usual profusion of pears, plums, peaches, figs, apricots, almonds, and filberts, but a solitary small plate of very indifferent gooseberries. *Sic transit gloria mundi.* The inn here (the Poste) is small and unpretending, but does not appear dirty, and I have found a passable supper and a really good bottle of claret.

"*Wednesday, July* 28*th*, and legions of bugs, which are giving me a degree of itching quite intolerable. Left at five, and pro-ceeded five posts to Avallon. After this the country improves to Auxerre, and the vineyards are of immense extent. . . . From Auxerre about five posts brought me to Joigny, and I then fell into the road I had passed in setting out to Sens, which I reached at eight o'clock. . . . I hope to reach Paris by three to-morrow afternoon, being to an hour the exact month since I set out, in which time how much have I seen! But I am not very sanguine in this hope, for the carriage is so very crazy that it is next to a miracle if it does not tumble to pieces before I can reach Paris, or at least if something does not break, to repair which will require considerable delay.

" *Thursday, July* 29*th.*—Left Sens at four o'clock, and after a journey which offered nothing remarkable, having passed through Charenton and by the castle of Vincennes, where the Duke D'Enghien was shot, I arrived at my friend Baron Merian's, at the same hour and day on which I had departed a month ago, and found him ill in bed. He rose, however, to dinner, and we passed the evening most agreeably.

  •   •   •   •   •

" *Saturday, July* 31*st.*—Left Paris at six, arrived at Amiens at ten at night, and saw its magnificent Cathedral, but little inferior to Rheims, by moonlight. Arrived at Calais at nine o'clock, August 1st, and found near a hundred people fighting, scolding, entreating, demanding, and tearing Madame Meurice to pieces for beds. At last, after an hour's delay, I got one two streets off, clean and quiet.

"On Monday, August 2nd, I left Calais at half-past nine; and after a most delightful passage in the French mail, the officers and sailors of which are remarkably civil and attentive, I arrived in three hours and twenty minutes at Dover."

CORRESPONDENCE, AUGUST 5TH, 1819—JULY 10TH, 1820.

FROM THE REV. S. TILLBROOK.

"*August 5th,* 1819.

*   *   *   *   *

" My own time has been spent leisurely enough. I have been a little while at the Lakes, and to Scotland for a season, and am now going to see old Cheviot put on his nightcap. By the end of this month I hope my caravansary will reach Salop. My rod has had harder duty than yours since we parted, and has tickled up the Poissons in grand style. I have been a vagrant and a vagabond ; have been suspected of passing forged banknotes—once all but apprehended in Yorkshire, with no one to give me a character but my dog Pepper—and no bail at hand. Almost forced to pawn horse and gig."

*   *   *   *   *

TO MR. BROOME, CHURCH STRETTON.

"SHREWSBURY, *August 20th,* 1819.

" Dr. Butler feels extremely obliged to Mr. Broome for his attention in removing the coachman who overturned the Hereford coach, when his boys broke up at midsummer last. The man has been to Dr. Butler (whom he did not see), and has stated ' that he has been fifteen years on the road, and has never before been intoxicated nor complained of to Mr. Broome, but that Mr. Broome will not restore him without Dr. B.'s concurrence.' If this statement be correct, Dr. Butler would wish Mr. Broome to consider him as not disposed to object to the man's restoration, should he be inclined to reinstate him, but he wishes by no means to be considered as making a request to this effect, or as doing more than merely leaving the matter wholly to Mr. Broome's consideration, to whom he begs to return his very sincere thanks."

FROM BARON MERIAN.

"*August 30th,* 1819.

" DEAR SIR,—It is, by Jupiter, not permitted that in A.D. 1811 an erudite editor of Shakespeare should be ignorant of the meaning of the word *child* applied to knights, warriors (see *King Lear*, III. 4), and wonder like a silly ninny hammer ' how that came to pass' (p. 413, Chalmers). Why, on the Continent a child knoweth that yon *child* is nothing in the world but *held, heros, hero,* a most common German word, and by mere chance resembling your , child,' *infans,* which again is corrupted from the German *kind.* I say corrupted, because *kind* has an original signification, which

child has not. It is a most unconceivable thing that your
dictionaries, at least such as I saw, give not *child, hero*. I dare
to say that it is ridiculous to let boys and scholars believe that
child, infans, and *child, hero*, are one and the same word, or
teach, like Miller, that *child* is sometimes applied to princes and
kings in the same way as *Infante* is in Spain.

" This is a long speech about a single word, but it leads me or
a most serious, and I believe important, reflection. The English
grammarians and learned men will as a matter of course fot
ever be in the dark about such matters, if they continue in that
unaccountable neglect of the German languages of which they
are more than any people, and with much less excuse, guilty to
the present day. I wrote to you once upon this subject—I do it
again, for it is crying aloud. How the excellent Johnson writes
an etymological dictionary of the English tongue, and, forsooth,
knows not one word of German ! ! ! Would you write a similar
work on the Italian, and not know one word of Latin ? You
laugh at the idea : give us leave not to laugh at a man like
Johnson, but to be stupefied at the phenomenon.

"Give us further leave to tell you that since Lewis XIV. you
lean altogether a great deal too much, in more than one aspect,
to French, and similar culture. Smooth Alex. Pope, for instance,
is not an English but a French poet, and will therefore not
survive among you ; and merely for running after idle wenches
the noble English maiden is grown forgetful of her own venerable
mother. I pretend no man can say ' I understand English '
unless he understand German, and I engage to show you in a
trice twenty English words which you, my dear friend, do not
understand, and which I do. What, *e.g.*, is *jeopardy*, and *buxom* ?
And do you know what your *mole-hill* is ? A tautology, and no
better than hill-hill ; for *mole* is by no means an animal, but a
little rising ground,—in German *maul, meil* ; in Russian *mogila* ; in
Latin *moles*. . . . You borrow daily words from the French which
are not French but German, and by passing through that filthy
medium have lost their original purity and lustre. . . . *Ex. gr.*
you had an old ' sicker '—the German ' sicher.' No, faith, that
would not do ; but you must run after ' sĕcŭre,' which, with
ἐχυρός, is nothing but cant for *sicher* and *sicker*—and you give
it a nonsensical accent ; for mark that every true English word
has its momentum on its radical syllable—bewilder, unlŭcky—a
quality which no language in the world has, except the German
and its offspring. And so strongly does this innate (why not
inborn ?) notion act on English minds and throats, that without
being aware of it they alter foreign words, and draw the accent
against foreign rule to its right and natural place. Thus *senatus*
became senate, *papyrus* paper, so deeply are you German, and
yet neglect German. It is wicked.

"'They ought, I repeat it, to look seriously back to the place from which they sprang, and consider the three eternal partitions of Europe, which are so well described by Madame de Stael in the beginning of her book *De l'Allemagne,* and which, in spite of contrary wars, treaties, and dictionaries, will and must forcibly break through and pop up *in sæcula sæculorum.* Amen.

"And lastly we beg you will show this to Dr. Parr, τῷ πάνυ, by whom we should of all things like to be a little scourged."

FROM BARON MERIAN.

"*September 9th,* 1819.

"DEAR SIR,—Here's one morsel of Morcellus.* The other will follow always at Rothschild's. Be not angry at my late letters, but consider that if I scold 'tis only because I love England and its literature. Now let me give you another striking instance to support the truth of my 'grand' letter; take peace and war. Ask of any English schoolboy to explain peace, he will soon say, Peace, paix, pax, pactum, pangere. Right. Then ask about war. He cannot answer. And yet war is of your mother tongue, and peace is foreign, and introduced by the Conquest only, for *fred* is the right word that answers war. I do not recollect : does Johnson or any new lexicographer explain war and *fred*? I doubt; for to say they are Anglo-Saxon is not to explain. Why is *bellum* called war? and why is, or was, *pax* called *fred*?

"If we inquire, we find that the very same notion or observation which created the Latin pax created also the German *fried* or fred, both meaning originally a stick, or term of separation : *palus solo impactus ; septum.*

"This and a hundred similar questions your short but profound vocabulary might explain, and by doing so astound many a learned professor, who never fancied there could be sense anywhere but in Greek and Hebrew. Now the fact is the very contrary. Greek and Latin are corrupted German."

FROM THE REV. S. TILLBROOK.

"*MILLBROOK, September 15th,* 1819.

"DEAR DOCTOR,—Finding the ale still incomparably good at Shiffnal, I desired the landlord to forward a two-dozen hamper of it to your cellar. Drink the health of the donor, and save one bottle for him till next year.

"Report—*i.e.* the waiter at the King's Head, Coventry—assured me that at the Bear and Ragged Staff at Daventry I should

---

* Morcellus wrote a work entitled *De Stylo Inscriptionum.*— ED.

find the ale as good as in Shropshire. The name of this *auberge* amused me, so I determined to hobble to this interesting shrine of Sir John Barleycorn. Under cover of the night I sneaked into the *auberge* aforesaid, and found, as I opined, that the ale of Daventry bore no comparison to that of Salop.

" I consider my summer travels at an end now, and shall begin to celebrate them in Hudibrastic doggerel when I resume my armchair at St. Peter's. I am afraid, excepting to such ready wit as your own, that Monte Pulciano, Alleatico, Siracuso, Alchermes, Curacoa, Maraschino, etc., offer insurmountable difficulties, and yet it would be unpardonable to omit them."

From Baron Merian.

[*End of September*, 1819.]

"The Scotch family of Elphinstone is of German origin ; the Counts of Helfenstein are well known in Germany, and suffered much in what they call the War of the Peasants.

" Your *Utis* has on my brains the effect of I do not know whose victories on the brains of Themistocles : he could not sleep. But the difference is that Themistocles soon equalled those victories : I never shall your *Utis*. Οὔτις εἰμί.

"Whatever you undertake you never fail of executing in a masterly way. I have read the introduction and part of *Charlemagne*. I have but this to say : if I had not been told so, I should never have taken that poem for a translation. Yet on this occasion I must lament once more—do, only for the love of me, not fetch your Saxon mythology out of French phials. *Irmensul* is no more a god than General Hill's column is one. Bless us ! *Sul* (?) is a column, and *Irmen* is not ascertained yet, but conjectured to be Herman. Such mistakes look very pretty in French productions ; but you noble Saxon progeny ought to look elsewhere for the *cultus* of your forefathers. Suppose an unlucky German was to travel through England, and then write down, *Habent in istâ regione deum sive idolum cui nomen est Hillicolumnus* : what would you say ? Thus formerly a French lawyer used to quote with great respect the German lawyer *Harcomannus*. Now let it be known that he mistook the word *Herkommen*, which means *custom, law not written*. I beseech you, my dear friend, take all these criticisms and witticisms *in bonam partem*. Your great superiority is acknowledged ; if you take one flight more, you will be, not what Saumaise or Scaliger were, but what, each in his sphere, Bacon was or Newton. You may give grammar a new turn, and language a new foundation, *i.e.* the old and only right one. Your eyes will become sharp-sighted, and you will be struck with thousands of errors and mistakes round about you which hitherto have escaped your sight. Dr. Hodgson, for instance, writes Ădălgüise quite wrong ; it is Ādĕl-wēīs, *nobilis, sapiens*—for mark, that anciently, and still now in the Orients, all proper names were and are *appellative* ones, having a clear signi- fication. Bagatelles, very true, but they show and demonstrate the truth of the assertion which lies at the bottom of my scolding letter, viz. *that since Lewis XIV. you have considerably leaned to the French side in literature,* and to your vast detriment ; for French (politics, manners, and) literature are, and must for ever be, foreign to you ; 'twould be alloying copper to your silver. *Ergo istæ bagatelles,* si non seria ducunt in mala, tamen arguunt ista adesse mala. Let levity be far from German characters ; it becomes them not : what becomes them hath been marked out by Schiller : *Ernst und Liebe, die Beyden Ziemen dem Deutschen.*

"The second morsel of Morcellus goes with this to Messrs. Rothschild, London."

The "old Utis" in the foregoing and sundry other letters of Baron Merian refers to an explanation given by Dr. Butler of a passage in Shakespeare.

In a commonplace book, dated 1816, I find the following :—

" ' By the mass, there will be old Utis ; it will be an excellent stratagem ' (*King Henry IV.*, Part I., p. 241. Ed. Malone). ' "Old Utis" signifies festivity in a high degree ' (Steevens). ' "Utis," a merry festival, from the French "huiet," "octo," "the octaves" ' (Pope). I conceive Shakespeare alludes to the story of Utis in the *Odyssey.* The Prince and Poins are going to disguise themselves, and impose on Falstaff as two waiters or drawers. Shakespeare, who had heard probably of the story of Ούτις and Polypheme, means to say that they will renew the old story of Utis (as it would be written in the translation) in their imposture on Falstaff."

FROM BARON MERIAN.

"*October 4th,* 1819.

"DEAR SIR,—I continue my reading and remarks. General Hill's column gave me much pleasure ; you wrote admirably, but why is your beautiful CIVI SUO and POPULARES EJUS not expressed in the English inscription ? ' Contemporary ' is sorely vague, and kills the interesting sentiment of concitizenship. Besides, why Masonry?* What was that good for ? Such secret societies are

---

* Dr. Butler must have sent Baron Merian Captain Moyle Sherer's

either dangerous or ridiculous. *Non datur tertium.* For if they and their leaders have no idea but of doing good, assist the poor, teach children, why for heaven's sake cannot they act *sub dio?* There is no reply to this. .Now all their signs, and marks, and shots, and aprons are fiddle-faddle and kickshaws fit for boys. All that part of the story is a miserable cant a serious man ought to be ashamed of, for 'tis not even ingenious. And what signifies their brotherhood? Arrant nonsense likewise.

* * * * *

"That incoherent meddling of masonry has brought me off my theme, which was your Latin composition. I doubt whether Morcellus has any one thing finer than that—so short, so strong, so plain, so properly rising, and exit with a thunderclap. The English inscription—I don't know who wrote it—I think very fine too (the exposition of merits is delightful), only I repeat that 'contemporary' is too weak, since something more forcible and engaging might have been said. The Englishman does not tell us that the hero is a Salopian."

* * * *

The preceding letter makes it clear that Dr. Butler wrote the Latin inscription on Lord Hill's column, but I have found no draft of either Latin or English among his papers. The English inscription is generally believed in Shrewsbury (probably with truth) to have been also written by Dr. Butler. The Latin inscription runs :—

CIVI . SUO . ROLANDO

DOMINO . BARONI . HILL . AB . ALMARAZ . ET . HAWKSTONE

POPULARES . EJUS . EX . AGRO . ATQUE . MUNICIPIO . SALOPIENSI

COLUMNAM . HANCCE . CUM . STATUA . P.C.

A.S. MDCCCXVI.

IS . IN . RE . MILITARI . QUEMADMODUM . SE . GESSERIT

TESTES . SINT . LUSITANIA . HISPANIA . GALLIÆ

NARBONENSIS . AC . BELGICA

ARTURUS . DUX . A . WELLINGTON

SOCIORUM . ET . QUIDEM . HOSTIUM . EXERCITUS.

---

description of Lord Hill's column in Shrewsbury, etc., where the fact of one of the principal contributors being a Freemason is expressly stated. He was Mr. John Straphen, a builder in Shrewsbury, and he gave the internal staircase.

The English inscription is as follows :—

TO LIEUTENANT-GENERAL ROWLAND LORD HILL,
BARON HILL OF ALMARAZ AND HAWKSTONE, G.C.B.
NOT MORE DISTINGUISHED FOR HIS SKILL AND COURAGE IN THE FIELD,
DURING THE ARDUOUS CAMPAIGNS IN SPAIN AND PORTUGAL,
THE SOUTH OF FRANCE, AND THE MEMORABLE PLAINS OF WATERLOO,
THAN FOR HIS BENEVOLENT AND PATERNAL CARE
IN PROVIDING FOR THE COMFORTS AND SUPPLYING THE NECESSITIES
OF HIS VICTORIOUS COUNTRYMEN,
AND FOR THAT HUMANITY AND GENEROSITY
WHICH THEIR VANQUISHED FOES EXPERIENCED AND ACKNOWLEDGED,
THE INHABITANTS OF THE TOWN AND COUNTY OF SALOP
HAVE ERECTED THIS COLUMN AND STATUE,
AS A MEMORIAL OF THEIR RESPECT AND GRATITUDE TO AN
ILLUSTRIOUS CONTEMPORARY,
AND AN INCITEMENT TO EMULATION IN THE HEROES AND
PATRIOTS OF FUTURE AGES.

A.D. MDCCCXVI.

FROM BARON MERIAN.

"*October 9th,* 1819.

" DEAR SIR,—The ENGLISH *language* is of a *singular nature* Every other *language* has some *foreign* words *admixed* to it, *comparatively few* (peu), but the ENGLISH is *composed* of two *distinct* and *belligerent parts*, which no time will and can ever *amalgamate*, the GERMAN part and the FRENCH part—for a very few remainders of ancient BRITISH are hardly worth notice. Yon two *parts* are at *present* (xixth *century*) a match for one another, the *second*, however, *gaining continually* ground, for your fine *people* think themselves *prodigiously* witty and happy when they may thrust in some *fashionable* FRENCH *expression*, some of which by *degrees* stick fast, and are at last *reputed* to be ENGLISH. I say reputed, for in fact they are not and never can be. It is to me a wonderful thing to look *attentively* at an ENGLISH page : I there *perceive distinctly* two *languages* instead of one (*very* often two words instead of one, and now and then a third one—' kingly,' ' royal,' and besides ' regal.' Now what's the *use* of that ?), and am in *search accordingly* for two *dictionaries*, a GERMAN-ENGLISH one and a FRENCH-ENGLISH one. To *illustrate* this *impression* I have used italics for words of FRENCH *origin*. In any quite new *composition* you'll find *proportionally* more of such words, and this *circumstance* shows you the path you are now in, for *style* is man.

"There is, however, this one great difference : the German is the foundation, the French the superstructure, so this may one day be blown away. . . . Your plan for 1820, 1821, is delightful. *Je ferai mon possible pour le réaliser.* I have other things in view besides in which I shall once more beg of you to assist me. . . . There will be old Utis. My respects to great Dr. Parr."

FROM THE SAME.

"*October 24th,* 1819.

" DEAR SIR,—I have received *Etymologicum Universale,** 2 vols. Splendid : a very fine book indeed, and for which I am deeply indebted to you. . . . Is Whiter still conversant on this globe, and where ?

"Ten thousand thanks at least for your kind answer concerning our Calypso ; your advice will be strictly followed. You have most probably by giving it saved a very worthy man from ruin. . . .

"Champagne. I suspect it to be in England long ago. Have you asked Dejex about it ? and has he answered ? You must and shall have it, *Mehercle !*

" I look with great impatience for the printed accounts of the triumphal γάμος.† Such honours are true honours, for they proceed from free-will. No authority can command, no money can purchase, them. Your benevolent mind, your great activity in forwarding whatever is καλοκαγαθόν, have now met with a due and public reward ; and you might, if pride was admissible, be justly proud of testifications, which, in exalting the daughter, tend to exalt the father.

"Where lives now this said fair and dear daughter ? Do reflect about marrying your elder daughter too. It is not fit that she should long be a looker-on. Such cases engender bitterness of heart. You are not surely one of those parents who fancy children are born to make their tea for ever."

FROM THE SAME.

"*November 24th,* 1819.

"DEAR SIR,—Ecce my notes on the sermon. [Dr. Butler's Installation Sermon of 1811, referred to on pp. 66-71.]

*   *   *   *   *

" Page 31. Engine [referring to what Dr. Butler had written about confession]. It became so by abuse. Originally to confess, *i.e.*

---

* By the Rev. Walter Whiter.
† The marriage of Dr. Butler's second daughter, Harriet, to T. J. Lloyd, Esq.

to tell one's misdeeds to an aged worthy person, ask for counsel, and even submit to opposite restrictions (as fasting for gluttonry), is no doubt one of the best remedies, and safest. Do you not teach your children to come and tellen you freely whenever they did amiss? You are the father of your children. Well, from the day you take away the parental and filial connection between priests and laics, you have done away the whole establishment of religion. *Abba, pater, father, papa,* is and was throughout the universe the appropriate, the first name of the priests. Unless I can consider and reverence him as a father, I have no occasion for a priest. *Atqui* to a father I may, nay I ought, to confess my failings. Ergo . . . You, for instance, Dr. Butler—I treat you as my friend and equal : we are about the same age, both of cheerful disposition, and yet be assured that beyond this level intercourse, and behind it, there is still something other of respectfulness in me towards you which cannot and shall not be in you towards me. I am perhaps older than you. I have been furiously thrown about in this world, and so forsooth am not deprived of experience, and yet I would most willingly repair and fly to you, not only for advice, but for admonishment—not only for admonishment, but for correction. And why? Because that you are a priest and I a laic. The next year will probably evince the truth and explain the purport of these words, and old Utis will then become very intelligible.

*   *   *   *   *

" Champagne. Not cheap, faith ; but let Parliament answer for half the price. Here's the proportion : Buying and carrying from Epernay, Champagne, to Calais, 415 francs. 5 francs a bottle on the spot where it grows. But now follows shipping and taxes, 395.21. Consequently nearly as much again.

" If the wine, on tasting it after some rest, prove not exquisitely good, write to me, and you will hear at Shrewsbury the tremendous tempest I shall raise at Epernay.

"Homer with fifty-eight drawings is preparing for his journey to M. Rothschild's, London. *Et iterum munera ? Quoadusque tandem ?* To a thousand I cannot answer one. I only wish you could see me blush like a virgin at fifteen.

"Be tranquil of mind. Robortellus must and shall be yours, though 'tis harder to come at him than at a quadriphyllous trefoil.

" I pity Whiter. A great etymologist—perhaps the greatest that ever lived. A genius certainly ; but it seems, like most eminent artists, dissolute. Ten thousand thanks for your Hamletiana. After such intelligence only, we understand a poet. I entirely agree with you after due rumination. Homer and Shakespeare are the only two poets in the wide world."

FROM DR. WOOD, MASTER OF ST. JOHN'S, CAMBRIDGE.

(Original in Cambridge University College Library.)

"*December 24th,* 1819.

*   *   *   *   *

" Your liberal offer of assistance to such as want and deserve
it I shall certainly bear in mind, as there is no man living in
whose hands I would sooner place a boy than yours."

*   *   *   *   *

TO DR. PARR.

"SHREWSBURY, *January* 25th, 1820.

"DEAR DR. PARR,—After long and very serious consideration of the case in the joint letter I received from yourself and
Dr. Maltby, and after every allowance for the claims of private
friendship and public respect due to you both from me, I find
myself obliged to say that I cannot admit the boy.

*   *   *   *   *

" One more objection, and that of high importance, remains.
From the horror in which the conduct of the boy who stole from
his schoolfellows, whoever he might be, was held, I am convinced
that, except those *furta Laconica* which you and I flog boys for
with a grave face, and inwardly laugh at, or admire for their
intrepidity and spirit of adventure, no meanness of the kind prevails among my boys. Pickle boys rob an orchard, but they
would scorn to steal a shilling. Now is it just to introduce among
them one of a different description? And if anything should
happen, would not parents justly reproach me for the result ?

*   *   *   *   *

" To-morrow we celebrate your birthday. With your present
vigour of mind and body it is reasonable to hope that you may
long be spared to enjoy its recurrence with your friends. God
bless you, my dear Dr. Parr ; accept our kindest united congratulations on its return, and believe me yours very affectionately,
"S. BUTLER."

FROM THE VERY REV. THE DEAN OF HEREFORD.

"DEANERY, HEREFORD, *February* 4th, 1820.

" MY DEAR FRIEND,—I have proof enough that in your com-
mendations of my son Fred you did not flatter me. . . . If
I had the ear of his mathematical master (you can *vellere et
admonere*), I should beg that he would enjoin upon Fred not to
read any proposition of Euclid in the book before it had been
clearly demonstrated to him and the scheme drawn, and no
finished figure as in the book shown him. Thus in the first
term I learned four books of Euclid *vivâ voce,* and thus for

upwards of thirty-six years I taught geometry, and never among my asses did one boggle at the *pons asinorum.* When Charles Luxmoore was superannuated at Eton, I offered the Bishop my services, and his son learned—well, three books of Euclid in a fortnight : from college he soon wrote to his father that by reading he puzzled himself and despaired; but if his tutor would teach him as I had taught him, he and 'the old carpenter' might have jogged on together very lovingly !

"I believe I followed this plan from a sentence of good old Postlethwaite : ' Write, write, sir ; many a man reads without sense and talks nonsense, but few are such fools as to write nonsense !' . . . All a lecturer in mathematics should do or can do is to direct the march of his pupil's intellect; he is no post-horse to carry the lad, but a guide-post to prevent him going out of his road. *Eh bien !* where is my hobby carrying me ?

" I did not examine the tradesmen's bills before this morning. I contented myself, as well I might, with your sum-total, and your P.S. testimonial of ' *bene meruit* '; but lo ! I find a note of thanks, and I think from the pen of dear Mary, date December 15th, for venison, two hares, and three partridges, folded up among the bills. 'Oh,' said Kate, ' I remember them leaving, and that Dr. Butler thanked you in September—and one of the hares I think you intended for Mr. Griffiths.' ' True, Kate, be it so ; the season is well advanced, and I will look out for a puss fit for a classic's *regale*, inasmuch as *sapiens sectabitur annos.*'

"I seem to hear you say, 'I am glad the Dean is in good spirits.' Why, my good friend, as you approached your home on your return from Warwickshire, did you not feel your spirits elated at the prospect of rejoining your family ? And is not the near termination of the long journey of life an object as exhilarating as the near termination of any stage of it ? Do I not hope to rejoin those whom I have loved—with whom I have lived ? With these hopes you will say, ' Vade, vale '; and do not, I beseech you, omit to add, 'Cave ne titubes.' Ever yours most affectionately,   " George Gretton.

" P.S.—Dross of my gratitude, my pecuniary debit, is enclosed. Corrigenda.—In the *mollia tempora fandi*, a man is often well corrected. Therefore at dinner I have been informed of and correct my error. No hare was sent hence to Mr. Griffiths since July last ; therefore both were yours. Nevertheless a gravid hare (if I can beg one) shall, as before said, be sent to Mr. Griffiths. The three partridges (were they salted ?) were sent to you by the rector of Nantwich. Alas ! what a chasm fell on Saturday last between you and my Henry ! From Hereford to Salop, thence to Adderley, and so to Nantwich. My old friend the rector of Adderley, whose regard I possessed during sixty years, from a child on his knee to the *olim meminisse* of our age, died last Saturday. Good as our old King was. If kings have chaplains in heaven, surely the coincident translation of both together from earth would make me, what?—wish that a country parish priest who deserved to be a bishop may be near the person and enjoying the bliss of the best prince who ever exchanged a temporal for an eternal crown."

Dr. Gretton died about three weeks after the foregoing letter was written.

To a Pupil who was Leaving.

"April 3rd, 1820.

" Dear ——,—You judged rightly in supposing that great inconvenience would arise were such communications frequent as that which I received from Gladstone on your departure. And for that reason I should not have replied to it, had I not just received your note enclosing the two guineas for yourself and your brother. As I now send you a reply which you may produce in your own defence if necessary, it would, I think, be inconsistent with the friendship I feel towards you not to answer that communication.

" I give you full credit for the contempt you express for dishonourable boys; and though I have forgotten any particular occurrences * of your earlier years here, I am fully satisfied they were exempt from any acts of meanness. The cause which made me wish your removal was the influence I observed you to have over A——, which he himself acknowledged, and which I perceived was highly prejudicial to him. In fact, I did not think it possible to keep you both, and the relationship between myself and A—— made me prefer letting him return of the two. How far I might have succeeded in keeping you both, had he not gone to India when you returned, I do not know, for I certainly should not have looked over some things, had he been here with you, which while you were here alone I considered of less importance.

" In arranging the places of the boys I never pretend to infallibility. Impartiality is my aim, and that I confidently claim. I decide upon the evidence of their exertions which appears before me. Boys may have much better talents than those above them, and yet lose ground if those talents are not accompanied with proportionate exertion. I have no doubt that, had you chosen to put forth your strength, you would have done much more and have been much higher; but I am not to blame because you were not industrious; nor is a boy to stand so much upon points with

* From an erasure in the draft, it appears that there had been some " particular occurrences " which Dr. Butler had not forgotten.—ED.

his instructors as to fancy himself ill-used when he finds others placed above him whom the master believes to have used more exertions. This, I know, is a common error with boys, which is best unlearned by experience in life.

" I certainly could have wished for your own sake that you had kept more to the spirit than to the letter of your promise ; for I cannot say that your behaviour, though not actually contumacious, has been altogether satisfactory—by your own acknowledgement it was not all it might have been, nor what my own goodwill towards you had led me to expect. Do not understand me to say this as upbraiding you ; my object is to show you why I confine the note which you may produce when necessary to as few words as possible. You know that you were not dismissed, and you know the precautions I took to prevent such a supposition; but you should also bear in mind that where it exists it has probably originated in some rumour about your general conduct here latterly, and especially just previous to your leaving me, and this may help to convince you that it has been injudicious. What you have heard me say sometimes to the boys I may now repeat to you with more probability of your attending to it, which is, that here, as well as at all other public schools, there are plenty of people who have little to do but amuse themselves with prying into the transactions of the master and boys, and magnifying all the faults they find. Nothing is so easy as to find fault, and wherever there are boys there will of course be opportunities of doing so. It is fortunate when these misstatements can be corrected, but this opportunity is not always found. I have thus replied at some length to your parting letter, because I am persuaded the time will come when you will be convinced that the course you latterly adopted here was rather headstrong than becoming, and because, if you are in consequence led to reflect, you may be saved from similar errors in your academical course, where you may perhaps not find similar indulgence. I am your sincere friend and well-wisher,   " S. Butler."

The letter enclosed, that was " to be shown if necessary," ran :—

" Dear ——,—In reply to your note of last night, I have only to say, what is well known to your schoolfellows, that you did not leave me in consequence of a dismissal or any application made on my part to your father, but in consequence of a note from him requesting that I would send you home, in order that you might be equipped to go to college. You are at full liberty to show this note to any person to whom you may think proper to make the communication. I am your sincere friend,

" S. Butler."

From the Rev. S. Tillbrook.

" King's Head, Coventry, June 1st, 1820.

" Without being sent I find myself among the noisy descendants of peeping Tom, and shall be very happy to turn my back upon them to-morrow.   I have just been reconnoitring from my bed-room ; in front of it stand fourteen caravans containing all sorts of beasts of the brute or human kind.   The Devonshire giant is drawn up alongside the Flemish fairy—I know not why, except that οἱ πολλοί may compare great things with small.   The wilder beasts are roaring for their prey, and the rabble for the showman. What a curse to be kept here twenty-four hours among the *feræ naturæ*, without a chance of earning a penny by exhibiting one's own beauties or deformities.   I think, however, that I might have excited popular curiosity as the descendant of a fire-eater whose nose had been likened to a furnace by a certain learned doctor, and which was capable of being converted at will to a fire or candle lighter.

" Talking of fire, I have had a visit from the Poet Laureate * at Peterhouse.   He stayed three days, and I had a dinner in honour of him.   I was glad to find he liked my stock, and swallowed it more greedily than I do his poetry.   He was going to Oxford to meet Lord Hill and the Duke of Wellington—an honorary degree was to be the payment of his travelling expenses.

" But we can talk of this when we meet.   I see no reason why I should not reach your dinner-table by four o'clock on Sunday next.   Bishops travel on Sundays, so I suppose *à fortiori* B.D.'s may do the same.   Have the goodness to send John to bespeak a stall for my horse, and a bed for myself in my old room adjoining the upstairs dining-room at the Raven.   Mind, I do not and cannot think of troubling you for anything but larder and cellar provisions, and as much of your native good-humour as you can spare.   I give you a day or two's warning that you may announce my intended arrival to the Serjeant.   I have letters to a gentleman at Ludlow, and to Mr. Knight for Leintwardine, and long to be at the grayling and trout.   If I am not with you by Sunday, some accident will have happened to me worse than wind or weather."

From the Rev. T. Sheepshanks to Mrs. Butler.

"July 2nd, 1820.

*   *   *   *   *

" I am glad to hear Tom is diligent ; he shall have a week's decent drilling from me at Shrewsbury before the examination, and after that he must trust to good luck and his own brains.

*   *   *   *   *

---

* Southey.

" I have read *The Fortunes of Nigel*—would I had not ! The author seems to me to have taken final leave of his senses, and I trust has or will pay the same compliment to his readers.

*   *   *   *   *

" I can't say I have been very successful in the way of obtaining boys to fill up the vacancies (this being the most interesting subject, I ought to have mentioned it sooner). I had one nibble at Worcester, which I think may possibly catch a gudgeon. I had a bout the other day with an honest gentleman, who wanted a private tutor for his son. I recommended him, of course, to send him to Shrewsbury, where I would (for a consideration, of course) be his private tutor myself. I enlarged, as in duty bound, on the superiority of schools over private tuition, and on the superiority of Shrewsbury over all other schools. He said he wanted his son to have exercise and cleanliness, etc. I observed that we had the Quarry and the Severn—the best walk and river in the kingdom; but I took especial care not to say that the one was out of bounds, and being caught in the other a flogging. He reckoned, however, that he wanted his son to have a little wine—not too much, of course, after his dinner. In order that he might have no excuse for making his son a dunce, I said that a private tutor would take him for £200 per annum, whereas your terms were only forty-six guineas, and offered (what could I do more ?) that for the remaining £151 14s. I would myself take care that he had wine daily, and not too much. Of the quantity necessary I was to be sole judge. This plan altogether he did not approve, so I was obliged to let him go. You see, however, I have spared no efforts. Of Mr. White I know nothing, except that as proproctor he behaved very ill to a friend of mine. If, however, he sends some boys who are acquaintances and private pupils of mine, I will forgive him all his sins. Pray give my best regards to Miss Butler, and Mrs. John Lloyd and Mr. John Lloyd, and Tom and Lizzie, and Mrs. John Lloyd's little baby, and Mrs. John Lloyd's little baby's little finger—in short, to the whole concern.

" Believe me, my dear madam, yours most sincerely,

"T. Sheepshanks."

To a Parent.

"Shrewsbury, *July* 10*th*, 1820.

"Dear Sir,—At the time of the breaking up I learned that an attack was meditated by some boys on your son and some other of his schoolfellows, the result of some party quarrel, in which it is generally most advisable for a master not to interfere, because the disputes of boys are best settled among themselves, and the interference of the master tends to perpetuate ill-will.

On this occasion, however, finding that there was serious and vindictive aggression on one side, and a steady determination to resist it on the other, I felt it my duty to prevent the mischief by separating the contending parties. I have since learned that your son, who appears to have been on the defensive, not the aggressive side, was armed with so deadly a weapon as a loaded pistol. I have therefore to request that you will insist on his most faithfully promising you and me that he will never arm himself with a similar weapon during his continuance under my care, and will give up to you that which he now has.

     *   *   *   *   *

"When two boys quarrel, though battles ought not to be encouraged, perhaps the most desirable thing is that they should settle it between themselves by a trial of mastery, which generally puts a stop to all further squabbles. But no master can either say this or encourage it. I am only giving you my opinion, which is for your private consideration, not for promulgation."

     *   *   *   *   *

CHAPTER XIII.

THE LETTERS TO HENRY BROUGHAM, ESQ., M.P.

Correspondence, September 20th, 1820—December 16th, 1820.—Appointment to the Archdeaconry of Derby.—Correspondence, January 1st, 1821—December 3rd, 1821.

TWO Bills were introduced by Mr. Brougham in the summer of 1820 which threatened to prejudice the interests of almost all future masters of endowed grammar schools throughout the kingdom. The schools of Eton, Westminster, Winchester, Harrow, the Charterhouse, and Rugby were exempted, and as the Bills were not retrospective Dr. Butler was not affected; believing, however, that the Bills would lower the tone of public education, he attacked them (or rather the second of them, dated July 14th, 1820) in two vigorous letters to Mr. Brougham himself, the first of which was published in 1820 and the second in 1821. The first dealt with the effects of the measure on education generally, while the second urged the claims of Shrewsbury to be added to the list of schools excluded from its provisions. Among the objectionable clauses was one empowering those who had the appointment to the mastership of any school to limit the number of boarders which the master might take, or, if they chose, "to forbid altogether the taking, receiving, or entertaining of any such boarders." By another clause the master was liable to be compelled "to teach, either by himself or by an usher or assistant, reading, writing, and accounts," should those who appointed him see fit to

194

so require.   The Bills were abandoned after having been amended in committee.   I need not therefore give any analysis of the arguments advanced in the first of the two letters.

A few extracts from the earlier ordinances for the government of the school (commonly called Ashton's ordinances), and Dr. Butler's synopsis of the course of instruction for the fifth and sixth forms in his own time, comprise all that is of present interest in the second letter.

" 1. Schoolmaster not to frequent alehouses.

" 2. Master's families to quit, on vacancies, within three months.

" 3. Item.   The head schoolmaster's degree of the said school for the time being shall be, at the time of his election, a Master of Arts of two years' standing at the least, well able to make a Latin verse, and learned in the Greek tongue.

" 4. Item.   The second schoolmaster of the said school for the time being shall be, at the time of his election, a Master of Arts at the least, and well able to make a Latin verse, and learned in the Greek tongue, before he be admitted to teach in the said school.

" 5. Item.   The third schoolmaster of the said school for the time being shall be a Bachelor of Arts at the least, and well able to make a Latin verse, and of such sufficient learning as that place requireth, before he be admitted.

     *   *   *   *   *

" 21. Item.   Every Thursday the scholars of the highest form before they go to play shall for exercise declaim and play one act of a comedy, and every Saturday versify, and against Monday morning give up their themes or epistles ; and all other exercises of writing or speaking shall be used in Latin.

     *   *   *   *   *

" 24. Item.   That no scholar shall be admitted into the Free Grammar School before he can write his name with his own hand, and before he can read English perfectly, and have his accidence without (book ?), and can give any case of any number of a noun substantive or adjective, and any person of any number of a verb active or passive, and can make Latin by any of the concords, the Latin words being first given him.

     *   *   *   *   *

" 33. Item.   There shall be read in the same school, for prose, in Latin, Tully, Cæsar's *Commentaries*, Sallust, and Livy ; also two little books of Dialogues drawn out of Tully's *Offices* and

Ludovicus Vives by Mr. Ashton, some time chief schoolmaster
of the said school; for verse, Virgil, Horace, Ovid, and Terence;
for Greek, the Greek Grammar of Clenard, the Greek Testament, *Isocrates ad Demonicum*, or Xenophon's *Cyrus*; and those
authors, or some of them, mentioned in the table for the manner
of teaching to be read in this school,* according to the head-
master's discretion and choice, as shall seem best for the
children's capacities."

*   *   *   *   *

The weekly course of instruction for the fifth and sixth
forms, under Dr. Butler, was as follows :—

Monday.—1. Chapel.   History, Grecian, Roman, English.
Repeat Greek Grammar.
2. Dalzel's *Analecta Majora*, sixth and upper fifth only.
The parts read in this class are Thucydides, Plato,
Greek Orators, Aristotle, Longinus.   Lecture on
Greek Grammar.
3. Cicero's *Orations*.
4. Virgil.   Shell attend.   Chapel.
Tuesday.—1. Chapel.   Repeat Virgil.   Show up Latin theme.
2. Dalzel's *Analecta Majora*.   Parts read are the Greek
plays, Pindar, Theocritus, Callimachus.   Subject for
Latin verses given.   Remainder of Latin themes
shown up.   Half-holiday.   Masters of accomplishments attend.
Wednesday.—1. Chapel.   Tacitus, Demosthenes, Greek play or
Plautus, for sixth and upper fifth ; Pitman's *Excerpta*,
lower fifth ; and repeat Dalzel of Tuesday.
2. Greek play.   Examination of a class of the lower boys.
3. Horace, *Odes*.
4. *Scriptores Romani*.   Chapel.
Thursday.—1. Chapel.   Repeat Horace.   Show up Latin
verses.
2. Homer.   Shell attend.   Lecture in Algebra to sixth
and upper fifth.   Remaining verse exercises shown
up.   Half-holiday as Tuesday.
Friday.—1. Chapel.   Repeat Homer.   Show up lyrics.
2. Juvenal or Horace, the *Satires* and *Epistles*.   Shell
attend.   Show up the remainder of the lyric
exercises.
3. Tacitus, Demosthenes, Greek play or Plautus, to sixth
and upper fifth only.   Lower fifth Pitman.
4. Virgil.   Shell attend.   Chapel.

---

* This table was not in existence in Dr. Butler's time.—ED.

Saturday.—1. Chapel. Repeat Juvenal or Horace. Lecture
in Euclid to sixth and upper fifth.

2. Open lesson, generally English translated into Greek
or Latin prose, or lesson in Greek play. Prepostors
of the week show up Greek verses.

Sunday.—Church in the morning. Chapel in the evening.
Upper boys examined in Watts' *Scripture History*
or Tomline's *Theology.* Lower boys examined in
Catechism.

*Examination for the Sixth and Upper Fifth Forms, commencing
August 7th, 1820.*

Monday.—1. English theme.

2. Latin theme.

3. Greek metres; adjustment and translation into Latin
verse of a Greek chorus.

Tuesday.—1. History.

2. English translated into Latin.

Wednesday.—1. Geography.

2. Euclid.

3. Philology.

Thursday.—1. Latin translated into English.

2. Latin verses.

Friday.—1. English translated into Greek.

2. Greek translated into English.

3. Algebra.

Saturday.—1. Religion.

2. Arrangement of classes. Distribution of prizes.

The questions are all given and answered in writing,
in the presence of the head-master, who never quits
the school during the period of examination, and
each subject takes on an average two hours.

CORRESPONDENCE, SEPTEMBER 20TH, 1820—
DECEMBER 16TH, 1820

TO THE HON. H. G. BENNET, M.P.

"*September 20th,* 1820.

*   *   *   *   *

"Writing to you on a previous occasion I claimed that Shrews-
bury School should be put on at least as favourable a footing as
Eton, Westminster, or any other. I now see that in this Bill
Eton, Westminster and Winchester, Harrow, Charterhouse and
Rugby, are excepted as being public schools. I claim the same

exception for Shrewsbury on that ground also, and I beg to state my reasons.

" If by a public school is meant one to which persons from all parts of the kingdom send their sons for education—and I cannot conceive any other meaning of the term—then I beg leave to say that there is now, and usually have been during my mastership, boys at Shrewsbury School from almost every county in England and Wales, some from Scotland and some from Ireland.

" If reference is made to the extent of the foundations and exhibitions, I beg to say that this foundation is far more extensive than Harrow, and has more numerous and valuable exhibitions than Rugby. For particulars I refer you and Mr. Brougham to Mr. Carlisle's books on endowed schools.

" If to merit, it is tender ground and invidious for me to speak, but there are more prizemen at Cambridge from Shrewsbury School in proportion to numbers than from any other school in England, and more in actual numbers than from any school but Eton and Charterhouse.

" If to numbers, there are now a hundred and fifty-eight boys, and the number is limited for want of room.

" I see no right which any of the excepted schools have to their exception, or to the title of public schools, which does not equally belong to Shrewsbury, and I therefore claim the same exception and the same distinction."

* * * * *

From the Rev. T. S. Hughes.

(In reference to the letter to Henry Brougham, Esq.)

"November 1st, 1820.

" My dear Doctor,—I should have written to you before this on the subject of your letter if I had not known that old Till intended to do so, and had agreed with him in some opinions which he expressed.

" I have the pleasure to tell you that I never knew a thing so well received ; the observation of all who read it is that the arguments and statements are quite unanswerable. I have lent my copy to go round a large circuit of houses. I have introduced the subject in all quarters, and have found no dissentient opinion. I only heard one person say that he thought one or two of the remarks were a little too caustic."

* * * * *

From W. H. Butler, Esq., of the Stone House, Kenilworth.

" Kenilworth, November 5th, 1820.

* * * * *

" We have not experienced any disturbance here or at Warwick since you left us, and the electioneering goes on smoothly.

The only incident I heard of yesterday was that one of Mr. Spooner's friends from Coventry being over-fatigued by his exertions, and unwilling to walk home, proceeded at dusk to the Saltisford Common with a string formed as a bridle, caught a horse, and rode away briskly through the outskirts of Warwick towards the Coventry road. But the animal became restive and set off full-speed into the town, making a dead stop at the bridewell door. The keeper, being accidentally on the outside, recognised his own horse, called the turnkey, and had both horse and rider immediately secured."

FROM THE RIGHT HON. J. C. VILLIERS, M.P. (AFTERWARDS EARL OF CLARENDON).

"EUSTON, *November 7th*, 1820.

*　　　*　　　*　　　*　　　*

"I must recur to what I mentioned in my former letter,* and I only do so for the further credit of your school—you may depend upon the fact that the principle of tuition by the boys is with success carried to a greater extent than is thought of in any other classical school; and you may rely upon its general utility to the scholars upon the testimony of so competent and great an authority as the eminent Etonian whom I mentioned, and whose testimony has satisfied me upon the subject."

*　　　*　　　*　　　*　　　*

FROM BULKELEY WILLIAMS, ESQ. (A FORMER PUPIL).

"MAGDALENE COLLEGE, *December 3rd*, 1820.

"REVEREND SIR,—It is with considerable concern that I inform you that I am again refused a scholarship on Dr. Millington's foundation. I am the more disappointed as Mr. Crawley held out great hopes of success to me, expressing himself satisfied with my performance at the examination. He gave me a paper of questions, and said that if the answers to them were not satisfactory he would give me another such paper. The first answers, however, seemed sufficient, as he gave no more questions. Upon this I began to feel sure of success, but some time after he informed me that he had written to the Master on the subject, and observed that he was afraid I could not have the Millington Scholarship, but that I should have some other; his last account, however, informs me that I can have none at all. As he really thought me deserving of a scholarship, I am at a loss to conjecture why the Master should give a different decision, who, being at his living in Flintshire, can have no idea of the result of the examina-

---

* I did not find the letter referred to among Dr. Butler's papers. —ED.

tion, but from the account he has received from Mr. Crawley. Bray is also deprived of his scholarship, being rusticated for a very slight offence without been convened, and merely not having an opportunity of saying anything in his defence. I trust that this will not appear irrelevant to the subject, as there seems to appear in it a wish on the part of the College to have as many scholarships as possible vacant. Shall I under these circumstances beg the favour of that advice which you have so kindly offered me? I should wish to change my College (and should prefer Peterhouse to all others here); in this step however I shall be happy to be ruled by you.

" I am, Reverend Sir,

"Your most obedient and grateful pupil,

" BULKELEY WILLIAMS.

" P.S.—A line to my father on the subject would be thankfully received by him."

FROM THE REV. P. WILLIAMS.

" BEAUMARIS, *December* 16*th*, 1820.

" DEAR SIR,—I have received a letter from Mr. Crawley since I troubled you before about my son Bulkeley regretting that he had not been able to recommend his election into the scholarship on Dr. Millington's foundation, and, after paying him some compliments on his regular conduct in College, says ' that by some unaccountable means he has left school so exceedingly ill-informed as to the first principles of grammar, that I have found it absolutely impossible to support his pretensions without violating that duty which I owe to the College and that respect for the institutions of the founder which I conceive ought in all such cases to be the primary consideration.'

" Mr. Crawley had Bulkeley before him some time after the examination, and told him in direct terms he must not expect the exhibition, and Mr. Neville has written to the same effect to Lord Bulkeley: we must therefore give it up, but my son is so much mortified and disappointed, and conceives himself so much ill-treated, that I cannot prevail on him to remain at Magdalene. He is very ready and willing to go to any other College at Cambridge you may recommend, to which Lord Bulkeley has also consented, and his Lordship agrees with me that my son has been ill-used and deceived. Bulkeley has intimated a wish to go to Peterhouse, but as I am not competent to judge what is best now to be done with him, I shall be exceedingly thankful to you for your friendly advice on this occasion, and be so good as to let me hear from you soon, so that I may write to Bulkeley, who remains at College during the Christmas recess, to arrange his plans for his removal and to have the benefit of the terms he has kept.

"My son John has just arrived at home, and was sorry he could not contrive to stop at Shrewsbury and call upon you, but I find he has no means of judging of the examination of his brother, who has kept no copy of the papers he brought up to Mr. Crawley. Upon the whole I fear nothing can now be done but to remove poor Bulkeley from a College where the sons of great men only are encouraged, under the government of the Tutor as well as the Master. I hope you will excuse my troubling you on this occasion, and remain, with our united and best regards to Mrs. Butler, yourself, and family, dear Sir,

"Your obliged and faithful servant,

"P. WILLIAMS."

Dr. Butler does not appear to have kept any drafts of the answers which it may be taken as certain that he wrote to both the foregoing letters, probably because the letters reached him just at the end of the half-year, which is always a busy time.

Early in 1821 Dr. Butler was appointed by Lord Cornwallis, then Bishop of Lichfield and Coventry, to the Archdeaconry of Derby, which office he held till he was himself appointed to the See of Lichfield and Coventry on the death of Bishop Ryder.

CORRESPONDENCE, JANUARY IST, 1821—DECEMBER 3RD, 1821.

FROM BARON MERIAN.

"*January 1st*, 1821.

"DEAR SIR,—Pray where is that verse of Homer in which a person is commended (or blamed) for being very expert in swearing? I believe and am almost sure the verb ὁρκίζειν is in that verse. The sense of the line is equal to those where a man is quoted for being a good runner, a wise judge, a rich farmer. I have asked two Greek professors here, but they could not tell me. I am, however, quite certain of the existence of such a Homeric verse."

●   ●   ●   *   ●

The passage referred to is in *Odyssey*, xix. 392, etc., where Autolycus is mentioned as singularly expert at thieving and false-swearing.

Dr. Butler sent the required reference, and on March 9th, 1821, the Baron wrote, "The verse of Homer is *ipsissimus*: now I shall beat my French doctors."

To an Old Pupil.

"SHREWSBURY, *March 5th*, 1821.

"DEAR BRAY,—We have examined the decree under which you hold your exhibition, and can find no power given to the Master and Fellows to deprive you of it. All that appears is that, if you do not keep the greater part of each term, you forfeit for the first offence one-half the exhibition for that year, and for the second offence the exhibition is made vacant. The utmost penalty, therefore, which you have incurred is the loss of one-half your exhibition for the present year, and if you keep the present and next terms you ought certainly to have the other half. If the Master and Mr. Crawley have declared your exhibition vacant, your remedy lies in an appeal to the visitor.

"It is true that the visitor is the Master's father; but still, were I you, I would appeal to him: you cannot be worse off by so doing; you may be better off; and you will either obtain justice, or subject the visitor to the same suspicion of partiality as the Master and Mr. Crawley now labour under. Some legal advice is necessary on making the appeal, and I think you should first consult your father on the subject and then apply to some respectable lawyer at Cambridge. By all means go to some one who ranks high in the profession, and not to an understrapper. He will draw out your appeal, which cannot cost you much, and if you succeed it will be a great triumph for you. When you have consulted your father, which I wish you to do without delay, write to me upon the subject. If your father consents to your appealing, I presume the first step you have to take will be to call on Mr. Crawley with your lawyer, ask him whether your exhibition is declared vacant, and demand a decisive answer. If he says No, then you have no need to appeal. If he says Yes, then tell him you shall appeal to the visitor. In all this I give you my advice as a friend, not as a trustee: it is my own opinion unconnected with the trustees, and they are not responsible for it. Nor will it be in their power or mine to allow you anything from the trust funds towards the expense of the appeal, whatever it may be. Of course I write all this to you confidentially, and do not wish to be mentioned in the College or to any one but your father as having given any advice in the matter, though I shall always be ready enough to avow my opinion of Mr. C—— when called upon."

FROM THE REV. S. TILLBROOK.

"HUSTLER'S ROOMS, JESUS COLLEGE, *May 6th*, 1821.

"MY DEAR DOCTOR,—Since I wrote to you some days or even weeks have elapsed, yet I have heard no tidings of your convalescence. Pray write to tell me you are well again, and mean to keep so. My Easter was spent mainly in Hampshire—trouts and fishing-rods the order of the day. There are some glorious streams in the neighbourhood of Andover and Stockbridge, and I mean to have a legal right over their inhabitants as soon as any of the piscatorial liberties are offered for hire.

"By-the-bye, Mr. Madox and Colonel Leighton, as I understand, have hired the fishery of Llyn Ogwyn. What is now to become of me? Unless I can carry on the war I may as well keep out of Wales, and remain free from the contaminating influences of envy and covetousness; for though Gwyned and Tally Llyn be very good reservoirs, yet Ogwyn is far the best of the three. When you see Mr. Madox, present my *angular* and *circular* compliments to him, *i.e.* come round him if you can. My present intention is to be in Wales during August, and to return to Salop at the beginning of September, so as to give the grayling a benefit at Leintwardine.

"Ask Mr. Madox if he be acquainted with the new fly called 'the coachman'; it is much used in Hants, and, as I suppose, took its name from whipping—its wings are white, body red hackle and peacock neck [?], hook middle size. I know you love these minutiæ. I could tell of some other peculiarities, and promise to let you into the *arcana*, provided always that you reward me accordingly. You do indeed know some of the best baits for a fisherman, and sauces for his fish; but as I have already put you into a stew, I will leave you there for the present to fatten with any odd fish you may chance to fall in with. It is ten to one but he or some one of his connections will know me and my haunts and otter-like propensities.

*   *   *   *   *

"I have tried to get you some dotterel, but have been at present unsuccessful; but I do not despair, and think they will be of use to your inner man. If I can do anything for you here, pray let me. And I promise not to bore you again about fishing till we find ourselves at least at the riverside, or in the middle of it, as I was last week in Hertfordshire, when I was properly *duck'd* in consequence of a *green drake*. Good-night."

The letter to which the following is an answer was sent

by the boys without Dr. Butler's knowledge: see letter to Sir B. Bloomfield, December 1821 :—

FROM WELD FORESTER, ESQ.

(Original in possession of Mrs. G. L. Bridges and Miss Butler.)

"SACKVILLE STREET, *June 18th,* [1821 ?].

" Mr. Weld Forester presents his compliments to the gentlemen at Shrewsbury School, and begs to assure them that, should his Majesty come to Willey on his way to Ireland, he will with pleasure state their request, and communicate the King's answer to Dr. Butler, but at the same time begs to acquaint them that at present his Majesty's intentions are to go to Ireland by sea.

"TO THE HEAD BOY OF THE FREE SCHOOL, SHREWSBURY."

FROM THE REV. REGINALD HEBER, AFTERWARDS BISHOP OF CALCUTTA.

(Original in possession of Mrs. G. L. Bridges and Miss Butler.)

"*July 27th,* [1821].

" DEAR SIR,—I feel I am taking a great liberty with you, but I trust that the anxiety I naturally feel for the success of my brother in his present contest for the University of Oxford may be my apology for thus intruding to request your friendly interest in his favour with any of your pupils who have votes for Oxford. Great as is the number of the distinguished scholars whom you have sent to your own University, I am well aware that ours is also beholden to you for many, and I know too well the affection and respect with which all your pupils regard you in after-life not to be convinced that your good word (should you think fit to exert it in favour of my brother) must be of very considerable service to him. At all events, in a contest which ought at all events to be swayed by opinion, and success in which has generally had some reference to literary reputation, it will be a material encouragement and comfort to us, whichever way the struggle is decided, to believe that we have the good wishes of Dr. Butler. I arrived in Shrewsbury too late to call on you this evening, and must set out again for town to-morrow at six, which must plead my excuse for this hasty note.

"A letter will reach me at any time during the next fortnight at 18, Charles Street, St. James's."

FROM LORD SPENCER.

"PLYMOUTH DOCKS, *August 5th,* 1821.

" DEAR SIR,—I received your letter of the 31st of July just as I was setting off from the Isle of Wight to come to this place by sea, and I now take the earliest opportunity of thanking you for it, as well as for your former one of July 3rd, which I postponed acknowledging till I judged you were returned to Shrewsbury from your northern excursion ; and I should have written to you in a few days even if I had not again heard from you. I have to return you very sincere thanks for your description of the Greek Testament of 1638, which I have no doubt must be an edition of considerable rarity, notwithstanding the low price assigned to it by Brunet. I am pretty sure that I have not a copy of this edition, but I am unwilling to deprive you of it, as it is so well calculated to hold a place on the shelves of a scholar and a divine. However, if you are not unwilling to transfer it to my collection, which is already rich in editions of the Scriptures, perhaps you will allow me to propose to you in exchange some Aldine edition of which you may be in want, and of which I have several that are duplicates, besides those which were sold at my late sale, most of which, as I am informed, have been purchased for you, which induces me to suppose that you are collecting that class of books : if this proposal should suit you, I will take measures for sending you a list of such as I may have for your selection, and shall be very happy to find that I can offer you anything you may want in return for your very obliging offer to give me up this Testament.

"I am well aware (though I never saw it) of the existence of the copy of Walton's Polyglott with Castellani's Lexicon on L. P. in the library of Shrewsbury School. It is very seldom that the Lexicon is to be found with the Polyglott in that state, and I myself know but of two other such copies—namely, that in the British Museum, which was a presentation copy to Charles II., and that in the library of St. Paul's Cathedral, which was a presentation copy to James II. when Duke of York. I have a copy, which I bought at Paris, which wants the Lexicon, and there is another similar one in our late King's private library at Buckingham House : there is also one in the royal library at Paris equally defective. I should be glad to know whether the Shrewsbury copy has the dedication to the King, as also whether in the preface it has the original paragraph acknowledging the remission of the paper duty by the Protector, or that paragraph as it was corrected after the Restoration, in which the Protector's title is omitted. My copy is of the latter description."

*   *   *   *   *

The letter of August (?), 1821, to an assistant master has been already given in the introductory chapter.

A copy of a letter *re* the alterations made by the committee in the inscription written by Dr. Butler for the monument to his ever most affectionately remembered master Dr. James now in Rugby Chapel, with the inscription as originally written by Dr. Butler and again as it stands at present, will be found in the British Museum among Dr. Butler's papers under date October 5th, 1821. The original is at Rugby School.

FROM A PAPER HEADED " STATEMENT OF S—— E——'S BEHAVIOUR."

" October 31st, 1821.

*   *   *   *   *

" A preposter is one of the first eight boys to whom the master delegates a certain share of authority, in whom he reposes confidence, and whose business it is to keep the boys in order, to prevent all kinds of mischief and impropriety, and to give up the names of offenders to Dr. Butler, either when called upon by him, or without such requisition as often as they see cause."

The spelling of the word " prepostor " occasions me some uneasiness. I believe it is usually spelt either " pre-" or " præ-postors," but Dr. Kennedy used always to write " præpositors," while Dr. Butler, generally if not always, in his drafts, wrote " preposters." In his printed papers I see he spells it " prepostors."

Stoves, it seems, were only beginning to find their way into churches, and that not without opposition.

TO THE REV. H. SIMS.

"Tonstall, Derbyshire, October 31st, 1821.

" REV. SIR,—I beg to acknowledge the favour of your letter yesterday. Having in my charge recommended the adoption of stoves in churches, you may be sure I can have no objection to the use of them ; but as I do not infer from your letter that the stove in your church, though generally acceptable, was approved by the vote of a parish meeting, it would, I think, save much trouble and uneasiness were you to adopt this measure now, which appears to me the most ready and indeed regular way of proceeding. If it is approved by the majority of your parishioners in vestry, I trust all altercation and dispute on the matter will be at an end; if rejected, you would, I presume, hardly wish to persevere in a measure which is not acceptable to the greater part of your parishioners."

*   *   *   *   *

The charge above referred to does not appear to have been published. There is no copy in the British Museum, nor have I found it among Dr. Butler's private collection of his published charges and sermons, nor yet among his MSS.

FROM MISS MONEY.

"*November* 13*th,* 1821.

"As you are one of the gifted persons who know everything (either by inspiration or industry), so it is very fair you should pay the penalty of being wiser, wittier, and cleverer than your neighbours by submitting to have the knowledge you possess plucked out of you. As I scorn little insidious ways, I shall, John Bull fashion, bolt my battering-ram in your face at once; and if the matter I am in pursuit of is in you, I have no doubt of its flying out at the first fire. A friend of ours has got a coin of which he cannot obtain any authentic knowledge, and therefore he concludes it to be scarce. It is a gold angel of James II., of very pure ore, and in perfect condition. It is the size of a half-guinea, now weighs one pennyweight and six grains, and has a hole drilled at the top, by which it seems to have been worn as a charm. One side represents St. Michael and the Dragon, with the inscription 'SOLI DEO GLORIA,' or 'Soli Deo Gloria,' for I have not patience to write the characters properly; the other side has a ship in full sail, and in the same characters 'Jaco II. D: G: M: Brit: et . Hi: Rex.' When this piece was coined is a doubt. Ruding does not allow there was a coinage of gold angels in England after Charles, I think; but these letters are particularly clear and unworn. If you can throw any light on this momentous question, I shall feel obliged; and if you can point out any book where the little gentleman is depicted, still more so: the numismatists here are all at fault.

"It is so long since we heard from you, and I am sure the fault does not lie on my side, though I do not insinuate where I think it does. I scarcely know what inquiries to make. You may have had a half-dozen children and a dozen grandchildren—buried one wife and married another—bought an estate and built a conventicle—turned Methodist, or accompanied the King to Hanover —or, what is much more likely, like the poor little innocent mouse, 'have set fire to your tail, and burnt down your house'—in fact I do not know how the world has wagged with you at all."

On inquiry at the coin-room of the British Museum,

I learn that the coin above described was one of those struck specially for touching persons afflicted with " the king's evil."

FROM BARON MERIAN.

"*November*, 1821.

*   *   *   *   *

" Have you received the *Tripartitum* from M. Nicholls, Cambridge? They are now come to the manifest apprehension that there is and ever was but one language in this world, and that whatever we call tongues, idioms, dialects, etc., are nothing else but forms and modifications (by time and distance) of the said universal language, which, as H. Grotius says, *nullibi est integrum sed ubique sparsum.* And you will own that this way of considering the matter not only perfectly agrees with Scripture, but is the sole one which does so. For if you admit different springs of language, you must admit different Adams. Now, *ex opposito*, if one Adam has been sufficient to procreate in the course of centuries the Englishman and the Negro, I should like to know why one type of oration might not have spread and branched out successively into those numerous lingoes we perceive to-day.

" But say you, Very well, *a priori sed, quæritur a posteriori ;* where is the resemblance? Where are the lineaments, the family features, the analogy, between the Samojed's and the Welshman's chatter?

" It is everywhere, my dear friend; it is most striking, most irrefragable, not resting upon reasoning and *atqui ergo*, but upon plain palpable facts, numberless instances, and an indivisible thorough concatenation. Vide the *Tripartitum* and its 2nd and 3rd vols., which comprehend the Orient.

*   *   *   *   *

" I gave Mr. H[ughes] a book and map for you you'll not dislike—the Geography of the Greek Prepositions.

*   *   *   *   *

" Consummate scholars like Dr. Parr cannot relish this mode; it is too different from what they have learnt and taught for many years with applause. It throws together what they carefully distinguish ; it is only a base and foundation, and they are busy about the top and ornaments."

TO SIR B. BLOOMFIELD.

"*December 3rd*, 1821.

" Dr. Butler presents his compliments to Sir B. Bloomfield, and begs to say that he was not aware that the boys of Shrewsbury School had presumed to petition his Majesty.

" Dr. Butler will be most happy to testify his duty to his Majesty by obedience to his Majesty's commands, but he humbly begs leave to state that the vacations at Shrewsbury School are already long ; and that if he were allowed to divide the fortnight between the Christmas and summer vacations, it would be attended with less disadvantage to the boys, and indeed with much more convenience to himself, as it would give him an additional week for a journey to the Continent next summer. If Dr. Butler hears nothing to the contrary from Sir B. Bloomfield, he will adopt this arrangement at the ensuing vacation."

CHAPTER XIV.

UNIVERSITY REFORM.

Two Pamphlets signed "Eubulus."—Correspondence, January 30th, 1822—June 16th, 1822.

EARLY in 1822, when the movement in favour of establishing a Classical Tripos at Cambridge was gathering to a head, Dr. Butler, writing under the pseudonym of "Eubulus," published a pamphlet entitled *Thoughts on the Present System of Academic Education in the University of Cambridge.** So strictly did he preserve his incognito that he did not confide the secret even to his most intimate friends resident in Cambridge, Tillbrook, Hughes, and R. W. Evans. The only persons whom he appears to have taken into his confidence were Baron Merian, James Tate of Richmond, and Francis Hodgson.

Moreover, he adopted a *ruse* on this occasion which shows him to have been particularly anxious to conceal his identity. He invariably spells "judgement" as it should be spelt, *i.e.* with an *e* in the middle of the word. He would as soon have written "enlargment" as "judgment"; in this pamphlet, however, he has allowed "judgment" to stand, no doubt as believing that no one who saw the word thus spelt would dream of suspecting him to be the author. This anxiety to escape detection shows that the writer knew himself to be writing treasonably; he must have

---

* Longmans, 1822,

known that what he was saying about mathematics applied quite as forcibly to classics; and that if his principles were once admitted, they could end in nothing but in the system of modern sides, and of·other practical reforms, the progress of which, though rapid in these last years, leaves still room for development. Indeed, from several of Baron Merian's letters, it appears that Dr. Butler intended to pursue the subject of University reform as far and as fast as prudence would allow; and probably he would have done so had he not ere long undertaken the conduct of the School lawsuit, of which I will say more later.

It was no doubt because Monk scented its want of finality that he was so bitter against Dr. Butler's pamphlet. What Dr. Butler meant to convey was that the education of his time was too like the horny tip which an embryo chicken grows to its beak in order to break through its shell, and then throws away. The foremost classical teacher then living in this country could hardly be expected to disparage openly the system which it was his duty to adopt. I have heard the late Canon W. G. Humphry say, " Dr. Butler certainly did succeed in making us believe that Latin and Greek were the one thing worth living for." It was his business to do this, but he would never have succeeded as he did if he had appeared as the author of a pamphlet the scepticism of which was so transparent. Hence no doubt the, for him, very unusual reserve he manifested on this occasion.

The following extracts may suffice to show the drift of the pamphlet :—

" On an average for the last three years a hundred and forty-six men enter the senate-house annually at the usual degree time.

" Of these fifty-two obtain honours, of whom nineteen are wranglers or proficients in mathematics, nineteen are senior optimés or second-rate mathematicians, and fourteen junior optimés or smatterers.

" What are the remaining ninety-four? What have they to
show for an education of three years and a quarter, at an expense
which cannot be short of £700? What have they got in religion,
ethics, metaphysics, history, classics, jurisprudence? Who can
tell? For except the short examination of one day in Locke,
Paley, and Butler in the senate-house, the University must be
supposed to know nothing of their progress in these things.
Their University examination for their degree is in mathematics;
and if they have got four books of Euclid (or even less), can do
a sum in arithmetic, and solve a simple equation, they are deemed
qualified for their degree—that is to say, the University pro-
nounces this a sufficient progress, after three years and a quarter
of study.

" So much for the πολλοί, the *vulgus ignobile* of the mathematical students, among whom I include what are commonly
called gulph men—that is, men who can answer and will not, and
who are therefore entitled to no distinction in the view now taken
of an University examination.

" Let us look back to those distinguished with academic honours.

" Of the junior optimés, do any bring their reading in mathematics to after-use?

" Of the senior optimés, do any two in each year keep up and
pursue their mathematical learning, so as to make farther proficiency in it after they have taken their degree?

" Of the wranglers, do many of the lower wranglers, and all or
nearly all the higher, pursue their mathematical studies farther
than to qualify for fellowship examination, which at some colleges,
as at Trinity, for example, are partly mathematical? In fact, do
more than two-thirds of the wranglers pursue their mathematical
studies after they have taken their degrees?

" If they do not, then all the fruits of the three years and a
quarter of study, and all the expenses of a hundred and forty-six
men, amounting to above £100,000 (which, indeed, a juster
computation would reckon as £136,000), are concentrated, as far
as any literary benefit results from them, in about twelve or
fifteen individuals.

" Of these I cannot be supposed to speak or think disrespect-
fully, when I ask, Of what use to them are their mathematics,
without the walls of the University, in common life?

" How many Cambridge mathematicians distinguish themselves
by bringing their mathematics to bear upon the useful arts?

" Is it true that they, generally speaking, turn their mathematics
to any account, except that of speculative amusement or academic
contention?

" They may be, and no doubt often are, very ingenious and
acute men; but does that ingenuity and acuteness tell, for the
most part, to any great moral, political, or social purpose?

" Are not, in fact, the greater number of calculations and

combinations by which mathematics are brought to bear upon the arts made by men who have not received an academic education ?

"Are not practical mathematics the great source of useful inventions? and are not the Cambridge mathematics almost exclusively speculative?

"Take a junior or senior optimé, or even a wrangler, into an irregular field with a common land-surveyor, and ask them severally to measure it ; which will do it soonest and best?

"Let one of each of these academic graduates and a practical sailor be sailing towards an unknown coast; which will soonest make a correct observation ?

"Build a bridge across the Thames ; who will do it best—Mr. Rennie, or a committee of Senior Wranglers?

"If it should happen that in these cases the practical mathematicians would have the advantage, may it not be said that our mathematics are more for show than use?

"It may be urged that we point out the principle, and leave the practice to others.   This may be very true ; but I believe the laugh would be a good deal against the speculative academic who was beaten by the practical clown ; and though I admit that ridicule is no test of truth, there would in this case be a good deal of reason on its side.   I can see no grounds for neglecting practice because we understand theory ; and if we profess to make mathematics our prime pursuit, surely we should comprehend not their principles only but their application.

"Enough of this.   Let me be permitted to make a few observations on the examination itself, especially that which respects the higher class of honours.

"Ever since the days of Samson, riddles have been thought a great test of the acuteness of the human mind.   Samson puzzled the Philistines, the Sphinx puzzled the Thebans, and the Queen of Sheba tried to puzzle Solomon.   It is in conformity with this custom, in which sacred and profane histories alike concur, that the examiners still propose riddles to their examinants.

"What is the greater part of that examination but a set of mathematical conundrums, in which each examiner tries to display his ingenuity by quibbling subtleties, by little niceties and knackeries and tricks of the art, which are for the most part exceedingly clever and exceedingly unprofitable, and which bear a close, I may say a very close, affinity to those hair-breadth theological and metaphysical distinctions, which baffled, and perplexed, and expended in the most abstruse and idle speculations, the intellectual faculties of schoolmen and Aristotelians in the middle ages?

"Alas! all their labours are now considered but idle paradoxes and waste of pains.   What will future ages say of our own?

"But there is one melancholy fact. It is a certain sign of incipient decay in any people when their refinements begin to be excessive. As soon as the true and legitimate standard of taste and judgment either in morals or science is exceeded, it is even more difficult to retrograde towards perfection than it was before to ascend to it. It is hard indeed to save ourselves when, having climbed up the mountain on one side, we have begun to topple down the precipice on the other.

"There is another point well deserving our consideration, on which I have not yet touched. Suppose mathematics not to be the exclusive branch of academic examination in this University, would there be any deficiency of great and eminent mathematicians? I cannot conceive that, were a fair and due degree of honour given to mathematical pursuits without an exclusive preference, there would be any want of persons sufficiently inclined to cultivate and excel in them. I do not know and do not believe that, in the days of Barrow, Newton, and Cotes, the same exclusive attention was paid to mathematics as at the present time, nor do I conceive that any modern names can be disgraced by a comparison with these. The same stimulus which was then sufficient to produce a Newton would always operate to produce one, although there were no exclusive preference given to mathematics and no exclusive rewards.

"A university is a society of students in all and every of the liberal arts and sciences. How, then, can that society deserve the name which confines its studies almost exclusively to one? This exclusive preference militates against the very spirit of our institution, and certainly damps the ardour and cramps the genius of many a man who might excel in classical or metaphysical pursuits, by compelling him to adopt a course of study for which he has neither talent nor inclination, but in which he is compelled to delve and toil if he wishes to attain any academic reward.

*   *   *   *   *

"In truth it is known and acknowledged that the severity of the senate-house examination, and the dryness of mathematical pursuits, induces many men after one or two years' trial, or even more, and after having with infinite toil and labour made some progress on their cheerless way, to abandon all competition for mathematical honours, and content themselves with barely getting their degree.

"Of what use are all their studies to them? It may be said that they have only themselves to blame, and that they might and should have persevered; this is true in the abstract, but, like many theories, fails in the application.

"With human beings allowance must be made for human failings and human imperfections; and if the mind sinks under the load that is laid upon it, they who lay that load are themselves not exempt from blame.

"What then do I advise? The relinquishment of mathematical pursuits? By no means. I would give equal honour, nay, concede all that can be fairly conceded, to long-established habits and prejudices; I would give precedence to mathematical studies, but not exclusive privileges and rewards. *Nec nihil, neque omnia.* I would give a large and liberal share of honours and rewards to classical studies, not only in the distribution of classical prizes at present existing by the benefaction of various founders, but in the senate-house examination, and in the classification of academic degrees.

*   *   *   *   *

"I must add a few words on the classical examination. It would of course comprise not merely the construing Greek and Latin, but a variety of questions connected with the passages selected, and depending on history, antiquities, chronology, geography, metrical and philological criticism, and ancient philosophy. And this leads me to a remark which will perhaps be unpalatable to some of our distinguished scholars, but which truth compels me not to omit. I mean that our range of Greek reading is at present too much confined. We labour about the dramatic writers too much to the exclusion of the rest. We weary ourselves with adjusting iambics and trochaics and anapæsts, and twisting monostrophics into chorusses and dochmiacs, and almost seem to neglect the sense for the sound. I do not mean to disparage these labours, which are sometimes learned and often ingenious, but I wish merely to hint that, if these things are good, there are also better things than these. We must not forsake the critics, philosophers, orators, and historians of Greece for a mere branch of her poets; and I say without risk of contradiction from the most able and competent judges that Plato, Aristotle, Xenophon, Thucydides, Polybius, and Demosthenes afford more improvement to the taste, more exercise for reflection, more dignity to the conceptions and enlargement to the understanding of the student, than all the Greek tragedies that were ever penned. Not that I affect to slight the noble monuments of the Grecian Muse left us in the works of her dramatists, but I underprize them in comparison of the mighty names I have enumerated, and think too much is sacrificed to them if these are neglected in consequence."

*   *   *   *   *

Dr. Butler's pamphlet was at once followed by another in the form of a letter to the Bishop of Bristol by a writer signing himself "Philograntus," and dated February 1st,

1822. In a contemptuous and angry postscript the writer, who evidently did not guess who " Eubulus " was, attacked him with great asperity. Dr. Butler knew Monk, then Dean of Peterborough, to be the author ; the two were fighting on the same side, and he was displeased that Monk of all people should attack him. He rejoined fiercely in *A Letter to Philograntus by Eubulus.**

At this time Dr. Butler was incensed with Monk about another matter which need not be gone into here. This, in fact, was the date of the second serious estrangement between the two men. There is not a syllable in Dr. Butler's rejoinder that refers directly or indirectly to anything except the matter in hand, but I do not doubt that Dr. Butler's attitude was more hostile than it would otherwise have been for the reason above hinted at. He dedicates his reply to Monk himself in a pointedly sarcastic preface. The cause of Dr. Butler's displeasure was ere long happily removed, and from that time forward I find no want of harmony between the two men.

CORRESPONDENCE, JANUARY 30TH, 1822—JUNE 16TH, 1822.

FROM BARON MERIAN (AFTER PRAISING " EUBULUS ").

"*January 30th*, 1822.

*　　　*　　　*　　　*　　　*

" Let me make one observation. What you Englishmen tell now we foreigners told twenty years ago. Not one traveller who has visited Cambridge but sighed, ' It is not an University (or ' a University '—is it ' an' or ' a ' ?) ; it is an (or ' a ' ?) Euclidity."

*　　　*　　　*　　　*　　　*

To a Parent.

"*March 8th*, 1822.

" DEAR SIR,—I have had a great deal of uneasiness about your

---

* Longmans, March 1822.

son this evening, and am induced to send a purpose messenger requesting that you will come over. The circumstances are these : I had particularly desired the masters in the large school, in order to preserve silence and attention there, to send down to me for punishment any boys who were noisy. I had also warned the boys in the school of this, and told them that when sent down they would be flogged. Mr. Sheepshanks sent your son down this morning for making a disturbance ; but as I had had some correspondence with you about him in the holidays, I thought I would treat him with marked indulgence, and I desired him to bring me his Homer to set him a punishment. He told me that Mr. Sheepshanks had already set him sixty lines of Virgil, whereupon I let him go.

"This evening two more boys were sent down by Mr. Sheepshanks for being noisy, and he at the same time inquired whether I had received your son's name this morning. On my informing him that I had, and that I had let him go, in consequence of his having a punishment already, Mr. Sheepshanks informed me that he sent him down because after the punishment had been set he again struck the boy he had before been striking. This so completely altered the state of the case that I felt bound in justice to the two boys then sent for punishment, and in order to support the authority of the master, to send for your son, and tell him that circumstances were so much altered that I could not avoid punishing him. His reply was that he could not submit to punishment, as he was not guilty. I requested him to consider of the matter, but in vain. I warned him that I had no alternative when a boy refused to be punished but to expel him, and I begged him to reconsider the matter and weigh the consequences. Still he persisted in his refusal. Determined, however, to give him every chance, I have had him in my study, and have been arguing the matter with him in every point of view—I am sorry to say without success. I have, however, brought him to acknowledge this : First, that it is essential for me to maintain my authority as a master, and that I have no alternative but expulsion if a boy will not submit. Secondly, I have got him to state the grounds of his refusal, which are these : He says he did not strike the boy, nor indeed mean to strike him, and that therefore, if he submits to be flogged, he shall acknowledge himself guilty when he is innocent, and by so doing shall sink in the estimation of many of his schoolfellows. I have endeavoured for more than an hour in vain to make him understand that this is a point of romantic boyish punctilio ; that his schoolfellows are not to decide what boys the master is and what he is not to punish ; and that if he is punished unjustly, as he calls it, the fault is the master's, not his. I have got him to acknowledge more than this. He admits that, though he did not strike the boy, he put out his hand with an intention of laying it on his head ; that the boy withdrew his head, thinking he meant to strike him ; and that the master, who saw his hand put out, and saw the boy withdraw his head, could have no means of judging what his intentions were, except from appearances ; and that if the master, having first given him a puni-hment for making a disturbance, saw him apparently recommencing that disturbance, and submitted to that apparent defiance of his authority without acquainting me, it would be impossible to preserve discipline and authority. That therefore, though his intention might be innocent, the master's conduct was not unjust.

" Having allowed all this, one might be puzzled to conceive how he could any longer hesitate to submit ; but still he does, though I have exhausted every argument I could think of on the subject. As his resistance appeared to arise from foolish punctiliousness on this head, I shifted the ground, and told him that had he been ten times innocent that part of the question was gone by from the moment he said he would not submit ; that it then became a question whether I or the boys were to govern ; and that after his public defiance of my authority it was essential for me to punish him. He still reverted to the original question, and replied that after all it would be said he was punished for that which he did not do. At last I moved him so far as to say he did not like to rely on his own judgement altogether, but did not know how he could avoid it. I then told him, if that was the case, instead of expelling him at once, I would send for you, and that he should have the benefit of your advice, by which he said he would be entirely guided. I have therefore despatched a messenger to you with this, requesting your attendance as soon as possible.

" I presume I need hardly observe to you that, if boys are to decide when and how they are to be punished, or to be guided by the suggestions of their schoolfellows instead of the authority of the master, all discipline will be at an end, and that in every well-regulated school in the kingdom there can be no alternative between submission and removal. Your son I have no doubt will tell you how exceedingly averse I am to punish when it can be avoided, though perfectly inflexible when it is necessary, and I am quite sure will have the candour to acknowledge that, although I consider his submission indispensable in the present instance, not for his own sake only, but for the support of discipline and example, I have sought to avert the unhappy alternative by every means in my power.

" I remain, dear Sir, yours faithfully,

"S. BUTLER."

From the Rev. T. S. Hughes.

"Cambridge, *April 16th*, 1822.

*   *   ·   *   *   *

"How go on agricultural distress with you? I expect we shall have no dividend this year. Farms are thrown upon our hands, and the Bursar is become a kind of journeyman bailiff. In spite of all this great improvements are projected, and I really believe, if you delay much your next visit to Cambridge, you will find King's new buildings, Bennet College, and the Museum all begun in the great range of Trumpington Street, and the Observatory complete. I hope you approve of our new examinations, which passed the Senate last term. Perhaps you will think that enough is not demanded; but if more had been asked, we should have gained nothing. In all these cases I believe it is best to begin gently, and to add as necessity may demand. The next step to be taken is a reformation of the examination of the οἱ πολλοί for the A.B. degree, and this will very soon be brought into discussion.

"I suppose you are by this time beginning your arrangements for your summer excursion. As I am sure to be in England, you will not forget that I shall feel most happy in taking your school for as long a time as you please at the beginning of the ensuing half-year. I see no reason why you should not for once take 'a free and lofty range'; you must not go again into Italy without seeing Rome and Pompeii."

*   *   *   *   *

It was intended that Dr. Butler should prolong his holiday until the end of September 1822, and that T. S. Hughes should take his place during the first two months of the ensuing half-year. In that case he would have visited Greece as well as Italy. Hughes, however, was so seriously unwell in June that he was ordered absolute rest, and the plan had to be abandoned.

To the Rev. T. S. Hughes.

(First sheet of this letter not found.—Ed.)

"The Odes and Essays are supposed to be decided by the Vice-Chancellor.

"The University Scholarships by the Regius, *Hebrew*, Greek, *Law*, *Physic*, and *Divinity* Professors, and the Public Orator.

"The Medals by the V.C., the Masters of St. John's, Trinity

Provost of King's, Peterhouse, Clare, Christ's, the senior resident Medallist of Trinity, Public Orator, Greek Professor, and Professor of *Modern History*.

" Now all these may be very fit men for their respective situations; but by no means, with the exception of those not underlined, does it follow that they are fit or likely to be fit as classical examiners. They may be so now, but hereafter may not. To have these examinations efficient, there should be five examiners appointed by the Senate and paid. It should be a *sine quâ non* that all of these should be or have been either University Scholars, Senior Medallists, or at the very least Second Medallists and Bell Scholars.

" It may be said that the examiners are in some cases appointed by will, and therefore cannot be altered: that difficulty might be got over by calling these five examiners deputies to the present examiners, or assessors.

" If it be objected that the V.C. is thus not sufficiently considered, I would appoint six examiners, and in all cases of equality give the V.C. the casting vote. This would suffice *pro dignitate officii.*

" The style of the examinations should be changed. A Greek play, Greek historian, Greek orator, Greek philosopher, and Greek poet not dramatic should be subjects for five separate papers. A Latin historian, poet, Cicero, should be the subjects of three more papers ; Latin theme, Latin verse (an original subject, not a translation), translation from English to Latin prose, translation from English to Greek verse or prose, for four more papers. There should also be a paper of philological questions in Greek, another in Latin, and a paper of historical or geographical questions. These make fifteen papers, or three from each examiner.

" The verses ought always to be long and short. It is a farce to examine in any other. None but these show a man's resources. Sometimes a translation might be required instead of an original copy.

" This would be a severe but effectual examination. I defy the devil himself to succeed in this by good luck.

" Now for some of the disgraceful Anglicisms sent forth to the world as Latin in the shape of odes.

" First of all, the nature of the ode is generally misunderstood. The odes are all too long. There is a want of mythology, allusions, philosophical reflections, and that transition from the subject to the inculcation of some great moral sentiment which is so great a charm in Horace.

" Then want of imagination, want of phraseology, and that singular pedantic and contemptible machinery in the Greek odes which consists in stringing together a set of phrases from different writers and different periods—Pindar, the Tragedians, Homer,

Theocritus, and fragments of the lyric poets gleaned by the help of *indices*—and calling this a Greek ode. Sir Thomas Browne was considered a great ass in his day by all his sensible contemporaries, but his having founded a medal for a Sapphic ode, of which we have such very scanty specimens, would have sufficed to prove him so without any corroboration. We want a prize for Latin hexameters, and much more for Latin longs and shorts, and then we should be complete. Any additional prize would be too much. After all, Latin verse and much more Greek verse are but ornaments and elegancies. Latin prose—Ciceronian prose—clear, luminous, correct, chastened prose, is the sterling ore; it is this that stamps the scholar, and that will come into play in after-life, and mark the man.

"What are we to think of such expressions as the following? I take them at random as I open the pages: *Jura Libertatis* for *justam libertatem—mundumque pacatum futuros—deseruit minitans furores—malignæ victima gloriæ—seditio improborum virûm—o qui sceptra nostro nobilitate tenes amore—te tuorum procerum cohors cingens triumphante ordine—aurea vox cantus.* All these occur in the ode for 1820. *Tranquilla libertatis arva—horas lætitiæ—timores, implacidos animi tyrannos—vernantis ævi in limine flores—singultu frequenti luctûs—latronum victima—Hymen corollam texerat uvidam non imbre verno sed lachrymis,* etc. *Venti effræna noctis numina turbidæ*—and almost all the rest of this and the subsequent stanza—*ostendit undantem Oceanum jubar redux diei—amoris soliciti resides querelas—amorem gentis inhospitæ—nutus tyrannorum terrificus—fœdus hospitii et amoris*—the whole stanza '*o nata*,' etc.—*dolor sparserat canitiem inter capillos aureos—Rosas marcentes genarum*—the whole stanza '*Vos, quæ*,' etc., and the next, *invidiæ venenum.* All these occur in 1821.

"I meant to have taken 1822, but cannot find it—some Greek odes and essays; but I find that two odes in which I have not noticed one-half the faults have exhausted my paper—this specimen may serve. There is nothing in style, phraseology, thought, or construction like Horace. They are writings *sui generis*—Browniads, or what you will.

"Lawson told me that the Provost of King's, then V.C., adjudging the medal to a Browniad against a very good classical ode of his which I saw, assigned as a reason that his ode had not got *the Eton roll*/// If you do not use this letter, show it to Dr. Blomfield and Mr. Dobree; but I hope you will use it. When I say 'use it,' I do not mean that you should copy these phrases or instances, but they serve as a specimen of what I mean. I have not seen the ode for 1822, but suppose it is like the rest."

The foregoing letter was probably written, like the two

pamphlets signed " Eubulus," with the view of effecting still further modifications in Cambridge examinations over and above those which had passed the Senate, May 30th, 1822. It probably should be dated either at the beginning of June 1822, shortly after the publication of the Odes, or not till August or September of the same year, after the holidays were over.

From Baron Merian.

" May 11*th* (?), 1822.

"Dear Sir,—A letter for Milan, one for Florence, and one or two for Rome are ready. May you come soon, stay long, depart late, return quick !

"I congratulate you most sincerely on the success of ' Eubulus ' (your true and appropriate name). There you have again done a great thing. Do not forget, I beseech you, to bring me the several writings *pro* and *con*, and your last year's charge too ; and if you hit, by the way, on some American vocabularies (old or new, but of the indigenous chat), place them, pray, between your half-a-dozen of shirts and black silk breeches. I shall ever be very glad to hear of the thrivation of your wise and benevolent plan, and, let me add, most necessary, if rulers and compasses are not definitely intended to become surrogates for extensive and liberal learning, and the deep-mouthed precepts of scansion to eliminate the understanding of the meaning of the author, and its application to private and public practical use. Never drop that important matter till you have brought it to perfection and execution. You are in the right, and therefore you must succeed, and will succeed, in spite of all monks and friars whatsoever.

*   *   *   *   *

" If the Catholic question step backwards, you will allow me to say that reason, justice, policy, and gospel step backwards too. The foes of Britain will rejoice to find her know so little of the savour of the present day. You wrote a word I could not read : ' B—— will *rat* soon.' "

*   *   *   *   *

From the Rev. James Tate.

"Richmond, Yorkshire, *May* 22*nd*, 1822.

*   *   *   *   *

" A thousand thanks for the present of your ' little book of maps.' It is exactly what I have been sighing for during the last twenty years of my life. We are all of us your debtors, but the masters of schools yet more than the pupils. The young rogues are now without the shadow of an excuse for ignorance in geography : one could not say so before."

* * * * *

The foregoing refers to the Ancient Atlas just published by Dr. Butler. The Modern maps had been published in 1813.

FROM THE REV. HENRY DRURY.

(Original in the Harrow School Library.)

"HARROW, *May 29th,* 1822.

"MY DEAR SIR,—Never was a warmer letter penned by the hand of man than yours to me, and I should do ill, in return for it, if I could go and read your books and drink your wine in your absence. No, I must wait till you have recrossed the Ponte Molle, and then I hope we can have about us at Shrewsbury some of our ancient and mutual friends—Hughes, Heber, and Hodgson.

"Satisfaction and joy to you on your tour. 'Twere much to say how I envy. I got one stage on the Roman road towards Florence, but the rebellion then existing in two Papal cities, Forli and Benevento, and still more the formidable accounts which reached us daily of the malaria, put all my pedantry to flight, and sent me across the Mediterranean to Genoa. But then my endeavour to see Rome was in the '*grave Autunno.*' Beware the Lungara, and return to yours full of life and spirits."

FROM THE REV. T. S. HUGHES.

"CAMBRIDGE, *May 31st,* 1822.

* * * * *

"I am going to Peterborough to-morrow with a German professor named Miller, who has been quartered on me some days past—indeed for the last month past I have been daily devoured by lions, and if I stay here much longer shall die no other death. Poor Clarke actually did die of it. The new examinations passed the Senate yesterday, one for altering that at the B.A. degree to a more respectable footing, and the second a classical tripos for all who have taken honours after degree. These do not supersede the Little-go, which passed last term ; so we are now in a state to defy the censures of the world.

"By-the-bye, let me not forget to request you to leave out the books that may be wanted by me when the school opens, and a written paper of directions in full. Let me beseech you not to hurry home—stay as long as you like—and I promise to do my utmost in keeping up the credit of Shrewsbury School in your absence. Remember that you may possibly never have another opportunity of seeing Rome and Pompeii, the two greatest lions in the world except Athens and Jerusalem.

"I shall write to Walter Whiter from Peterborough, and will send him your message. We are all in hot water here. The heads wish to nominate to the Mineralogical Professorship, and have tried to do it by stratagem. The M.A.'s are all up in arms, and we shall possibly bring it into the proper Court of Trial."

*   *   *   *   *

FROM MISS MONEY.

"LINCOLN, *June* 16*th*, 1822.

"What a glorious thing it is, when a letter has remained long unanswered, to have a specific subject ready to begin scribbling upon! Such is my fortunate case. So have at you, Doctor! Only think of my having seen Mrs. Monk! Ye gods, how we did talk! If the top of your right ear swelled, inflamed, looked glossy, and burnt intolerably on the 17th of last May, it was not St. Anthony's fire I pronounce, but it was the fire of our tongues perpetually hissing round your devoted head. Well, it was a real pleasure to meet a person who knew you all, and to find her so unaltered— as good-humoured and merry as ever, not quite so pretty perhaps, but who is, after nine years' wear and tear, and a love affair into the bargain, which of itself adds ten years' wrinkles to every twelve months of human existence? Bachelors and old maids whose fates are decreed have much the best of it. But people never know when they are well off. We are all born with a natural inclination to burn our fingers, though we don't much like the succeeding smart. Those soul-physics so much recommended by the pious are more wholesome than palatable.

"But to return to the cloisters. Our Monks had starving weather during their visit, so that Mrs. Monk saw Lincoln to every dis-advantage, but all those who saw her were pleased. He was very polite and gracious. But powder is sadly unbecoming to his personal charms. We agreed you were very tiresome not to put yourself into the little shoe, and walk down to us last Christmas. I do believe we never shall catch you by the leg, although in the winter we could supply you with preference to your heart's content; the old gentleman will tell you dismal tales of age and infirmities, and sit up night after night dealing, and calling, and shuffling, and throwing up till after twelve o'clock as merry as a grig. I always consider preference as a sort of dram-drinking—the more you play the more you want to play; though the noses do not actually turn red, the senses are somewhat muddled at times. We are all as

well as three months' north-east wind allows us to be.   Mr. St.
Barbe, who leaves us for the commencement if he is well enough,
is the greatest sufferer ; he has been very indifferent all his visit,
and is a mere shadow to behold.   If we have another cold summer,
I will migrate to Lapland.   With kind regards to Mrs. and Miss
Butler."

The Mrs. Monk referred to in the preceding letter was
sister to the Rev. T. S. Hughes, and a frequent visitor to
Dr. and Mrs. Butler, with whom she was a great favourite.
Her husband had some months earlier resigned the Greek
Professorship at Cambridge, on his appointment to the
Deanery of Peterborough, which he exchanged in 1830 for
the Bishopric of Gloucester.

CHAPTER XV.

VISIT TO ROME.

Third Foreign Tour.—Correspondence, August 12th, 1822—November 30th, 1822.—Praxis on the Latin Prepositions.

THOUGH unable to be absent for so long a time as he had hoped, Dr. Butler was still not baulked of seeing Rome altogether, and spent a fortnight there during the seven weeks' summer holidays of 1822. The following extracts are taken from a transcript of his letters made by his elder daughter, and now in the British Museum. I only found one page of the original letters.

"*June 12th*, 1822.—Left Dover and embarked in the *Dasher* steam-packet for Calais ; but the roughness of the sea not allowing the vessel to get into that harbour, we put in at Boulogne, after a passage of three hours and five minutes.

"*June 13th.*—Arrived at Paris after a most fatiguing journey in a diligence with five very disagreeable dirty French people, and found most comfortable apartments provided for me at Meurice's hotel by my friend the Baron, who had also engaged an exceedingly good and nearly new carriage, and one of the most agreeable intelligent servants I ever met with. From what I have seen of Paris, it appears much changed since I was here last, several new streets having been built. I drove to the Bois de Boulogne from the Champs Elysées, and dined there capitally ; among other good things, we had a fine brace of partridges, no game laws existing here as to the time of killing them.

        *   *   *   *   *

"*Milan, June 24th.*—A great change appears in Milan since I was last here ; every shop is shut [during church time—ED.] with even Presbyterian strictness, and I cannot be allowed so much as to go to the top of the Cathedral or to see the body of S. Carlo in the splendid chapel beneath the high altar. But by a singular contrast to the general strictness, the first thing after service in the Cathedral is a drive to the Corso, and the next to the opera.

*   *   *   *   *

"*Rome, June* 29*th.*—At three o'clock yesterday morning I left Radicofani, which is situated on a hill about as high as Cader Idris, and did not get to Viterbo till three [?], having found the mountains much more tedious than I expected. From thence I was obliged to drive most furiously for seventy miles, in order to get to Rome before the dangers of the Campagna are at their height. I caught a glimpse of the Immortal City about a mile and a half above Baccano—that is, I had seen the cross and the cupola of St. Peter's, and the city bearing away to the left. I then closed all the avenues to the air to avoid the *mal'aria.* On reaching the Ponte Molle, and finding by the sound of the wheels that we were going over a bridge (which I knew could be no other) two miles from Rome, I threw open the windows of my *calèche*, knowing all danger was over, and saw on my right hand St. Peter's one blaze of light. This being one of the greatest festivals of the Romish Church, the eve of St. Peter's is kept as well as the day.

*   *   *   *   *

"At five this morning, June 30th, I rose and got into my carriage with a very intelligent guide. I drove first to the Capitol, and ascended its tower. I could not contemplate from this spot, which commands all the monuments of Antient Rome, without feeling very strong sensations ; in short, I could not refrain from an actual gush of tears. I stood on the Capitol : on my left was the site of the Temple of Jupiter Capitolinus," etc., etc.

*   *   *   *   *

"At half-past ten I drove to St. Peter's to grand mass—that is to say, to the most imposing ceremonies of the Catholic Church in the most august temple in the world. . . . I must not omit a circumstance which had a ludicrous and almost profane effect. Just after the cardinals had descended the steps of the high altar, and were preparing to accompany the Pope * up them again previous to the consecration of the mass, two dogs came and sat down on the very seats their eminences had just quitted, and I was really in pain for the gravity of the procession when it returned. I thought they would have flown at one of the cardinals who shook his robe at them.

*   *   *   *   *

"The Church of S. Giovanni in Laterano . . . contains many highly interesting antiquities, and many that are not a little comical. Among the latter, as I was a favoured visitor, I saw among the reliques the very table upon which our Saviour celebrated the Last Supper, which is large enough in the present

---

* On this occasion represented by one of the cardinals.—ED,

times to hold four people, so that the world cannot have degenerated so much as some people suppose : one corner of this table is
decayed—they say that Judas sat there, and the place where his
elbow leaned is become corrupted. . . . I have seen a thousand
such fooleries ; but the better class of people appear wholly to
disregard them, and I never saw any but the most squalid and
miserable objects pay them attention."

  *   *   *   *   *

The following passage goes far to explain why Mr.
Philip Browne's eyes twinkled when he was asked if Dr.
Butler knew anything about the art of painting :—

" I have seen an immense number of fine paintings, as well as
all the *capi d'opera*, which seem to me to have a faded appearance.
Beautiful indeed they are, but they all seem past their prime.
They will, however, be preserved in the freshest beauty in the
mosaics of St. Peter's, which are eminently beautiful in themselves, and will be highly interesting when their originals, with
which they will bear the strictest investigation, are no more."

This can only be surpassed, if indeed it is surpassed, by
Dr. Arnold's taking the *terra-cotta* figures of the Varese
chapels for waxworks, and mistaking an Assumption of the
Virgin (to whose ascending figure the eyes of all present
are directed) for a visit of the Apostles to the tomb of
Christ.*

"The people in the ecclesiastical states are certainly more
wretched and dirty, and probably more unprincipled, than in any
of the northern states. I believe every third person one meets
is ready to be an assassin. The look of lurking malignity, which
arises indeed from poverty and oppression, is not to be mistaken.
  *   *   *   *   *

" Amid all these ruins and trophies of ancient grandeur not a

---

* The passage runs : " In one of these chapels, looking in through the
window, we saw that it was full of waxen figures as large as life,
representing the Apostles on the Day of Pentecost ; and in another
there was the sepulchre hewn out of the rock, and the Apostles coming,
as on the morning of the Resurrection, ' to see the place where Jesus
lay.' I confess these waxen figures seemed to me anything but absurd ;
from the solemnity of the place altogether, and from the goodness of
the execution, I looked on them with no disposition to laugh or to
criticise " (Stanley's *Life of Arnold*, 1844, Vol. II., pp. 367, 368).

sound was heard, nor a human being, except the sentinel at the gate of the Colosseum, could be seen. The moon fell upon the foundations of the palaces of the Cæsars and the cottage of Romulus, upon the temples of the greatest people in the world, and on the humble shrine of their founder: all was buried in the same repose. A gulf seems to separate antient and modern Rome; yet turn but a corner, and you find yourself once more in a city whose temples and palaces, unrivalled for grandeur, for number and magnificence, for the precious works of art which they contain, and for the splendour with which they are still decorated, proclaim her to be imperial and immortal. Rome is the only city in the world which has survived every change, every convulsion, every calamity, and which may therefore so far deserve the epithet of 'eternal.'

  *   *   *   *   *

"I then (July 4th) drove through a very extensive wood of antient olives (the site of Tibur) to the modern town of Tivoli, which is of considerable extent, and beyond all comparison the filthiest and most horribly disgusting specimen of an Italian town I have ever seen: the inn, however, is pretty fair. . . . I tasted the wines of Tibur, but they have greatly degenerated since the days of my friend Horace. I returned partly by day and partly by moonlight. The heavens were red-hot, and the wind blows like a flame.

  *   *   *   *   *

"*July 6th.*—I went at six this evening to the Quirinal to see the Pope * take his airing, and had an excellent view, being rather less than two yards from him. He seems excessively feeble, bent almost double, and quite unfit to be dragged out of his apartment. Indeed he is so ill that this day for the first time he came through the gardens of the Quirinal instead of the usual way, being unable to bear the fatigue of going downstairs. His carriage, drawn by four black horses, proceeded only at a foot's pace, and I followed in mine about eighty yards' distant to see the people great and small; and those who were in carriages got out and knelt in the dust. The Pope was dressed in light buff-coloured clothes; his hair is grey, but not white: he is eighty-six years of age. I went about a mile and a half to watch this procession.

  *   *   *   *   *

"*July 9th.*—From Arezzo to Florence is but little more than forty miles, but I took more than twelve hours to perform it without losing an instant. It is a succession of ups and downs, and yet I am at a loss to conceive how I could have been from two in the afternoon till half-past two in the morning about it."

Pius VII., who was succeeded in the following year by Leo XII.

Dr. Butler continued his journey to Pisa, Lucca, and Massa, intending to go on to Genoa by the coast road from Lerici to Genoa.   On arriving there, he found that he could not proceed.   He therefore returned to Pisa.

"*Pisa, Saturday evening, July* 13*th.*—I am safe and well, but am obliged to retrace all my steps.   By to-morrow morning I hope to reach Florence once more, from whence I shall in one hour commence my journey homewards.

"The case is, that a storm which happened the night before last has utterly destroyed fourteen miles of the road to Genoa just made, so that for six months it will be impassable ; and when I got my carriage embarked at Lerici in order to proceed by sea, which was as clear and as smooth as a looking glass, an accidental, or I may rather say providential, delay in signing my bill of health of Genoa saved me from a sudden hurricane that must have been fatal if I had been out at sea.   The captain of the felucca refused to go (but he got my money), and I find these sudden hurricanes are very frequent at this season on this coast.   I have now renounced all intention of going by sea, or of going to Genoa at all ; and owing to this adventure, I have taken in vain a journey of two hundred and fifty miles at an expense of £30, and the loss of four good days."

It seems, then, that there were three violent storms within a few days of one another.   From the foregoing passage the most violent appears to have been, not the one that occurred on the 8th, in which Shelley lost his life, nor that of the day on which Dr. Butler was writing, but an intermediate one on the 11th ; for it is not likely that he is confusing the 8th and the 11th.   He must have perfectly well known of the disaster which had been fatal to Shelley ; but Shelley's body was not found till the 22nd : it was not yet therefore absolutely certain that he had not been picked up and saved.   Dr. Butler would naturally say nothing about what had happened, for fear of alarming his wife and daughters ; but it is curious that there should be no reference in a very long letter from the Hon. W. Hill (dated Genoa, August 12th, 1822, and dealing almost entirely with the real or supposed effects of the storms in question) to an event which is now held as epoch-making in the literary annals of the century.

" *Bologna, July* 16*th*.—After a long, harassing, and fruitless journey from Pisa to Florence, my carriage broke down at the gates of the latter place, and it cost me a day to repair it. I set off last night to cross the Apennines ; and though the road is good, yet it took me sixteen hours to accomplish fifty miles.

* * * *

" *Wednesday, July* 17*th*.—Thank God! after many difficulties and never having had my clothes off once but to change them since Saturday, I am now arrived safe at Turin, tolerably well, but fatigued and heated to death. I have now done with the dangers of banditti and malaria. . . . I am just going to the ramparts to take an evening view. I shall then go to bed for six hours, an immense indulgence which I have not had anything like since I left Rome—nor indeed ever more than that there, having been in bed at ten and up at four regularly. It is surprising with how little sleep (for I do not sleep half the time I am in bed) a man may live in a hot country. I believe what has kept me alive and well is the tepid bath—which I always feel a great relief from fatigue.

* * * * *

" *Paris.*—I am just arrived here safe and well, and have sent immediately for my letters. My disappointment is extreme ; I have not heard from England once since I left it. I hope to be at Shrewsbury on Tuesday the 30th."

CORRESPONDENCE, AUGUST 12TH, 1822—NOVEMBER 30TH, 1822.

FROM THE HON. W. HILL.

"GENOA, *August* 12*th*, 1822.

" MY DEAR FRIEND,—I had been rather unwell before you fixed your time for being with me, when I worked day and night to prepare some despatches for your conveyance, that I might have the entire enjoyment of your society for the few hours you meant to give me. My labours and anxiety of mind at your non-arrival affected my health deeply, and I am now but just crawled out of my bed, to which or my room I have been confined ever since. Not having tasted food for twelve days consecutively, during the progress of my illness, and having been nourished by broth and jellies only, I am still in such a state of weakness that I scarcely know how I shall get through this letter. Thanks to an English physician lately settled here, oceans of bark, and diminution of heat, I recover a little strength daily, and the first use I make of it is to express my regret, and (may I add without reproach after all your own sufferings ?) my astonishment at our curious misfortunes. When three or four days had elapsed after the latest time fixed, I turned to my nephew and said despondingly that I could not guess what had happened, but that I gave you up. He laughed and said, What were two or three days' delay to a traveller ? I acknowledged in every other case he might be right, but he did not know Dr. Butler or his engagements, and that I was sure you would be punctual if health permitted. Among my conjectures I expressed my fears that you had been induced by some felucca rascals to abandon the road for their own interest, but Noel, who likes the sea, would hear nothing against the sailors.

"I had prepared a passport for you to go 'en courrier' with despatches for the British Government, which, without obliging you to go faster than you pleased (and you might have slept every night on the road), would have given you innumerable advantages between this place and Paris, where you would have left the letters with Charles Vaughan or carried them on as you liked. You would have had the right to pass every other carriage, to be served first with horses, exemption from every search of baggage and stoppage whatever ! ! ! For this I hoped to have screwed out of you another day, if not two; and as it was, you had better have given me six days than have turned back from Lerici, except to go to the Spezia, and so on to Genoa by land or even waited for the wind. I can easily conceive the fidget you must have been in, but a moment's reflection must have convinced you that I would not have recommended that road upon light grounds, in spite of the foolish information of Prince Engarin [?]. Prince Leopold's sister went over that road in the winter; Lord and Lady Bradford in April or May ; Lord Clare went from my house to see his old schoolfellow Lord Byron at Pisa, and returned and dined with me again, carrying letters for me to Paris ; the Prussian envoy's wife and daughters, and innumerable persons you do not know by name, were going and coming every day. It is true Lord William Russell, who was living with me when I expected you, told me that the road-makers, where reparations are wanting, like to be tipped for moving machines and carts out of the way when a carriage passes, but this is all. Lord William prefers a felucca—a strange taste, like Noel, and the wind had been east and south-east for two months consecutively, as it frequently is at this time of year, and perfectly fair from Lerici. It might have been too boisterous the day you were there, but twelve hours would have settled it, and perhaps it was so only in the Gulph, or not at all, but some rascality of the felucca-men, who wished to go to some fête, when they had secured your carriage, and found you frightened about the road. If your bargain was written and made in a proper manner I could make the rascal vomit up all your money. You may guess how painful it was to learn your adventure and determination when every day before and every day after numerous feluccas arrived under my windows, bringing different passengers, some of my acquaintances, some with letters of recommendation, etc. Last year, at the very time you arrived, I passed twice myself before the road was finished, but where there was no carriage road there was an excellent horse road, and delightful mules and horses, for about two hours only. As Noel preferred the sea I gave him my carriage baggage and a servant, and went with Mr. Hamilton and one servant in a carriage of the country from Spezia, except where we rode. I remember the innkeeper at Massa telling me I could not cross some torrents. I never saw them, at least the water. You had better have remained two or three days at Lerici than have done what you did, or sent an estafette to me, or threatened the rascally felucca-man with complaint to me. It is but seven or eight hours with a fair wind, but you might have landed at Sestri —in four, five, or six, according to its state.

"You could not certainly know what arrangements I had prepared for you here, but there was one thing above all which must have struck you with your road book in your hand continually, and your different calculations, if your agitation and anxiety had not blinded you. I am an old resident of the country, and must have known (as I dare say you have) that Alexandria is but nine hours from this place. If I had not been certain of my fact, and that it was an immense saving to you to avoid the dreadful hills of Bologna, I would have advised your coming from thence and returning, particularly as you had preceded your time, and indeed you might have turned long before you got to Alexandria. I go through that place five or six times every year, and the waiters there are my oldest friends, by which means I got your letter the next morning. As I had by that time given you up, it gave me no disappointment, but relieved me as to any anxiety for your personal safety. My first impression was to send my despatches after you, but I must have been too late, as you would have even left Turin. My illness made such rapid progress I could not even direct a purpose messenger with them for some time to Paris. For the want of two or three hours' sober reflection or inquiry, you have missed seeing a beautiful country, a singular and beautiful city adorned with the finest palaces in Italy and many fine pictures, of which you have seen enough; but what is worse, you have hurried, fatigued, and vexed yourself to death, and lost much precious time and your health and money to avoid seeing them. We have both suffered sufficiently, so God bless you, and pray believe me to be yours always truly and affectionately,

                                                        "W. H."

FROM THE REV. WALTER WHITER.

"CAMBRIDGE, *August* 13*th*, 1822.

"DEAR SIR,—I must express to you my best acknowledgements for the trouble which you have had in conveying to me the literary packet from your friend Baron Merian. The packet arrived safe on Sunday last at this place, where I have now taken up my abode for a few months.

*   *   *   *   *

"Let me take this occasion to express what I think on the support you have given to the *Etymologicum Universale.** It appears to me that your zeal in the cause has introduced the work to the Continent, and I shall always be prompt to declare this opinion. In our own country these studies are not cultivated, and it would perhaps be difficult to discover in what pursuits our literature consists. Yet there are some men in our country of the genuine stamp, whose scholarship is of the highest order, and who read and meditate with unceasing diligence, urged by no other motives than those which the love of literature supplies. I have been fortunate enough to obtain the favourable opinion of some men who do honour to this order of scholars, and I rejoice at the occasion which the present letter affords me of expressing to you with acknowledgements of my gratitude what I feel on this subject.

"Your friend Baron Merian is full of zeal in the cause of good letters, and ardent to proclaim and to applaud what he conceives to be well and diligently performed for the advancement of truth. To you, sir, I owe this auxiliary who is at once so able and so willing to promote the cause which he espouses. I have looked over the little pamphlet on language by the Russian [Gulianow], and agree with you that it savours of mysticism. You say that the author and the French Institute are at loggerheads on the subject. I tremble for a subject when the loggerheads of Institutes, Academies, etc., etc., have taken it under their care or jurisdiction, either as athletes or arbiters.

*   *   *   *   *

"I have no copy of this work [the *Etymologicum Magnum*†] here, nor do I know where a copy is to be had. Poor Billy Lunn told me that when the price of this book in one volume was reduced to its fourth part—five shillings—and became an inhabitant of the stalls about London, the copies suddenly disappeared, and came into the possession of those ambulating readers who hang about the stalls in the capital—a powerful, numerous, contemplative body of stu·dents, of more weight, as I am told, in deciding the final fate of books, than the greedy collectors of libraries are disposed to imagine.

"So unknown is the *Etym. Univ.* in this country that Todd,

---

* Cambridge, 1822—1825, 3 vols., 4to.—ED.
† Cambridge, 1800, Part I. (no more published).—ED.

the editor of Johnson's dictionary (whom I know a little), a
regular bookman, seems to be ignorant that such a work exists.
He quotes always, as I believe, the former work—*Etym. Mag.*
The traffic of literature, as it reigns at present in our own country,
is, I am informed, alike potent and active in its sway.   Whether
it executes its province of publishing, or exerts its propensities to
conceal—not to be enrolled in some band of literary conscripts is
to suffer the penalties of proscription, and to be banished from
their roll of fame."

Memo in Dr. Butler's First Letter-Book.

" August 17th, 1822.

   " Went to Harwood with Mr. Sheepshanks and told him that
I had strictly forbidden the boys to hire boats, and that if any
accident happened in consequence of his letting them have boats
after warning, the blame would rest with him, and that he was
hereby most earnestly requested by me not to let them.   He
replied that he kept his boats for hire, and should let them whenever desired to do so.   Upon this I called on the Mayor with
Mr. Sheepshanks, and was promised by the Mayor that he would
see Harwood this evening, and inform him that if he did so in
defiance of this warning, the law should lay hold on him."

There had been no boating at Rugby, and Dr. Butler
was afraid of the boys getting drowned ; hence a pro-
hibition which was for some years a fertile source of
trouble, and in connection with which my good old friend
and tutor the late Rev. Richard Shilleto once told me the
following story.   Dr. Butler was reprimanding the boys
about the boating, and spoke with a slight hesitancy, which
Mr. Shilleto told me was habitual with him when pre-
tending to be more angry than he really was.   " If the
men," he said, "will let the boys have boats, I will have
them up before the magistrates."

   As these words fell gradually from the Doctor's lips,
Shilleto wrote on a scrap of paper :—

> " Quando velint homines pueris conducere cymbas,
>   Ante magistratus Butler habebit eos."

Having done so, he slid them on to Dr. Butler's desk.

" Psha, boy, psha," was all the answer made him ; " but,"
said Mr. Shilleto, " the Doctor folded the paper carefully
up and put it in his pocket. I knew 'conducere' was
wrong, but it was the nearest thing I could get at the
moment, and I have never been able to set it right since
without spoiling the whole thing : so it must stand."

From the Rev. Authority Norman.

" Brailsford, *August* 26*th*, 1822.

" Rev. Sir,—I think it my duty to inform you that a practice
which prevails in this part of the country of deteriorating the
Church property under the guise of repairing it has now reached
this parish. Since I mentioned to you at Derby the condition
of my church, it has been determined to repair the roof after the
practice of which I speak, by taking away the lead and covering
it with slate. The old lead I am told will sell for sixty pounds,
and the cost of the slate will be about twenty—and these repairs
are only over the aisle. The roof of the church body will soon
require to be repaired, and the lead which covers it will sell for
upwards of a hundred pounds.

" At the vestry meeting, where this measure was proposed, I
stated my opinion of its illegality, and begged that no such step
might be taken without Mr. Mott's advice. I was answered that
it must be done 'under the rose,' and that I need not to
notice it, as other clergymen had not ; and it was held out to
me that I should have a vestry built if there was money to spare.
Since that time it is determined without a public meeting to
pursue this plan. Yesterday the churchwarden informed me of
it, and I think it imperative upon me to make you acquainted
with it. But should you in consequence deem it proper to
pursue any measure, may I beg that the source of your information be not named, as it would certainly be followed by every
vexation and hostility to me, with which the troubles of the present
day are so familiar ?

*   *   *   *   *

" I named the promise of building a vestry, as I also spoke
to you concerning one. My house is distant half a mile from
the church, and I often have to walk through the wet grass,
but the personal inconvenience is not so much to be regretted
as the consequent loss of official dignity by being obliged to mix
with the people before the service, and even by putting on and
off the surplice and gown in their sight. I have refrained from
asking for a vestry in consideration of the difficulty of the times,

but after such an offer on the part of the parish it needs no further delicacy on mine. I trust that the nature of this case will excuse the liberty of my address."

FROM THE REV. WALTER WHITER.

"CAMBRIDGE, *August* 27*th*, 1822.

*   *   *   *   *

" You ask whether any analogy can be traced between the form of letters and the position of the organs of speech that utter them in any of the earliest written languages, and you add that you can trace none. No more can I. I think, however, that many of the things that have been frequently repeated on the formation of letters are sufficiently true, and such observations as occur to me at the moment without looking into any books I shall write down till my paper obliges me to stop.

"I do not think that attempts were made to form figures according to any conceived resemblances of those figures or letters with the organs of speech. In hieroglyphical writing something of this kind may have occasionally taken place, but in general I imagine nothing of this sort was attempted or conceived. The marks adopted were such as were suggested to the inventor at the moment. They were straight lines, not curves, which were more difficult to mark on stones, etc.—as most seem to agree. The resemblance of letters in different alphabets has been observed by all, but they do not seem to have perceived the full extent of this resemblance—especially in letters supposed to have a different power. I think that more dexterity has been exhibited by reformers of alphabets in noting this resemblance than is commonly imagined. I think that we shall discover similarities before hidden if we turn our curves into straight lines forming angles.

"The passage in *Don Quixote* (I have brought my *Don Quixote* with me) in which Cervantes describes the mode of forming the name of Dulcinea del Toboso always appeared to me to contain words which admirably described this dexterity of these inventors of alphabets, though the artifice adopted by these inventors and Don Quixote proceeds on a different principle. ' Buscandole nombre que no desdixasse mucho del suyo, y que tirasse, y se encaminasse al de Princesa,' etc. In the formation of cognate letters it is contrived that they do not much gainsay each other, as it were,—that they draw near to each other in their forms and traces; that they walk, as it were, in the same track, or that they are entrack'd with one another, if I may so put it; or, in other words, that cognate letters are traced or drawn not much different from each other. You have justly seen that B and ⅃ belong to each other. Turn the curves of our English B into straight lines and you have E (two Hebrew B's, ⊏ ⊏), which, accommodated to the Hebrew mode of writing from right to left, becomes ℶ ℶ, the Hebrew Beth ב.

"Let us examine the other labials. The English F is the Æolic digamma ϝ, and the P turned into straight lines becomes F.

"The V or V V, U or u u, contain the Beth cavity ⊏ ב. When the parallel lines in ⊏, ב, or ב form angles > < V, the M is M or two V V inverted, Λ Λ; hence the cognates μ and β.

"Mu and beta are, as you say, almost indistinguishable from one another. The modern Greeks represent the sound of B (English) by M B. The Greek Π is another ב n, in Hebrew ב. The Greek Φ represented by straight lines becomes ‡, which is two F's or ꟻF.

"We cannot but note how S, etc., appears under a similar form in various languages: ש (Heb.), ש (Ægypt.), Σ or M or Ξ, ξ or ш, س, the Arabic س ـ, in Russian Ш. N is an organical appendage to M in many cases, and hence it is like it in shape. In modern Greek N before Π becomes as M, τὸν πατέρα, tom batera.

"There is a mingled sound of the guttural and labial in the human voice, and hence the Q and U are united with each other in Latin words, so that Gualterus becomes Walter, guerre war, etc., as all understand. Hence G and F are sometimes like each other, as Γ, F, or F, and hence F is called the two gammas, or digamma. This muffled sound is expressed in Hebrew by ע (Aïn).

"Those who wish to know anything about the nature of this mingled sound of G and U or V or of the digamma would do well to study Mr. Owen's dictionary among the Welsh words beginning with gw, where they will see how in each word the two forms are adopted, of the guttural G and the labials w and [letter illegible] beginning the word, and from hence they will pass to their parallel words in other languages, and see how terms apparently different in form belong to one another.

"Thus 'Gwener'—'that confers happiness, Venus'—becomes Wener, and hence we have the Latin Venus, Vener-is, and understand how *gun* in *gune* may belong to the *Ven* in *Venus*, and how in other dialects of the Celtic the name for woman appears under the labial form Bean, and sometimes under the guttural form Gean (see Shaw's dict.). *Wenin* is another form of queen, quean, and this is the origin of the *en* in Helen, etc., *quasi* Olwen, the Celtic Venus (see Owen's Welsh dictionary). You will at once call to mind the passage in Herodotus that the temple dedicated to a foreign Venus in Egypt was no other than the Grecian *hEL-EN.* The war of Troy was a war of two states rivals in religion and commerce, and if Paris ravished away from Argos a material personage of flesh and blood called *hEL-EN*, a priestess of Olwen, whose name she bore, he like-

wise, we may conjecture, may have taken away the mistress—
the goddess Olwen, the deity of the temple without flesh and
blood, under form of a statue.   The people of Argos might have
considered this insult to their religion a more reasonable cause
of war than the insult offered to Menelaus by taking away his
wife.   Herodotus would have been altogether of the same opinion.
This will account for the story of the image of Helen in
Lycophron, Euripides, etc.   By examining Gn in Mr. Owen's
dictionary, you will see that it means whatever is delightful,
beautiful—what is white, bright, fair, etc., and you will agree that
it belongs to the Greek Gan-os (Γάνος), which is explained in
Prelim. Dissert. to *Etym. Univ.*, page 121.   The Olwen is
supposed to mean the person with fair or beautiful traces of
countenance, and thus by considering the sense of Ol, the track,
trace, and by examining the words connected with *ala*, etc., in
Mr. Shaw's Gaelic dictionary, you will see how Ol belongs to
Hole and to αὔλαξ, Ἑλκός, οὐλη, etc.   Such is the composition
of the Grecian *Hel-En*.   These observations have drawn me from
the remarks on letters, with which I will fill the remaining part
of my paper.

  "It might be asked whether the cavity of כ and ף belongs to
the cavity of Beth ב, and whether their similarity arises from the
connexion between the guttural and labial sound.   Though the
figures of letters are not taken from the supposed resemblance
to the organs of speech, yet their names may, and the Hebrews
might have called these letters Beth, Capa, Coph, from בת, the
hollow, as a den, bed, etc., etc., כפה [or rather כף], the hollow of
the hand, as some have conjectured, and such might be the
Hebrew idea.   Yet Beith is the Irish name for B, and this signifies
a birch-tree, though we are reminded of the Irish *Both*, a cottage
or booth, which corresponds with the sense of בית.

  "Some tribes of the Celts called their alphabet from trees,
and the twigs of trees under certain relations to parallel horizontal
lines represented the letters.   This species of writing was called
the Ogham.   From this the notation of musical sounds is derived,
and by this Ogham we take our degrees in Cambridge.   These
twigs were sometimes put loosely upon the tablet, and hence, I
imagine, is the story of the Sibyl's books being dispersed by the
wind.   In Vallancey's grammar the forms of the Ogham may be
seen, and in other books on alphabetical writing.   These are very
hasty remarks, which I should have only ventured to write from
your desire to hear what I think on a subject, on which I have
only thought enough to convince me that nothing satisfactory
can be made of it.   I am, my dear Sir, your most faithful servant,
                                             "WALTER WHITER.

  "There is still a little room left.   The Rho of the Greeks and
the English P are alike P.   Hence I should conjecture some

relation in their sound, and should conceive that the Greek Rho had sometimes a vowel breathing before it in the beginning of a word with a labial kind of sound. Our rudiments tell us in the same article that ὐ and ῤ have an aspirate, ὕδωρ and ῥῆμα, where the labial and the ρ are brought into contact with each other. We find that many words beginning with R in some languages have a vowel breathing before the R in others, as Rapio, Repo, Roof, ἁρπάζω, ἕρπω, ὀρόφη. The rough breathing would be the due accompaniment. I cannot but think that this observation on the P is of some weight. These are only the slightest sketches of very many things that might be said on the same subject, but I fear that even some of these things may appear fanciful. Something, however, of this sort I think must exist, if it was only developed, or if there should be evidence enough belonging to the subject to ensure conviction."

To a Lady.

"*August 28th*, 1822.

*   *   *   *   *

"I am myself a loyal member of that Church in which I have the honour to hold an office of some importance. I aim at nothing better, and in truth I know nothing better. I cannot comprehend the meaning of the term 'evangelical,' which some of those who profess to be its ministers assume to themselves in exclusion of the rest. I teach those principles of religion to my pupils in which I have been educated myself, and in which I believe myself, and I teach no more."

*   *   *   *   *

To the Venerable Archdeacon Blomfield.

"*August 31st*, 1822.

"I know nothing likely to remove me hence if I have my health till this boy shall have completed his education, but of course he must take his chance as to my continuance. My belief is that I shall remain here till he is fit to go to college, and longer, but one cannot look so far into futurity, and all that I can promise is that as long as I am master of this school he shall have his board and education gratis. I should not have mentioned this had I not been tormented lately with letters of inquiry, owing to a report that I had expressed an intention of becoming a candidate for Rugby, which is, and always will be, the farthest thing from my intention."

I presume there must have been some rumours about Dr. Wooll's intending to resign the head-mastership of Rugby. As a matter of fact he did not do so till 1828.

To the Editor of the "Sheffield Independent."

(Original written on the back of a document which I destroyed.—ED.)

"*September* 21*st*, 1822.

"SIR,—Observing a paragraph in the *St. James's Chronicle* of September 19th quoted from the *Sheffield Independent*, which states that the Vicar, churchwardens, and constable of one of the most populous parishes of the High Peak had attended a large cattle fair for the purpose of selecting a bull to be baited for the pleasure of their parishioners, I beg leave to say that I shall feel much obliged to you if you will inform me which parish in the High Peak you allude to, and am, Sir," etc.

*   *   *   *   *

From Dr. Parr.

(Signature and address only in Dr. Parr's handwriting.)

"*November* (?) 30*th*, 1822.

"In general terms I scouted the tale, and of course I did justice to the calm and genuine virtues of your venerable mother. I anticipated in my mind all and more than all that you have written in detail. Her whole life was a course of preparation for everything which is intelligible and credible in a future state. I quite approve of the word 'veneration' which you propose, and should disapprove of any epithet affixed to it. The term is strong, sufficiently strong, and it harmonises with the general simplicity and seriousness of the inscription.

"As to the contest in your county, I certainly exult in the victory gained over Toryism, and from the events which are passing among us and around us, your sagacity must perceive that Toryism has endangered the Church and State. I shall always reprobate the invidious and indiscriminate application of the word Radical. They who opposed the French war were called Jacobins ; they who censured the measures of administration and dread the servility and corruption of Parliament are now called Radicals. This perversion of language is convenient for the very worst purposes and the very worst rulers. No man of common sense would suppose for a moment that I would co-operate with such miscreants as Hunt and Cobbett; yet I hold that Hunt was cruelly punished, and I further hold that Cobbett has diffused the knowledge of many substantial and important truths. Many of his disciples will in practice be found wiser and better men than their master. They will separate the tares from the wheat, and they will apply to good ends what the wretch himself proclaims for very bad ones. As to myself, I am a man of too much research and too much discernment to be even in speculation a republican, and in practice I hope to die as I have hitherto lived, a constitutional Whig. I divide my hatred among the Ministerialists and the Radicals in portions nearly equal, but as matters now stand my fears of the Ministerialists are greater than my fears of the Radicals. I observe, too, that when men are preparing to apostatise they disguise their latent views under the pretence of condemning and resisting that which is indisputably evil. You, namesake, have too much sincerity and too much magnanimity for such paltry artifices. Again, I dislike the doctrine that all statesmen are rogues, and I have observed that doctrine employed as a pretence for joining those rogues who are in power at the time. In the present state of Europe nothing can be adiaphorous to a wise man. I have been, and ever shall be, a partisan, but my approbation of the Whigs is not indiscriminate, and they know it. My good friend, no man will undertake to defend the system upon which the English Government has been conducted since the accession of George III., and surely the party which for more than sixty years has deliberately sacrificed power gives the best possible pledge for sincerity. The Radicals are shrewd in their generation when they inculcate distrust and dislike of the persons with whom I sympathise. The Tories, by long success, have multiplied perils to the Church and State; the Whigs will not be permitted to save them; the Radicals would subvert them to-morrow. Namesake, I decidedly prefer Canning to Londonderry, and do not you believe that Romilly would have been a more desirable statesman than Lord Eldon ? Let us talk these matters over when we meet. I hear a favourable account of the four Cambridge candidates, and particularly of Bankes, but I detest the principle on which Bankes relies. Among the Herveys, from the time of Pope to the present hour, there never was a dunce nor a worthy, unless your correspondent forms an exception. Grant has a large share of talent and virtue. Scarlett's integrity in private life is adorned by his steadiness in public, and if he had played fast and loose he would have risen to the situation which is now filled by Abbott. Respect him at least for his consistency, and prefer him you must to such deserters as Charles Warren, Copley, and Gifford. If Scarlett fails, as I think he will, the death-blow is given to the cause of freedom in Cambridge. That the young men should have caught the contagion of servility from the old is a dreadful spectacle; but the plain truth is that, to an extent quite unprecedented, the Church and both the Universities are corrupt to the very root. Your grandchildren will be eye-witnesses of the mischief. I have lived, and happily my head will be under the sod when the storm bursts."

*   *   *   *   *

The inscription referred to in the preceding letter is the

one written by Dr. Butler for the mural tablet that stands
—unless the modern practice of moving old monuments has
found its way also to Kenilworth—in the old church on
the south side of the chancel arch.   It runs:—

NEAR THE PULPIT ARE INTERRED
THE REMAINS OF MR. WILLIAM BUTLER AND LUCY HIS WIFE,
THE FORMER OF WHOM DEPARTED THIS LIFE
MARCH 21, 1815, IN HIS 87TH YEAR,
THE LATTER NOV. 2, 1822, IN THE 84TH YEAR OF HER AGE.
THEY WERE UNOSTENTATIOUS BUT EXEMPLARY
IN THE DISCHARGE OF THEIR RELIGIOUS, MORAL, AND SOCIAL DUTIES.
THIS MONUMENT IS ERECTED BY THEIR ONLY SON,
SAMUEL BUTLER, D.D.,
ARCHDEACON OF DERBY AND VICAR OF THIS CHURCH,
IN VENERATION FOR THE MEMORY OF HIS BELOVED PARENTS,
AND IN HUMBLE THANKFULNESS TO ALMIGHTY GOD,
WHO VOUCHSAFED TO GRANT THEM
LENGTH OF DAYS, ESTEEM OF FRIENDS, CONTENT OF MIND,
AND AN EASY, GENTLE PASSAGE TO ETERNITY.

I see Professor Mayor places here among Dr. Butler's
works *An Essay upon Education; intended to show that
the Common Method is defective in Religion, Morality, etc.*
(8vo, London, no date); he queries it, however, as by another
author.   This is the case; it is by one S. Butler of Bristol,
and was first published in 1753 as "By a gentleman of
Bristol," though later editions are signed S. Butler.   In the
British Museum catalogue it is rightly excluded from the
list of Dr. Butler's works.

Of the *Praxis on the Latin Prepositions*, published in
December 1822, Professor Mayor says:—

"The book held its ground about twenty-five years, but seems
to have been superseded by Mr. T. K. Arnold's and other exercise
books, which follow the dry, mechanical system of Ollendorf.
There is great reason to believe that the quality of the elementary books used in many schools has fallen off: it may well

be questioned whether this Praxis might not be re-introduced with advantage."

I am not philologist enough to know whether the derivations given by Dr. Butler of the several prepositions will in all cases be held correct, but the book is pleasant reading from its clearness and from the excellence of the translations given as examples. These translations from a Latin writer are intended to be re-translated into Latin by the student, and the master is furnished with a key containing the original passage.

CHAPTER XVI.

AN ARDUOUS UNDERTAKING.

The School Lawsuit.—Correspondence, January 4th, 1823—July 3rd, 1823.—Kennedy takes the Porson Prize whilst still at School. —His Remarks upon the Shrewsbury System.—Correspondence, August 17th, 1823—April 19th, 1824.

IN January 1823 I meet with the first traces among Dr. Butler's papers of a lawsuit which, originating in the reign of James I., had been continued intermittently from that date till Dr. Butler took it in hand. The successful strangling of this suit was perhaps the most arduous and important of the many services he rendered to Shrewsbury School, and it is evident from his letter to the Master and Fellows of St. John's, written in 1835, and announcing his intended resignation, that he so considered it himself.

After a period of repose that had lasted for some years, there had been a recrudescence of legal activity between the years 1806 and 1823, which brought the school property into such serious difficulties that on the 6th of January, 1823, the trustees unanimously resolved to reduce by 50 per cent. the salaries of the masters that had been augmented since the passing of the School Act, and also to reduce by 50 per cent. the head-money allowed for each boy on the foundation. At the same time they declined, on the score of want of funds, to render assistance in the matter of closing the school-lane thoroughfare, which passed along the whole front of what are now the Museum buildings, and so into Castle Street.

Dr. Butler, knowing that the suit would never be ended as long as it was in the hands of the trustees, and seeing that things kept on going from bad to worse, determined to get the matter into his own hands, and accordingly wrote to the trustees asking them to make an order that should give him access to all documents in the hands of their bailiff and solicitor relative to the lawsuit, which he might have occasion to consult.

At their meeting in July 1823 the trustees made the necessary order ; and from that time until the final settlement of their claims, in the early months of 1827, the direction of the whole matter was practically left to Dr. Butler. It should be remembered that the very arduous task on which he now entered—a work more than sufficient to occupy any man's whole time—was undertaken in addition to the wearing labours of his school, then entering on its most brilliant period, and the by no means light business of his archdeaconry. I have heard my aunt, Mrs. Bather, say that her father's health, at no time robust, never fully recovered from the strain now put upon it.

CORRESPONDENCE, JANUARY 4TH, 1823—JULY 3RD, 1823.

FROM THE REV. T. S. HUGHES.

"YARMOUTH, *January 4th,* 1823.

" I have just accidentally heard the pleasing intelligence, and send you a line instantly to tell you, that I am elected Christian Advocate in the room of Lonsdale. I am writing this before going to bed, having come from a dinner party where the master of the house put me into no small surprise by wishing me joy of my new honours. Upon expressing my total ignorance of his meaning, he produced the paper which announced the appointment, very gallantly cut out the paragraph, and presented it to my dear Maria. The fact is that about three months ago I sent in my name, but . . . I gave up all hopes of success, and had really almost forgotten the whole affair.   How I came to be chosen is yet a secret; I suppose I slipped in through contending interests.   The appointment is very gratifying to me, especially as it may promote my success in the world wherein I am now going to settle; and I well know that no one will rejoice more in my good prospects than you, my oldest and dearest friend."

* * * * *

FROM BARON MERIAN.

"*January 24th*, 1823.

* * * * *

" Pray push Mr. Whiter to send me his letter.   'Tis a great drama we are about, and he has opened the scene.   Whatever is printed here of that sort shall be sent to you.   It has been found that nine hundred years ago the Chinese had paper money (bank-notes) just as we have, and with the same vicissitudes of rising and falling, the same wry remedies, etc.   But that's another chapter.

* * * *

" Two circumstances make a man rise: favour, which you disdain; and merit, which you possess—but merit often subsides when it is not supported by what the French call 'la force des choses,' a power infinitely more powerful than the '*force des hommes.*'   We Christians might call it the views and decrees of Providence.   You will never get a bishop's mitre and crook for your sake: you will get them for the sake of your flock—not because you have friends, but because you are a bishopable man."

* * * * *

TO THE REV. T. S. HUGHES.

(Original in possession of addressee's representatives.)

"*March 12th*, 1823.

* * * * *

" What you tell me about your projected review * interests me much more.   If you can effect a change in the present disgraceful system of public classical examinations and awards of prizes you will do a great thing.   I have lately conversed with Parr, Dobree, and Blomfield on this subject, who are all quite of my opinion. The utter ignorance of all Latinity which allows such detestable verse and prose to go forth to the world under the shape of odes and essays is an *æternum opprobrium* to the University.   I must write to you again on this subject if I can.   I know that 'Eubulus' had an intention of putting forth a pamphlet on that subject, and that he was deterred by fearing he should be misunderstood by the young men, who might suppose he was criticising them instead of their judges.   I suggested a plan to him by which this

---

* I was unable to discover what review was here contemplated —ED.

difficulty might be avoided, but other occupations, I believe, will prevent him from undertaking it. And here, in strict confidence, let me give you a piece of advice which you may do well to profit by. If you are disposed to fall foul upon ' Eubulus,' read temperately and dispassionately his two pamphlets, and do not petulantly think to write him down. He is not one whom it is wise to provoke, and I know he has an esteem for you, and is your well-wisher, and inclined to think of you as highly as I believe he does contemptuously of ' Philograntus.' I give you this piece of advice in the strictest confidence, but you must profit or not by it as you please. And let me give you another hint : do not toady anybody in your review. I heartily wish you well on your marriage and your subsequent plans."

* * * * *

From Baron Merian.

"*May* 13*th*, 1823.

" Dear Sir,—Nothing can be more judicious than the rules which you lay down for the investigation of Analogy. I am bound to say so, because they are the very same which we follow. Nay, we make use of a printed formulary (first sketched by the Empress Catherina II.), containing about three hundred chief words of the identical classes which you mention. Bread, however, is perhaps not quite proper, as being an *artefactum* which many nations have been and some are still without.

" Grammar (inflexions) is less important than Roots ; roots are the inalterable stuff, grammatical accidents are the variable forms ; it signifies little that the Germans say *hack*-end and the English *hack*-ing, or the Romans *por*-orum and the English ' of the *por*-es,' the first syllable, *i.e.* the root, being decisive. I call here *por* a root, though, strictly spoken, gutturals only can form roots.

" The expression ' fas coming from fa ' is not quite in our style ; fas comes not from fă, and fă comes not from fas. They are not father and son ; but, as you yourself perfectly indite, they are ' brothers and sisters ' sprung from one general idea and primitive verb, *fa*, *pa*, or *ba* (cry, speak), which you will meet with in fifty distant places, modified into φά-ω, φη-μί, fa-or, for, bo-o, βο-άω, as you justly observe. The Chinese have preserved fa and pa (Deguignes, 1118, 1157, 11683).

" *Lex* (legs) belongs not to *lego* in the sense of ' read '; it might belong to λέγω in the sense of ' say '; but in fact it belongs to λέγω in the sense of ' lay,' ' lay down.' (Compare the second line of this letter, and Ge-setz, setze, statutum, statuo, θεσμός, θέω, etc.)

* * * * *

" At present and in the meanwhile, if you should not be convinced of the truth of the axiom that all languages are one language (which you may well doubt of, since you have yet seen but a very small part of the proofs), pray let me ask you but one moderate favour—suspend your judgement. Say not No. The axiom is not to be demonstrated—it is already demonstrated on this side the Channel ; and you and your English friends, who in a short time must become the chief supporters and most zealous proclaimants of a doctrine which the immortal Whiter (whom, by-the-bye, his countrymen did not understand, and therefore not extol) roused—you, gentlemen, I say, will once thank an old honest Continental correspondent for having preserved you from an otherwise unavoidable retraction. Fight against us as much as you can day and night, you will please and oblige us, but do not condemn us unheard. No jury would."

FROM THE REV. (AFTERWARDS ARCHDEACON) R. W. EVANS.

"TRINITY COLLEGE, CAMBRIDGE, *June 8th*, 1823.

"MY DEAR SIR,—You have learned from my brother that Dobree has announced himself a candidate, and the πτηνῶν ἀγέλαι have all retired before the μέγας αἰγυπιός. I called upon him the morning after my arrival, and found him busily employed about his sermon (as he terms his inaugural thesis). The Master of St. John's received me most kindly, and wished me to stand in competition with Dobree; but this I never could think of for a moment. I called upon Dr. Parr, and sate ' enshrined in cloudy tabernacle ' with him for about an hour, and he wished me to mention to you that he approved highly of my retiring before Dobree, and that in any other case he would gladly exert his influence with the Provost in my favour. From what I see I feel confident that, had not Dobree come forward, I should, late as it was, have carried the election. I think the Professor elect will in no long time be sick of the duties of his office, and in case of another vacancy shall not hesitate a moment.

"Ever your sincere and grateful
"R. W. EVANS."

Professor Dobree died in 1825 ; but Mr. Evans, finding that he could not attend both to his duties as a tutor of Trinity and to those of the Greek Professorship, did not offer himself as a candidate.

FROM BARON MERIAN.

"*June 16th*, 1823.

" ' *I believe we mean pretty much the same thing in most respects.*' *—Dr. S. Butler.* Most certainly, and this is my pride. Could it be thought that I should maintain any literary scheme which you, upon examination, had rejected? Never. Truth is the same everywhere, and what men like you cannot acknowledge to be truth *is not truth*, and therefore no food for me.

* * * * *

" The name of ' Eubulus ' I shall not mention ; but it is so very characteristic that children, I think, might guess the man.

" I consider your *magna et præclara Cantabridgiensia* as of the greatest importance. Cambridge by these means, and by these alone, can speedily overtop Oxford. Cambridge must enlarge its basis. Classic studies are very fine and elegant, and mathesis is a very sure and certain discipline. But they are both small— nay, very small—parts of human knowledge, all the chief parts of which ought to be taught at such places as call themselves *Universitas*. Let every branch take its appropriate place, but let not some, like parasitic plants, eat up the tree. Besides, even classical studies cannot be carried 'on as they ought without more general views, nor without previous notions of the whole of which they are a fraction.

* * * * *

" Young has stung Champollion. About a month hence Champollion will sting Young. But I conjecture that the English sting will be the deeper, for 'tis one thing to discover, and another to improve. *Cura ante omnia ut valeas. Eris tunc ex omni parte beatus. Have.*

" P.S.—A true French invention. You have heard of the Zodiac of Denderah which is now at Paris in the Louvre, but has not answered the expectations of the savants. Well, to provide it with an antiquity which it has not, what have they imagined ? In the royal Louvre a sculptor has been ordered to *add a face* behind a face already insculpted on it, and so we *now* see a Janus instead of the former simple face."

FROM B. H. KENNEDY, ESQ. (AFTERWARDS REV.).

" BIRMINGHAM, *June 28th*, 1823.

" DEAR AND REVERED SIR,—My father and myself feel extremely grateful for your kindness in sending the certificate to the Master of St. John's, and in suggesting the corrections, which were sent the same day to Mr. Hastings Robinson, and will, I hope, answer in time. I wrote without any idea of success, and of course the news was most unexpected ; but I may safely say that I then felt, and still feel, more pleasure in being the first Johnian and the first Salopian who has gained the Porson Prize than in any consideration of a personal nature, and that in my academical career the honour of my school and college will predominate over every other feeling. I trust my present success will not lead me into folly of any kind, but will rather prove a stimulus to future exertion. Of course I feel, and every one knows, that I am indebted to you for any honour I obtain, and this will be an additional excitement. I have now nearly regained my strength, and country air has done all the good that Dr. J. Johnstone promised. I regretted my illness principally because it removed me from school before I could express my warm gratitude to you and Mrs. Butler for all your kindness to me while under your care.

"With kindest remembrances to Mrs. and Miss Butler and Tom, I remain your grateful and affectionate pupil,

"BENJAMIN H. KENNEDY.

"P.S.—I will send copies of the prize compositions when printed and the Latin Ode by Marindin."

The following note was appended to this letter by the late Professor Kennedy about a month before his death, nearly sixty-five years after the original letter was written :—

"I had sent from school a translation for the Porson Prize, and also a Latin Ode. Both were selected for the Prize, but the Porson Prize only was adjudged to me, because a grace had already been passed restricting the Browne medals to candidates in residence. My letter refers to these matters."

FROM BARON MERIAN.

"*July 3rd,* 1823.

*   *   *   *   *

"You have been unwell; it is not right. Every fair cause, every good and just thing, wants and finds your support. You cannot be spared in these times. Cambridge is deeply indebted to you. But is your life perhaps too full of agitation? Are your pursuits too numerous? Be not too eager; coolness and diet make long lives, and Nestor was more useful than Achilles. Your family, your friends, England cannot spare so much learning and so much sense and so much probity. Greet the stout and nuptial defender of the Greeks. How is his sister? Still *incloistered?*"

"Still incloistered" refers to Miss Hughes's marriage with the Dean of Peterborough (Monk).

The affectionate pride which Dr. Butler took in his illustrious pupil will appear more fully later, when it will be seen how ardently desirous he was that none but Kennedy should succeed him, nor can I remember without pleasure how fully his sagacity was justified by the event.

Kennedy's triumph in 1823 was only once surpassed in Dr. Butler's time : I mean in 1831, when Brancker, while still in the sixth form at Shrewsbury—a boy in jacket and turn-down collars—came up to Oxford, where he was not yet entered, and took the Ireland Scholarship against the whole University, and among other candidates the still living and ever-youthful Mr. Gladstone. When Kennedy took the Porson, Cambridge changed her rules, so as to protect her resident *alumni* from being beaten by schoolboys, however brilliant. I have always heard, but must confess that I have not verified the statement, that Oxford did the like as regards the Ireland Scholarship on its being taken by Brancker. I believe, therefore, that Dr. Butler may claim to have been the only schoolmaster who ever compelled both Oxford and Cambridge to change their regulations in consequence of defeats inflicted upon them by his as yet non-resident pupils.

How warmly and generously Dr. Kennedy to the end of his life recognised the assistance rendered to his own great talents and exertions by his training under Dr. Butler will appear from the following letter (already partly quoted from in my Introduction) to the Rev. G. Sandford on the system at Shrewsbury during his own schooldays.

"*May 5th*, 1887.

*   *   *   *   *

"Homer was always one lesson a week. Some Greek play was always in hand. Demosthenes was a favourite author of his, and we did some Thucydides, but not a great deal, and no Plato that I remember. In Latin Cicero, Virgil, and Horace were his favourite books, always to the fore.

"History and geography were never neglected. He had the upper fifth along with the sixth to most lessons. He was of course an excellent scholar, and no ordinary teacher, but his crowning merit was the establishment of an emulative system, in which talent and industry always gained their just recognition and reward in good examinations.

"This it was that made his school so successful and so great. Added to this he always advised and recommended private reading, and to my obedience to this oft-repeated recommendation it was that I owed my scholarship and my success at Cambridge, for I had read a great deal privately before I went to college—all Thucydides, all Tacitus, all Sophocles, and Æschylus, much Aristophanes, Pindar, Herodotus, Demosthenes, and Plato, besides Cicero.

"I think I have said all that I can say, and you may be sure that Dr. Butler had no pupil more appreciative of his merits, or more grateful for his teaching, or more anxious to follow his steps than I have been always."

CORRESPONDENCE, AUGUST 17TH, 1823—APRIL 19TH, 1824.

FROM THE REV. WILLIAM SHEPHERD.

"GATEACRE, NEAR LIVERPOOL, *August 17th*, 1823.

"MY DEAR SIR,—In making a trespass on your kindness I must beg you to pardon the liberty which I take, to which, however, I am emboldened by the recollection of friendly communications with which you have honoured and gratified me in former times.

"I have been requested by the congregation of Protestant dissenters meeting in Moseley Street, Manchester, to write an epitaph on their late minister, Mr. Hawkes. This epitaph, contrary to my advice, they will have in Latin. Well knowing how keenly these compositions are examined, I am anxious not to commit myself by any violation of taste or of grammar; and I wish to submit my labour to your critical judgement. To any communication you may please at your earliest leisure to make to me on the subject I shall pay the most deferential attention.

MS.

GULIELMI HAWKES
HUJUS ECCLESIÆ
OLIM ANTISTITIS
VIRI GRAVIS
LITERARUMQVE SACRARUM
DOCTISSIMI
QUI PRÆCEPTA VIRTUTIS
QUÆ ORATIONE
LUCULENTER EXPOSUIT
ACERRIMEQVE SUASIT
VITA
ILLUSTRAVIT

"I am aware that *ecclesia* in the sense of a church (*i.e.* a building) is rather divinity than classical Latin, though it is so used in the Pandects. But is not *templi* too ambitious for a Presbyterian meeting-house? In fact, as you probably know, we attach no sacredness to our buildings. The essence of our system is the congregation (in this we differ from the Church of Ireland, where congregations are scarce articles), to which *ecclesia*, if admissible, will well apply. I have no books of topography or collection of epitaphs to which I can refer for authority."

To THE REV. W. SHEPHERD.

[*About August* 18*th*, 1823.]

"DEAR SIR,—If you use 'ecclesia' in theological Latin, you must use 'antistes' in theological Latin, and as far as I know it is generally used for that abomination of your flock—a bishop. Therefore I object to 'antistes.' I object to 'ecclesia,' unless you mean to say that you are members of the Established Church --which you do not.

"Don't mistake me—I do not mean to say that you, as a congregation of Christians, are not a Church in that sense; but if you were the Established Church in this country, and we were not, you would be right in using the word, and we should be wrong. I should say that I had no right to use the words 'hujus ecclesiæ' in writing the epitaph of a clergyman of the Church of England who officiated in an episcopal parish in Scotland or in Italy. You will tell me that an ἐκκλησία is an assembly, a congregation. So say I—but I say that the usage of ἐκκλησία in this country is to designate a church, not a meeting-house, and I therefore object to 'ecclesiæ.' In my supposed case I should say 'sacelli,' but I hardly think you can in yours, because you have no consecration, and reject the idea of sacredness in connection with a building. What can you do? See, your detestable heresies exclude you from the use of the Latin tongue. I therefore say repent, repent, and be converted. If you won't, what can you do but describe yourself by a periphrasis?

"I should say something of this sort:—

"'Legis divinæ per . . . annos
In his ædibus interpretis.'

"Or I should prefer:—

"'Legis a Christo institutæ
In his ædibus ministri.'

"I mention these forms not as those which I would recommend to your adoption, but as conveying a notion of my meaning. You will easily adopt better.

"'Acerrime suasit.' So says Paterculus (?). 'Gravissime' would perhaps be the phrase of Cicero, but you have had 'gravis' already.   I should prefer :—

> "' Is quæ præcepta virtutis
> In docendo luculenter exposuit
> Suis ipse moribus pulcherrime illustravit.' "

An inscription, to the scholars of those days, was like the sound of the bugle to a war-horse. I have heard my father tell how Dr. Parr once said to my grandfather, " It's all very well, Sammy, to say that So-and-so is a good scholar, but can he write an inscription?"

FROM THE REV. W. SHEPHERD.

"GATEACRE, *August 24th*, 1823.

" MY DEAR SIR,—Whilst I most cordially thank you for your kind and prompt attention to my draft upon your critical acumen, I congratulate myself on my prudence in resorting to your judgement and assistance.   In epitaph-writing, as in larceny, a private whipping is certainly preferable to a public one.

" I can assure you that on setting to work on this composition I was struck with the fact that we *non cons* are, to a certain degree, as you say, debarred ' the use of the Latin tongue.' This is the case in more senses than one.   I never envied you your deaneries and bishoprics, but I have often envied you the advantage of your public schools and universities.   Conscious of a power of industrious application, and of a delight in the pursuits of classical literature, I have often regretted and still regret the lack of opportunity in early life of being initiated into those niceties and minutiæ of the languages of Greece and Rome which are to be learned in our public institutions alone, and which are despised by none but the half-informed and the presumptuous.

" Of these niceties must be reckoned the exclusive application of *ecclesia* and *antistes* to churches and clergy of the Establishment. On that ground I had rejected *templi* and *sacerdotis*.   It is well you saved me from dubbing my late friend a bishop.

" After I had despatched my letter I was alive to the jingle of *qui* and *quæ*, and fully expected your objection to it.   But I was not aware of the use of your *cardo* ' Is ' in composition of this kind.   I don't think indeed I have read a dozen Latin epitaphs in the course of my life.   My short sight precludes my reading them on stone or marble, and books of topography have not been an object of my study.   Is there any collection of Latin epitaphs I could procure as a guide in future contingencies of this kind?   With your correction Mr. Hawkes's epitaph will stand as follows :—

MS.

GULIELMI HAWKES

LEGIS DIVINÆ

PER XXXI ANNOS

IN HIS ÆDIBUS

INTERPRETIS

VIRI GRAVIS

LITERARUM SACRARUM

DOCTISSIMI

IS QUÆ PRÆCEPTA VIRTUTIS

IN DOCENDO LUCULENTER EXPOSUIT

SUIS IPSE MORIBUS

PULCHERRIME ILLUSTRAVIT

NATUS EST IV ID FEB MDCCLIX

OBIIT KAL AUG MDCCCXX

" With your permission I will inform any scholar who may converse with me about it that you were so kind as to revise and materially correct it. As to the *profanum vulgus*, they will care nothing about it.

" I have written to my Liverpool bookseller to send you two volumes of Mr. Hawkes's sermons, which I beg you to accept as a token of my sense of your friendly attention to my request. If you have time to read one or two of them, you will find that he was worthy of a permanent memorial. He was upwards of thirty years minister of the Moseley Street congregation."

· To the Rev. W. Shepherd.

" Shrewsbury, *August 27th*, 1823,

" My dear Sir,—I think the inscription in its present form will do, but I should rather incline to put EA before SUIS IPSE MORIBUS. It may be omitted, but it corresponds better perhaps with the relative *quæ* to have it in. Neither is wrong.

" There are some little minutiæ in cutting inscriptions which give them a classical air, and which, as you say you have never turned your attention to the matter, I will take the liberty of mentioning.

" 1. The letters should be all of the same height.

" 2. Diphthongs should be resolved.

" 3. J and U should be always written I and V.

" 4. Compound words should be expressed in a rather more learned form than they are generally written (as *inlustravit* for *illustravit*).

" 5. A full-stop should be put after every word, except at the end of a line.

"6. After numerals, and at the end of the inscription, it is optional to put or omit it.

" 7. Numerals should have a line drawn over them.

" I will transcribe it on the other side as it should be engraved (except as to calligraphy), and you can copy it for the engraver.

"There are but two books on inscriptions which I can safely recommend, both scarce, and one of them very scarce.   The one is Fabretti—*Raph. Fabretti Inscript. Antiquæ* (Rom., 1702) ; the other is *Morcellus de Stilo Inscriptionum.*   Morcellus was very rare indeed : I gave ten guineas for my copy (Rom., 1781) ; but there is another enlarged edition, printed at Padua in 3 vols. in 1819, for which I gave a great deal of money in Italy (having been dandy enough to chuse fine paper) when I was there last. Perhaps it may be obtained in England by this time.   I suppose a tolerable copy could be got for about six guineas.

" Guiter's immense mass in 4 vols. Fol., and Muratori's supplement in four more, are not nearly so valuable as Morcellus.   I have them all, and have thumbed them decently.

" I need not tell you, after the trial you have had, of the extreme difficulty of writing inscriptions, and I believe there are very few persons indeed who know anything about the matter, and therefore you need not be much afraid of criticism.   Our friend Parr is supreme, ΖΕΥΣ ΥΨΙΒΡΕΜΕΤΗΣ—his knowledge in this respect especially, as well as in all other points of classical literature, is transcendent.   Many thanks for your kind present. I shall take an early opportunity of looking into it.   I see there is a sketch of his life by our friend John Corrie, from whom I heard about ten days since. . . .

" P.S.—The inscription will stand as follows :—

MS.

GVLIELMI . HAWKES

{ LEGIS . DIVINAE

{ PER . XXXI . ANNOS

{ IN . HIS . AEDIBVS

{ INTERPRETIS

VIRI . GRAVIS

{ LITERARVM . SACRARVM

{ DOCTISSIMI

IS . ALIIS . QVAE . PRAECEPTA . VIRTVTIS

IN . DOCENDO . LVCVLENTER . EXPOSVIT

EA . SVIS . IPSE . MORIBVS

PVLCERRIME . INLVSTRAVIT

NATVS . EST . IV . ID . FEBR . A . S . MDCCLIX

DECESSIT . KAL . AVG . A . S . MDCCCXX.

" *Quere*, whether by putting the two lines I have bracketed in three instances into one, the tablet would not be better filled up. I think it would. You must remember then to put a stop after *divinæ, ædibus*, and *sacrarum*.

" I suppose you have no objection to A.S., Anno Salutis or Anno Sacro—if you have, you may omit it. On revising I found *suis ipse* was so marked as to require some word opposed to it ; I have therefore inserted *aliis* between *is* and *quæ*; and thus I believe the whole is now complete."

FROM BARON MERIAN.

" September 29th, 1823.

" DEAR SIR,—A thousand thanks for your *Charge*, which, though your name had not been prefixed, any man would have attributed to you, such is its force, elegance, and that particular argumentative closeness which no antagonist can escape.

" But I could not help smiling when, immediately after, according to your prescription, I read Dogberry's speech, and the famous allocution of the second watch, ' Well, masters, we hear our,' etc. Bless me ! I hope those you addressed did not say ' *Well, masters,*' when you were gone. But that is *entre nous.* Your explanation of the *two o'clock* is a very fine because a very simple and natural one. My compliments to the late Mr. Malone ; his melons are not of that savour. He was no more a commentator than I am an astronomer. Are your remarks to be lost ? or do you collect them somewhere as a garland on Shakespeare's tomb ?*

*   *   *   *   *

" Your *Praxis on the Prepositions ? Pappæ !* you never men-tioned a word of it to me. If there be left one spark of virtue in your bosom, you will send me the very first copy drawn of the said Praxis. Gail has printed one of the Greek prepositions, which succeeded well."

*   *   *   *   *

FROM B. H. KENNEDY, ESQ.

" ST. JOHN'S COLLEGE, November 4th, 1823.

" DEAR AND REVERED SIR,—I return you many thanks for your kind and welcome letter, which I received from Miss Butler at Birmingham. I shall preserve it as a talisman amidst the trials and temptations of Cambridge. I have indeed found its

---

* I found no notes on Shakespeare among Dr. Butler's papers, nor have I seen the charge above referred to. There is no copy of this in the British Museum, nor yet in Dr. Butler's private collection of his charges.—ED,

utility already; for having made an acquaintance with Praed, Townshend, and Ord, the leading members of the Union Debating Society, I have been repeatedly invited to join it, but through your kind advice have been enabled to resist the temptation. I feel convinced that there is nothing to fear from me on the ground of politics; my feelings on the subject are neither strong nor warm, and my opinions are not such as can injure me. I never make them the theme of conversation, take in no newspaper, and subscribe to no newsroom.

    *   *   *   *   *

"I am now reading the eighth play of Aristophanes, the *Ranæ*. If, as I am given to understand, the three others, the *Lysistrata*, *Eccles*, and *Thesmophor*, are unnecessary to be read, I shall feel greatly relieved. I shall then have time for Demosthenes, which I have not yet opened, and, if you recommend it, a little of Plato. I have read Thucydides twice through, besides marking and reconsidering all the difficult passages. I wished to inquire how much Homer it will be desirable for me to read, and whether Plautus is useful."

    *   *   *   *   *

The question asked in this last sentence raises obvious reflections. Dr. Butler, in a " Plan for Reading " which he drew up in 1822, but which is too long and too much out of date to allow of my printing it, insists that far more is gained by mastering all that has been left of a single author than by more discursive reading. This last, however, so long as the Universities continue their present system of examinations, is imperative alike on schoolmasters and students.

FROM NICHOLAS CARLISLE, ESQ.

"SOMERSET PLACE, *November 18th*, 1823.

    *   *   *   *

"MY DEAR SIR,—I hope you will not relinquish your design of having drawings of all the churches in your archdeaconry, and copies of the monumental inscriptions; they may hereafter be treasures of great value, and by the opportunities which are afforded to you may furnish a genealogical collection of more importance than has ever been made by the most diligent inquiries."

    *   *   *   *

Mr. Philip Browne told me he drove round the archdeaconry with my grandfather in two successive summers, and sketched every church, at his desire. The drawings are now, I believe, in the offices of the archdeaconry of Derby, but no copies of inscriptions appear to have been made.

To the Churchwardens of a Parish Unknown.

[1823 ?]

"I fear you are under some misapprehension as to the archidiaconal powers in regard to ecclesiastical buildings. They rather act as negatives upon any alteration than as positive sanctions for such things. The archdeacon may recommend improvements, but he cannot compel them. I will endeavour to explain myself by an instance. If a gallery has been duly erected in a church and becomes out of repair, the archdeacon can compel reparation, and can fine the parish, from which fine no appeal is allowed in the temporal courts, till that repair is made ; but he cannot compel the erection of an additional new gallery, he can only recommend such a measure to the parishioners. In like manner, if the customary fences of a churchyard are out of repair, he can compel the persons on whom such repair falls (generally the parish at large) to make those fences good, and to keep the churchyard neat, but he cannot compel any alteration in the direction or nature of those fences, or in the general boundary of the churchyard. I trust you see the distinction. I cannot therefore order the alteration you propose, though I approve it and recommend it ; but I can order the churchwardens to repair the present fences of the churchyard wherever they are out of repair ; and in compliance with your request and the discharge of my official duties I hereby order them to be repaired accord-ingly, and a certificate of such repair to be made to me at my next summer's visitation.

"I direct this letter officially to the churchwardens. Of course they will have the goodness to communicate it to the steward."

From Miss Butler, afterwards Mrs. Bather.

"January 11*th,* 1824.

*   *   *   *   *

"My private opinion was that this concert went off very flatly. Lindley was out of humour ; Mrs. Salmon was ill, or at least she was a bottle or two short of her usual allowance, and she frequently sang deplorably out of tune. However, it was agreed *nem. con.* that it went off remarkably well, and was very pleasant, etc. The ball was a pleasant one, and remarkably select. There

was not a single vulgar person present—plenty of diamonds, great affability, much dancing, and a good deal of beauty.
                        *   *   *   *   *

"We got excellent places at the Circus on Friday evening, though our party was large and the house filled early. It was warm and comfortable, and very full and fashionable; but I believe we were too tired, generally speaking, thoroughly to enjoy it. I was much amused with hearing mamma and Mr. Drury laying their unmusical heads together, and wondering, as indeed I often did myself, what the performers would be at. I admire Phillips, the new base singer, extremely; but Mr. Sutton thought fit to criticise him severely in his best song, Shield's *Wolf*, and Mrs. Sutton said loud enough to be heard by the three next benches, 'Ah, Sutton! I have often heard you sing that song far better.' "
            *   *   *   *   *

The Mrs. Sutton alluded to in the preceding letter was a general favourite, but very eccentric. She used to do whatever she liked, and no one dared so much as lift up a finger against her. Lord Hill was dining at her house once, and there was nothing but pork in one shape or another for the meat dishes. She said, "You see, my lord, we have killed a pig." Lord Hill is reported to have laughed good-humouredly, and answered, "Only *one*, Mrs. Sutton?" I have heard my father say that he was once seated next her at dinner, and had the thigh of a woodcock on his plate. Mrs. Sutton espied it, and instantly transfixed it with her fork. "Young man," said she, "I know you don't like that," and in a second the woodcock's thigh was on Mrs. Sutton's plate.

Kennedy's taking the Pitt University Scholarship in his second term of residence was another of the brilliant triumphs which he achieved both for himself and Shrewsbury. He wrote February 11th, 1824 :—

"You have no doubt heard ere this the news of my unexpected success. I should have written to you on Monday, immediately after the announcement, had not Mr. Hughes appeared to wish that I should defer my letter and suffer him to give you the first news of my success. I need scarcely say that I now feel more than ever indebted to you, and sincerely hope that the pleasure of this moment may be some compensation for your kindness.

*　　　　*　　　　*　　　　*　　　　*

" Whether I can sit for the Bell is a debated point; but I think my right is clear, and precedent is certainly in my favour. The Bell cannot be considered an University scholarship, for it is not open to all the undergraduates of the University, and Waddington certainly held the Pitt with the Bell, though the words of the regulation are: ' The Pitt scholar shall not hold any other University scholarship.' "

*　　　　*　　　　*　　　　*　　　　*

Professor Kennedy never quite forgave my grandfather for having refused to sanction his going in for the Bell. He spoke about it to me a few weeks before his death, and with his own hand added the following note to the original letter :—

" This refers to my success in gaining the Pitt University Scholarship. Dr. Butler dissuaded me from going in for the Bell Scholarship as *infra dignitatem*. I do not think that his advice was sound, as it left that scholarship to an inferior man, and deprived me and my father of a pecuniary benefit without good cause. The precedent was not followed in other cases—for instance, in 1856."

Yes, but surely it was by Dr. Kennedy's own advice given to his old pupil, Arthur Holmes, that the precedent was not followed.

From E. Baines, Esq.

"Christ College, Cambridge, *March* (?), 1824.

" My dear Sir,—There was a report that the classes would be out to-day, and I accordingly waited to see the truth of it. However, they are not yet visible, and I understand that the examiners find as much difficulty in deciding as they have done in examining, for I hear there was nothing but *fracas* among them the whole week, owing to that brute Scholefield, who has succeeded in making the examination give entire dissatisfaction to all parties. We were pressed for time in a most disagreeable manner, so that some papers made it more hand-work than head-work. We had no Homer, but a gloriously long and hard lump of Pindar, and you will smile at the piece they gave us as the representative of Cicero's works."

*　　　　*　　　　*　　　　*　　　　*

FROM THE REV. S. TILLBROOK.

"OLD HOUSE, *March* 12*th*, 1824.

* * * *

"Your scholastic fame spreads like wildfire here. Nothing is talked of but Shrewsbury School, Dr. Butler, Lawson, and Kennedy. I really think you ought to raise your terms, nor can I think that your numbers would be diminished.

"In about three weeks I start for Herefordshire, and hope to turn over a dappled trout or two. By-the-bye, can you not send me a good copy of longs and shorts on this subject, and immortalise old 'Till? There is an excellent simile in *Ronan's Well* which, if the length of line mentioned had been twenty instead of twelve yards, would, I think, have applied to your humble servant. 'He could cast twelve yards of line with one hand, and his fly fell like the down of a thistle on the water.' Versify this and put it to our adventure on the Dovey—a pretty subject for a few hexameters and pentameters—and I will insert them in my interleaved and adnotated edition of Honest Izaak. I am to be made a member of the Walton and Cotton Club next month.

"Here and hereabouts there is no particular news stirring. Our classical examinations gave great dissatisfaction. A few of the authors altogether omitted may be found in the following list: Homer, Plato, Euripides, Sophocles, Herodotus, Lucian, Theocritus, Lucretius, Virgil, Horace, Ovid, Cicero (with the exception of perhaps a letter to Atticus), Tacitus, Livy, Terence, Juvenal, etc. The examiners ought to have been all of them well flogged."

* * * * *

FROM THE TRUSTEES OF THE SCHOOL.

[*April* 19*th*, 1824.]

"The Governors and Trustees of the Free Grammar School having attentively perused Dr. Butler's able memorial relative to the Albrighton Tithe Cause, beg leave to return him their best and unanimous thanks for his kind and laborious exertions on the occasion, and to request his further assistance in framing a memorial to be presented to the Barons of the Exchequer, praying their judgement on the case before a total ruin of this excellent foundation takes place."

The sheet on which I found the above was undated; reference, however, to the trustees' minute-books at Shrewsbury enables me to fix the date as above. No copy of the memorial itself was found by me. It was, however, immediately drawn up, and presented through the Bishop of Lichfield and Coventry, with such effect that the case came on for hearing in June 1824; but the Lord Chief Baron, Sir W. Alexander, deferred judgement till after the vacation.

CHAPTER XVII

CORRESPONDENCE, MAY 13TH, 1824—DECEMBER 1824.

FROM THE REV. T. S. HUGHES.

"CHESTERTON, *May* 13*th*, 1824.

*   *   *   *   *

"MR. TILLBROOK is very well and very jolly, just come from his fishing in Hampshire, where he killed a hundred and sixty trout. We had a very pleasant day at St. John's Port Latin this year. The College is in earnest, I believe, about building, but I am afraid about the situation. They talk of placing the new court in the walks. Have you heard of the intention of the Pitt Club to grant us a donation from their funds to erect a Pitt Press at Cambridge, as a rival to the Clarendon? Really Cambridge will soon be able to hold up its head."

*   *   *   *   *

TO THE BISHOP OF LICHFIELD AND COVENTRY (DR. RYDER).

[Probably May 1824.]

"MY LORD,—I take the liberty of sending my three charges to your lordship, that you may become acquainted, so far, with my proceedings as Archdeacon of Derby. I was enabled by great exertion during the whole of my vacation last summer to make a parochial visitation of about one-half of the county. I hope in the course of the approaching summer vacation to complete the undertaking. I shall set out for Derbyshire on Monday, June 21st, when my vacation commences, and intend to spend the whole of it in Derbyshire; and I take the liberty of mentioning that, if you are likely to be at Eccleshall on the day I have mentioned, or on my return, which will be at the end of July, or at the very beginning of August, I could by making a little detour have the honour of paying my respects to your lordship, and showing you my papers. I very much regretted not being able to attend your lordship at Lichfield, yet I am thankful that I was prevented, for on the Wednesday, when I wished to have been there, the school tower caught fire, and probably, if I had not been on the spot, the whole of this fine and venerable structure would have been burnt down. A quarter of an hour

later no assistance could have preserved it, as the wind was very
high. My principal assistant was also that day confined to his
bed by severe illness.

"I understand that you have been so good as to express a wish
to see my statement of our unfortunate lawsuit. I have just
received some papers (a large basket full) which throw light on
the business, and which I must examine as well and as soon as
my engagements, now unusually pressing, will permit. As I may
probably make considerable alterations or additions to the present
statement in consequence, and shall be some months before I can
complete them, I could wish to defer sending it to your lordship
till this is done."

FROM THE REV. T. S. HUGHES.

"CHESTERTON, *August 5th,* 1824.

❋   *   *   *   *

"All my pupils are arrived and work begun, as I suppose it is
with you. I, like yourself, am very far from disliking my occupation. Indeed I in some measure consider it as a piece of
good fortune to be forced to reperuse the immortal works of these
jolly old heathens—thus mixing the *utile dulci* in a very agreeable
manner.

"It is time, however, that I should immediately set about my
second part of the Defence of St. Paul—which I will do. I have
been thinking on the subject, and have noted down some of my
thoughts. The way I intend to treat it is as follows—to stick
to the *Miracles.* Gamaliel Smith denies their reality. This now
I must prove. He also denies the conformity of the doctrine
they are intended to prove with that of our Saviour. I think,
therefore, that to complete the subject I must show that it is so.
This you will perhaps think sufficient without attending to his
scurrilities and impertinences.

"Can you then (1) intimate any books for me to consult?
(2) Do you know in what author is contained a diatribe against
St. Paul's sailing to, and performing miracles in, Malta, which is
said to have been Meleda in the Adriatic? (3) Can you tell me
anything about a certain Peter Annet? I have an anonymous
tract, said to have been written by him, from which it seems that
Gamaliel Smith has culled all his arguments. It is called *The
History and Character of St. Paul examined in a Letter to
Theophilus,* etc. It has no date, and has been torn out from
a volume containing other tracts.

"Thank you for your portrait, which is extremely like you. I
need not say—for I know you cannot doubt—how much I shall
value it."

"Gamaliel Smith" was a pseudonym for Jeremy Bentham,

who in 1823 published a work, *Not Paul, but Jesus*, under this assumed name.

The portrait above referred to was an engraving by William Ward, A.R.A., from the picture by Thomas Kirkby, now in the head-master's house at Shrewsbury School. This is much the best portrait that was taken of Dr. Butler, and is reproduced (by direct photography from the picture itself) as the frontispiece of this work.

FROM THE REV. S. TILLBROOK.

"LEINTWARDINE, *August* 15*th*, 1824.

"MY DEAR DOCTOR,—Do not be alarmed if you see me or my ghost hastening towards Salop on Thursday next. If I come, I shall choose the time of day generally devoted to dinner; but if my ghost only should arrive, it matters not when, you will know it by its red face and limping gait. Use it well for my sake, and have it laid to rest in your wine-cellar.

"I have been staying here since Friday last, and have killed good store of trout and grayling, neither of which fish, in my humble opinion, are fit to set before an archdeacon or a tutor of a college, otherwise you would have received a few of both sorts. I catch them and give them to my landlady, Dame Evans, who in return for my liberality feeds me as daintily as the fabled chaw-bacons of old did Apollo. I begin the day with broiled ham, dine on beans and bacon, or eggs and bacon, and sup on the same. This diet provokes great thirst, which I am doomed to allay with a drink which the Goths called 'gripen-gutten-Wein,' and we 'cyder.' This is the penalty of my vice, as you call it. But this is not all, for the very plumage of my artificial flies reminds me of the volatile delicacies—snipe, woodcock, partridge, dotterel, and grouse. Pray pity me, if you can, and pardon any little excess which I may commit upon your larder and cellar—'date poculum Tilbrogio.' . . .

"P.S.—As my stay must be so short, I shall prefer sleeping at the Raven with my suite and my servants—being in all one— *egometipse* to wit. Vale!"

FROM MR. W. HONE, AUTHOR OF "HONE'S EVERYDAY BOOK."

"45, LUDGATE HILL, LONDON, *October* 5*th*, 1824.

"SIR,—Perhaps I ought to have thanked you for the politeness and urbanity of the note I had the honour to receive from you in February, in answer to mine accompanying a copy of the pamphlet I published in that month. But from your expressions I was led to think you had not then read the tract, and I deemed it more respectful to abstain from troubling you with a notice which, after its perusal, might not altogether have been accepted at that moment. I knew, however, sir, that you appreciated the civility of my intentions, and that your liberality would not assume unworthy motives for a questionable silence. If there were a sentiment in that pamphlet regarding yourself, as I fear there may have been, to occasion you an unpleasant feeling, I desire to assure you that I shall feel sorrow at the mishap, and a sorrow the deeper because the compliment you were pleased to pay me on my volume respecting the Mysteries was most generously gratuitous and wholly unexpected. From such a hand, on such an occasion, it affected me far otherwise than those who have chosen to ' wound by hearsay ' would be pleased to imagine, or at least to represent, if they knew it. Good treatment I have been so little accustomed to that your kindness overcame me. In fact I am ruled by the law of kindness, as I believe most men would be, if they were acquainted with the nature of the obligation, and it were proffered them for their acknowledgement."

*   *   *   *   *

To Mr. W. Hone.

(The original was so much cut about, and had evidently given Dr. Butler so much trouble, that I destroyed it.—Ed.)

[*October 6th* or *7th*, 1824.]

" Sir,—I should be wanting not only in common civility, but in feelings of a much higher and better nature, if I deferred to thank you for the very courteous and candid letter which accompanied the small packet I was favoured with from you last night.

" The sentiments which you so well and feelingly express are in unison with the best sympathies in our nature, and I give you full credit for sincerity. I shall therefore deal very plainly and perhaps at some length with you in reference to your letter.

" I must premise that, if I had taken offence at anything you had said in your pamphlet, I could neither have so long retained it nor in any case could have remained offended after the letter I yesterday received from you. But I assure you I never felt offence. I was quite aware that a man who throws stones must not expect his enemy to throw him roses in return ; and had you spoken more harshly than you did, I should still have felt no animosity—in fact I think I see in all you have said a wish to have said less, and something more than mere absence of personal hostility.

*   *   *   *   *

" You avow yourself a Christian, and your letter is written in a tone which forbids my doubting your assertion. What your peculiar religious opinions may be I have neither the right nor the wish to ask. They are probably materially different from mine ; but I have not the slightest wish to make you a proselyte, and only send the little book that accompanies this letter as a means of conveying to you my sentiments on an important point of practical Christianity, and at the same time of offering you a little acknowledgement for your courtesies and a token of my good-will. You will, I hope, accept it as such, and believe me to be, sir, your sincere well-wisher and obedient servant,

" S. BUTLER."

No doubt "the little book" above mentioned was the sermon on Christian liberty, already mentioned.

FROM BARON MERIAN.

" *November* 1st, 1824.

" DEAR SIR,—I will now write you a long letter in two parts. 1. Answer to your two last. 2. A matter concerning you. I begin. It was not my intention to jest when I sent you the printed notice of your *Aischylos.* I had no idea of your reading or even knowing of the *Bulletin Universel,* which is indeed a very commodious collection and still improving. I was rather grieved at the very improper moment when my lines arrived ; it had, however, been impossible for me to foresee an event like that you witnessed then unfortunately.* To all those I love I use to write gaily ; this is in my nature, which partakes of the nature of Shakespeare clowns. I cannot help it ; to be or look grave is a restraint upon me which I put off as soon as I can. The world to me is no object of serious contemplation. Pug's exclamation hums for ever about my ears : *Basta.* Your perfect quietness as to criticism is as it should be ; you need fear nobody, but yet it may be acceptable to you to hear of the general approbation your works meet with. I am glad to find my opinion of the Halls confirmed. Basil writes and acts like a man of genius. Pray do not forget to send me the *Curate of Derbyshire,* whatever he be about.† *Sufficit a te laudarier.*

*   *   *   *   *

" Part II.—You are acknowledged to be the best classical scholar of England. Suppose you added to that merit the merit of becoming the first synglossical scholar ? You know by long experience I

---

* I have not succeeded in finding out what Baron Merian alludes to.—ED.

† Probably this refers to a book called *Literæ Sacræ,* by the Rev. Authority Norman, Curate of Brailsford.

am not hot-headed or light-brained, nor propose whimsical things to my friends. The matter I mention is of the highest importance to learning in general, to philology in particular. Believe my words, of the highest importance, of indispensable necessity. What interest would I have to amuse you with fictions, or how venture it? No, ten years later what I now recommend will be a common practice. But would you not anticipate? Would you not march before, *dux gregis*? I demand no labour, not a great deal of your time ; you are, if any, capable of performing the task by preparing the minds of your countrymen. 'Tis like walking out of a beautiful garden (classic) into an open, spacious, and fruitful field (synglossic)."

*   *   *   *   *

From Baron Merian.

"*November 20th*, 1824.

" I beg your pardon. Verbs are before Nouns, and there is not a single noun on the globe but had a verb preceding. Certainly many verbs are formed of nouns, but those nouns had come from other verbs older and simple. You mention ' to blacken ' and ' to fire.' That is from *black* and this from *fire. Concessum.* But whence is *black* and whence *fire*? From verbs. There is an old verb ' firlo,' to cover, to daub, to darken (velo, velas), which made *falak, balak, black.* I believe this ; but suppose you should not like it, would that prove that there exists or existed no verb *fal*, or *bal*, or *pal*, or *bl*, from which you might conveniently derive *black*? Indeed not. I may be unable to assign the source, but will that destroy the source? Never."

(About two pages are omitted here.)

" P.S.—If you like authorities, here are two English ones. Whiter, *Prel.*, p. 88 : ' I am firmly enlisted under the party of the verbs.' Murray, I. 326 : ' It is certain that the verb was invented before the noun.' Here, however, I protest against the word ' invented.' Man no more invents or has invented words than he has invented voice. You may modify, compound, sever, but never invent."

The following letter and the one already given on pp. 131, 132, are the only two of his letters to Baron Merian which Dr. Butler drafted :—

To Baron Merian.

"Shrewsbury, *November 25th*, 1824.

" Most Excellent,—Why do you talk to me about English authorities in particular? English, French, German, are all of equal weight with me if they are on the side of truth.   As things stand between us, our friend Whiter, thrown into the scale together with your good self, weighs just nothing.   People are fond of novelties, and become attached to systems which look so pretty in their arrangement on paper that it is quite a pity to disturb them.   But I will put a plain question to you.   I believe you change your habitation about as often as I do my coat; still I presume, whether you move weekly or monthly, you live in a house composed of stones held together by mortar.   Now verbs are the mortar of sentences, but are no more the materials of them than lime and sand are the materials of the house.   The stones are the substantial part of the house, and the nouns are the substantial part of your sentences, which are held together and connected by the verbs as the stones are by the mortar.   But as the stones existed before the mortar or the house, so did the nouns before the verbs and sentences ; and the more I think on this, the more I am convinced that this is true, and that the system which you and Whiter and your learned coadjutors adopt is and must be false.

"You give me a long string of derivations in several languages. What does that prove ?   Nothing.   Admitting for the sake of argument, what I am not going to assert or deny, that there is only one primitive language, of which all other languages are dialects, it does not of course follow that the radical term in that language is the procreative principle of all the terms for the same thing in these different dialects.   For one nation may give a name to a thing from one circumstance and another from another. Thus one nation may derive the name of gold from its colour, another from its weight.   We call gold a precious metal, and we might form a name for gold from this circumstance ; a savage Indian might call iron his precious metal, and form his name for it accordingly.   What would become of our elementary radicals for gold and iron then ?   But, as I said before, this proves nothing —our dispute is, Which were first in the formation of language, nouns or verbs ?   I say nouns, because the things themselves, or the qualities of things or persons, *i.e.* nouns substantive or adjective, must have preceded those things or persons in certain states of action or suffering, *i.e.* verbs.   You say that verbs are not the names of things or persons in action or passion, and say that I cannot prove it.

" Now pray observe that I do not fix upon any two letters as an absolute and real root in the radical language, but I am assuming two letters just to argue upon and illustrate my position ; and whether they be real or hypothetical radicals does not matter one jot.

" Let us then suppose that in this radical language ST represents the elements to which we annex the notion of firm or quiescent position.   I say that these two elements, combined with

ω or ϵ, fragments of ἔγω, or with ϵμι, or if you prefer it with ' or
י, fragments of אני, form a verb signifying to fix, to place, or to
make to stand or to set. That is to say, that the verb ΣTaΩ
or ΣTaEMI in Greek, or the verb שׂתי in Hebrew, is derived
from the elementary form for a firm or quiescent position, combined with the pronoun or fragment of the pronoun signifying I,
and so of the other inflexions of the verb ΣTaειΣ, שׂתה, etc.

" This is my view of the subject, which I cannot help thinking
more simple and philosophical than that which you adopt, and
which your arguments, such is my stupidity, do not appear to me
to prove. For they only show, what I do not dispute, that there
is often a great affinity between the elementary terms for the same
thing in different languages, which may possibly therefore be
derived from some more [word lost] and primitive common stock.
But if you derive fire, for instance, from the principle of burning,
and say that in all languages FiRe contains the elementary principles of the verb to BuRn, even admitting the fact (which I do
not), I should say that it is not philosophical to derive the thing
from its qualities, which is like tracing the source of a stream
downwards instead of ascending ; and I would maintain, on the
contrary, that the verb to BuRn is derived from FiRe, of which it
is a quality, just as much as the effect is derived from the cause.
In fact, if nouns were derived from verbs (primitively I mean),
there would be no need of a noun at all, for verbs themselves
would be the names of things, which they are not—but names of
certain modes of action or suffering incident to things, and the
things must have existed previous to their having any mode of
action or suffering ; and so nouns must have preceded verbs in the
formation of language, and I cannot argue myself out of the belief
if I cannot argue you into it.

" I am sorry to tell you that the *Lexicon Ægypt. Lat.* is not to
be had for any quantity of love or money that I can offer. Still
I will not give up the search. I am writing to the Dean of
Christ Church, who is omnipotent at Oxford, on the subject, and
if it is possible to be got you shall have it.

" Believe me, my dear Baron, yours most truly,
" S. B.

" Barometer yesterday 27·89 in., the lowest, I believe, ever known
in this country. Violent tempest from the S.S.E. It has risen
to-day to 29·34 in."

The Baron's rejoinder would fill six whole pages, and I
must refer the reader to the original in the British Museum.
It is, I believe, accepted now that the terminal inflexions
of verbs are added pronouns in a changed and decayed

state. As for which came first, nouns or verbs, I am no philologist ; but may we not imagine that the earliest spoken symbols were neither purely nouns nor purely verbs, but did double duty, and more than double, becoming differentiated as the art of speech advanced ? Is it not a repetition in another form of the old question, Which came first, the egg or the hen?—the fact being that both have come from a something that was wholly neither. Or again, are they not like desire and power, which begin as mere sound of a going in the brain, too incoherent and inarticulate to be recognised as either power or desire ? The vague, indefinite sense of mere disturbance becomes first more coherent, and then assumes two alternating states that act and react upon one another and are called desire and power. I am aware, however, that I am venturing beyond my depth.

COPY OF A LETTER FROM SIR UVEDALE PRICE, BART., TO
    DR. PARR, IN WHICH CASE THE DATE IS PROBABLY 1820—
    1824.

" I have always regretted that from some misinformation or misconception of my own I should have fancied that you were to be absent from Hatton the whole of the time that I was at Guy's Cliffe, or I should not have been satisfied with a single visit. I might perhaps also have been lucky enough to meet Dr. Butler, whom I should have been very glad to have known, and among others on a very trifling one, but the circumstances of which, if they should be new to you, may afford you some amusement. In the neighbourhood of Sunning Hill, where I used to be a good deal, and very near George Ellis, there was a gentleman who wrote little erotic poems to Celia in an arbour, or to Chloe by a fountain, and these namby-pamby verses of his he printed—not published—in a neat volume, each poem having a page to itself with a large margin. He gave a copy to Ellis : and Gally Knight coming to Sunning Hill, and finding this volume on Ellis's table, was much diverted with the style of the verses, and being tempted by the broad margin he wrote under one of the poems :—

'Coughing in a shady grove
    Sat my Juliana ;
Lozenges I gave my love,
    Ipecacuanha.'

The fourth line is inimitable. I thought, however, that a sequel was wanting, and there still being room in the margin ventured to add another stanza :—

> 'Full half a score th' unwary maid
> From out my box did pick;
> Then turning tenderly she said,
> My Damon, I feel sick.'

"I thought this joint production of ours had remained snug in Ellis's library; but I find—now comes the πρὸς Διόνυσον—that Dr. Butler somehow got hold of them, perhaps without knowing whose they were, and amused himself with putting them into Greek and Latin hexameters and pentameters, in which languages ipecacuanha being neither in the Dispensary of Hippocrates nor of Galen must be '*ignota indictaque primum,*' and to suit the metre must be in regard to accent (*i.e.* quantity) *parce detorta,** though not '*Græco fonte.*' Charles Luxmore, the Bishop's son, has seen them, and promised to get me a copy, but has not yet, and I am very curious to see how Dr. Butler has managed it—I dare say very ingeniously and very differently from the way in which certain Greek hexameters were managed. These last, I fear, were very unfit to meet any critical eye, much less such a one as yours ; and I wish they may not have acted upon you as the lozenges are supposed to have done on the supposed damsel.

"With our best regards to yourself and Mrs. Parr,
"Believe me, my dear Sir,
"Most truly and respectfully yours,
"U. PRICE."

* Horace, *Ars Poetica*, 53.—ED.

CHAPTER XVIII.

CORRESPONDENCE—CHARGE—LAWSUIT.

Correspondence, February 18th, 1825—April 18th, 1825.—Extract from a Charge delivered June 22nd and 23rd, 1825, at Derby and Chesterfield.—Correspondence and Progress of the School Lawsuit, August 28th, 1825—December 15th, 1825.

CORRESPONDENCE, FEBRUARY 18TH, 1825—APRIL 18TH, 1825.

FROM J. P. HIGMAN, ESQ. (AFTERWARDS REV.), FELLOW AND TUTOR OF TRINITY COLLEGE, CAMBRIDGE.

"TRINITY COLLEGE, CAMBRIDGE, February 18th, 1825.

"REVEREND SIR,—Accustomed as you have long been to receive accounts of the very remarkable success that has attended all your pupils in our University examinations, it will give you little surprise, though I have no doubt very much pleasure, to learn that your pupil * is the University Scholar, and what is still more, that Eyre, another scholar from Shrewsbury, was next to him in the examination. You may naturally suppose that such extraordinary distinctions obtained in successive years by the pupils of one master has given rise to much talk in the University, respecting the distinguished abilities and high classical attainments of the present Master of Shrewsbury School. Amidst the general voice of praise, I hope you will allow mine to be heard ; particularly as it proceeds from a College which in former times and under the government, or rather intrigue, of a faction was not disposed to do justice to one whose exertions in the cause of literature and ancient learning deserved somewhat more than flat jests and pert, superficial criticism. That day, sir, is gone by; the party is gone, and with it have disappeared all feelings of coldness to the editor of Æschylus."

FROM DR. BUTLER TO —— (?).

[February or March, 1825.]

"SIR,—I am directed as chairman of the committee for

* T. W. Peile, afterwards Head-Master of Repton

275

improving the entrance into Shrewsbury by the Castle gates to acquaint you with the great advantage which Lord Darlington's property will receive thereby, and to solicit a subscription on his lordship's account.

" It is proposed to give Lord Darlington that portion of the street adjoining his two houses opposite the school gardens, according to the annexed plan extending even beyond the present channel, and to build up a retaining wall, so as to form a terrace for the houses and a driving way to the Castle.

" Mr. Pelham as tenant of the Castle has very liberally offered to build this wall to the level of the intended terrace, which will cost him about eighty guineas, besides subscribing £50 to the general purposes of the improvement."

[Rest of draft not found.—Ed.]

To the Trustees of Shrewsbury School.

" *March* 1st, 1825.

" Gentlemen,—It was proposed at the last meeting of the committee for improving the street and lowering the hill from Mr. Palin's to a point below the old Castle gates, to ask the trustees of the school to be at half the expense of Mr. Carline's estimate for taking down the present boundary wall of the school garden, and rebuilding it in its present form, using the old material. His estimate amounts to £68 18s., the half of which is £34 9s. The committee came to the resolution of making this proposal to the trustees on the score of the great and highly important benefit which the school would receive from shutting up the thoroughfare through the school lane, and the actual increase of ground which would be gained by the school by exchanging part of the present school garden near the street for that part of the school lane which is given up by the public in consequence of stopping the thoroughfare.

" I have had a survey made, which I enclose, of the land which it is proposed to exchange, by which it appears that the school will gain sixty-five and three-quarters, say sixty-six, square yards. This will be purchasing the ground at near half a guinea a square yard, which I conceive is a pretty good price. Still, however, I am satisfied that the benefit which will result from stopping up the thoroughfare through the school lane is so important that it would be well worth while for the trustees to give four times that sum in order to accomplish this purpose. Besides which, a great public advantage will be gained by lowering the hill.

" The estimates for lowering the hill are not yet made out, but the expense will be very considerable ; and unless the school, as well as other neighbours and the public at large, come forward liberally, I think it will not be effected. I propose on my own part to contribute £50, if the thoroughfare through the school lane is stopped up, but not otherwise.

"What I wish earnestly to press on your consideration is, that you should never allow the work to be begun in the school garden till the stable which is to be price of Mr. Dixon's concurrence in stopping up the school lane is bought and transferred to him. The work must be done before the magistrate can sign the order for stopping up the school lane ; but you can stipulate with the committee, of whom I am one, that it shall not be begun till this transfer is completed, and I shall be greatly obliged to you if you will do this, because I thought I saw in a leading member of the committee a strong inclination to escape from this obligation, which would effectually destroy all hope of stopping up the thoroughfare.

"Having now purchased Mr. Gwyn's house and all the others in the school lane, I have no difficulty with the other tenants ; and I should hope—when I am able to examine the houses (which will be at Lady Day) and arrange my plans—that I may be able to find enough space at the upper extremity to make a porter's lodge, and in that case should wish to remove thither the fine old gateway from the bottom of the lane—which I shall then ask the trustees to put up there and furnish with gates in proper style, so as to admit of a carriage to drive under them. I should give the porter's lodge free of expense as long as I continue here, and whenever I quit—without wishing to pledge the trustees to any engagement on their part—I have it in view to make them the first offer of all the property I have purchased in the school lane on liberal terms. This is of so great importance to the schools that I hope they will not be easily deterred from availing themselves of that opportunity ; but if they should decline it, I could wish it to be understood that in such case the space occupied by the porter's lodge must revert to me, and the gates must be removed by the trustees to a point below, or at the termination of, my property, as they might injure the sale of the houses to strangers."

Besides other and more serious evils arising from the fact that there was a thoroughfare through the school grounds, difficulties used to arise between the boys and any passer-by who for whatever reason attracted their attention. My old friend and schoolfellow Robert Taylor, Esq., late of the Indian Civil Service, was told by the late Rev. G. W. Rowland that there was a certain exciseman in Shrewsbury who was very trim and neat in his attire, but who had a bottle nose of more than usual size. As he passed through the school lane the boys used to call him "Nosey," and this made him so angry that he complained to Dr. Butler, who sympathised, and sent for the head boy, to whom he gave strict injunctions that the boys should not say "Nosey" any more.

Next day, however, the exciseman reappeared even more angry than before. It seems that not a boy had said "Nosey," but that as soon as he was seen coming the boys ranged themselves in two lines through which he must pass, and all fixed their eyes intently upon his nose. Again Dr. Butler summoned the head boy, and spoke more sharply. "You have no business," said he, "to annoy a man who is passing through the school on his lawful occasions; don't look at him." But again the exciseman returned to Dr. Butler furious with indignation, for this time, as soon as he was seen, every boy had covered his eyes with his hand till he had gone by. "What would you have me say to these fellows?" said Dr. Butler. "Can you not see that they will obey, and yet evade, every order that I give them? Had you not better keep out of their way by going up the public street instead of going through them?" And, as the story ends here, I suppose that this was what the exciseman eventually decided on doing.

FROM THE REV. JOHN LYNES.

"HATTON, *March 7th,* 1825.

"MY DEAR SIR,—Dr. Parr expired after a short, but not painful, struggle at six o'clock yesterday evening. You are earnestly requested, in a paper directed to his executors, to preach a very short sermon on the day of his funeral, which is fixed for Monday the 14th inst.

"The number of friends I have to make acquainted with the event will, I hope, excuse this short notification."

Many letters from Dr. Parr's bedside, written by Dr.

John Johnstone and the Rev. J. Lynes, will be found in
due order of date amongst Dr. Butler's papers in the British
Museum.   Dr. Butler preached as requested, but I must
refer my readers to Professor J. E. B. Mayor's pages for
an account of the sermon itself.

FROM THE MASTER OF ST. JOHN'S COLLEGE, CAMBRIDGE.

" ST. JOHN's, *March 11th,* 1825.

" MY DEAR MR. ARCHDEACON,—I have read your memorial
to the trustees with very great interest, and hope there are few
cases on record in which there are symptoms of similar intentional
and fraudulent delay, or culpable negligence.   Sorry I am to
say that, as far as I can form an opinion, the judges are not free
from the latter imputation.   The fears which the parties may
have of exposure may operate upon them to bring the suit to
a conclusion, which but for your memorial and petition would
probably have gone on for another century.   From the House of
Commons little further advantage can be expected beyond the
exposure.

" I will send your statement back the first favourable opportunity
I have, and if I can procure a copy of the Bishop of Peterborough's
case respecting the Rector of Byfield, I will enclose it in the
same parcel.   It is drawn up with very great moderation, but it
leaves an impression on the mind unfavourable to our judges,
who seem to have constantly in view the lowering of Church
authority—which object they pursue *per fas atque nefas.*   But
to turn to a more agreeable subject, I congratulate you most
sincerely on the success of your scholars.   In truth you stand
at the head of all public schools in this kingdom.   May the
Master of Shrewsbury be rewarded as he deserves.

" The measures you have taken with the orators is the most
prudent and likely to be the most effectual that can be adopted.
In confidence I assure you that the Master of Trinity has done
more harm to the University discipline than any other individual
in the memory of man.   Concessions to young men are frequently
like concessions to Roman Catholics, never to be recalled or
remedied.

" I have had little leisure to look into the book you had the
kindness to send me.*   I shall, however, give particular attention
to it.   I apprehend I must condemn the spirit which has of late
appeared, and which your author shows, of lowering the value
of natural religion.   The arguments brought forward are not

---

* Probably *Litera Sacra,* by the Rev. Authority Norman.

conclusive, and if they were, they would only have the effect of undermining instead of supporting revelation.

" Give my kindest remembrances to Mrs. Butler.

" Most truly yours,

" J. Wood."

From the Rev. Samuel Tillbrook.

[Undated—probably end of March, 1825.]

" My dear Doctor,—I wish you well through all your troubles, and condole with you for the loss you have sustained in the poor old Doctor. Report says you are Dr. Parr's sole executor: if this be true you are more to be pitied than envied. Do not forget your promise to secure a pipe for me as a keepsake ; I will hang it alongside Dr. Clarke's Turkish tube.

" Have you as yet fixed on a successor to your late curate ? Beware of Master ——. I heard one of the Fellows of Emmanuel College say that he should feel half inclined to speak in false praise of him, for the sake of getting him removed from the College. Can you guess from what country the sincerity of this man sprang ?

" We were all delighted at Baines's success. Do you want a funny rogue to succeed him ? We have an A.B. with a nose like the devil's : a wrangler of this year, and an honest, well-disposed man—sound in mathematics, but not a very good classic. He would make a better indoor than in school tutor.

" Sheepshanks is a great man now. He told me with a voice like one of the tuned singers of St. Peter's, Rome, ' that although he was not quite the plenipotentiary, yet he was almost so among the folks at Falmouth.'

" I am off to the trouts to-morrow. I shall kill, but not eat. *Apropos,* the lamperns were served up *à la maître d'hôtel,* and delicious they were. I shall soon have to write to you on the subject of Izaak Walton's monument. I have had a most kind-hearted letter from the Dean of Winton, and an invitation to spend a few days at the Deanery while selecting the site for the erection of the bust or statue. But more of this anon. Good-night, and joy go with you. I am dead tired, and ever yours truly,   " S. T."

To Mr. W. Hone, 45, Ludgate Hill.

(Original draft, with four abortive beginnings, destroyed by me.—Ed.)

" April 2nd, 1825.

" Sir,—Whatever may be the difference of religious and political opinions between us, I am confident you will not be displeased at my offering you the sermon sent herewith as a proof of the favourable impression made on my mind by the letter which I received from you some time ago, and of which I spoke in the terms I thought it merited to the dear and revered friend whose character I have attempted to sketch in the pages now sent you, the very last time I saw him before he was on his deathbed.

"Believe me, yours faithfully,   "S. BUTLER."

FROM MR. W. HONE.

"45, LUDGATE HILL, LONDON, *April 4th,* 1825.

"SIR,—To say that I am obliged and flattered by the honour you do me through the kind note accompanying a copy of your sermon at the funeral of Dr. Parr, would be a cold expression of my feelings on receiving them this morning. My alacrity in acknowledging the unlooked-for favour would be, if I had the pleasure of being known to you better, an assurance of my warm and, I would almost say, my affectionate respect on the occasion.

"Shut up with my books at the back of my house in the midst of London, I scarcely know but from a daily newspaper what passes within the world, and I was ignorant that it had devolved on you to 'bury Cæsar'—I speak so of him whose vast intellect commanded my admiration, and whose childlike simplicity so attempered his greatness that I would say of him whom most men feared, I know not whether I most reverenced his greatness or loved his gentleness. A hero, it has been said, is no hero to his valet ; but this is because the valet is not also a hero. There were men about Dr. Parr to whom he seemed only a little higher than themselves, because he descended to the meanness of their capacity, and who, when his mind soared to the source of light, imagined it lost in clouds. These were babblers of anecdotes concerning him in his lifetime, and will be tale-tellers of his table-talk now—gossips of what they call his 'common' table-talk, who never talked commonly because he never talked ill. So, at least, I infer he could not talk, who, in the few interviews I had the happiness to be indulged with, uttered wiser things than most can bring forth in the course of their existence.

"I remember that when I first saw Dr. Parr, on his invitation to me to breakfast with him, I went from Warwick to Hatton with delight and trembling, and approached him with indescribable awe after I had been announced by his man Sam. The Doctor rallied me on my embarrassment, and in five minutes I was astonished by finding myself as intimate with him as if I had been known to him for years. He had the art, by being without art, of making a man easy in his company immediately, and the four or five hours I spent at Hatton Parsonage that morning were the most delightful I ever enjoyed—save on my next visit, which the Doctor insisted on my making to him the Sunday following at dinner, when I had the felicity of hearing his conversation till all the party left in the evening, leaving me to sleep there. After supper the Doctor challenged me to meet him as early as, he was pleased to say, I should please in the morning; this we settled should be at six o'clock. At that hour I left my room, while the clock struck, and descended to the library, where the Doctor awaited my arrival, gave me most cordial greetings, and then, telling me he had stayed the lighting of his pipe till I came, he sat down and said, ' Now to business.'

"That morning interview, sir, was brought to my recollection (it never can be erased from my memory) by your sermon, and especially by its fifteenth page. He lighted his pipe and said, 'Now, Hone, to business.' 'In what way, sir?' Withdrawing his pipe and slapping his hand on my knee, he answered by a solemn look (one of his looks), 'You must answer me a question, and answer it honestly and truly—What is your creed?' It was an unexpected and irresistible requisition, and I answered your, and allow me to add, sir, my, excellent friend honestly, truly, and fully. He was the only man to whom I ever did, or perhaps could, disclose myself, and not a secret of my heart was hidden from him. The remembrance of those three hours before Mrs. Parr came down to breakfast brings tears to my eyes. Dr. Parr, sir, was the noblest-hearted man I ever talked with, and the wisest I have ever known, and wiser than any I can know ; that is my conviction and belief. I loved him more than any human being of whom I saw so little ; his death was a blow upon my heart. The last time I saw him was at Hatton, in the autumn of 1823, where I spent about three hours, and nearly one-third of the time was occupied by himself on the subject of human decay and death. His mind then was vigorous as a giant's limbs in full manhood. Pardon me, sir, for having scribbled so much and to so little purpose, seeing that your letter required I should briefly and respectfully acknowledge your remembrance of me ; and let me add, I account it a happy circumstance that what I thought an evil has been a good to me—I mean the accident that procured me the distinction of your regard. I hope, sir, I may cherish it, and that no act of mine will ever occasion you to think of me otherwise than as, sir,

"Your most respectful and sincerely obliged servant,

"W. HONE."

FROM BARON MERIAN.

"*April 5th,* 1825.

"Good news ! I have spent all your money, and more, I believe. We have bought all Venice. The books are coming, and I look for them every day, which made me postpone writing to you, dear sir. Having the advice, I wanted to have the chest too, which I shall keep at your disposal, till you come or com

mand, and then we shall settle our accounts.   But do me a favour
if you please, and τᾰχὺ too.   Klaproth wants a little money,
some £20, which is no wonder, his stay being so much protracted.
Pray send them to him some way or other, and take and seize
me for your debtor.   He was quite enchanted with the care you
took of him.   Accept my best thanks for that.   You behaved
indeed very kindly.   Now as to our *prælia gigantum.*   I say my
ally TIME must decide.   Meanwhile I humbly ask whether *sedile*
is from *sedeo,* or *sedeo* from *sedile?*   And then I remain your in
comparable friend for ever, in spite of the American affairs.
Have."

FROM LORD CLARENDON.

"N. AUDLEY STREET, *April* 16th, 1825.

＊   ＊   ＊   ＊   ＊

"I do not know whether there is at present an evening sermon
at Kenilworth.   If there is not, there surely ought to be in such
a place.   I have a strong idea that the bishop would recommend
it, should it not exist at present; but it will be infinitely preferable, on many accounts, that it should originate with yourself
on the present opportunity."

TO LORD CLARENDON.

"*April* 18th, 1825.

＊   ＊   ＊   ＊   ＊

"P.S.—None of the parishioners have ever expressed to me a
wish for two sermons.   If the curate is willing to try a sermon
from Lady Day to Michaelmas, and the inhabitants are disposed to
make him an adequate compensation, there can be no objection
to his making the attempt next year.   I conceive that he will do
it with more effect when he is a little known to them than on his
first coming."

The postscript as originally drafted stood : "I am quite
sure it would be perfectly useless at Kenilworth to have
an evening sermon in the winter half-year."

- -

EXTRACTS FROM A CHARGE DELIVERED BY DR. BUTLER AS
    ARCHDEACON ON JUNE 22ND AND 23RD, 1825, AT DERBY
    AND AT CHESTERFIELD.

"REVEREND BRETHREN,—At our last meeting I informed you
that I was about to commence a personal visitation of every
parish within this archdeaconry.   I have been able to accomplish
this, not indeed without considerable exertion, and a progress of

about twelve hundred miles, in the course of the two last
summers; and I conceive that it may not be uninteresting to
you if I make the result of that inspection the subject of our
present consideration.

"The archdeaconry of Derby is, as you know, commensurate
with the county and divided into three deaneries, Derby, Ashbourne, and Chesterfield. There are, however, about thirty
churches which, being either peculiar or donative, are not under
archidiaconal jurisdiction. The greatest part of these lie in the
north-western side of the county, from about Bakewell, towards
Buxton and Ashbourne.

"Of the remainder, being a hundred and sixty-three parishes,
there are, in the deanery of Derby, ninety-one; in that of
Ashbourne, twenty-one; and in that of Chesterfield, fifty-one
churches.

　　　*　　　　*　　　　*　　　　　　　*

"Of the above hundred and sixty-three churches, ninety-one
have houses fit for the residence of a clergyman; twenty have
houses, but unfit for the residence of a clergyman—and, indeed,
nearly all these last mentioned are mere cottages, just capable of
accommodating a labourer and his family; and fifty-two have no
house. So that, in fact, there are seventy-two churches which
virtually have no place of residence for their minister.

"On the ninety-one livings which have houses, there are
resident sixty incumbents and twenty-one curates. In the remaining ten cases, in which neither incumbent nor curate appear
resident, the incumbent, generally, is so virtually; either living in
his own house in the parish, instead of the parsonage, and himself
doing the duty, or residing on an adjoining living, and doing also
the duty of that on which he does not reside.

"Of the twenty livings which have no fit houses, and the fifty-
two which have no house at all, many are of small value; and
being themselves insufficient for the support of a clergyman, and
of small population, requiring only single duty, are served by
the curate or incumbent of a neighbouring parish. There are,
however, five of these which have their incumbent and five which
have their curate resident in the parish, and of the remaining
sixty-two the duty, in thirty-nine cases, is performed by the
incumbent himself.

"There were educated, in schools connected with the Church
establishment, at the time my survey was completed, eleven
thousand seven hundred and fifty-nine children; but owing, I
hope in some degree to my own previous recommendations, and
no doubt much more to the zeal and earnestness with which our
able and excellent diocesan has taken up the subject during his
last year's visitation, I trust this number, large as it appears, is
now considerably augmented.

"At the time of my own survey there were twenty-nine parishes, containing fourteen thousand inhabitants, without any school whatever.

* * * * *

"The charges for dilapidations, even where the houses are even in tolerable repair, are of late years seldom light ; but where they have fallen at all to decay they are so serious, that it is highly for the interest of every clergyman to preserve his family as much as possible from these demands, by preventing the necessity for them.

"Claims of this nature always come at the most unfavourable time ;—when a family is in affliction from the loss of its head, and not unfrequently reduced from comparative affluence, or at least competence, to a narrow income. When a heavy sum is demanded at a time like this, and is to be paid from means already straitened, the hardship is great indeed ; and it is often equally hard on the succeeding incumbent, if he does not receive a sum which he cannot afford to lose, and which in turn must be paid by his own family to his successor.

"The best way of obviating these difficulties is by a slight annual sacrifice of income, which is so connected with our present subject that I cannot consider the mention of it irrelevant either in time or place.

"Circumscribed as the incomes of the clergy generally are, they are called upon by every endearing tie, and every domestic duty, to make some sacrifice, even for a moderate income, in order to provide for their wives and children after their decease. Every man who enjoys only a life income is peculiarly bound to this duty, that when he is taken from his family, and the great means of support derived from his appointment are also taken from them, they may not be left wholly or comparatively destitute. · A lamentable case, which within the last few months has fallen under my own observation, has led me more particularly to make these remarks ; and I trust, my Reverend Brethren, you will not think me wandering from the topics which ought to form matter for our consideration on these occasions, when I recommend to you the importance of Life Assurance.

"If this is done at a tolerably early period, the expense is comparatively small, and the advantage is in time considerably increased. But even at what may be considered as the middle age of life, it is not too late, and there are some societies, I believe, which are better adapted to this age than others. These, how-ever, it is not for me to point out—you can make your own inquiries and arrangements, if you have not already done so. But I may perhaps be allowed to state that one is recently instituted exclusively for persons who are or have been members of either of our Universities, and is patronised by many of the first characters in the Church; the details of it I need not enter into here; but its institution being recent, and its admission of members confined exclusively to academic persons, I have felt it but reasonable to make known to you its existence.

"Such, Reverend Brethren, is a succinct account of the general result of my survey. I will not detain you now with observations on other topics, but content myself with expressing a hope that the labours I have undertaken in the last two years may be acceptable and useful to you. And while I thank you for the kind attention which I received in many instances, on my progress, and which were offered in many more than I was able to accept, I beg leave to assure you of my earnest desire to promote, as far as I can, every object connected with your own comforts and respectability, and the welfare of that venerable establishment to which we all belong."

CORRESPONDENCE AND PROGRESS OF THE SCHOOL LAWSUIT, AUGUST 28TH, 1825—DECEMBER 15TH, 1825.

FROM THE REV. S. TILLBROOK.

"Ivy Cottage, *August 28th,* 1825.

"Dear Archdeacon,—As you feel disposed with your usual good sense and kind indulgence to overlook my transgressions and allow me, like a true Petrensian, to 'go a-fishing,' I will send you a salmon fresh or dried, or a pot of char, *si modo fata,* or something as good.

*   *   *   *   *

"I expect the Bishop of Chester here in a day or two to consecrate the new chapel—and also Lady Le Fleming. She has been very polite and attentive to me, granting the use of the boat and lake, and very dearly do the pike and perch pay for renewing their acquaintance with old Till.

"We had a delightful day yesterday at Wordsworth's ! ! ! Prof. John Wilson, Lockhart, and the Great Unknown. Sir Walter is really a delightful fellow, full of life and anecdote—a walking collection of novels and interesting stories. He knows everything modern, and everybody of note—is mild, unassuming, kind and affectionate in his manner even to children. I wish you would come and see me here some summer. I could entertain four or five well. 'Tis a charming spot, I promise you. Wilson is as wild as ever, but more of this when we meet.

*   *   *   *   *

"I was pleased with your account of the salmon of fifty pounds.

I cannot kill you one so large, but if I kill one at all, great or small, he shall be sent to my Salopian brother of the angle. Hildyard shall have rooms. Our new court gets on famously. I should like to see it finished during my bursarship."

I have already explained that one wing of the " new court " of Peterhouse bears Mr. Tillbrook's initials, S. T.

To the Rev. Francis Hodgson.*

[*August* or *September*, 1825.]

" My dear Friend,—Nothing has occasioned my silence but incessant wearing and exhausting occupation. My papers now lie in heaps two feet high on two tables. I am in the midst of drawing petitions to both Houses of Parliament respecting our lawsuit, the perusal of papers for which is enough for a moderate man's life; the assistance I am giving to the Memoirs of Parr; the dreadful labour of doing, what no man has ever yet done, ascertaining the quantities (by reference) of proper names for an index to my maps; besides my usual labours with a fifth and sixth form of a hundred and twenty boys,† and the care and superintendence of all the rest; and of my archdeaconry, the latter a far more troublesome office than you may imagine ; add to this some thirty or forty workmen, who require some little superintendence (and even a little adds to what is much), and who have been now near five months at work building me a house in the school lane, the whole of which I have purchased, pulled down, and am rebuilding, and you may well imagine I am not able to reply by return of post.

" I have fresh plagues at Kenilworth, which in the course of the last eight months will have cost me near four years of the clear income in produces. I heartily wish I had resigned it ten years ago. But a truce to torments which irritate me of late by their apparently endless multiplication."

It would not have been surprising if failure had attended some one or more of the many enterprises above alluded to, but throughout Dr. Butler's life everything that he set his hand to prospered. The boys taught at this time were the terror of all other head-masters with clever pupils. As

---

* I have taken this letter from the *Life of Francis Hodgson*, by the Rev. J. T. Hodgson (Macmillan), 1878, Vol. II., pp. 189, 190.

† Dr. Butler took the fifth form as well as the sixth himself.

for the lawsuit, that had baffled so many generations, he carried it to a triumphant conclusion in what was for those days an incredibly short time. The extracts above given from his charge of 1825 will show the thoroughness with which he worked his archdeaconry. Furthermore, any extra demands on his time and patience seem to have been invariably met. When the approaches to the north side of Shrewsbury were to be improved, Dr. Butler, as we have seen, was chairman of the committee appointed for the purpose. If any one wanted to know anything about anything, Dr. Darwin, Mr. Blakeway, and Dr. Butler were the local encyclopædias to one or other of whom the whole country-side would immediately appeal—and of this excellent triumvirate Dr. Butler was perhaps the hardest worked of all.

FROM DR. MALTBY, AFTERWARDS BISHOP, FIRST OF CHICHESTER, AND THEN OF DURHAM.

"BUCKDEN, *September 1st,* 1825.

"MY DEAR DR. BUTLER,—You will render a most acceptable service to all scholars as well as students by giving us as perfect a list of geographical names, with their quantities marked, as can be reasonably hoped for. I have often felt the perplexities which you mention in reading Cæsar, etc.

*   *   *   *   *

"I have often suspected that the Roman poets used these barbarous names as suited their verse. How can we lay down any rules why it should be Axōnes, Suessōnes, yet Pictŏnes, Senŏnes, etc.? In Asiatic names it is an almost invariable rule, I think, that penult. in ānes, āres, and ātes is long, and in ăces, ămes, and ăges short. You of course remember Virgil's Morĭni, where you and I, without such authority, should be disposed to say Morīni."

*   *   *   *   *

TO THE EDITOR OF THE "SHREWSBURY CHRONICLE."

"SCHOOLS, SHREWSBURY, *September 7th,* 1825.

"SIR,—As you may perhaps like to have an account of the gold coins lately found at Holyhead, as noticed in the *Shrewsbury Chronicle* for August 26, one of which I have obtained by your kind interference, I beg leave to say that the following remarks are much at your service.

"The coin in my possession is of gold, and weighs three penny-weights and a half.

"On the obverse is the head of the Emperor Constantine the Great, in very excellent preservation, wearing a diadem (strictly speaking, for it is a simple band) of pearls and jewels, with this inscription, CONSTANTINVS. MAX. AVG., *i.e.* Constantinus Maximus Augustus.

"On the reverse is a wreath very neatly executed, within which is the inscription VOTIS XXX ; and on the exergue T S E.

"The words VOTIS XXX mean *votis tricesimis*, or the thirtieth time on which vows were offered for the prosperity of the Emperor ; in other words, the thirtieth year of his reign. This will be the year 335 of the Christian Era, and, as Constantine reigned about thirty-one years and a half, will bring the coin to a period within the last two years before his death.

"The letters T S E on the exergue have been thought by Bandurius to mean *Trevirensis secundæ quintum*, or the fifth bounty given to soldiers of the Legion (or, as I should rather say, of the Cohort) called *Trevirensis secunda*. The Emperors on their birthdays, or days of accession, and on some other solemn occasions, used to distribute a largess of money to their troops, and if we adopt this interpretation we must understand that the gold was coined for the purpose of distributing among the soldiers of that cohort. I confess I do not incline to this opinion, though supported by such high authority ; nor indeed do I know anything of this cohort, except that no such cohort appears ever to have been stationed in Britain. This however will not be proof positive that it might not have been coined for their use. That there was a Roman station at Holyhead cannot be doubted. In Gough's *Camden*, Vol. III., p. 204, we are told that the walls of the churchyard of Holyhead are evidently Roman workmanship. Holyhead (in Welsh, Caer Guby) derives its name from the adjacent mountain, which was inhabited by St. Kibius, a disciple of the great Hilary of Poitiers, about A.D. 380—some thirty-five years after this coin was minted.

"The interpretation, however, which I prefer giving to these letters is, *Treviris signata, in officina quinta*—coined at Treves in the fifth minting-house.

"Treves was one of the six cities of Belgium which had the right of coinage under the later Emperors. The letter E, the Greek numeral for five, is constantly thus used in ancient mint-marks ; and it was also the custom of the ancients to mark the minting-houses by letters, as in the present instance.

"Thus we find T. ARL., *Tertia Arelatensis officina*—the third minting-house at Arles ; ROM. T., *Romæ in officina tertia*—the third minting-house at Rome ; and to come to the point still nearer, *E. SIS.*, *Quinta officina Sisciæ*—the fifth minting-house at Siscia ; S. M. SISC. E , *Signata moneta Sisciæ in quinta officina*— money coined in the fifth minting-house at Siscia ; so KRT. E., *Karthagine in quinta officina*—at the fifth minting-house in Carthage. And to put the matter beyond all doubt, we find S. M. T. S. E., *Sacra moneta Treviris signata in quinta officina*— sacred money coined at Treves in the fifth minting-house, or, as we might say, in Mint E.

　　　　" I remain, Sir, your very obedient servant,
　　　　　　　　　　　　　　　　　　　　　　　　　" S. Butler."

Mr. Grueber, of the British Museum, tells me that TS has been now ascertained to mean, not Trêves, but Thessalonica. He also tells me that, though Dr. Butler was right in rejecting Bandurius's explanation of the E, the letter nevertheless refers not to the number of the minting-house, but to the number of the issue from the minting-house, and means that the coin bearing this letter was a coin of a fifth issue, such letters, in fact, being private marks for the information of the mint.

From Baron Merian.

" September 26th, 1825.

" Dear Sir,—Johnson, in his grammar concerning *a* and *an*, where he rightly calls *an* older than *a*, has not fixed the principle of the use of *a* or *an* before *h*. Examples are not rules. The rule, however, is very simple : place *a* before words of German origin beginning with *h* ; place *an* before words of Latin, French, etc., etc., origin beginning with *h*. I suppose your actual grammarians know this rule, but it is evident that Johnson knew it not, though his examples coincide neatly with it. And mark, this is the chief difference between the old and the new way : the former tells you, Do so and so, to get this and that by heart ; the latter *tells you why*, and speaks, not only to your memory, but likewise to your judgement. The former commands, the latter explains. The former gives you examples, the latter principles.

" The neglect of those principles has, among the rest, occasioned a strange mistake concerning Samskrit[*sic*], which the learned ones of divers countries placed far above (higher up in antiquity) its proper place, considering it as a mother of the other Hindoo dialects—nay, of whatever is spoken between Ceylon and Iceland. Now this, considering its thin and long forms, it cannot be. Very ancient forms (words) are, on the contrary, thick and short. The said Samskrit (the very name means worked together, worked up, perfected) is an artificial embroidering placed upon precedent rough and popular forms, which are still to be found in many parts of the East Indies (or Hindies), exactly as old English or French terms will be found in dales and on hills, and are the solid rude stuff which has been successively rubbed and polished into polite and classical language."

* * * * *

FROM THE REV. S. TILLBROOK.

"*November* 15*th*, 1825.

" DEAR ARCHDEACON,—Are we to keep a metropolitan Christmas again this season, or do you remain in scholastic durance on the banks of the Severn? *flumina amem* as usual—let me know your intended movements. I spent such a happy summer in my Ivy Cottage that I feel half inclined to go down and kindle the Christmas log ; if, however, I could be sure of a fortnight or three weeks in town and Brighton with your cheering wit and good fellowship, I should be tempted to march with you into any winter quarters you might prefer. What think you of our old nook at the Hummums ? *Apropos*, the landlord told me that you had written to him for a room and had never appeared to tenant it. Was this so ? I offered to pay any demand he might have upon you, but the sly fellow said he hoped to see you again, and that the matter might be settled then—from me he would take nothing, apprehensive no doubt that it might turn out a quitrent payment.

" Tom [Dr. Butler's son] and I are better friends than neighbours, for he is too far off for me to gossip much with him. He, however, comes and sits and sups with old Till whenever he feels inclined, and I heartily trust he will continue to do so. I will give him the best of anything I have, not forgetting advice to freshmen ' gratis.'

" I have, I am glad to say, received great benefit from the operation Alexander performed on my right eye, which had been wrong for a year and a half. I must practise self-denial, mortify the flesh, drink little, move about more, and in short consider my eye as the safety-valve of my whole body—never committing excess of any kind. *Tertia pars morborum jejunio sanantur*, or veal broth and *potage au vin*.

" Write me word, I beseech you, and give my orders for the Winter Campaign. With regards to Mrs. Butler and all friends, believe me, dear Doctor,

" Yours very faithfully,

" S. T."

Towards the end of 1825 Dr. Butler, dissatisfied with

the Chief Baron's delay in announcing his decision, prepared a petition to be presented by the Bishop of Lichfield
and Coventry, the Master and Fellows of St. John's, and
the Trustees of Shrewsbury School, to the House of Lords,
stating the facts very briefly and clearly, and praying for
" such relief as to your honourable house shall seem fit."

The memorial, the draft of which is in the British
Museum, says nothing about the lawsuit having been
commenced in the reign of James I., but begins with the
year 1779, when it probably became active again after a
period of quiescence. It had been going on ever since
1779, with the exception of a space of ten years between
1796 and 1806, during which the Albrighton estate had
escheated to the Crown; between 1806 and 1825 the
trustees had paid over £3,000 in legal expenses.

I do not think this memorial ever can have been presented, for on the 22nd of November, 1825, the Chief Baron
gave judgement in favour of the trustees, giving them also
four-fifths of the cost.

At a special meeting of the trustees held November 26th
a vote of thanks was passed to Dr. Butler. The defendants
appealed, but on December 15th, 1825, the Chief Baron,
after hearing a three hours' argument, confirmed his former
decision.

CHAPTER XIX.

CORRESPONDENCE—CHARGE—CORRESPONDENCE.

Correspondence, December (?), 1825—June 15th, 1826.—Extracts from a
Charge on the Education of the Poorer Classes delivered at Derby
and Chesterfield, June 15th and 16th, 1826.—Correspondence, June
16th and 17th, 1826.—Vote of Thanks from the Trustees, October,
1826.

CORRESPONDENCE, DECEMBER (?), 1825—JUNE 15TH, 1826.

To the Hon. G. Neville,* Master of Magdalene College, Cambridge.

[December (?), 1825.]

" DEAR SIR,— . . . When you informed me last spring
of the probable vacancies in the Millington exhibitions, I
used the utmost pains to send you two first-rate scholars as
candidates, and in this I flattered myself that I had succeeded. I
find the names of both of them have since been withdrawn from
your boards. Since that time I have pressed the parent of another
of my pupils, also of very high promise, to send his son as a
candidate, which he has declined, though an exhibition of sixty
guineas would be a material object to a clergyman with rather
a large family. You will naturally imagine that there must be
some foundation for this reluctance, and the object of my present
letter is confidentially to tell you what I believe it to be. I think,
then, that there is a general persuasion among the young men
educated at this school that they are not favourably treated at
Magdalene College, and that one of the principal examiners,
whose opinion is supposed to have much weight with you, not

---

* The Master of Magdalene's name is given in the University
Calendar as the Hon. and Very Rev. George Neville-Grenville.
In Dr. Butler's letters of March 10th and 15th, 1826, he is addressed
as the Hon. G. Grenville. In his own letter of June 16th, 1826,
he signs himself George Neville.

293

only does not encourage, but does not look with a friendly eye, on the candidates who come for examination. Pray understand that I do not state the fact to be so, but am informing you of a general opinion, which I have no means of contradicting."

*   *   *   *   *

FROM J. S. COPLEY, ESQ., AFTERWARDS LORD LYNDHURST.

(Original in possession of Mrs. G. L. Bridges and Miss Butler.)

"GEORGE STREET, *January* 16*th*, 1826.

"DEAR SIR,—I thank you very sincerely for your obliging letter. With the contents of it I am, as I have reason to be, perfectly satisfied, and I beg you will so consider me and accept my acknowledgements. Everything as to election matters being thus over, allow me to ask a very great favour. If I could prevail upon you to give me the pleasure of your company at dinner on Friday or Saturday, I should feel very highly flattered. Not a word of what we said about votes, canvass, election, or anything connected with these things; and after this pledge perhaps you will allow me the opportunity of making your acquaintance.

"Should it be equally convenient to you, Saturday would be the day that I should prefer, as being the freest from care."

FROM BARON MERIAN.

[*January* (?), 1826.]

"DEAR SIR,—Your letters are never short; for when of six lines only, they still contain so much good and friendly information or wit or learning, that, like British sterling gold, drawn to French wire, they would through pages shine. The various packets your kindness intended to gratify me with I have not received yet—among them I chiefly regret your epitaphs on my premature death. What about the Parrian memoir by Johnstone? Is it a biography? Has Dr. Parr left some treatise achieved upon language in general, or was he a pure classic rigorously? What are his inscriptions? I hope nothing of so great a scholar will be lost. You are a terrible spendthrift. . . . Eighty guineas for a MS., £600 for Aldines, eclipse Lord Spencer ! What shall I say to all this? Why, *bene est, si te voluptate afficit ac literis prodest.* . . . Your '*Columna*' Longman has a parcel for you, containing, 1°, the first volume of Raynouard * Aldines, which Mr. Klaproth lays at your feet, and the following volumes are to follow. Farther, some notices of Langle's famous library; item, a battery

---

* I presume Renouard the publisher, who wrote a book about Aldines, is intended.—ED.

directed against Arrowsmith's maps, which Mr. Klaproth begs you will, *amore veritatis perductus*, excuse, though it is *nonnihil* smart. But in faith Arrowsmith made abominable work. Klaproth has finished his *Table hist. de Persie* (?) (vii numbers), and is very busy about his *Description of China* in English, to be printed with maps and figures, London.

"As to Russia, look upon the events of December 26th as *non avenus*. They can have no immediate influence. The system that hitherto prevailed in and out will continue to prevail; it is the system of patience and abstinence. *Apropos*, the packets you promised me were, 1°, your own works from 1822 to 1826 (I have your ancient maps only of 1822); and, 2°, some *palatable Parriana*. Have you not heard of the Turgenews? Yours *pectore, animo, visceribus cunctis*.

"You have distinguished very well in your *Geography*, 1822, p. 118. But let me now combine. Those islands and fifty others might be called, and may be called, Mona, for 'Mon' is not a proper name, but a mere Welsh word for an island. The Romans mistook it for a noun proper.

"My humble respects to Miss Butler.

"What a wonderful residence have you chosen! 'Old Hummum's!'"

To a Parent.

" DEAR SIR,—A school of two hundred good boys would be a paradise upon earth which no master was ever happy enough to meet with. Among many boys there will be many dispositions, and we must have our share here as well as at other places.

"'That boys sometimes rob orchards and are always punished for it when discovered is perfectly true; that they go out of bounds often without discovery because no master can be in twenty different places at once is perfectly true; that they sometimes get liquor is perfectly true, and it is equally true that if I discover this I always severely punish it, and if I find a boy has a habit of the thing I dismiss him.

"That cases happen here which happen at no other school I must deny, and that more happen at other schools than at this I must confidently affirm.

"That the boys get their lessons out of school is perfectly true of the upper boys, and partially true of lower boys, and not true at all of the lowest. The same is the case at all other schools, and how it can be otherwise no practical man can show.

"That no control is exercised over the boys out of school is not correct. The lower boys are made to show themselves every hour for the summer half-year, and the upper can never be absent more than two hours; they are called over also at locking up, and visited in their bedrooms.

"That your son Richard was grossly ignorant of Latin I knew well, but he was put in a class where he was to learn Latin as fast as he could, with his Greek, which was merely elementary. I have now put him since his return in a lower class, at his own request, and promised him every encouragement if he will take it up.

"The strongest argument against the canting gossip you have heard is that I wrote to beg you would remove Richard if he did not reform, lest he should corrupt his brother and others, and this is my practice in all cases where I find boys viciously inclined. It would be a real service if you would give me the names of any of the bad set with whom Richard associated, and I should keep the utmost secrecy while I dealt with them according to circumstances, and should feel deep gratitude.

"I could wish all parents to be satisfied—at least I am sure that my exertions to the utmost of my power are never wanting to do my duty—but where they feel dissatisfaction, and distrust and vindicate their children at the expense of the master and his other pupils, I can only regret that when they feel they have misplaced their confidence they do not withdraw it. You, my dear sir, I hope have no reason to repent of yours in the instance of your eldest son.

"Let me add, with regard to boys being flogged regularly twice a week, that to the best of my belief I have never flogged the same boy twice a week more than three times in twenty-six years, that the whole number of floggings inflicted in a half-year (of which I have a correct account for the purpose of referring to in cases of bad behaviour) never amounts to two a week, though some weeks may have half a dozen, and some not one; and that, so far from destroying the moral feeling by the infliction of mere bodily punishment, I have a great aversion to the infliction of bodily punishment, though it is an evil which is sometimes unavoidable. I always avoid it when I can; but for boys who are too sulky or too stupid to feel the force of remonstrance and lenity, I know no more effectual remedy. Still, I wish there was one."

From Two Churchwardens.

"*March 4th*, 1826.

"Reverend Sire,—The Reverend Mr. W——, Vicar of ——, has taken the liberty of getting the coal from under the vicarage land, and was preparing to get the same under the vicarage garden and house, and near to the church, whereby the same would have been in danger, as the offices belonging to the vicarage house is already injured by the coal being got too near them by Mr. Sutton. We, as churchwardens, thought it our duty to remonstrate with him against such proceedings, but he gave us evasive answers, saying it did not become a prudent man to say what he intended to do, nor a brave man to say what he had done. We also asked him to what purpose he intended to apply the money he had sold the coal for that is already got, to which question he refused a satisfactory answer. We therefore think it our bounden duty to acquaint you, sire, with such proceedings, and humbly beg your kind instruction how we are to proceed in this case, and shall be thankful if you will be kind enough also to send us a statement of regular surplice fees. So shall we remain, reverend sire,

"Your very humble and obedient servants."

I found no draft of Dr. Butler's answer.

TO THE EDITOR OF THE "SHREWSBURY CHRONICLE."

"*March 8th*, 1826.

"SIR,—I send you an account of the gold coin which you have been so good as to show me, and which you state to have been found near Aberdovey.

"It is a noble of Henry V.

"The obverse has a figure of the King armed and crowned, standing in a ship, which differs from those of preceding princes by having no streamer at the masthead, and only two ropes instead of three. In his right hand he holds a naked sword, and has an annulet under the right elbow; in his left hand a shield, bearing the arms of France and England quarterly. There are but three fleurs-de-lis in those of France.

"On one side of the ship, immediately under the deck, are three lions and fleurs-de-lis in a single line, interchangeably. I say three lions; for though only two are very distinct, there are traces of the third, and this is the only blemish in this remarkably well-preserved coin. The inscription is, HENRIC'. DI'. GRA. REX. ANGLI. Z. FRANC'. DNS. HYB., *i.e. Henricus Dei Gratia Rex Angliæ et Franciæ Dominus Hiberniæ.*

"The reverse has a cross fleury, voided, in a double tressure of eight arches, with very small trefoils in the outward angles. Over each limb of the cross is a fleur-de-lis, and in the quarters between these a crown, with a lion passant, gardant, beneath. In the square void of the cross is the letter H. The inscription is, IHS. AUT'. TRANSIENS. PER. MEDIUM. ILLORU'. IBAT., *i.e. Jesus autem transiens per medium illorum ibat.* This is followed by a single fleur-de-lis. The separating points between the words on the obverse are made by small fleurs-de-lis; on the reverse by annulets. The weight is 106 grains.   "S. BUTLER."

To Dr. Butler's Son, who had been sitting for the
Bell Scholarship.

(Original in possession of Mrs. G. L. Bridges and Miss Butler.)

" *March 9th,* 1826.

" My dear Tom,—Before you receive this you will know your
fate. The two lines about Priam and the horse no scholar has
ever yet understood, nor the double ' et.' Some read ' tutet,'
a strange word for ' tutetur,' instead of the second ' vivat.'
' Vivat ' has probably crept in instead of some other verb, if
Ovid did not write carelessly.

" Your verses are fair—not surpassingly good—not bad ; the
fourth stanza is the worst.

" Your Latin prose is but moderate ; it is too verbose, and the
right phrase is often missed, though sometimes caught.

" Your Xenophon in the last sentence is very wrong.

" But then you must recollect that others were liable to make
faults as well as you. I hear that you have done yourself credit,
and from what I see I am convinced of it.

" G. Johnson was second for the University Scholarship at
Oxford, and declared to be very near and all but first.

" God bless you.

"S. B."

Postscript by Miss Butler, afterwards Mrs. Bather.

" My dearest Tom,—We have this morning received your
parcel, for which we all thank you. I hope you will be quite
reconciled to your fate against you receive this letter, and now it
is over pray think as little about it as possible. Papa seems quite
satisfied with you, and therefore you may be easy on that score.
We have been laughing at Mrs. Bromfield for a dream she had a
night or two ago. She fancied you and Marindin, and a fair-
haired young man, who I tell her is Bland, were all sitting in a
large college room with clumsy tables and chairs. You had two
of your fingers bound up, and were about to lose the nail of one
of them either from a cut or some other cause. Poor Mrs. Bromfield was in great distress to think how you could bear to have
your nail taken off, when Marindin came up and knocked it off
in a minute. But her greatest distress was that you had your hat
notched all round ; however, she was relieved from that misery
by seeing another man come in with his hat notched also. She
was so anxious for an interpretation of this wonderful dream that
she consulted her dream-book, but in vain. Papa inquired
whether the wreath round your head might not signify laurel,
especially as you had a companion crowned also—an explanation

mighty satisfactory to Mrs. Bromfield. I told her I should tell you
her dream, and she particularly begs I will ask you whether any
accident has happened to your fingers. Papa has just been playing at patience, to see whether you will get a good place, but unless
you have better luck than he you will have none at all. Mrs.
Bromfield bears your account of yourself better than I expected,
but when you sit for anything again I think we had better not let
her into the secret. . . . We had a party of boys on Tuesday night,
consisting of Cameron, Payne, James Hildyard, and Bonett. The
last since his battle with Shilleto has gone on very comfortably with
the boys. Cameron was in the highest spirits, and we had altogether
a very pleasant evening. Mrs. Bromfield desires me to tell you
she is happy to say Wakefield [a new under master] is beginning
to be a beast. He has kept order with considerable success for
the last day or two, owing, I believe, to a talking to he got from
papa lately, and Mrs. Bromfield really hopes he will soon be as
great 'a beast' as herself. . . . We have got some very nice
plants in our windows now, such as Persian lilacs, geraniums,
tulips, narcissus's, and a beautiful Camelia japonica. You have
never told me whether you would like any drawings. I have
begun one of a ship scene for you. There is the famous
Captain Murray Johnson here now, with his condemned goods
from the custom-house—some of them are beautiful. Papa
bought a beautiful French workbox, fitted up with gold and
mother-of-pearl, as a present for Miss Maltby, who is delighted
with it. Mrs. Carless, with the Suttons, is here to-night playing a pool. Mr. Blakeway has been dangerously ill nearly
all the week with an abscess on his side, and is still, I
believe, in a very alarming state. The children are all well.
Harriet made me laugh yesterday with an account of Lizzie and
Lucy conversing together in bed on the subject of their prayers.
Lizzie said she wondered what was meant by the 'power and the
glory.' 'Why, don't you know?' said Lucy; 'it is the same as
to pour down rain and to pour out tea.' A most satisfactory
explanation truly. Why did you not send Kennedy's song in the
parcel? Papa was very glad to have the Bell papers, and also the
law papers Dr. Cory was so good as to send. What a wretchedly
dull magazine the last *Metropolitan* was! We had it in our
reading society, but papa has countermanded it for the future.
Papa desires me to request you to purchase for him four pounds
of mangel-wurzel seed, which you can get at the place where
Dr. Cory used to purchase it. Also please to buy at Deighton's
two new Cambridge calendars for this year, unless you should
be in the habit of taking it in yourself, in which case papa only
wants one; at all events let them both be put down in Deighton's
bill, and send one in a parcel with the mangel-wurzel, and keep
the other till you can come down to Shrewsbury. I rather think it
is not published till the 21st. Remember, by the way, when you

send a parcel that the Birmingham coach only leaves Cambridge on Mondays, Wednesdays, and Fridays. . . .
" P.S.—Pay for the seed if you can afford it; it will only be a few shillings.   By the way, how goes on the money ? "

I have elsewhere said,[*] but would repeat here, that Mrs. Bromfield, who had been my father's nurse, and was then matron of one of the schoolhouses, coined perhaps the most thunderclap word that was ever struck out of the English language.   She came into the hall one night when the boys were noisy, and, singling out an offender, told him he was the rampingest-scampingest-rackety-tackety-tow-row-roaringest boy in the whole house.   Then, after a moment's lull, she looked round the hall in triumph. "Young gentlemen," said she, " prayers are excused," and left them.   I had this from my aunt, the writer of the letter just given.

From the Rev. T. S. Hughes.

[*About March 9th,* 1826.]

*   *   *   *   *

"What a triumphant year this is for you !

*   *   *   *   *

" I hear that Tom has done himself credit in his examination whether he succeeds or not.   He is very unfortunate in having the strongest competitors that were ever known for these scholarships.   He is a very good youth, and everybody speaks well of him.   So that crafty old fox Watty † has nearly got his tail into the trap at last.   Well, I think we shall all give our consent *nem. con.* to the match ;—but ' be burst ! ' as old Barnes says, I wonder how he let you run off with the damsel that evening in the hackney coach, or how he endured old Till's incomparable flirtation."

From the Rev. S. Tillbrook.

"*March* 10*th,* 1826.

" My dear Archdeacon,—Salop schools and Dr. Butler for ever ! !   You have carried off the Bell [Scholarship].   Horatio

---

* *Universal Review,* May 1889, p. 136.
† The Rev. R. Watkinson, afterwards of Earl's Colne: cf. letter under date April 10th, 1836.

Hildyard is 'primus inter omnes'! Tom was next to him,·but the injunctions of the founder compelled the examiners to give the second scholarship to Scott of Queens', his circumstances being very narrow. Nevertheless your son Tom was, I believe, the second best among forty competitors, and a good token of your approbation does he deserve, and *I know* he *will have it.* He must be named as highly distinguished. What a proud fellow all these honours will make you, and make you IN YOUR OWN RIGHT, which is everything to an *independent soul*!

"I have had the pleasure of congratulating Hildyard's father, and I have done it most cordially : perhaps he will think me an extravagant eulogist—I do not care twopence if he does. I have drunk bumpers to Horatio and to Tom, and I hope they may live to return the compliment to me.

"I am in haste. Ten thousand thanks for the immortal spotted lampern—never was anything so good ; if I can I will send you dotterel in return.

"I spent two days with Watky, who introduced me to Miss Harvey. What a sly fellow! Thank God I did not go back in the coach with her ; I might have talked more nonsense than might have been agreeable to the lady elect of one of my dearest friends —and I was in the vein for it, as Falstaff said, which is right now.

"I am buying books piscatorial from the Haworth collection now selling in London. I shall be caught, I fear—never mind.

"Kind regards to all, and I may add *sincere congratulations,* for Tom's name *is up* now, and the 'Sirenum Voces' will sound sweeter than ever. Farewell.

> "Ever yours faithfully,
> "OLD TILL.

"P.S.—Send me a letter and the *fishing book* by coach, and I shall be eternally grateful."

TO THE HON. GEORGE GRENVILLE.*

"*March* 10*th*, 1826.

"DEAR SIR,—Understanding from Mr. Dayrell, who called here two days since, that you are at Hawarden, I direct my letter there instead of to Cambridge. Mr. Blakeway and I duly received your letter, with the College notice of the 15th of December, and before the expiration of the time allowed by the decree (six months) I shall send you two candidates for exhibitions. One of them is a boy of first-rate talents, the other is not remarkable for more than ordinary attainments, but is a well-behaved and respectable boy, and great-nephew to that most distinguished ornament of your

---

* See note to the first letter of this chapter.

College, Dr. Waring. The decree says that the candidates thus sent to the College are to be elected after two months' residence. Now before I proceed to acknowledge the communications from the College officially, I wish to consult you by this, which you will be pleased to consider a private letter, respecting these boys.

* * * * *

" I had heard of Massie's removal, but was exceedingly surprised at finding, when I was at Cambridge at Christmas, that Smith had either not put his name on the boards or had taken it off.

" Both he at Cambridge and Massie at Oxford were candidates for University Scholarships this year, the latter I know with much credit to himself. I am shocked to tell you that since I began this letter Mr. Blakeway is dead. The moment new incumbents are appointed to St. Mary's and St. Chad's I shall proceed to have a new deed of trust drawn out, in which your name must be inserted."

* * * * *

DR. BUTLER'S ELDER DAUGHTER, AFTERWARDS MRS. BATHER, TO HER BROTHER.

" *March 15th*, 1826.

" MY DEAREST BOY,—We were all delighted beyond measure at the receipt of Mr. Tillbrook's letter yesterday, which contains the good news of the credit you and Hildyard have gained for the Shrewsbury men. You should have heard the huzzas of the boys, and have seen the capers and frolics and delight of us all. I confess your representations had brought us almost all down from expecting you would get the Bell, and we little thought you really would be second, which in point of credit is just the same as if you had the scholarship, and gratifies us as much. Mrs. Bromfield said to the very last you would have it, and I believe papa had his hopes, but I own I had none, and I do not think mamma or anybody else had. Mrs. B. is very anxious to know whether Scott or Chatfield have light hair. *Vide* my account of her miraculous dream. And now we can talk of nothing but the delight of seeing you, which will be worth all the rest. I think we shall scarcely sleep till Monday next. Old Till says your name is up now, and the Sirenian voices will sing sweeter than ever. I have been laughing at the idea of your receiving my letter of condolence on Sunday morning, when in fact I should have sent you one of congratulation. Mamma says every minute she wants to see you. If she eats an egg, it is ' in honour of Tom.' If she takes wine, it is to drink your health, and almost whenever she opens her mouth it is to talk of you. Mrs. Bromfield too is crazy to see you ; so is papa, and so are John and Harriet. The last has just been here to inquire about you, and begs her best love and congratulations. . . . I believe papa has told you of poor Mr. Blakeway's death.   The town is full of candidates for his vacancy at St. Mary's."

*   *   *   *   *

To the Hon. George Grenville,* Master of Magdalene College, Cambridge.

"Shrewsbury, *March 15th,* 1826.

" Dear Sir,—I never ask favours for myself, and am sorry to have troubled you with a petition on behalf of two parents who can ill afford the expense of a term which will tell for nothing towards their sons' degrees.   I shall send the two candidates to Magdalene College immediately at the opening of next term.

" B—— is going on fairly.   He is a well-behaved boy, but not possessed of first-rate talents.

" I have the honour to be, dear Sir,

" Your obedient, humble servant,

" S. Butler."

From Baron Merian.

" *March,* 1826.

" Dear Sir,—If you wish to read a very good book connected with the history of England, take Depping, *Les Normands* (1825), 2 vols., 8vo, price 12 francs at Paris.   It would be a much more laudable attempt for your translating steam-engines to translate such works than all this miserable French and German stuff, which is laughed at in the countries where it pullulates, but, by means of fine plates, milk-white paper, and hot press, *necnon* elegant binding, are sold, read, and admired in Old England.   It grieves an honest heart to see the proceedings of most of your eminent booksellers, how they are so astonishingly ignorant, not only of what is good or bad abroad, but even at home, and how in their foolish speculations, never considering the intrinsic value of a performance, they exclusively ask, ' Will it sell well ? ' ruining by this Armenian principle not only the taste of the bulk of their readers, but also frequently themselves and their families, since at the least difficulty or stop ensuing (*ecce hodie*) here sits Master Bookseller on the top of a heap of nonsense, which none but idle extravagance would ever have purchased, and which now, where bread is more in request than smooth paper, nobody calls for ; whereas, if the books had true lasting merit, were moderately printed, and on reasonable terms, they would sell successfully for ever.   *Ecce* Constable at Edinburgh and his bombast of novels.   For, in spite of the genius of Walter

---

* See note to the first letter of this chapter.

Scott, his works will pass, and not remain, because the genius is false, and a mingle-mangle of history and fiction in prose narration can never become classic, even if it was written by Gabriel himself.

" Here's a philippic. .All for the good of the United Kingdom, to whom I am an old and most sincere well-wisher, though I perpetually attack, not its great and glorious parts, but its amazing prepossessions, errors, and want of information. Look, by Jupiter, at Arrowsmith's maps ! ! ! Look at your geography, your philosophy, your poor Lockes and poorer Dugald Stewarts ; look at your own national English dictionaries (*proh pudor*) ; look at your whole extra classic (for as to classic I bow in respect) philology. Fifty years *en arrière*, my dear friend, *pour le moins*. Let me quote here *ad confirmandam rem* a certain writing of a certain Dr. Butler, who, they say, is one of' the solid and zealous and enlightened friends of his country, a *vir bonus* in the highest degree, a most eminent scholar, concerning the *lacunæ* of university instruction ; read that small writing attentively, and you will soon discover *unde meæ lacrymæ*. Latin and mathematics ! there's the magic circle ! Would it not be worth your while, and a benefit to British youth, to write an amplification of that sheet of yours ?

" One of my friends said the English furrow deep. Very sensible and very true. But, replied I, I could wish they would, at the same time, look somewhat far and wide also. Pray read, in order to understand what I mean, the annexed ' Un homme,' etc. It is in these *idées universelles* (which we must not confound with *idées superficielles*) that I believe the English at large to be deficient.

" One instance of typographical folly. The Laws of Menu have lately been edited, intended for schools, for boys to learn. They form two magnificent vols., most beautiful paper, and cost I know not how many guineas. There's a book for schoolboys to try their pens on, and knock at each other's heads. Let now booksellers complain ; they cannot sell.

" *Jam satis est.*

" (Enters Zephyrus, breathing sweetly.)

" Two of your letters, February 8th, 25th, are before me, *pro more*, full of interesting information, good-humour, and marks of that inalterable friendship which has now filled a space of thirty years. The *petit paquet blanc* contained some little manuscripts and prints for your collection. I do not think it has been lost by inadvertence. It has rather been classified, perhaps in France. I find you have made truly brilliant acquisitions. Is it your intention to make, or get made, any public use of those MSS.—for instance, Suidas and Lucanus ? Are any new editions preparing ? I have lately been told that it was no longer fashionable in England to employ such active participles in a passive sense as ' preparing' for being ' in preparation '; therefore pardon my solecism, for, in fact, it is one, though very common. Klaproth is, as you

know, one of your devoted clients, and is ever glad to hear that
you remember him.   It is true his criticism on Arrowsmith
(*Journal Asiat.*, XLIII., XLIV.) is 'very severe.'   But is it not
a 'just and necessary war'?   Is it lawful to cheat people, not
only of their money, but also of their time and knowledge, by
selling for £4 (?) a map, and under royal patronage, which map
is not worth fourpence?—for surely it is much better to have no
map at all of a country than to have one which is completely
false and most ridiculously stupid.   You will not, dear sir, think
these terms too severe when you shall have read the said *Journal
Asiat.*, Cahier XLIII., XLIV. Is it lawful to print lies, but not lawful to discover and expose them?   Is it right for a man to lie in
ambush and rob, but not right for another man to warn a traveller
and tell him, 'If you walk that way you will be robbed'? How?
to do wrong is not severe, but to say (with perfect truth) that it
is wrong is very severe?

"Courageous critics, like Klaproth, ought to be encouraged
by any means, for truth and science can only thrive when fiction
and ignorance are removed.   It is an unfit comparison, yet how
did Christ treat the vendors of falsehood?

"Klaproth has attacked and overthrown in the same manner
two or three Russian 'savants.' I could not but approve of it,
notwithstanding my connections with Russia.

"In all this, I can assure you, is not the least personality.
For what is dead Arrowsmith, for instance, to living Klaproth,
who never saw him in his whole life? Sed *fiat justitia, pereat
mundus.*   The impositions and frauds of book and map-makers
are so common and so grievous that, as in China, public tribunals
need to be erected to check them.

"(Enters Boreas, and, finding that Zephyrus is out of his cue,
gives him a slap on the ear, and vanishes.)

"Zephyrus continues.   I rejoice in the prospect of receiving
soon your new praxis, new geography, and sermon.   No broken
b (?) or *d* (?) will prevent me from acknowledging the true value
of whatever drops from your solid and elegant pen.   'Maps
engraved on steel'—I do not remember to have seen any such
yet.   It is a new improvement.   Rennel, I believe, was the first
man who added an index to maps—a very excellent idea, especially
as he executed it, by drawing squares which showed the *locus ubi.*
I shall be very glad, too, to see the Parrian catalogue. . . . Parr
surely was one of the very top gardeners of the classic garden.
The red beads have two stages of life, like mahogany—red, and
then brown.   And the brown are preferred, as heads of tobacco-
pipes, when smoked for some time.   But the beads should not
lose their lustre ; they should be brown now, but still shining.
If they are so, they are right.   Keep them very dry and cold ;
'tis their native climature.

"I beg old Hummum's pardon for having made free with it ;

the inelegance of the name had seduced me. And should I ever be able to contrive to look at the City of London again, none but old Hummum should have the honour of harbouring the great Hudibras of lingo, who, by-the-bye, was most egregiously flattered by your epitaph ; for simple he is born, simply he lives, simpleness is in all his doings, he strives never to step out of simpleness, and hopes to die simply too, meaning by this word the very contrary to intricate, the true Ζῆν καὶ πράττειν ἁπλῶς."

To the Rev. W. Crawley.

(Then at Magdalene, afterwards Archdeacon of Monmouth.)

[*March* or *April*, 1826.]

"Dear Crawley,—I enclose a draft for £63, for which be so kind as to send me a stamped receipt. I thank you for your congratulations ; I wish more of them were applicable to my pupils at your own College, but there is a cloud there which makes me uncomfortable. You may depend upon it that first-rate scholars will be very reluctant to go where they find the claims of their schoolfellows, who, if less brilliant than themselves, are yet worthy of attention, are repulsed. I have now sent up one very superior scholar, and one who, though not likely to be distinguished by University honours, is certainly respectable. I mention this to you now, as a friend who I know feels kindly towards myself and my pupils, in the hope that whenever you come to take a part in College concerns, which you may do if you are elected into a foundation fellowship, it may have its weight. At present I neither wish it to go farther than yourself, nor to draw any expression of opinion from you. I content myself with stating a fact, that there is a great reluctance among Shrewsbury men to go to Magdalene College, where several of their schoolfellows have been repulsed, and where, though I admitted Massie and Smith, two excellent scholars in June last, neither have remained. I am not so much surprised at the former withdrawing to Oxford, because it was always his earnest wish to go there, but I never was more surprised than on finding Smith at St. John's when I was at Cambridge at Christmas. I do assure you that it is always my wish to send good men to Magdalene, but I cannot always succeed, notwithstanding the advantages they have a claim to.

"With regard to your fellowship, I beg to observe that, having carefully read the last decree, I find it contains, as the decree before it did also, not only no clause requiring the fellow to reside, but one exempting him from all forfeiture, except that of his commons, for non-residence. I therefore request that in future you will not send me a certificate of residence, lest it should grow into a custom, but merely state that you are still fellow, and request payment. The exhibitioners are bound to residence.

> "I remain, etc.,
>
> "S. BUTLER."

As these pages are going through the press, Archdeacon Crawley, to whom the foregoing letter was addressed and who was the oldest surviving pupil of Dr. Butler, has passed away, January 12th, 1896, in the ninety-fourth year of his age.

FROM A CLERGYMAN AND FORMER PUPIL.

"HIGH STREET, SHREWSBURY, *April* 13*th*, 1826.

*   *   *   *   *

"I have taken the liberty of sending you some of my old school exercises, one of them the last which I wrote whilst under your care, which I have accidentally (I had almost said providentially) kept. They will enable you to judge where my performances stood in the scale of merit, a point which must naturally be obliterated by the hundreds of exercises you have seen since I left the schools. I can warrant them genuine, and testify on oath that they are my own. Should you hereafter hear me upheld, in any assembly from which custom excludes me, as a person of singular stupidity, I trust you will stand manfully forward and at least do me the justice of delivering the following character of me, which sincerely and upon my honour I consider most just and true : 'He was a duck-stealer, yet he had some shreds and patches of honour ; he was far from being a boy of shining abilities, but he was not singularly stupid nor very deficient in sense.' In the former part of this I will bear you out with anecdotes, if necessary; of the latter part the accompanying exercises are evidence. I wish at least not to fall from that station of life in which I was found on entering the world. By such an honest statement you will not, I think, diminish from the respect which others may have for you, and you will confer an obligation upon,

> "Reverend Sir, your obedient servant,
>
> "——— ———

"I will thank you to return the exercises after you have read them. I set, perhaps, too high a value upon them, but I cannot help regarding them fondly."

With regard to the foregoing letter, I should explain

that the writer was a candidate for an appointment then vacant in Shrewsbury, and believed Dr. Butler to have disparaged him, and to be lending the weight of his influence to an opponent. Dr. Butler drafted an answer in three lines, saying that he returned the exercises, and *was glad to learn that they had been the writer's own,* but he put the words " Not sent " against what he had written. Whether he gave his correspondent a testimonial to the effect that he had been an efficient duck-stealer does not appear, but I know that there was a good deal of duck-stealing going on at one time. Dr. Welldon told me the boys used to fish for ducks with a baited hook and a line from behind the wall of any farmyard that lent itself to their operations. One farmer's wife, he said, was nearly driven out of her mind by seeing a duck waddle hurriedly across the yard and then walk up a perpendicular wall—she not suspecting that there was a hook in the duck's mouth, and a boy hidden behind the wall. I do not remember any duck-stealing in my time.

From the Rev. James Tate.
" Richmond, Yorkshire, *April 29th,* 1826.

" My dear Sir,—Since your letter of October 5th, now before me, nothing in the way of correspondence has passed betwixt us, unless my despatching a copy of *Origination of the Greek Case, etc.,* the other day be so considered.

" *Horace* is at present the object of my lucubrations in his life and localities, in his metres also, obliquely perhaps, but not in anything at all like a regular treatise. You will forgive me, therefore, if I ask how your intentions in that way proceed, and what use you are likely to make of my article in the *Classical Journal* on the Alcaic stanza of Horace. It may be that I shall allude to the neglect and ignorance of Horace's metres, so miserably shown in by far the greater part of his avowed imitators. *Statius,* you know, the first writer after Horace perhaps in the Alcaic and Sapphic stanzas, had no idea of Horace's variety in the Sapphic at all, and in the Alcaic copied his best forms with something like stiff uniformity. Can you pursue the subject from *Statius* downwards to the revival of letters ?

" By-the-bye, after *Virgil* had given its last finish of varied harmony and grandeur to heroic verse, next comes *Ovid*, who hardly ever deviates by any possible chance from the two standard forms,—

> Tityre tu patulæ ‖ recubans sub tegmine fagi
> Formosam resonare | doces ‖ Amaryllida sylvas.

Not very unlike this you may consider Pope coming after Dryden, and hardly ever admitting, much less seeking, that fine variety in English verse, when the sense of the first distich flows over into the second.   Dryden perhaps has it too much—that is, at times rather carelessly done.

" Horace has one stanza of the Sapphic kind which exhibits all his legitimate forms (*Carm. Sæc.*, vv. 13-16) :—

> A. Rite maturos ‖ aperire partus
> C. Lenis Ilithuia | tuere | matres,
> B. Sive tu Lucina | probas ‖ vocari
>   Seu genitalis.

" The forms A, B, C, occur in every 12, as 9, 2, 1, throughout Horace, or more nearly in every 15, as 12, 2, 1.
" Horace has but another form of the verse,—

> Laureâ ‖ donandus | Apollinari ;

and that only once.   It is ridiculous to see the distortions of this pretty little stanza committed by *Buchanan, Casimir,* etc., etc., and in the *Musæ Etonenses*, passim.
" Some few imitators, on the other hand, have been as stiffly correct in adhering to the one form, A, as old *Statius* himself chose to be.
" All improved knowledge, and practice too, in the Alcaic stanza I consider as owing to Charles Burney, Samuel Butler, and James Tate.   There have been worse triumvirates of men—or of scholars.
" Can you give me any idea, from Cluverius or from any good source of geographical knowledge which you so completely command, whether, from the use of the *Via Valeria* in the days of *Horace, Mecænas* was likely to pass by Vicobaro across the Apennines to the eastern side of the Peninsula on any public business, or to any place of political importance whatsoever ?
"You know the old tradition, I. *Carmm.* XX.
" *Vile potabis, etc.   'Mecænatem, in Apuliam iturum Horatio significasse, se in itinere in ipsius villam Sabinam deversurum.'* Of course, if his journey was into Apulia, we know there was another road, though perhaps more circuitous.
" Have the kindness to tell me what you think on the subject. *Cluverius* I have not.   *Domenico de Sanctis's della villa di Orazio*

Flacco lyes before me.   Had the Via Minucia anything to do with the points proposed in this question?

"At what age do you think it likely that old Horace would carry his son from Venusia for education to Rome?

"Forgive all this freedom in consulting the oracle at Shrewsbury, and pardon my importunity if I request the earliest response you can give.

> "I am, dear Sir, most faithfully yours,
> "JAMES TATE.

"P.S.—On receiving your letter of October 5th, I did write as you requested to Sir James Mackintosh.

"Have you seen Sir William Jones's *jeu d'esprit* in Greek on his friend Parr in the year 1780? And what do *you* think is meant by τριγγίζειν ἀτριγγισμόν?

"That one word *structure* as applied to Latin verse carries with it the whole secret of Horace's metres murdered by his followers. They were taught the *scansion*, and even that not always correctly. For the rest, except where a good ear sometimes got the better of the general *ignorantia recti*, we all know what sad havoc was made."

FROM THE REV. S. TILLBROOK.

"PETERHOUSE COLLEGE, *June* 15*th*, 1826.

"DEAR ARCHDEACON,—If I could manage to reach Derbyshire by the 1st or 2nd of July, in what manner do you think of travelling afterwards? My plan was to drive my gig towards Shropshire, and then to find some mode of forwarding it or of providing for my pony, till I should return in the autumn. At all events I cannot start before the end of June—say the 23rd or 24th. My reason for inquiring as to your mode of travelling is this—I cannot bear in hot weather to be stewed up in a common coach, and I dare not ride on the outside of one. We should easily manage when we got to Rydal, where all would be ready to receive us and glad to welcome us. Could we start from Salop and pay Blomfield a visit on our way to Westmoreland? I am sure the relaxation and ease which you would enjoy at the Ivy Cottage would be of service to you."

*   *   *   *   *

EXTRACTS FROM A CHARGE DELIVERED AT DERBY AND AT
CHESTERFIELD, JUNE 15TH AND 16TH, 1826, UPON THE
EDUCATION OF THE POORER CLASSES.

*   *   *   *   *

Speaking of a date some fifty years earlier Dr. Butler
said :—

" It is now almost as unusual to meet with an adult (unless
in the most abject state of poverty and neglect) unable to read,
as it was then rare to find one of the lower orders who possessed
that acquirement. If to reading the accomplishment of writing
were added, the peasantry of those days generally attached the
name of scholar to the possessor of those attainments. A great
step has been gained, therefore, and a great intellectual improvement has been effected in the mass of the people, by the very
general diffusion of the one and at least the much-extended
acquisition of the other of those useful attainments. How far
the lower classes should be educated beyond this is the great
point of debate. For my own part I am not afraid to confess
that I think there is something too vague and indefinite in the
benevolence of those who would wish to go much farther. I
stated, I think, when I last addressed you, that we live in an
age of all others the most experimental. I cannot but add, and
I wish to give offence to none while I say it, but truth compels
the assertion, that we live also in a time unexampled for morbid
sensibility. This is the natural result of wealth, luxury, and
indulgence. I grieve to subjoin that, as far as my observation
and historical reading go, this symptom of disease in the moral
feeling has not unfrequently been the precursor of decline in great
and powerful states, and without attention and counteraction
may produce the most serious ill-consequences.

" It is the result of that prosperity which has been at its highest,
and therefore must begin to be on the wane. It does not appear
when the vigorous energies of a great people are yet in action
towards their full development, nor when the powers of an
enfeebled and sinking nation are exhausted and decayed ; but
it is the natural effect of security and inaction, the enervation
which comes on after great excitement, and which demands some
stimulus that may administer relief to the lassitude of unhealthy
and unnatural repose. To this cause I think we may attribute
the innumerable schemes and societies for the improvement of
mankind—many, we may say almost all of them, springing from
virtuous principles, and directed, in their intention at least, to
benevolent or pious purposes—which of late years have sprung
up among us.

*   *   *   *   *

" Real learning requires time, patience, talent, and opportunity
to its attainment. How much of these can be commanded by
the lower orders, who must always be under the necessity of
working for their daily bread, and whose intervals of labour must
generally be spent in that rest which is necessary to qualify them
for its resumption? If, captivated by a laudable thirst for knowledge, they devote even a portion of those hours which they
can ill spare from their employments or their necessary repose
towards its acquirement, what is to repay them for the sacrifice—
for giving them new wants which they cannot gratify, and opening
to their view new hopes which must end in vexation and disappointment ? For it is perfectly hopeless to suppose that they
can, except in some very rare instances, arrive at any profound
depths of science, and mere superficial attainments, however
gratifying, on their first acquisition, to the vanity of their
possessor, will lose their charm with their novelty, and will
neither afford permanent utility, nor even gratification. But this
is not the worst. They who know the least in any science are
generally the most dogmatical and presumptuous. They are continually prone to mistake the information they receive for the
discoveries of their own sagacity, and because a new light has
broken in upon their own understandings, they fancy that other
men have always been as much in the dark as themselves. We
may smile at the result of such notions in abstract science or
verbal criticism, but we must contemplate them with fear and dismay when we see their effect in those matters in which the highest
concerns of mankind are implicated—in the laws in which our
temporal, the morals in which our social, and the religion in
which our eternal interests are at stake. Men of cultivated minds,
and competent or affluent fortunes, whose education has trained
them for the acquirement of knowledge from their earliest years,
and who have found every accession of it attended with advantage
and delight, when they wish that all their countrymen should participate in the same benefits, appear to overlook the disparity of
circumstances between themselves and the great mass of the
people. They seem to forget that the progress of all real knowledge is gradual, and sometimes almost imperceptible ; that the
preparatory steps to it are tedious and difficult ; and that to plunge
the uninstructed into science without due and early elementary
preparation will be only to perplex and astound, not to instruct
and edify them.

*   *   *   *   *

" Let me add that nothing appears less likely to promote great
discoveries in science, and bring forth men of lofty and commanding genius, who stamp their names on the age in which they live,
than multiplying these helps to learning. Mighty difficulties make

mighty minds: it is the struggle with obstacles apparently insurmountable that strengthens the intellect, that throws it upon its own resources—baffled, it is true, in many a conflict, but still rising with fresh vigour from every fall. But when the road is smooth and easy, when resources are everywhere at hand, and even when the spur of ambition is blunted by the facility of attainment, it is in vain to expect great and towering minds. The stream of knowledge necessarily becomes shallower as it is spread ; it occupies, indeed, a more widely extended surface, but it is stagnant, vapid, and powerless."

* * * * *

CORRESPONDENCE, JUNE 16TH AND 17TH, 1826.

FROM THE MASTER OF MAGDALENE.

"RECTORY HOUSE, HAWARDEN, CHESTER, *June 16th*, 1826.

" DEAR SIR,—It will give me much pleasure to hear that some young men will be entered this commencement at Magdalene College from Shrewsbury School.

"There are still vacancies on Dr. Millington's and Mr. Millington's foundations, and considering the goodness of the endowments, it is greatly to be regretted that we have not eligible candidates sent to us upon whom we may bestow them. I feel most anxious to have all the vacant scholarships in Magdalene College filled up at the next election ; at the same time I must acknowledge that I am determined not to elect any one who cannot pass a tolerable examination.

" I have the honour to be, dear Sir, your faithful and humble servant, "GEORGE NEVILLE."

TO THE MASTER OF MAGDALENE.

[*June 17th* or 18*th*, 1826 (?).]

" DEAR SIR,—There seems both now and heretofore a degree of dissatisfaction conveyed in your letters respecting the exhibitioners from Shrewsbury School to Magdalene College, which I am very desirous as far as I can to remove. Allow me, therefore, once more to enter upon the subject.

"You appear to entertain an opinion that I am not disposed to send you the best candidates in my power : any such disposition I beg leave most distinctly and unequivocally to disavow. I have sent you many whom I consider fair scholars, and who I know would be well received in other Colleges; and I must repeat, whatever representations may have been made to you to the contrary, that Bird, who I find is not elected to an exhibition, was at the time he left Shrewsbury, in June last, a fair and rapidly improving scholar, and if he has been thought unworthy of an exhibition at the late examination, the fault is not in my tuition. What he has done since, or what he has been expected to do, I know not—I have no means of forming a judgement, and cannot blame either him or any one else, but I must be allowed to vindicate myself so far as to say that he left me, not a first-rate, but still a respectable scholar.

"An opinion, I know, prevails among my young men, though it has received neither origin nor confirmation from me, that the exhibitioners are not countenanced at your College, and the rejection by the examiner, whether justly or not, of some boys who were candidates for exhibitions has so rooted this opinion in their minds, that I meet with nothing but discouragement whenever I propose to parents to send their sons to Magdalene. I do not say that this cause will always operate, but it operates now in spite of all endeavours on my part to the contrary, and the rejection of Bird, who was known to all the boys when he left Shrewsbury (and I may add to all the masters, as well as myself) to be a boy of promise, will, I fear, strengthen this prejudice to a great degree.

    *   *   *   *   *

"I do not wish these exhibitions to become sinecures, nor can you do me a greater wrong than by supposing that I do not wish to send you good scholars, or could send you better were I so inclined. Permit me to assure you that I deal most frankly and candidly in this respect, and the explanation on which I have entered may serve to prove it. I have the honour to be, dear Sir, your faithful, humble servant,   "S. Butler."

July 26th, 1826.—At a special meeting of the trustees a conference was proposed as to the payment of arrears due from the occupiers of Albrighton, to be held between the solicitors to the trustees and the executors of the late occupier. Resolved that Dr. Butler be requested to lend his invaluable assistance on this occasion. On the tenth of the following October a vote of thanks to Dr. Butler was passed, for his report on the above subject.

CHAPTER XX.

THE CLERICAL SOCIETY.

Correspondence, September 13th, 1826—February 15th, 1827.—Conclusion of the School Lawsuit.—Correspondence, April or May, 1827 —December 14th, 1827.

CORRESPONDENCE, SEPTEMBER 13TH, 1826—FEBRUARY 15TH, 1827.

COMMENT of any kind on the very interesting series of letters about the formation of a Clerical Society that here follows would involve my entering on matters which are beyond my scope ; the letters themselves, however, so clearly reveal the inner mind of the wiser clergy of the time that I have not ventured to exclude them.

FROM THE REV. JOHN WOOD.

"SWANWICK, *September* 13*th*, 1826.

●   ●   ●   ●   ●

"MY DEAR SIR,—To-morrow my Lord Bishop will take his silver trowel in hand to lay the first stone of the new church at Derby ; and on Friday, after visiting Ilkeston and Heanor, he is to fix upon a site for a new church at Alfreton Riddings. He is to drive with Coke, who has desired me to give him the meeting. Since my return I have received a polite circular signed by Pole of Radborn and Simpson of Derby, requesting my attendance at a meeting of the clergy to establish a society to meet occasionally, but for what purpose did not clearly appear ; and as caution is necessary in these days, I declined the invitation. I am glad I did so ; for I do not find that those whom I should conceive most proper, from age and talent, to take the lead are at all forward in the business, or indeed can give any information as to what is the intent or proposed end of the society. When we hear of extempore prayers being proposed, and discussions on

315

abstruse points of doctrine, in my humble opinion no good can come of it; but we have so many zealous young sprigs of divinity springing up on every side of us, that I fully expect we shall be told by-and-by that we are hardly capable of directing the concerns of our own parishes without their assistance."

*   *   *   *   *

FROM THE REV. JOHN WOOD.

"SWANWICK, *September 25th,* 1826.

*   *   *   *   *

"With respect to the Clerical Society, any information I can give you I shall be happy to communicate—at the same time I must request it may be strictly confidential.

"Since I received your letter the plot begins to ripen. On the 8th a few of us dined together after the Clergy Widows' meeting, and the subject was started by Cotton, who, very contrary to his inclination, had been named President for the next meeting—fixed, I believe, for the 17th of October. He seemed quite at a loss whether to attend the meeting or to withdraw his name; it was recommended to him to call together the committee originally appointed, but who had not acted, and to take their opinion as to the future arrangement of the society.

"Last Friday I was in the bookseller's shop writing, and Cotton with Pickering brought Pole there, and they entered upon the business. Pole as secretary declined calling together the committee; he said he had done so both personally and by letter, and they would not attend. If they had met, he said, of course the future regulations of the society were in their hands; but as they had refused, a general meeting had taken place, and certain things had been determined upon, and therefore it was not in his power to make any alteration, but a circular was now publishing which was to be sent to the clergy, and if they did not choose to attend it was not his fault. If the thing ended in a party business, the committee might thank themselves for not giving the proper directions as to the formation of the rules, etc.

"As I, being present, became in some degree a party in the conversation, I mentioned that I had found when I returned home a note of invitation from him, and I wished to know what was the end proposed by the society. He referred me to the circular, the rough copy of which was produced and read. I begged to ask him one question—whether it was intended that religious points of doctrine should be discussed and argued upon at their meetings. He said it had been so determined; and I immediately said, if so, I should beg to decline being a member, as I thought it calculated to produce no good whatever. Pickering declared himself quite of the same opinion. As to this circular, it is not yet come out, but I will endeavour to quote from memory (observing first that I am told the subjects proposed are some of them different from what was proposed at the meeting—but by whom altered, or when, did not appear).   After certain commonplace orders as to forming a society to meet four times a year, you are appointed President, and I think that all clergy acceding at the next meeting to the rules and regulations laid down are members.

"I am told it was proposed to begin the meeting with extempore prayer, but Pickering would not hear of it, and it was fixed that he and Simpson were to arrange some prayers from the Liturgy for the purpose.   The subjects for discussion proposed in the circular, I think, are six—the First Article, Sponsors, then the best way of bringing back dissenters ; the others I have forgotten, but you will see them in the circular, which will as a matter of course be sent to you as President—at least I should suppose this would be the case.   I am told that Heath, Anson, Johnson, and several others have declined.   I put the question to Pole whether the Archdeacon approved of what was doing, but had no answer to the purpose.   Cotton, whose name stood alphabetically first at the last meeting, and on that account was elected chairman, seems terribly hampered ; I told him that, were I in his place, when he had got the circular, I would send it to you, and say that, as many of the elder clergy seemed to disapprove the thing, he wished you to give him your advice.   You will thus have the circular, should it not be sent to you by the secretary, and can then decide what steps, if any, you will think proper to take.   I hope this letter will give you some hints which you perhaps would not otherwise have obtained. '

FROM DR. BUTLER TO THE REV. CHARLES E. COTTON.

"*October* 11*th*, 1826.

"DEAR SIR,—Pray accept my very sincere thanks for the favour of your communication.   I am afraid the proposed Clerical Society will assume a very different form from that which I contemplated, and I certainly do not feel at all confident as to its utility.

"I must observe that its very preamble is in some measure incorrect.   The natural inference to be drawn from the heading of the circular is that the society originated with me.   Now that is incorrect.   Mr. Pole mentioned to me that it was the wish of some of the younger clergy of the archdeaconry to have more intercourse with their seniors, for the purpose of obtaining information on many points which arise in the discharge of their parochial duties, and he did me the honour to ask my approbation of a plan to effect this, stating that, if it had my concurrence, he should write to propose the formation of such a society.   Conceiving that a society of this nature would form a bond of union between the younger and elder clergy, besides affording them much useful information in point of their parochial duties, I signified my assent; but the original suggestion was from him, not from me, and all that I did was to signify my approbation.

"It was then agreed that a committee should be formed, consisting of several very respectable gentlemen, whose names and number I do not exactly recollect; but I think that few were at the meeting, except Mr. Curzon and Mr. Pole, unless you and Mr. Norman were also present.

"Not a word was said about doctrinal subjects; and if I had had the least idea that they were to be introduced at the meetings, I should have argued strenuously against them.

"The objects which I then publicly stated that I understood the society to have in view besides those of friendly intercourse were principally connected with the discharge of parochial duties, and the discussion of such difficult and peculiar cases as often arise, and in which a young clergyman may wish to have the advice of others with experience longer than his own.

"The subjects of which you have sent me a list may perhaps be said for the most part to be within the range of the above plan —except the second, which I think highly objectionable.

"I speak in this qualified way of all the subjects but the second, because I did not contemplate the formation of a debating society on specific subjects regularly proposed three months before. I contemplated that each member of the society who had occasion should propose at the meeting any cases of difficulty which had arisen in his parish, and take the opinion of his clerical brothers upon them. This I conceived would be really serviceable. A regular debate such as you propose may involve ingenious and possibly instructive exercise, but is not likely to be of much practical use. And in fact I consider such debating society to offend at least virtually, if not actually, in some respects against the seventy-second and seventy-third Canons. A debate on the First Article respecting the august and incomprehensible essence of the Deity is one which I most earnestly deprecate. It is a subject of too awful a nature to be discussed in debates at an inn. Forgive me for saying that I shrink with dismay from this familiar approach to a subject which I can never contemplate in my most private meditation without prostration of spirit and the most reverential awe.

"With regard to the prayers to be used at the meeting, if I thought any were proper I should say that none ought to be used but those from our own Liturgy, but I do not think that the meeting would act in conformity with the spirit of the seventy-second and seventy-third Canons by using any. In my humble opinion it would be much better to meet on a prayer day, attend as individuals at the regular service of the Church, and then proceed to business at the usual place of meeting.

"With regard to the office of President, which it appears the society have resolved that I should be requested to accept, I must beg leave to say that, although it was proposed to confer this unmerited honour upon me at the visitation in June last, I then declined it, inasmuch as I was not resident in the county, nor ever likely to be present at a meeting. I must also beg leave to say that no communication in consequence of the resolution I allude to has been made to me, nor have I been consulted as to the formation of the society, its rules or objects, since it was first mentioned to me at the visitation—so that I not only have not acted as President, but cannot even consider myself as a member of the society, nor could I with propriety belong to it under its present constitution.

"I trust I may be allowed to say that my own opinions are neither lightly taken up nor easily to be laid down. I am alarmed, I confess, at the discussion proposed; and even were it a less awful subject, I should say that any discussion of any of the Articles of the Church of England, to which we have already assented, is unnecessary, and, if unnecessary, can at best do no good. It is more likely to disunite than to conciliate. Now my object has always been conciliation. I am well aware that, although we all assent to the Articles, we do not all interpret them alike. Some consider them Calvinistic, and some do not. My own opinions are decided. I obtrude them upon no man, and I quarrel with no man for holding different ones. I know very well that, if I bring my opinions into discussion, I shall neither convince nor be convinced, and am likely to promote discord and ill-will rather than friendly intercourse and harmony. I therefore consider such discussions as ill adapted to further the ends of the society, and as foreign to its objects as understood by me when it was proposed at my last visitation.

"I have troubled you at great length, because I consider the subject of the highest importance to the welfare and harmony of the clergy of the archdeaconry, and I shall humbly think that it is better no such society should be formed than that it should embrace objects the discussion of which may lead to disunion, and which I think are hardly allowable by the ecclesiastical laws. I have felt bound to speak unreservedly, as I always shall, with every feeling of respect and good-will towards those who differ from me, but with a deep sense of the responsibility I owe to God and man in the faithful discharge of my duties. If you have no objection to state to the meeting on the 17th that you have communicated to me the resolutions passed on August 3rd, with a view to learning my sentiments previous to your taking the chair on that day, I have none whatever to your communicating this letter, with my hearty respects and good-wishes to the gentlemen then assembled. You and they will of course adopt such measures as may appear most eligible to yourselves with regard to the dissolution or continuance of the society, but I hope you will not be offended at my wishing, for the reasons already given, not to be one of its members.

" I could wish to add that, although your letter is dated October 7th, it has the postmark of 'too late' on it. I did not receive it till Monday afternoon, when I was occupied in preparing for two important public meetings in which I had to take a prominent part the next day. I was engaged from ten till near five yesterday in attendances on them, and returned with so severe a headache that I was unable to answer your letter till this day, when I have risen at six o'clock to begin ; but as it is a whole school day, and I am greatly pressed with other affairs, I doubt whether I shall have time to finish till the next day." *

FROM LORD STOWELL.

"LONDON, *October* 12*th,* 1826.

" MY DEAR MR. ARCHDEACON,—Many thanks are due to you for the charges with which you have favoured me, and I pay that debt of thanks with the most perfect sincerity. The charges are highly creditable to yourself and invaluable in information and use to your clergy. If duly applied by your clergy, they will produce real improvements within the extent of your jurisdiction.

" I am much less favourably inclined to our modern reformers and northern philosophers than you appear to be, for I attribute to them worse intentions. All this parade of the improvement of the education of the lower classes has, in my opinion, worse intentions for its bottom than what your candour is willing to allow ; they have a strong tincture of motives pretty plainly avowed by many individuals amongst them of changing the order of society, and of giving an undue preponderance to classes who cannot be trusted with it without danger to the public safety. I am just come from a neighbouring part of your country—Buxton—on account of a rheumatism by which I have been grievously annoyed. I have received benefit from the excellent baths there ; but I need not add that my time of life forbids the hope of a perfect cure."

FROM THE REV. CHARLES E. COTTON.

"DERBY, *October* 14*th,* 1826.

" MR. ARCHDEACON,—I have this moment received your obliging letter out of the post, and lose no time in making known

---

* I have taken the foregoing from the draft in Dr. Butler's letter-book, arranging it according to his own marginal notes, but retaining passages of some length through which he had put his pen, probably as thinking them too long.—ED,

to you that, upon the receipt of your letters yesterday, I thought it would be necessary to see Mr. Wood as soon as possible. I therefore sent a man over to him this morning, giving the heads of your most excellent letter, and requesting that he would do me the favour to dine with me at Dalbury on Monday and take a bed, when we might speak more fully upon the subject, and adding that, should that not be convenient, I would meet him at Derby at any time previous to twelve o'clock on Tuesday. I shall make a point to act according to your wishes ; and I feel confident that, should it be found necessary to read your admirable letter, it will give the greatest possible satisfaction to about two-thirds of your clergy in the Archdeaconry of Derby. I hope Mr. Wood will be returned by the time you mention ; but should that not be the case, I can rely upon Mr. Johnson of Aston and others attending, who have expressed themselves exactly according to what you have mentioned in your letter."

FROM THE REV. JOHN WOOD.

"October 19*th,* 1826.

" MY DEAR SIR,—Little did I think that I should have been found amongst the combatants on the 17th ; but so it was. Cotton's summons was so very pressing that I could not refuse him—so here beginneth the history of the first and last meeting of the Clerical Society for debating controversial points of doctrine. Precisely at twelve Johnson, Lowther, Hall, Murphy, Pickering, and myself made our appearance, to the surprise, I believe, of the long-faced tribe, who appeared to be fully equipped for the field, and panting to engage in the wordy war. So have I seen two men stripped into buff completely thrown into a state of derangement by the appearance of a set of fellows in the shape of constables, commanding them to keep the peace.

"The Bishop Blaze (no unapt name for the worthy secretary as far as outside is concerned) expressed his pleasure at our attendance, little dreaming at the time that his six subjects must be laid upon the shelf for future discussion. ' I have received from the chairman a letter from the Archdeacon, whom I thought it my duty to consult, particularly as he has been requested to be President of the society, which I beg leave to read previous to our entering upon business.' The letter was read, the Prayer Book sent for, the Canons appealed to, and I was in hopes we should have got rid of the concern altogether ; but Johnson and Lowther seemed to wish the rules to be new-modelled, and thought that, leaving out the objectionable part, the society might be a good thing. We divided upon the question equal numbers, but Mr. Dickenson wished the clergy to meet, and therefore altered his vote. The younger Shirley came in afterwards, and took the lead in conciliating the objectionable parts of the plan ;

and thus it now stands that a Clerical Society shall be formed, for friendly intercourse and conversation upon professional duties, to meet on a prayer day, and go as individuals to church previous to the meeting—open to all the clergy who choose to sign the rules.

"Very unsatisfactory all this, I believe, to a great part of the meeting. You will of course receive a communication. Our wise secretary freely confessed his errors and deficiencies : he ought to have written to the Bishop, but he forgot ; he would, however, amend his fault by a speedy communication of his proceedings to his lordship. He ought to have written to the Archdeacon, and sent one of the circulars ; but he did not get them printed till a few days before the meeting, and he had not time to receive an answer. I was accused of trying by a side wind to get rid of the society. Thinks I to myself, that is true enough, if I choose to confess it.

"When we divided, my vote and another were objected to by the secretary. I pleaded his invitation ; but Mr. Simpson informed me that I was asked to discuss the subjects mentioned in the circular, not to raise objections. This being the case, I voted myself useless, and took my hat, and other hats were apparently in motion to follow the example of mine. The secretary had found he had gone too far ; and I, being always meek and mild, was prevailed upon to resume my place. Thus at three o'clock I returned unenlightened as I came, leaving a considerable number, as the secretary observed, to discuss the merits of the soup and mutton, of which I have little doubt he would give a much better account than he could have done of his six subjects, had he been called upon for ideas about them. Between ourselves, I thought the party were terribly vexed the secretary had not written to the Bishop, hoping no doubt to have had a word of consolation which might have cheered them under the disappointment they experienced from the chairman's communication.

" Pray burn this scrawl."

FROM THE REV. AUTHORITY NORMAN.

" BRAILSFORD, *October* 20*th*, 1826.

" DEAR SIR,—As I have reason to believe that the scheme of a Clerical Society originated with myself, I hope you will suffer me to offer a word in explanation on the subject. My object was that which you express in your letter to Mr. Cotton, but the feeling of party was so strong that I was obliged to bend to circumstances. The orthodox kept aloof, and the low party carried the first meeting. The orthodox clergymen were dissatisfied with themselves, and at the last meeting came forward, and, I do trust, by steady perseverance carried their measures.

" Respecting the form of the society, a copy of whose rules was submitted to you, suffer me to say that I decidedly opposed the design of discussing doctrinal subjects, but was obliged to bend for a time, or the whole of the scheme had fallen away. When your letter was read, I was much struck with the sight of the danger which I had been running, must plead my ignorance of it, and sincerely thank you for my escape. Indeed, if no other good arises, I have been in one view the cause of much good to about a score of my brother-clergy in drawing from you that most excellent letter. I for one felt severely the rebuke which it put upon me, and I kiss the rod. But this single circumstance shows how beneficial a meeting for mutual information may become to the clergy generally. Here was half a dozen of the body with the best intentions, merely for want of information, about to incur the charge of the want of discipline and decorum.

" You will be pleased to learn that your friendly wishes were not lost upon us, and that we so modified our measures as, I hope, whilst we satisfied one party we did not offend the other. We are, alas ! much scandalised by the extremes of the parties. To attempt to unite them, I fear, is in vain. But they must be softened and lose much of their asperity by mutual and friendly intercourse."

FROM THE REV. JOHN WOOD.

"SWANWICK, *November* 13*th*, 1826.

" MY DEAR SIR,—Your letter of the 21st of October has remained unanswered till now, not because I have neglected or forgotten its contents, but from an expectation that something might occur which would render it necessary for me again to write to you, but not one word or hint have I heard respecting any further proceedings of the Clerical Society. The last meeting has probably cast a damper upon the zeal of a considerable portion of the members. The objections made were totally unexpected, and happy would it have been for us all had the entire dispersion of the society taken place instead of this remodelling plan—which although certainly better than to suffer them to proceed, yet sincerely could I have wished it had been entirely done away with. I should not be surprised if some letter had been written to the Bishop; indeed I think, if I recollect correctly, one of the party found fault with Cotton for his application to you, saying, if he considered it necessary to make any application, he ought to have applied to the highest authority (forgetting, I presume, that you had been requested by themselves to accept the office of President).

" I consider Pole in himself as a harmless animal, but possibly one that might be goaded on till he kicks at and annoys his neighbours. He regrets, I understand, nothing that took place at the last meeting, except his condescension in requesting me to return when I was leaving the room on account of the impertinent objection made by him to my vote about the alteration of the rules. Individually I sincerely wish he had not requested me to return, as I should in that case have entirely been clear of the business. The matter, however, must be made the best of; and as I have signed my name to their new rules, I shall make a point of attending—unless I see it assuming an objectionable form, in which case I shall not hesitate a moment in withdrawing my name.

"Thus what I have done and what I mean to do is easily determined; but when I come to the more material part of your letter, 'what I would do in your case,' I confess there appears greater difficulty. Your official situation of course totally precludes all idea of acting as a party man; yet I really think, after what has passed, I should not offer myself as a member unless solicited by the secretary, under the direction of a meeting, to become so. Your very friendly letter and the attention you have paid, though adverse to the plans intended to be proceeded upon, certainly demand this as a matter of courtesy--I perhaps should say of right. Should such an application be made to you, as the rules have been altered and the objectionable parts done away with—though it should be added that this was not done without a struggle, the members being equal on each side—I think I should not object to become an honorary member. As, however, the secretary had no order of this description (at least whilst I remained with them), it will give you an opportunity of seeing what may pass at the next meeting in January, and from what then takes place you will be better able to form an opinion whether you will like to become a member or not—saying this, I mean if solicited to do so—for in my humble opinion your official situation, independent of your kind attention to the clergy in general, demands this.

"I may be wrong, but I cannot help thinking that either Pole will write to the Bishop, and, if encouraged by him, will bring his letter to the next meeting, and the party will muster in force to carry his plans into execution, or they will let the matter sleep; and if they find they are watched, will by degrees suffer it, *as a meeting of the clergy* of the archdeaconry, to dwindle away, and after a few meetings to sink into oblivion. As some one observed, we shall soon have said all that can be advanced about marrying and burying, and then nothing will remain to be discussed but the merits of the soup and pudding.

"Be this, however, as it may, I cannot help considering it as a bold and daring attempt, though certainly not so intended by the original promoters of the scheme, to draw together the younger clergy, and induce them to become parties to the plans of a certain set, contrary, I shall always think, to the welfare and good order of that establishment which we have all sworn to

support.   I say this with all due deference to your better judgement ; but such are my feelings upon the subject, and I think you
would blame me were I not openly and candidly to declare them
to you."

The following letter is perhaps the only extant record
of Dr. Butler's manner of teaching, for no doubt the style
here adopted was the one most usual with him in school.
The letter was occasioned by an exaggerated report of
something said by Professor Scholefield about Dr. Butler's
having used *forte* for "perhaps" in the Latin notes to his
edition of Æschylus.

To Dr. Butler's Son.

"February 15th, 1827.

" Dear Tom,—That you may not be so ignorant a beast as
your father I beg to inform you
    " That *forte* is the ablative case of *fors*, and signifies by chance
or *by hap* ;
    "'That *forsitan* is the nominative case of *fors*, joined to the
verb *sit* and the conjunction *an*, and answers to the word *perhaps*,
which is not very different from *by-haps*.   But the difference in
the use of the two words is this : *forte* is used to express accident
or chance ; *forsitan* to express doubt.
    " *Forte* relates to facts.
    " *Forsitan* to opinions.
    "Thus when Horace says, ' Forte per angustam tenuis nitedula
rimam Repserat in cumeram frumenti,' or ' Ibam forte via sacra,'
he could not have said *forsitan* in either case, for he was relating
an accidental matter of fact, not a probable, but doubtful, matter
of opinion.
    "When Virgil says, ' forsitan illum Deducant aliquæ stabula
in Gortynia vaccæ,' he could not have said *forte*, because he was
not relating an actual matter of fact, but hazarding a probable
conjecture.   Furthermore ;—
    " You will generally find *forte* used with a past tense, *forsitan*
with a present.   This does not always hold, but from the nature
of their significations it must generally.   Furthermore, *forte* is
generally used with an indicative ; *forsitan* is used with a subjunctive only, or with an indicative future which is equivalent to a
subjunctive present.
    " A subjunctive after *forte* often depends upon a preceding
conjunction—as ' cum forte venissem.'   But though this is the
broad distinction between *forte* and *forsitan*, yet is *forte* sometimes

used instead of *forsitan*, though the converse may not hold. When Cicero says, 'Nisi forte magis erit parricida,' a doubt and not a matter of fact is being expressed ; but then you see *nisi* is being joined with *forte*, which brings it tantamount to *forsitan*, and in similar cases *forte* is used with these sort of conjunctions— 'Si quis vestrum forte miretur,' for 'Forsitan aliquis miretur.' In 'forte aliquis dixerit' doubt is expressed as much as if the writer had said 'forsitan aliquis dixerit'—but there is a question in this case whether *forsitan* should not be used instead of *forte*.

"Now I presume you know as much about *forte* and *forsitan* as the Greek Professor, and perhaps a little more.

"I have heard nothing from Cameron : I fear he has failed. I am your affectionate father,

"S. BUTLER.

"Every writer of Latin from Horace down to the present day sometimes makes a slip, so that I may very likely have written *forte* for *forsitan*, though I know not where ; and if I have done nothing worse than that, I shall not be very unhappy about it."

At a meeting of the School trustees held April 5th, 1827, the Rev. G. Maddock complained of a valuation agreed upon between the solicitors to the trustees and those who represented it as being too high. It was resolved that a special meeting be called to ascertain Dr. Butler's opinion. At the special meeting held April 19th Dr. Butler recommended that £250 should be accepted in lieu of £300, if paid at once. On April 26th the Rev. G. Maddock paid in this sum, and this was the end of the whole matter— roughly about three years and a half from the time when Dr. Butler took it in hand. In the course of a letter which the Master of St. John's wrote on April 30th to congratulate Dr. Butler, he said, "The School is wholly indebted to your exertions, and very few men, if any other, could have surmounted the obstacles which were opposed to an agreement."

CORRESPONDENCE, APRIL OR MAY, 1827—DECEMBER
14TH, 1827.

FROM THE. REV. S. TILLBROOK.

[*April* or *May,* 1827.]

*   *   *   *   *

" You have acted wisely and consistently with regard to the
Athenæum. William Hustler our registrary, and many others,
are just doing the reverse of Heber, and are backing out as fast
as they can. [Nothing more found on this subject.—ED.]

*   *   *   *   *

" Gordon has been unfairly used, I think. Had I been here,
he should not have tried for the Smith's Prize. Two of three
examiners Trinity men, so that it can only be considered a
College prize now. Besides Airey was private tutor to Turner—
a fact alone sufficient to turn the scale directly or indirectly in
Turner's favour. Now the Master of Trinity *ex officio* is an
examiner for the Craven Scholarship; but as his two sons are
sitting now, he very becomingly withdraws from the examination.
Gwatkin of St. John's told Melville of our College that if St. John's
had the senior wrangler next year, he would not allow him to sit
for the prize unless Airey appointed a deputy ; and he is right.

" I went last Friday to see the new comedy *School for Grown
Children*. On coming out I had my pocket picked—*i.e.* my gold
watch, chain, and seals (with fishing devices, club arms, etc.), all
snatched in an instant. I knocked the rascal down under a
hackney coach, and then just as I was hooking him two of his
worthy comrades pinned me against the walls of the Piazzas, and
the thief escaped. I went to the station, got bills printed, offered
a handsome reward, etc., but all to no purpose. *Tempus fugit,* or
the watch is flown.

" I hear that Tom and Hildyard have both done well at the
Craven examination. After two days (and they have had seven of
it) twenty candidates were dismissed : it is great folly in lads who
have no pretensions so to annoy the examiners."

*   *   *   *   *

To —— (?)

"*May* 3rd, 1827.

" DEAR SIR,—Your letter, which I had the honour to receive
yesterday, calls for some explanation on my part. Educated at
a public school myself for nearly nine years, and having been now
head-master of one for more than thrice that time, I must have
made little use of my opportunities of observation if I have
not learnt something of the habits and treatment of boys. But
anomalies sometimes occur, and when they do I am always

anxious to know how to treat them. I mean nothing invidious
to the masters of the other principal public schools in this
kingdom, with all of whom I am more or less acquainted, and
some of whom I know intimately, when I say that I think I am
at least as anxious as any of my brethren respecting the moral as
well as intellectual improvement of the boys under my care. I
cannot force them all to be first-rate scholars, because all have
not the same capacity; but if I train them to be honourable and
virtuous men, I am conferring a greater benefit upon themselves
and on society than by all the learning I can give them. With
this view I always exercise peculiar vigilance over boys while
their habits are yet unformed; and if I know them to be either
bad or good, the line of conduct to be pursued towards them is
easily marked. It is only in doubtful cases that I want information; and I feel it not only no trouble, but a duty, to communicate
with parents in such cases—which indeed are not very frequent.
I have now but two other instances out of above two hundred
boys. In general I have found such communications thankfully
received, and productive of material good, when met with corresponding frankness and co-operation. If they are not so met,
and if a parent is more anxious to justify his son than to approve
of the master's circumspection, I grant that no advantage can
result beyond what the master must derive from the satisfaction
of having discharged his duty."

*   *   *   *   *

From Baron Merian.

"*May* 31*st*, 1827.

"Dear Sir,—Your letters surprised and rejoiced me. Surprise:
Æschylus bis editur. You did not tell me a word of it before,
which reticence is not praiseworthy. Rejoicing: Your shooting
through Paris, which will be a most delightful thing to your
vetulus columbus. And to see your son will still enhance it. Let
him be as his father is, or become, and all will be right. Spadikins,
if there were many men like you spread all over the globe, bishops
and not bishops, what a life it would be, this human life!

"Yet I will not extol you for, I had almost said throwing away,
£100 for two old-fashioned books, one of which is worth just
fourpence. If your son happen to be not such an Aldinian as
you, those same gems will rust and rot, or be sold for a straw.
Or if you fix them at Shrewsbury (the celebrated mansion of
loud-voiced ladies), who will ever, in days to come, look at them?
Let libraries be small in quantity, and large in use. Here's my
sermon. You shall not have a right exclusive to preaching.

"There's bloody war about the piramids. [I humbly beg leave
to exclude the *y*, since the word has no more of fire about it than
the boot of a Dutchman, but is *pi* (article) and *ramad* (high

structure, tower. Stop, where am I got?), in spite of all the classics.] Young vindicates, not in person, his incontestable right of priority. Champollion, vain and silly like a peacock, thinks himself sole emperor of the Nile, and the rest of mankind doomed to hear and believe his fictions. I hope Mr. Drummond has sent you the first attack upon Champollion; a much severer one is just peeping out of the press. I am very glad Hughes is so well provided for; but how proceeds his amiable sister?—that I am still more avidulous to know. I might have said 'avid,' but you would have cried classically, 'Fy! Swift and Pope have it not: the diminutive is very good; *avidity* is excellent; but as to *avid* (which of course *must* have preceded both)—pugh! 'tis a shame; let me not hear it.' *Salvete* classics! your logic is admirable. Miss H. or Mrs. Monk has carried me far. As to your bridges under the sea, look first a little at French Master Brunel's *under* the Thames, and rather keep aloft. Now for Longman's banditti MS.; pray think no more about it—it has found another way. But *Smith-Barton* and the *Soosoo* vocabulary—that would be food for the hobby-horse of old οὐδείς."

FROM THE SAME.

"*June 5th*, 1827.

*   *   *   *   *

"Have you ever thought about *ambrosia*? It is literally 'immortal,' or giving immortality. The Indian form identical is *amritam*. Now *a* is the privativum—*mrit*, for *marit*, is *mors*, mort—*am* a mere termination. The Greek is to be spelt (Johnson knew not that to spell is to split) ἀ-μβρος-ία: where you finally deprehend μβρός, the mother both of *mort* and of βροτός; for the old ΜΒ split into M and B, and your ἄβροτος, ἀμβρόσιος (a- or immortal), are all but one word, a little diversified. And thus a poor mouse has offered to a great lion the Greek form for the Latin *mort-uus*, of which the lion was perhaps not aware. This is one instance of thousands. I could really wish that some of your youth would merely for the sake of *classicism*, merely in order to elucidate hard words and passages in Latin and Greek authors, betake themselves to the way I am showing. They and you would be surprised at the unexpected *real classic* profit (there's no hobby-horse in this), and at your next speech-day breakfast a little dissertation on facts of this sort would be, I trow, just as well as any *Quoadusque tandem*, or Ἄνδρες Ἀθηναῖοι.

"Now for *Venice*. If the matter may be delayed till September or October, I shall, I hope, be able to serve you. I shall then have some means of getting at the treasure of St. Mark. I would only request to be instructed how the collation is to be performed, and learn the shortest and surest proceeding, for those hesperidal *dottori* are amazing blunderers.

" Never in your life will you find the Soosoo vocabulary in a catalogue. It is called *A Grammar and Vocab. of the Susoo Language* (Edinburgh, 1802, 8vo), and was published by the missionaries (Bible-men), who do not sell, but gladly give it. Now pray get some good man of their fraternity to write to them and ask for two copies. Now there's a good boy."

From B. H. Kennedy, Esq.

"Paignton, Torbay, *July 22nd*, 1827.

" My dear Sir,—You said in your last letter it was probable that, instead of engaging an assistant immediately, you should wait till Tom had taken his degree. I am now writing on the supposition that you retain that intention. Without further prelude, if you think that I can in any way be useful to you for one year from October next my best efforts are at your disposal.

" You will not charge me with fickleness, for you will instantly see that my present proposal is not inconsistent with my former conduct in declining your original offer. For in the first place, although on mistaken grounds, I did expect a fellowship, and in that case intended to decline pupils and read law after the present vacation. But now I should be obliged to devote the greater portion of my time next year to pupils; and thus, supposing law to be my view, the sacrifice of time at Cambridge or at Shrewsbury would be the same. Again, could I then in my own opinion have spared a year, I should not have dreamed of offering myself to you for that limited period, still less have accepted the situation for that limited period with the intention of so soon resigning it, when I knew you desired an assistant who would stay with you at least for some years.

" And now I offer myself to fill up the interval (or the greater part of it) before Tom's degree, if you persevere in that plan; if you do not, I cannot expect that you will accept my offer. Of course I do not seek emolument, and therefore you would make your own terms; but if by a sacrifice of emolument I could obtain the more improving and intellectual employment, I should prefer it. My objects are to avoid the expense of residence in college, to live a regular life, and to free myself from the oppression of a numerous acquaintance; above all, to have the advantage of your advice and assistance in my studies and in the art of teaching. For Mr. Tatham has intimated to my father that the classical lectureship at St. John's College will be offered to me after my fellowship—which I shall probably accept, and enter upon its duties in October twelvemonth.

" I do not know whether you have ever thought of publishing *Musæ Salopienses*; but should you have such an intention, I should be most glad to devote some of my leisure hours to the selection and arrangement of the exercises. I think my eye sufficiently practised to detect most of the few *cabbaged* verses which may have crept into the Play-books.

"Should my proposal meet your views, I should be able to join you about the 14th of October.

"I trust the sea has proved beneficial to Mrs. Butler and Tom, to whom with the rest of your family I beg to be kindly remembered, and remain, dear Sir,

"Ever your grateful and attached pupil,
"B. H. Kennedy."

The arrangement above indicated was nearly frustrated by Kennedy's standing for Rugby on the resignation of Dr. Wooll. The appointment, however, of Mr. Arnold enabled Kennedy to stay the whole year at Shrewsbury, as originally intended.

From Dr. Maltby.

"Buckden, September 25th, 1827.

"My dear Dr. Butler,—Long before this time the trustees of Rugby School must have bitterly lamented the injustice done to you when they preferred Wooll to Dr. Sam. Butler, and the only reparation they can make to society is to elect the best man they can.

"As to your coming forward now, I consider it out of the question ; and no one could think of opposing you."

＊　　　＊　　　＊　　　＊　　　＊

From the Rev. James Tate.

"Richmond, Yorks, October 2nd, 1827.

"My dear Sir,—Fortunately or unfortunately, turn out as it may, I was so gratified with your letter and the permission to make any use of it that I pleased, that I dispatched it to Rugby on the very day it was received.

"But really, my dear sir, the game is already so deeply and cleverly played or playing in powerful recommendation through personal letters to the governors (not that I can raise any such engines), that even a pupil of yours, if he has yet to start, will find many fair chances of success pre-engaged.

"With regard to myself, I confess, if anything could encourage me to hope in this pursuit, it certainly would be the generous tribute of praise which a man so pre-eminent as yourself has bestowed upon my name.

"Forgive me, dear sir, if I state what my friend Archdeacon

Headlam knows to be true, that the periphrasis I use for the Head-Master of Shrewsbury is—the King of Schoolmasters.
"Ever faithfully and affectionately yours,
"Js. TATE."

FROM THE REV. H. A. S. ATWOOD.

"*October 8th*, 1827.

*   *   *   *   *

"The retirement of Dr. Wooll from Rugby, at least the notification of his intention to do so shortly, affords ample matter for conversation and inquiry in these parts. More than once your name has been mentioned. Mr. Leigh, who was with us yesterday, asked me if I thought you would accept it if strongly solicited by all the trustees. I said I thought certainly not."

The Mr. Leigh above mentioned is no doubt Chandos Leigh, Esq., of Stoneleigh Abbey, who was raised to the peerage by Lord Melbourne in 1839. Mr. Leigh was not yet one of the trustees of Rugby School, but was elected later, as Lord Leigh, in 1844. There cannot, I think, be a doubt that had Dr. Butler so wished he would have been appointed to the head-mastership of Rugby without opposition; but Shrewsbury had now nearly twice as many boys as Rugby, whose numbers at Christmas, 1827, were only a hundred and twenty-three, and Dr. Butler could not be expected to leave a school of his own creation, where the trustees now let him have absolutely his own way, for one in which there was no knowing what unforeseen difficulties he might not meet with.

FROM BARON MERIAN.

"*October 9th*, 1827.

*   *   *   *   *

"What a loss England and the globe have sustained since your last! But it is my belief that the benevolent and vast plans of Canning will be even better executed without than with him. His genius was too towering; 'tis now replaced by talent, and this does better in this world of mediocrity. Your King has shown himself gloriously in (*a*) creating and (*b*) maintaining the present gust. He was not fond of Canning, and yet he appointed him. That's

royal.   England has the respect of the universe ; if she proceeds
moderately in the present path, but without vacillation, she will
become the queen of nations.   But help Ireland.
  " *Paulo minora canamus.   Kärcher* is overjoyed at your sentence.
His dictionary will be all over Latin, and he implores your protection if, upon inspection, you find the work worthy of your
patronage.   Remember that, since the *obit* of yon other Samuel,[*]
you are the Ilion 'of classicism in Great Britain.   This I devoutly
acknowledge, yet it does not detain me a bit from fighting you on
another ground, that of universal palaver, where I strut and crow
as fierce as a game-cock.   Your letter has lit a sudden light.   I
find that you are a perfect Aristotelian, a declared synthetist, a
pilot that steers backward from the mouth to the spring, an
architect that thinks that gathering small pebbles will make a
palace.   Now I am the total reverse of all this.   *Hinc illæ lacrymæ.*
I begin if possible at the top, and sail downward.   If we agreed
in philosophy, we should agree in grammar immediately.   But
you place generalities at the tail of millions of particularities,
supposing parts to have been before the whole, and the human
mind to be at first an empty bag, or, if you please, a lump of
butter in July, impressible or implebile by those innumerable
exterior objects which surround us without control from the
cradle to the grave.   Consider pray what a confounded confusion would arise in the mind of men, if there was no previous
ruler within to receive and master and distribute the inroar.
Such a complete passivity, can it be the essence of a reasonable
mind, a spark of the divinity ?   No, the ruler is evident ; innate,
general, domineering ideas, simple and firm, precede the hurly-
burly of this world ; if not, the οἰκουμένη would be a Bedlam.
What you call abstractions are in fact precursions.   Does a man
laboriously abstract (*i.e.* collect) his notion of ' hollow ' from the
inspection of pots, cups, boots, and thimbles ?   Never.   That's
downright Condillac ; and if you could reject it, we should be
one in grammar, as we are in heart.
  " As to sound, it is of very little import, for every notion has
crept into every sound (or form).   There is no tie betwixt sense
and sound ; against onomatopoiia do but compare ' to bark ' in
divers idioms.   Lastly, you speak more of things, and I of names.
*Certe, ut lapides, lapide opus est ; sed etiam, ut lapis nomines, ratione
quâdam opus est ; hæc autem in verbo quodam, cui generalis notio
inest, latet.   Denominata enim res a prominenti quâdam qualitate,
cujus expressio semper e verbo simplicissimo hausta.*   Thence the
Chinese call the verb the living engendering word : the rest they
call *dead.*   No doubt there's a set of verbs—they call them
nominal, as to handle—which are plainly derived from nouns ; but

---

[*] Dr. Parr.

such verbs are of secondary formation, and their parent nouns had been preceded by those prior *simplicissima verba.*

"Suing . . . duco suspiria Soosoo, sodes, si Soosoo succurrit, suscipe Soosoo."

Here Baron Merian's letters come to an end. He died, as I have already said, on the 25th of April, 1828.

To an Assistant Master and Former Pupil.

"*October* [*2nd* (?), *3rd* (?), *4th* (?)], 1827.

"Dear ——,—All extremes defeat their own ends, and especially that of rigour. Jones in a fit of despair refused to be flogged. I did not choose to let him incur the mischief of expulsion, and I flogged him by main force. But he so utterly despairs of doing anything that may satisfy you that I hardly know whether by much and kind remonstrance I have brought the boy's mind into a right tone. I had him in my library for an hour to do his derivations for his evening Greek lesson. He did them well and correctly. I made him construe and parse it to me. He did so with some mistakes, but such as I considered venial, and in which it was much better to set the boy right by asking him a question or two, and making him think, than by intimidating him by threats and anger.

"I know you mean well, but you expect more than human nature is capable of; and not one, but one and all, of the boys, as far as they can venture to do so, make remonstrances when I come to punish them, that they are sent down for more slight offences than boys are usually flogged for.

"I have always flogged them that I might support your authority, but without always feeling that it was likely to prove a serviceable correction. I have more than once thought it was only hardening them, and that the despair of doing anything that would be accepted by you if it was not quite correct drove them to do nothing at all. The strong and serious case which I have had to-day induces me to beg that you will remit something of this extreme rigour without giving way to too much laxity. All great severity destroys its own effect."

To the Same.

"Shrewsbury, *October 5th,* 1827.

*   *   *   *   *

"I think every boy here knows my hatred of falsehood, and my indignation at any attempts to maintain it, and I also know that more general good is done by my expressions of scorn for the meanness of so contemptible a vice than by ten floggings to the individual who practises it.   Depend upon it, a fine perception of moral rectitude is better inculcated by example and exhortation than by blows.   It may be instilled into the mind, but cannot be beaten into it.

"Undoubtedly, if a boy persists in a flagrant course of lying, as in the instance of D—— G—— and the coachman, I should deem it my duty to flog him severely.   But to meet every petty excuse which a boy makes to save himself from punishment with the rod would in my judgement be not to correct but to tyrannise.

"Incessant flogging only hardens the offender.   It makes him callous to punishment, and takes off the edge of moral feeling instead of whetting it.   If the punishment of flogging is inflicted for petty offences, no greater remains for heavier ones, and the effect is destroyed by the frequency.

"Your own sense of honour leads you, as mine leads me, to detest falsehood as much as Paley or any other moralist can.   I am glad that you have it so keenly; for how much soever you may have cultivated it elsewhere, you must be sensible that I educated you in it; but I have also a sense of humanity, and an exercise of judgement and forbearance, which you do not seem to me to take sufficiently into the account.

* * * *

"With regard to your saying that I believed Jones's story in preference to yours, it is really going too far to answer you.   I never asked him his story, and to this hour I do not know what his story is.

"I punished him because you sent him down, and I wished to maintain your authority.   I remonstrated with you on your rigour, because the boy in a fit of desperation refused to be flogged, and because I knew that boys in general are not driven to this act but by some strong motive, and because I knew also that there is but one opinion about your severity; and were any confirmation necessary your present letter affords it.

"I once more repeat that I am persuaded no good arises from such frequent floggings for 'shirking,' as you call it, and I request that you will exercise moderation in the selection of cases of this nature.   Unquestionably some punishment is necessary, but not to that extent to which you carry it; nor is idleness to go unpunished, though an idle boy is not to be flogged every morning.   Our weekly conferences will pretty well point out the ordinary cases for punishment in the week ensuing. The extraordinary will occur either from cases of idleness and misconduct in boys not included in the ordinary cases, or in grosser idleness and misconduct than usual in those that are. An intelligent master can be at no loss in the selection of these, if he can govern his temper; and if he cannot, he ought not to hold an appointment which exposes him to continual irritation.

" P.S.—Since the above was written I have received your note. I am quite sure your intention is good ; but your *modus operandi* is too harsh, in my opinion—at least I know I should not myself punish boys where I punish them because you send them to be punished.

" As to my being an Egyptian taskmaster—Heaven forbid ! I do as I would be done by. But neither yourself nor all your coadjutors seem to be sufficiently aware of that golden maxim of Tacitus which I always wish to carry into effect : ' Omnia scire non omnia exsequi.' I ought to be made acquainted with everything, and left to my discretion in the selection of objects and cases of animadversion. I trust now we perfectly understand each other. Once more believe me yours truly,

"S. B.

" I have seen Jones again, and told him that he will not be allowed to be idle, but that no impossibilities are required of him."

This master resigned his appointment very shortly afterwards.

TESTIMONIAL FROM DR. BUTLER TO B. H. KENNEDY, ESQ., WHO WAS THEN STANDING FOR THE HEAD-MASTERSHIP OF RUGBY.

[About October 10th, 1827.]

" DEAR KENNEDY,—It is impossible that I can refuse a testimonial to your high and, I believe, unexampled merits as a classical scholar, and to your work and honour as a man. Of all my distinguished pupils, who have done honour to their teachers and themselves at the University, there is none who can compare with you in the splendour of his success.

" Two of the highest University prizes obtained in 1823 while you were at school—so utterly without my knowledge and assistance, that I felt it right to send a certificate to the Vice-Chancellor of my always discouraging boys from such attempts while under my care till they are actual members of the University.

" 3. In 1824 the Pitt Scholarship in the very second term of your residence, after an examination of unexampled splendour, leaving all competitors of two and three years' standing far behind you, and being declared *facile princeps*.

" 4. In the same year the gold medal for the Greek Ode.

" 5. The Latin Ode.

" 6. The Porson Prize.

" 7. In 1825 the gold medal for the Epigrams.

" 8. In 1826 for the third time the Porson Prize.

"9. In 1827 the first of the first class on the Classical Tripos; and, 10, the senior medal.

"More prizes than I gained myself—more than were gained by any other individual of my pupils.

"More than were gained by any one individual whom I can find in the records of the University within the same space of time.

"What can I say more, but that you are coming to me now to be an assistant for a twelvemonth, and that if elected to Rugby you know my system and will have the benefit of seeing all the details of it, and receiving my best advice, till the time of removal to your own station?"

To Dr. Butler's Son from Miss Butler.

"SHREWSBURY, *November 29th,* 1827.

"MY DEAREST TOM,—I have just half an hour in which I hope to give you a faint idea of the commotion your coming of age made yesterday in this place. Not a soul among the tradespeople knew of the event till Tuesday, but then active preparations were set on foot to celebrate it. Accordingly the bells began to ring at eight o'clock, and continued to do so most part of the day; cannons were fired; the band played; sheep were roasted; and a party of fifty of the friends and tradespeople of the family sat down to dinner at the Raven—tickets a guinea each. Mr. Braine and Mr. Iliff were the presidents, and the meeting was kept up till a late hour, and was a very respectable assembly.

"Nothing could exceed the warmth of the townspeople but that of the boys, who were literally beside themselves, and had a day of noise and fun to their hearts' content. They got up the three chapel bells and rang them, as well as all the breakfast bells, almost all day. They had a band and four rounds of cannon stationed in the school garden, which they never let rest for a moment; they had four flags hoisted on the school tower, and they sent up fireworks and squibs, and they shouted at every one of the family that ever ventured a head out of doors the whole day. This noise, together with the clapping, hurraing, and singing of the whole school, you may suppose made no small commotion; and as it was incessant, I hear many of the boys are to-day quite hoarse. They sung 'God save Tom Butler' with all their might, and the only thing they regretted was that they did not know it in time to have a flag with your name on it hoisted on the tower. Several houses were illuminated in the evening, and we had the hand-bells and singers at all the houses after dark. The boys enjoyed their roast beef and plum pudding and wine and dessert extremely, and were in the very highest spirits imaginable. The masters too were particularly cordial and good-natured. They all dined at the Raven except Hubbersty, who was engaged to a party at Greenfields, and Iliff was at the very head of the rejoicings. He did not know the event which took place till too late to provide a dinner like ours for his boys, but he gave them all wine and cut up two guinea cakes among them, which pleased them as well. Dr. and Mrs. Dugard dined with us, as did Harriet, and the three little girls came to dessert. They were quite wild, and kept saying, ' Oh, mamma, how happy I are ! What a very pretty, what an amusing day I have had !' etc., etc.

"The children drank tea with Mrs. Bromfield out of your silver teapot, and Sharpe of course was of the party. Harriet invited him to dine with her, which he did ; and all the children had their dinner downstairs. The masters all supped with us, as did Fred Cory, and John Underwood, who was in Shrewsbury ; and most of our friends either called or sent their congratulations, but none were kinder than Mrs. Maddock.

" Papa and mamma sent a dinner to the servants and workmen at each of their farms, with a quart of ale apiece to drink your health ; and Mrs. Jones and Mrs. Evans (the women there) had each a gown. We all came in for beautiful presents, as your keepsakes, which you shall see when you come down ; and, in short, I think nothing was omitted that could be thought of. But as we had no idea of receiving such a compliment as was paid in the rejoicings of the day, it is a wonder if nothing was omitted.

" We all unite in very best love to you ; and believe me, dearest Tom,

" Your most affectionate sister,

" MARY BUTLER.

" Everybody regretted that you were not present yesterday, but I think you would have found the attentions paid almost painfully oppressive, and were better out of the way. Papa sent a letter to the party at the Raven to thank them for their attentions, and they were much pleased with it."

FROM MR. JOHN PARDOE.

" LITTLE STRETTON, *December 14th*, 1827.

" SIR,—As some pupils of yours on their Way home yesterday passing through Little Stretton Took and threw a Quantity of round leaden Bullets at the Inhabitants Houses to demolish the Windows &c. And have broken several panes of Glass at several of the Houses, I myself have picked up five leaden bullets, and two white Peas, which they threw at my Windows, which I have taken care of them, the peas took me in the Face as they threw them. Them were they that went on the Outside the Coach, and those that threw the Bullets went by Chaise. It is requested you will Inform Me of the Names of these young Gentlemen and were their Parents reside, As we may know were to write to them and inform them of the Circumstance &c. such Conduct is not to be put up with. your immediate Attention to this and an Answer by return of Post will much Oblige

"Your most obedient servant
" JOHN PARDOE."

Note in Dr. Butler's handwriting :—

Kemmes
G. Lowe } by chaise.
Pardoe

Hoskyns *
Greenley
Newton † } outside coach.
Thomas ‡

Gill
Evans § || inside coach.

There was no draft of any answer.

---

* Chandos Wren Hoskyns, author of *Talpa ; or, Chronicles of a Clay Farm*, etc., and M.P. for Hereford 1869—1874.

† Sir Charles Newton, K.C.B., late Keeper of Greek and Roman Antiquities at the British Museum.

‡ Afterwards Canon of Canterbury and highly distinguished at Oxford.

§ T. S. Evans, Canon of Durham, and one of the most brilliant scholars of the time. See Memoir by Dr. Waite, published 1893.

CHAPTER XXI.

Correspondence, January 3rd, 1828—March 30th, 1829.—The "Beef
Row."—Correspondence, April 13th, 1829—May 25th, 1829.—Fourth
Foreign Tour.—Charge delivered June 18th, 19th, 1829, and Corre-
spondence, July 1st, 1829—December 16th, 1829.

CORRESPONDENCE, JANUARY 3RD, 1828—MARCH 30TH, 1829.

FROM THE BISHOP OF LICHFIELD AND COVENTRY (THE HON. H. RYDER).

"January 3rd, 1828.

"DEAR SIR,—The death of our valued friend Archdeacon Owen shocked and grieved me. It is a public as well as a private loss. May it please God to console and support his bereaved daughter!

"Would it be any ease or benefit to you to exchange the archdeaconry of Derby for that of Salop? It occurred to me that the long journeys might be inconvenient, and the immediate communication by conversation rather than by letter with the clergy under your superintendence might be more pleasant and satisfactory. Your acquaintance with the clergy of Salop, your knowledge of the late archdeacon's plans, etc., would make the entrance upon a new charge scarcely more troublesome than the continuance in an old one.

"You will, I am sure, be well convinced that your truly able, judicious, and assiduous conduct in your office is duly appre-ciated by me. I thought it right to make you the offer of the exchange first, in case it should be at all an object to you, before I proposed to fill up the vacancy in any other way, lest you should ever regret to have lost the opportunity of diminished labour.

"I remain, dear Sir, yours truly,
"H. LICH. & COV."

Dr. Butler declined the exchange, on the ground that he had already familiarised himself with the details of Derby Archdeaconry, and that his personal acquaintance with most of the Shropshire clergy might make it awkward for him to be as firm as it was occasionally necessary to be.

FROM MRS. HEMANS.

"February 19*th,* 1828.

" MY DEAR DR. BUTLER,—I beg to offer you my sincere congratulations on the approaching event which your letter announces. The name of Archdeacon Bather is well known to me ; and on mentioning yesterday in company the intelligence you have been kind enough to communicate, a lady exclaimed, with no little vehemence, ' Then Miss Butler is going to marry *the best of men* !' Still I can but too well imagine the mingled feelings with which you and Mrs. Butler must look forward to the event ; for I am about to lose in a similar manner my only sister, and I may almost say my only companion, since we have for years been linked together in a community of thought and pursuit which I must never hope to have renewed. Unfortunately for me, interchange of thought is an habitual want of my mind, and I pine without it, as the Swiss exile does for his native air ; so that I look with a feeling almost of alarm to the loneliness (not literal but mental loneliness) which seems awaiting me. But I know not why I should write thus to you, my dear sir, except that your kindness always encourages me to feel myself addressing a friend. My health is improving since I last wrote, under the care of *our* Esculapius, Mr. Bythell, who is, I believe, a friend of Dr. Darwin's. I did take to rearing geraniums some time since, by way of a less exciting amusement than my usual ones ; but I am almost ashamed to tell the result—in summer I forgot to water them, and in winter I forgot to shelter them, so the last frost these my ill-used adopted children all withered away. It would be too cruel to try similar experiments upon *live things* (though my conscience was sorely smitten upon reading the other day a gravely maintained opinion that plants can *feel*), so I fear I must not think of the bees and chickens.

" I do not know whether you are at all a lover of German literature, but there is in a poem in that language a beautiful nuptial benediction pronounced by a father over his child at the moment of his leaving him, which some parts of your letter recalled to my mind. I have copied Madame Stael's translation of it, and take the liberty of enclosing it for you.

" My poor Arthur !—I really know not what I shall do with him.

"With every good wish, believe me, dear Sir, most truly your obliged

"FELICIA HEMANS."

TO THE BISHOP OF LICHFIELD AND COVENTRY.

(Referring to the building and endowment of St. Michael's Church, Shrewsbury.)

"*March 23rd*, 1828.

"MY LORD,—Although the business on which I am about to write to your lordship is not strictly official—the parish which it concerns being a royal peculiar, and exempt from your lordship's jurisdiction—yet I feel it a point of respect to make the first communication to your lordship, and I have the greater pleasure in doing so because I know your zeal and activity on all occasions in which the interests of religion are concerned.

"For many years it has been my anxious wish to see an additional church with a great deal of free accommodation for the poor in this parish. It was a point on which I had many communications with my late lamented friends Messrs. Blakeway and Archdeacon Owen, and in which I am as cordially joined by their successor, the Rev. Mr. Rowland, as I was by them. The town population of this parish is about five thousand five hundred, and in the church there is only accommodation for the poor women of the almshouses. In this state of things it cannot be wondered at that some go to ranters, some to this and some to that description of dissent, and few, if any, to the church. There is therefore a most peculiar call for an additional church in this parish, especially in that part of it in which two great manufactories, one belonging to Mr. Marshall, the member for Yorkshire, and the other to Mr. Benyon, are situated.

*   *   *   *   *

"We have thought that the best way would be to appropriate at least £500 of the subscription towards challenging Queen Anne's Bounty, if that can be done, and appropriating the pew rents at first as a fund for repairs, and partly for liquidation of the money we may borrow, and, whenever the latter object shall be accomplished, in aid of the clergyman's stipend. It will take a large sum to effect all this, and we cannot hope to effect it unless we can receive important assistance from the commissioners for building churches. But as it is necessary in the first instance to know whether we can receive any (otherwise it will be in vain to attempt the subscription), and whether we may challenge the Bounty, as I have mentioned, with a part of our subscriptions, I write to ask your lordship's opinion on these two points, and remain, with great respect, my lord,

"Your lordship's obliged and faithful servant,
"S. BUTLER."

FROM E. MASSIE, ESQ. (AFTERWARDS REV.), WHO HAD JUST
    TAKEN THE IRELAND UNIVERSITY SCHOLARSHIP.

[*March* or *April*, 1828.]

"MY DEAREST SIR,—Thank you a million times for making
me the happiest fellow at the present moment under the sun.
I cannot tell you how very, very grateful I feel to you for enabling
me to make my father too so happy as he will be when he hears
of my success. When Symons came to me just now with the
information I was like a madman, and though only in my shirt
danced about like a wild Indian. Allow me, my dear sir, to
take this opportunity of congratulating you most heartily on the
marriage of Miss Butler. God grant she may meet with every
possible happiness! Pray remember me most kindly to her and
to Mrs. Butler.

"Once more, my dear sir, let me thank you from the bottom of
my heart, and assure you that I am most gratefully and affectionately attached.

"E. MASSIE."

FROM M. J. H. KLAPROTH.

"PARIS, *le* 6 *Juin*, 1828.
"5, RUE D'AMBOISE.

"MONSIEUR,—C'est avec un regret extrême que je me charge
de vous donner le premier une très-triste et affligeante nouvelle.
Nous avons perdu tous les deux un de nos meilleurs amis, et le
monde un savant distingué, et ce qui est plus à déplorer, un
excellent homme. Le Baron de Merian a succombé le 25
Avril, à une rougeole maligne à laquelle est joint une fluxion de
poitrine, qui l'a tué après une très courte maladie. Malheureusement ni lui ni son médecin sentaient le danger, et il est mort
dans le moment où tout donnait la meilleure espérance.

*   *   *   *   *

"M. de Merian vivait depuis un an à la campagne, et nous
étions en correspondance journalière ensemble. Je faisais tous
ses affaires, et à présent il me reste le triste devoir de mettre ordre
à son héritage et de m'occuper de la vente de ses livres."

From the rest of the letter it abundantly appears that
Klaproth had the ordering of all the Baron's papers. Many
were sent to Basle, and careful search was made among
these a few years ago for Dr. Butler's letters to the Baron
(which it appears from one of his own letters that he
preserved), but they were not found: they probably went
wherever Klaproth's papers went at his death in 1835.

It is unintelligible how Klaproth, who well knew how close and old the intimacy between Baron Merian and Dr. Butler had been, and who was himself personally acquainted with Dr. Butler, should have allowed six weeks to pass without letting him know of the Baron's death. The Baron's relatives in Switzerland found him already buried by the time they reached Paris on being apprised of his death, without having been previously informed of his illness.

To M. J. H. KLAPROTH.

[*June 9th* or *10th*, 1828.]

"CHER M. KLAPROTH,—Je suis vivement touché de la triste nouvelle que vous venez de m'annoncer. Je comptais le Baron Merian parmi mes plus chers amis. Notre amitié a duré plus de trente années avec une estime parfaite et réciprocale. Jamais n'ai-je connu un homme d'une âme plus simple et vertueuse.

*　　*　　*　　*　　*

" Je suis très fâché de la perte du pacquet qui contenait la grammaire et le dialogue dans le Soosoo. Je les trouvai extrême-ment difficiles à procurer et l'on m'avait assuré qu'il n-y-avait pas un trouvable. Ce n'était qu'avec beaucoup d'interêt et d'im-portunité que j'avais réussi à procurer une copie, et je suis presque désespéré de trouver une autre, mais je ferai mon possible, et je répéterai mes exactes recherches pour le pacquet qui est malheureusement perdu."

FROM THE REV. S. TILLBROOK.

"IVY COTTAGE, *August 14th*, 1828.

" MY DEAR ARCHDEACON,—I thank you over and over again not only for your good opinion, but for your spiritual reasonings and consolation. I have been very low at times, and have felt the want of society. Now I have two visitors with me—a son of my old friend Koch of Frankfort, and a worthy brother of the angle, Mr. Clutterbuck, Fellow of Exeter, Oxford. My thoughts and attentions are now turned to my guests, and I freely con-fess that society is better medicine than calomel and opium, which might be necessary for my bodily ailment, though their counteraction was very debilitating. My appetite is now return-ing, and I feel the benefit of a few glasses of red port and Margaret's mutton soup. I do not yet know how long I may stay here, for Clutterbuck is anxious to accompany me to

Leintwardine, to try his skill with the grayling, and I am nothing loth.

" Who is to be the new Dean of Norwich ? Bishopgate is given to Lord Grey's brother. I wish they would make you Dean of Norwich. I am very anxious to see you handsomely preferred. As for myself I have no claim, except it can be found in the character you have been so kind as to give me. Nor would I accept of any preferment unless I looked forward to sharing it with a helpmate. I should have enough to keep me and my angle, and might vagabondise to the end of my days ; but the fates seem to decree otherwise—and I think for my happiness, could that one obstacle, *res angusta domi*, be obviated. It is quite ridiculous to read the number of congratulations sent me, first on Copley's advancement, and now on Blomfield's, as if my fortunes were secured, and myself in the high road to clerical appointments and independence.

" I have jogged on nearly half a century, and a much shorter time will set all these worldly matters at rest. If I am not to be a Benedict in this world, I hope I may be so in the next. God bless you !

" Ever yours affectionately and gratefully,
" S. TILLBROOK."

TO DR. BUTLER'S SON.

[*August* (?), 1828.]

*   *   *   *   *

" We have had a great visitor to-day—the Duke of Sussex called and stayed two hours with me, though he said he could not stay a minute, and means to come at some future time and stay here, to your mother's infinite delight. We have set on foot our subscription for the church at St. Mary's,* and started with £700.

" Your affectionate father,
" S. BUTLER."

FROM THE REV. S. TILLBROOK.

" *October* 22*nd*, 1828.

" MY DEAR ARCHDEACON,—Our learned Caput, with Dr. Wordsworth as chief dissentient, have just thrown out the grace for admitting Pearson † to an *ad eundem* B.A. degree. This is hard and unjust, because no notice was given or grace passed previously subjecting Dublin to such contempt ; besides, I take the thing to be illegal, and have very little doubt but that Pearson might compel us by *mandamus* to confer the *ad eundem* degree. No objection under similar circumstances was ever taken before.

---

* *I.e.* St. Michael's.
† An old pupil in whom Dr. Butler took much interest.—ED.

" But it is no great matter, and Pearson, instead of being a B.A. of Peterhouse College, must be content to remain for the present a pensioner undergraduate. Dr. Hollingworth will allow him to attend his course of lectures, and you must do what you can with the Bishop of Hereford. I only returned to Peterhouse College on Friday last from Sussex, where I spent my time most agreeably. I went to Fulham to thank Bishop Blomfield for making me a Whitehall preacher. He was most kind, hospitable, and personally attentive to me. I staid three days, and was much pleased with the palace and grounds, which are contiguous to the river. We will go together some day and look at his larder and cellar, etc.

    *   *   *   *   *

" 'Tom has just popped in, and looks very well. He did not, however, report so favourably of your health as I could have wished. Let me hear better tidings soon.

    *   *   *   *   *

" Very glad the grayling proved good.

" Ever yours, etc.,
" S. TILLBROOK.

" P.S.—It would be an act of kindness in Mrs. Butler if she would consider me one of her boys, and buy for me six pair of Welsh fleecy hosiery lambs' wool stockings for the winter and forward them by coach.

" N.B.—Small foot, large calf ! "

Almost on the same day Pearson wrote a very sensible letter to Dr. Butler, telling him what had passed between himself and Dr. Wordsworth. This immediately drew from Dr. Butler the following proposed circular, addressed to Mr. Tillbrook :—

"*October 25th,* 1828.

" In consequence of the extraordinary refusal of the Master of Trinity College to grant an *ad eundem* A.B. degree to a member of the University of Dublin, whose character is unimpeached, and who produced a regular certificate from that University, some members of the Senate, who consider such proceedings to be arbitrary and illegal, and who are of opinion that it would be extremely hard to tax an individual with the expense of obtaining redress for an act of oppression and indignity hitherto unknown in the University, have agreed to subscribe the under-mentioned sums towards applying to the Court of King's Bench for a mandamus upon this occasion.

"S. BUTLER, D.D., ST. JOHN'S (£100)."

FROM THE REV. S. TILLBROOK.

"PETERHOUSE COLLEGE, *October 27th*, 1828.

" MY DEAR ARCHDEACON,—I never wish to fight under a better captain than you. I really believe that we could muster a good stout body of forces between us, for old Barnes always says that I am the best fellow that ever beat up for recruits under the keys of St. Peter. I must also do justice to this said veteran, who has been laying about the Caput most stoutly, and banging them into a sense of decency and justice. At the next congregation Dr. Davy, of Caius, Vice-Chancellor, will preside, and our Master has, I believe, overcome the scruples of Wordsworth. If at the next presentation of Pearson's grace his admission *ad eundem* be refused, it will then be time enough to take other steps ; and if it be not refused, the sense of the Senate will be shown when Wordsworth's threatened grace is offered.

" Besides, when Ds. Pearson is incorporated, we can *cudgel Wordsworth* without fearing his spite and malice. I would advise you therefore to wait patiently. If Pearson succeeds, you can write, if you like, a civil note to Dr. Davy, the ex-Vice-Chancellor, and you can, *si placeat tibi*, give Wordsworth a touch over the raw place with a little Salopian caustic. Pearson himself sent a very respectful and well-written statement of his case to Dr. Davy. Indeed, I have been much pleased with your old pupil's conduct generally, though in this particular instance his appeal to the Vice-Chancellor should have been through the father of the College, whose peculiar office it is to attend to matters of degrees, etc., etc.

" Do not let this matter annoy you. Believe me, the liberal feeling is all on our side. But as we can only ask, and not demand legally, we must not be too hasty. It is always at the option of the Caput to allow this privilege, though courtesy and custom have led some to conclude that it is a positive and legal right on the part of the Dublin B.A. The old tactic ' Cunctandi ' will suit our purpose.

*   *   *   *   *

" Thank Mrs. B. for taking care of my legs.

*   *   *   *

" P.S.—I have kept quiet because I saw that I could strike hard by waiting a little in ambuscade. I never yet in my life had to fight Vice-Chancellors and Proctors that I did not ultimately utterly rout them and put them to shame. Ask Le Blanc ; ask Dr. Proctor ; ask half the boys who have been Proctors. Our old house flourishes ; we have nearly thirty freshmen come up this term."

From a letter from Pearson to Dr. Butler dated

November 28th, 1828, it appears that on that day the Caput withdrew their opposition and admitted him to an *ad eundem* degree.

FROM THE REV. AUTHORITY NORMAN.

"BRAILSFORD, *October 22nd,* 1828.

"DEAR SIR,—I think it is due to you to state the alteration which has taken place in our Clerical Society, and led to the secession of the Revs. Hope, Gell, Wood, Swain, and a few others. Perhaps I had better speak plainly, and call them in modern language the Ultras of the High Church party. I hope I do this without any offensive meaning, as describing a party who would not give up something of their opinions for the purpose of uniting with their opposed brethren. The consequence has been that the middle party, to which I belong, has become more united with the party generally termed the Evangelical party in the purposes of the society.

"Discussions on doctrinal subjects were forbidden, and this restriction seemed to give a character of dryness to our meetings, so much so that the younger members broke through the order, and introduced questions on forbidden subjects ; and now there is no restraint except their own good sense over the discussion of the meeting.

"But I must say that great care has hitherto been taken to keep within the bounds of propriety. The last question was, The best means of establishing and maintaining the pastoral connection between the minister and his parishioners?—which led to many observations that must be useful to our body. But who can say that such discussions will be always conducted with prudence and decorum ? I thought it right to inform you of this step, to afford you the means of judging of the future. For my part, I scarcely know how to proceed. So long as I can carry moderation with me I may do more good than evil in attending the meetings. But assuredly I will not lend myself to any extravagance. At the same time I fear I am too fond of seeing the picture of human nature which such a meeting exhibits ; and this is something of an excuse for not having withdrawn myself, if I had not a better. But I do think that the two former of the gentlemen whom I have named should have consulted you before they retired, as by their secession they have assisted to change the character of the society, and leave you, the President of it, unconscious of that change."

*   *   *   *   *

To the Rev. A. Norman.

"Shrewsbury, *October 27th*, 1828.

"Dear Sir,—I thank you for your communication respecting the Clerical Society at Derby, from which you state several of our brethren to have withdrawn, in consequence of the admission of discussions on doctrinal points.

"I suppose they consider, as I do, that the society is dissolved by the alteration of its constitution in a most important and fundamental article, but at present I have not received any communication whatever on the subject except your letter.

"Be that as it may, I beg you to make known to the members of the present society, when you next meet, that, having originally disapproved and protested against the measure you state to be now introduced, I cannot consistently continue to have the honour of belonging to it.

*   *   *   *   *

"I am sorry to hear that you have been unwell. I have been a fellow-sufferer, and am still not in good health. . . .

"Believe me to be with much regard, dear Sir,

"Yours very faithfully,

"S. Butler."

From the Rev. J. Wood

"Swanwick, *November 1st*, 1828.

"My dear Sir,—Your letter found me at Swanwick after my return out of Wales, where I have been passing my three months, and one of my first inquiries when I came back was, 'How are you going on with the Clerical Society?' The answer, which did not surprise me, was, 'Your friends, So-and-so, have retired.' And as I was satisfied something or other must have happened to occasion this secession, without giving myself time to think much about it I wrote a note to Norman, assigning no cause whatever, but requesting him to withdraw my name; for as I expected to go back very soon to my family (with the Bishop's leave), I thought some queer new-fangled plans might be adopted, and I did not wish to have my name connected with a society of this sort, unless I knew precisely what their intentions and mode of proceedings were.

"I take shame to myself that I did not write to you before I withdrew my name—I certainly ought to have done so; but when we do things in the hurried manner in which I have been since my return, we sometimes forget things we ought not, and I trust you will forgive this unintentional omission of mine.

"With regard to the society being dissolved, I believe the matter stands as follows:—Mr. Hope fully intended to make a proposition of this sort, but he was overruled by Gell; for I understand there had been some hard raps on each side, and in some cases almost getting to personalities, and Gell said he was confident, if Hope had proposed the dissolution, it would have occasioned violent personal quarrels, and have exposed the nakedness of the land in such a public way that, for the sake of peace and quietness, and to avoid being made the laughing-stock of the dissenters, he persuaded Hope to withdraw quietly with the others. This is, I believe, the state of the case; but I speak only from what I hear. Your letter to Mr. Norman was put into the Derby office on Thursday. I saw Hope and Gell, and they both concurred in opinion about it.

"These very good folks certainly go great lengths, and many of them, begging their pardons, are very, very ignorant. What think you of W—— of Pinxton refusing (a coroner's warrant directing him) to bury a parishioner who hanged himself in a fit of insanity? The man's friends got Pepper to go over and talk to him; but he had seen the man sane the day before, and he must have better authority before he would either read the service or suffer it to be read in his churchyard. Luckily Pepper, in again looking over the warrant, saw that the man had hanged himself in a field adjoining Pinxton, but in Normanton parish; so he sent immediately the warrant to Doveton, and got the poor fellow put under the sod about nine o'clock. This is *sub rosâ.*

"I think I have not written to you since my son was at the ordination at Lichfield. I think six or seven were sent to the right-about. I was a little afraid, expecting some questions might be asked which might not be answered satisfactorily; but he found Hodson very gentlemanly, and the Bishop kind, though I believe they did not perfectly agree in opinion on some points."

To a Parent.

[*About November 5th,* 1828.]

*   *   *   *   *

"The ordinary expenses of a young man who is prudent, and yet lives respectably as a pensioner, are about £300 per annum. This includes his private tutor, journeys, and all expenses. I do not think it can be done for less. It is the allowance I make my son, who I am sure is prudent and steady; he finds it sufficient, but not superfluous. Now if —— were elected to one of our exhibitions at Magdalene College, he would still have £240 to provide. Under these circumstances I rather incline to recommend his being placed at Trinity College, Dublin, as a much less expensive mode of education. This, however, should depend upon his future destination."

*   *   *   *   *

From H.R.H. the Duke of Sussex.

(Published by permission of Her Majesty.)

[*Between February 25th and 28th*, 1829.]

" Dear Sir,—Many thanks for your kind letter of the 23rd of this month, with its valuable information, to which I will attend. What is to be the result of the Duke of Wellington's plans, with which I am acquainted, a few days will show. A more real and lasting service he cannot render his country, and I hope the grace will be conferred as generously as the conception is grand. The consolidation of the interests and the peace of a great empire is a greater service to a country than that of thousands of conquests by war. It is the triumph of justice and reason over bigotry and persecution. I look forward with pleasure to making you a longer visit on another occasion, when I trust we may congratulate each other on the success of events which must rejoice the heart of every honest man, of every sincere Christian, and of every true Briton. The game is not easy to play; for we must oppose calmness and reason to violence and misrepresentation; but as the former economises strength, and the latter wastes it, so we must tire out our antagonists. Poor, dear Drury! I wish he may succeed; * it would be a shame and injustice if he does not. He is a deserving, excellent man.

* * * * *

" I was very sorry not to see you when in town. Pray believe me, with great sincerity,

" Yours, etc.,
" Augustus Frederick."

* * * * *

To H.R.H. the Duke of Sussex.

[*About March 1st*, 1829.]

" May I be allowed to address a few more lines to your Royal Highness, both to express my gratitude for your condescension in so kindly replying to my last, and to make an observation on the point which I now find to be the clamour of the anti-Catholics in this neighbourhood?

" They say Mr. Peel has offered no security; and if I were speaking to them as between friends, I should be inclined to

---

* Mr. Drury was then a candidate for the head-mastership of Harrow, vacant by the resignation of Dr. George Butler. The electors passed over all the candidates who had offered themselves, and invited Mr. Longley, then a master at Westminster, to the head-mastership—he not having been a candidate.—Ed.

concede this in a considerable degree, though not perhaps entirely. But were I to declare my opinion in an assembly of statesmen, I would say that neither Mr. Peel's securities nor all the securities that any parliament can give will equal those that are to be found out of parliament. Parliamentary securities are but the securities of certain enactments which the next parliament may change ; but the real security is to be found in the Protestant feelings of the people, and if this security did not exist all others would be perfectly worthless, while if it does exist all others are unnecessary. Now the sense of the people of England as regards the Catholic religion is decided; their petitions against the admission of Catholics to political power speak to their faith, and every man who puts his name to one of those petitions does so far offer guarantees against the introduction of the Catholic religion ; from that point of view his petition against their being granted political power is not without its use, even though it tends to defeat one of his own arguments. I cannot find many here who understand this sort of reasoning, but I conceive it is intelligible to thinking men. I have not broached them here, nor shall I, for I hate to waste words to no effect."

From Dr. Burton, Regius Professor of Divinity at Oxford.

" March 21st, 1829.

"My dear Sir,—Having been employed in examining the candidates for Dean Ireland's Scholarship, I have great pleasure in sending you word that we have elected another of your pupils, C. W. Borrett, of Magdalen College. We were quite unanimous in giving him the preference, though the respective excellence of different candidates in different exercises made it more than usually difficult to decide. Johnson of Wadham has not, I should think, made so much advance since last year as might have been expected. Payne of Balliol has showed himself a very good Greek scholar ; and if he will work as hard in his Latin, he will have a good chance next year. You need not take the trouble to acknowledge this letter, unless you should wish for more particulars, which I shall be happy to send you.

    *   *   *   *   *

"Since I wrote the above I have learnt the name of another candidate who was considered by us to be second, and he is also a pupil of yours—Thomas of Wadham."

From the Same.

" March 30th, 1829.

    *   *   *   *   *

"The candidates generally were better acquainted with Greek than with Latin, and this tendency has been observed for some

years at Oxford.   I met with two fellows of Trinity in London
last week who told me that they had observed the same at
Cambridge. To what cause is this to be attributed, if there is
(as I believe) a free trade for both these languages in the two
Universities?   I am delighted to hear you are going to send us
so good a scholar to Christ Church."

The " beef row," as it is commonly called, was the second
and last case of insubordination which Dr. Butler had to
deal with in the course of his long head-mastership.   I
have found less about it than I expected, and am only
able to date it inferentially as having taken place on the
6th of April, 1829.   The outbreak occurred on the appearance of a round of beef on the dinner-table of the Doctor's
hall, whereon the boys one and all—by arrangement preconcerted among themselves before they had seen the beef
—left the hall, declaring that the meat was not fit to eat.
Dr. Butler required an apology from the prepostors, among
whom were several of his most brilliant pupils—Robert
Scott, James Hildyard, Brancker, J. W. Warter, and
Bateson, to mention no others.   As they all refused to
apologise he dismissed them, with the saving clause that
on apology being made he would receive them back.   Of
course the parents of the boys made them apologise, and
they all came back.   For further particulars I must refer
the curious to the MS. letters in the British Museum.

CORRESPONDENCE, APRIL 13TH, 1829—MAY 25TH, 1829.

FROM H.R.H. THE DUKE OF SUSSEX.

(Original in possession of Mrs. G. L. Bridges and Miss Butler.
Published by permission of Her Majesty.)

"KENSINGTON PALACE, *April* 13*th* 1829.

" DEAR SIR,—Many thanks for your obliging letter, and
hearty congratulations upon the great event which has recently
taken place [Catholic emancipation].   Were I never to receive

any other recompense but to have been permitted to see the success of a measure for which I have so long and earnestly laboured, I am satisfied and most grateful. I have undergone much fatigue of body and mind, as well as considerable anxiety ; but all is over now, and I trust in God that we shall before long witness the most happy results from this great act of justice. I hope I put the historical as well as ecclesiastical part in the proper way in which they ought to be viewed, and I think my principle is a right one, that our constitution is not founded on exclusion, nor our Church on persecution. . . .

" Believe me, with great sincerity, dear Sir,

" Most truly yours, etc.,

" Augustus Frederick."

From H.R.H. the Duke of Sussex.

(Published by permission of Her Majesty.)

" *May 22nd*, 1829.

" Dear Sir,—I have sent to Mr. Freeling of the Post Office a copy of my speech, in order that it may be forwarded to you post free, as it is above weight. I hope you will peruse it, and give me your unbiassed opinion on the subject. I wanted first to prove that I understood the subject ; secondly, I have endeavoured to explain my opinion to others, and to show that it was the result of study and reflection ; and thirdly, to impress upon the reflecting part of society the necessity of guarding against the mischief which might be produced by placing men of violent temper at the head of our ecclesiastical affairs. I have not stated where the spirituality of our Church resides, but I would venture to hint that it is nowhere to be found at present, since Government does not allow the Convocation to meet but *pro formâ*, and which, in my opinion, is very judicious. Thank God the question is now carried ; and if we can keep quiet some mischief-makers, which I think might and ought to be done, all must and will go on well. In this country it will not do to attempt arbitrary measures ; our lower orders are much too well informed, and can reason with sufficient acuteness to render such an attempt both useless and dangerous for the experimentalist.

" Believe me, dear Sir, with great sincerity and good-will,

" Yours, etc.,

" Kensington Palace."   " Augustus Frederick.

From the Rev. H. Drury.

" Harrow, *May 25th*, 1829.

" My dear Butler,—If there be a royal road to learning you have certainly found it, and your long, merited, and universal success makes us very anxious to follow you there.   There are, to drop a foolish metaphor, two or three questions which Longley and I wish to put to you, and which I will thank you to answer quite at your leisure in a letter which I may show him.

"It is our intention to give up the Eton *Scriptores Græci* and *Romani*, as they contain a great deal of useless and irrelevant stuff—*e.g.* the Lucian of the former, and the greater part of the Cicero of the latter—so useless for purposes of history, geography, etc.   I suggested that, in case of my having attained the mastership, I should have substituted a straightforward book at once—Thucydides, etc.   Now what do you do in this case?—for I have no doubt you have supplanted the old desultory method of school-reading for something solid and continuous.   Will you let me know your secret without buying it?   The question merely is, What Latin and Greek do you read with your sixth form (let alone Greek play and New Testament)? and how often and for what length of time in the week?

"Have you any composition in prose Greek?   Such is just introduced at Eton through the whole school.   And are any *tempora subseciva* employed in the cultivation of modern history, literature, etc.?   Have you declamations? and if so, do you find them succeed, or that the boys take an interest in them?

"Finally, I hear you have an excellent custom of frequent examinations of your upper boys in what they have read.   This we wish to adopt in some measure, and are anxious to hear the mode in which you proceed, and at what intervals.

"Excuse all this trouble.   I find Longley a very gentleman-like scholar, ready to listen to any proper suggestion, and as zealous as I could wish him.   We live very much together; and were the insult and affront of four of the governors a venial offence to me, I have no hesitation in saying that in other points I am fully satisfied with the decision.

"I beg my best regards to Mrs. Butler, and am
                    "Very faithfully yours,
                              "HENRY DRURY."

The answer to this letter was an immediate invitation to Shrewsbury, given to both Dr. Longley and Mr. Drury, which both accepted—both coming into school, and we may be sure being told all that Dr. Butler could tell them.

I mention the itinerary of a foreign trip taken in the summer of 1829 by Dr. Butler and my father, as showing that, though people had no doubt to travel with more fatigue, they managed to cover much the same ground before the days of railways as at present. Dr. Butler and my father left London on June 23rd. The route taken was Calais, Lille, Aix-la-Chapelle, Cologne, the Rhine, on which steamers were not yet running, to Frankfort, where a halt was made, and Dr. Butler was paid a dozen of 1611 hock won from his friend Koch, the famous wine merchant, in a bet as to whether or no Mr. Tillbrook would get married. This was the oldest wine the Kochs had in their cellars. I was given a taste of it in 1859; it was not drinkable, except as a curiosity, and for the remembrance that a bottle of the same vintage might have been drunk by Shakespeare and Cervantes. The travellers proceeded to Basle, Zürich, Coire, and over the Splugen to Chiavenna.

" At Chiavenna we were surprised to find ourselves in the best hotel I ever was in either in or out of England. This morning at six we started for the Lake of Como. . . . We had to row about twelve miles from the extreme upper end of the lake to reach the steamboat, which cannot come higher for some shallows. We then embarked on an excellent steamboat, and had a most delightful passage of four hours to this place (Como, July 12th). Among other places we passed the celebrated Villa d'Este, the residence of Queen Caroline when she was in Italy."

The two then went to Milan, where they stayed three days, and thence by the Simplon to Lausanne and Geneva. A trip was made to Chamounix and back to Geneva, from which place Paris was reached, *viâ* the Jura, Dole, Dijon, Sens, and Fontainebleau, on July 26th.

Much about this same time Dr. Arnold was also on the Lake of Como, and wrote the following passage, which I cannot resist the temptation to quote in full :—

                                        " *August 3rd*, 1829.
" I fancy how delightful it would be to bring one's family and live here ; but then happily I feel how little such voluptuous enjoyment would repay for abandoning the line of usefulness and activity which I have in England, and how the feeling myself

helpless and useless, living merely to look about me and training up my children in the same way, would soon make all this beauty pall and even appear wearisome.   But to see it, as we are now doing in our moments of recreation, to strengthen us for work to come, and to gild with beautiful recollections our daily life of home duties—this, indeed, is delightful and is a pleasure which I think we may enjoy without restraint.   England has other destinies than these countries—I use the word in no foolish or unchristian sense,—but she has other destinies ; her people have more required of them ; with her full intelligence, her restless activity, her enormous means, and enormous difficulties ; her pure religion and unchecked freedom ; her form of society, with so much of evil, yet so much of good in it, and such immense power conferred by it ;—her citizens, least of all men, should think of their own rest or enjoyment, but should cherish every faculty, and improve every opportunity to the uttermost, to do good to themselves and to the world.   Therefore these lovely valleys and this surpassing beauty of lake, and mountain, and garden, and wood, are least, of all men, for us to covet ; and our country, so entirely subdued as it is to man's uses, its gentle hills and valleys, its innumerable canals and coaches, is best suited as an instrument of usefulness." *

I cannot find that Dr. Butler and Dr. Arnold ever met, though they wrote to one another more than once. My father told me that Dr. Butler brought back with him four half-gallon bottles of water from the Rhine, Rhone, Danube, and Po, to make punch *aux quatre fleuves* on his return.   This gave a good deal of trouble at the custom-houses, the officials declining to accept the alleged reason for carrying four such mysterious bottles so great a distance.

EXTRACT FROM A CHARGE DELIVERED AT DERBY AND AT CHESTERFIELD, JUNE 18TH AND 19TH, 1829.

"REVEREND BRETHREN,—Whoever looks with any degree of reflection into the page of history will see that its various epochs are not more clearly marked by the reigns of princes and the lapse of centuries, than by certain modes of thinking and acting, produced by the influence of circumstance, habit, design, caprice, and, above all, example, upon mankind.   Thus one age shall be

---

* Dean Stanley's *Life and Correspondence of Dr. Arnold*, Vol. II., p. 366, ed. 1844.

characterised by its barbarism, another by its chivalric spirit, another by its superstition, another by its piety, another by its irreligion, another by its literature, another by its zeal for innovation. If I were asked what is the characteristic of the present age, I should say a morbid sentimentality, not to give it any coarser name, than which, I fear, there cannot be a stronger mark of a declining moral tact."

The rest of the charge, while betraying no sympathy with indifferentism, is marked by a not less evident dislike of the aggressive self-consciousness, and I may add bigotry, of the still dominant Evangelical party.

FROM THE REV. W. A. SHIRLEY.

"SHIRLEY VICARAGE, *July 1st*, 1829.

"MR. ARCHDEACON,—I gladly avail myself of the permission with which you favoured me to communicate my feelings to you by letter, as it gives me an opportunity of assuring you how sensible I am of the indulgence and kindness I experienced from you, and of apologising for whatever may have appeared irregular or unbecoming in the observations I ventured to make at Derby. I trust that I did not for one moment lose sight of the subordinate relation in which I stand towards you, and I believe that you will give me credit for having been influenced by a simple desire to state in candour the impression conveyed to my mind by your charge, and which prevented me from receiving it with that unqualified acquiescence which the request that it should be printed seemed to imply. I was aware how liable one is to misunderstand what is delivered only by word of mouth, and I was anxious, both for my own sake and that of others, that you should favour the clergy with some explanation of remarks which appeared, in the course of their delivery, to be of doubtful application I will candidly say that my fear was lest some expressions might be so taken as to leave men satisfied with something short of that earnestness and spirituality of mind without which there can be no sustained energy in the service of God, and lest by a similar misconception the indolent might be composed and the zealous discouraged—a deduction which I am sure you would be most desirous to prevent at a moment when the existence of the Church of England depends from hour to hour on the exalted piety and unwearied diligence of her friends and ministers.

"With regard to foreign exertions I could not help feeling that what you said implied something like disapprobation of a society which is supported exclusively by members of the Church of England, and has the sanction of many bishops. But I am unwilling to dwell on this point, or indeed on any other, because I have only my recollection of what you said to go upon, and also because the statement you were so good as to make after dinner, that German sentimentalism was the object of your animadversion, enables us to fix a precise meaning to the advice and caution which the charge contained. My only remaining hope is that you may deem it expedient to prevent others from falling into the error which misled me by appending to the charge some notice explanatory of your design, and thus the edifying confession of faith which it contained might produce the full benefit it was calculated to convey without the risk of any deduction."

To the Rev. W. A. Shirley.

"Shrewsbury, *September* 15*th*, 1829.

"Dear Sir,—I had the honour to receive your letter about five weeks ago on my return from the Continent, and only left it unanswered that my reply might be accompanied by the charge, which will best speak for itself. It is printed with scrupulous fidelity, and I have ordered my publisher to send you a copy immediately through the bookseller at Derby.

" I am aware that expressions, however clear, are liable to be misunderstood, and that intentions, however well meant, are not always equally well received. It is the common lot of all men, and I can claim no exemption.

" If this has been the case with my charge, I must still leave it to its fate without adopting the remedy you are kind enough to suggest. I conceive it difficult to make it plainer by any explanations; and as I am unconscious of having made any attack, and certainly am conscious of not having intended to make any, on the society to which you allude, I see no need of defending myself from an imputation which I feel I do not justly incur.

" In one part of your letter you say that 'your fear was lest some expressions might be so taken as to leave men satisfied with something short of that earnestness and spirituality of mind without which there can be no sustained energy in the service of God, and lest by a similar misconception the indolent might be composed and the zealous discouraged.'

" If I have used such expressions as justify lukewarmness or indifference in the cause of religion, I have greatly misrepresented my own feelings and conviction. But I am not aware that warmth of colouring is necessary to the language or cause of truth. I believe that many sincere and pious Christians suffer themselves to be led too strongly by their feelings—I mean so as to think that all those are lukewarm in the cause of Christianity or wavering in their faith, and deficient in 'earnestness and spirituality of mind' (if I may borrow your own expressions), who cannot believe that the essence of piety or the proof of inspiration consists in giving way to their emotions. Now when they think this, they are unjust to many truly pious and good men and sincere Christians, whose feelings are yet sobered down by their judgement, who believe that zeal should ever be tempered by discretion, and that the passions are bad and even dangerous guides in spiritual as well as temporal concerns.

"This is my belief. In this I was brought up ; it is confirmed to me by reading, observation, and reflection, and every day's observation of passing events strengthens me in it. In this, therefore, I hope to live and die ; and without impugning the opinions of other men, I trust I shall never change my own.

"I remain with much regard, dear Sir,
"Yours faithfully,
"S. BUTLER."

From the Archbishop of Canterbury (Dr. Howley).

"*September* 15*th*, 1829.

*   *   *   *   *

" I think your choice of a subject and manner of treating it equally seasonable and judicious. The publication will, I trust, do good in several ways, and particularly in contributing to discountenance the indulgence of that morbid sentimentality which is a dangerous as well as an inadequate substitute for the principles and feelings of genuine piety, Christian virtue, and benevolence."

From the Bishop of Hereford (Dr. Huntingford).

"*September* 26*th*, 1829.

" It is one of the most energetic and right-minded compositions which I have seen for years. In all you have written on that injudicious zeal for excessive and unsuitable instruction to the order of operatives I entirely agree with you. In private conversation I have again and again expressed my opinion on that subject, and on the effects of morbid and mawkish sentimentality. You have spoken out fearlessly, manfully, sensibly, justly ; and all who are anxious for the dignity of British character and genuine welfare of the community will be obliged to you for stemming a morally pestiferous torrent."

From the Rev. H. Drury.

"HARROW, *September* 14*th*, 1829.

*   *   *   *   *

" For any hints now and at any time I shall be much obliged ;

for one is never too old to learn, and many, and those the most important, of your excellent institutions have already been adopted by us.

*   *   *   *   *

" We are filling rapidly.

"Ever yours,
"H. DRURY."

FROM THE SAME.

"HARROW, *October 24th*, 1829.

" MY DEAR BUTLER,—If I have seemed to you very remiss in not answering your letters, it has not been from want of considering their contents and administering to them. Longley begged to write about French and dancing terms himself, as he said he had other things to write about. There was some delicacy in getting the latter, as the dancing-master has not had a pupil here these twelve years. I think the French terms are too high; but from the facilities of the Continent few boys learn now at school—at least here—as the *trajet* is so frequently made in the summer vacation.

" I read your charge with great delight; 'twas exactly what I should have liked to have heard, and to have seen in its effects on the sour visages of the 'serious.' I do not wonder they endeavoured to resent such home truths. The same spirit rages sadly among us. I had introduced Milman's *History of the Jews* to read with Paley's *Evidences* every Sunday morning. I found it gave sacred history and geography in such an entertaining manner that it riveted the attention of my boys surprisingly. This is daily denounced to Longley by Mr. Batten, as Cunningham's mouthpiece, as ' an impious book,' ' a gross misrepresentation of the Word of God,' ' an attempt to introduce German scepticism,' and what not—of all which Milman is as innocent as I am, and he has had the highest testimonials of praise and thanks from the first members of the High Church.

" I am happy that we shall have Hughes as our poser again, and in future. Our system works very well, and I thank you for the valuable hints we got from you during our delightful residence at Shrewsbury.

" Your quibbling verses are admirable; and Longley, though not given to the laughing mood, has laughed heartily over them with me. The last line delicious—*linendum cedro.*

*   *   *   *   *

" Malkin, who was with me yesterday, seems pretty certain of his election to the Historical chair at the London University. He tells me that the numbers in all the classes, save Lardner's, are likely to double, and that, with the exception of the medical squad, by far the greater proportion of the students are the sons of Regent's Park and Westminster gentry—which I am sorry to hear.

"I fully agree with you in the addition of the 4 [word torn off by seal] and one Philippic in our next edition. The *Britannica* of Cæsar those need not read who do not like it ; but it is part of our plan as text-book, and reference to our lectures. 'Twill take up but a small portion of space, and we have still room for another oration of Cicero, or other book of history—do you decide what it shall be.

"With most sincere and most complimentary regards to Mrs. Butler, believe me, my dear Butler,

"Ever most sincerely yours,
"H. Drury.

"I think I see you opening this at your sulky table. Best regards to the Dugards. The new Master of Westminster is not likely to live."

The "quibbling verses" referred to in the foregoing letter are as follows, and are of course inspired by Dr. Burney's *Tentamen*. The following prose passage is to be tortured into verse : "We must aver that Dr. Burney was a scholar of superior skill in scanning verses, and in all respects a clever man." The scansion is effected thus :—

> "We must aver
>   that Doctor Bur-
> -ney was a scholar of super-
>   -rĭŏr skill in scan-
>   -ning verses, an-
> -d in all respects a clever man."

I sent these lines to the *Athenæum* in 1891, but said there was nothing to show whether or not they were Dr. Butler's own. I had not then come upon Mr. Drury's letter, nor upon one from Dr. Hawtrey, August 6th, 1833, both of which prove the lines to have been by Dr. Butler—who nevertheless had a very profound respect for Dr. Burney's scholarship, and a great personal liking for him.

FROM DR. LONGLEY, AFTERWARDS BISHOP OF RIPON AND
ARCHBISHOP OF CANTERBURY.

" HARROW, *December 2nd,* 1829.

" MY DEAR SIR,—I send you the enclosed papers, to show
you how much I profited by my visit to Shrewsbury—not to
provoke your criticism, for I am well aware how deficient I am
in some branches of critical knowledge.

" I have been much gratified by the result of my first essay,
and am convinced that it may be made an instrument of great
benefit to our school."

  *   *   .   *   *

The " papers " above referred to no doubt were examination papers, which appear to have been then introduced
at Harrow for the first time.

TO THE REV. JAMES TATE.

"SHREWSBURY, *December 8th,* 1829.

" MY DEAR FRIEND,—When I saw you at Cambridge, I was
not aware of the import of your question, whether I had got the
new edition of your Greek metres.   I thought you meant whether
I had got your Greek Theatre.   From Cambridge I went to Italy
before I returned home, and on my return home I found your
new edition on my table, which is *tota merum sal.*   It is so
clear, so intelligible, so complete, and yet so free from being
overburthened, that I cannot sufficiently commend it.

" In your next edition will you think it worth while to put the
whole doctrine of *ictus* into a very short compass in a note, by
way of elucidating your remarks upon it, not one of which I wish
to see omitted?   I have long since found it useful to observe to
my boys that the infallible rule about ictus is, that it cannot fall
on a *short* syllable, except when the short syllable is one of the
two into which a long syllable is resolved—and then it must
always fall on the first of the two.

" I have found this rule very useful to them in their Greek
composition.   It makes them understand why in an iambic verse,
though they may use those short words τὰ, τὶ, σὰ, they must not
bring a tribrach of this nature, πὄλὔ δὶ, having two short syllables
in the first word and one in the next.   Nor in a trochaic verse
can they bring δὶ πὄλὔ, because in the former case the ictus
falling on the υ of πολυ, and there being necessarily a slight
though almost imperceptible elevation of the voice to pronounce
the separate word δε, the ictus would be overcharged, so that
the thesis could not be made with sufficient delicacy on the δε.
In the latter case there would be an undercharge on the δε and

an overcharge on the πο. See how much light they will throw on the antispastic forms—*verbum sat* to a real *sapiens*.

"Let me hope you will be encouraged to attack the choral metres.

Stanley, Butler, Burney, Herman, Wellauer, Bothe, Scholefield, Blomfield *rarely* differing from Burney, and a hundred commentators,	all give different arrangements of the same chorus—of all these, *only one can* be right.

"My belief is that Herman has written on the subject till he has puzzled himself; that those double-distilled asses Langé and Pinzger, who are so very sapient over their *Persæ*, know about as much of the matter as a cow does of playing on the pianoforte.

"We want something clear, sensible, and simple on the subject, to supersede the gothicisms of Seale, and to drive the ponderous German tomes (look for Heaven's sake at Boeckh's enormous Pindar!) out of the country. Something like an abridged Gaisford in English, as a sequel to your present book. Do it, I pray.

"Kidd wrote me yesterday to announce his election to Norwich School.   "Believe me truly yours,

"S. Butler."

FROM THE REV. ALEXANDER SCOTT.

"Rectory, Eremont, *December 14th*, 1829.

"My dear Sir,—Robert arrived here on Saturday, seemingly quite well, although he said that he had felt a little indisposed after the exertion of the play. At any rate there is no appearance of anything but good health now.

"Mrs. Scott and I were both much gratified by the favourable account you were so good as to give us of our boy's proficiency; and as he has now taken his final leave of Shrewsbury School, it becomes me to offer my sincerest thanks to you for the unvaried kindness and attention which upon all occasions you have shown him. Should Robert fulfil any of those flattering prognostications which you have expressed concerning him, we shall all know to whom he is indebted for those acquirements which have helped him forward, and I hope none of us will ever forget our obligations to you."

*   *   *   *   *

It is hardly necessary to say that the boy above referred
to was Robert Scott, who must rank as the most illustrious
and most engaging figure among all Dr. Butler's pupils, and
there was none, unless perhaps R. W. Evans, whom Dr. Butler
himself regarded with greater pride or warmer affection.
The Rev. Walter F. Scott tells me his father used to say
that the relations between himself and Dr. Butler were
more like those between son and father than between
pupil and master, and the letters that I can give from him
to Dr. Butler will show how cordial was the good feeling
that existed between the two.   The Rev. W. F. Scott has
kindly allowed me to copy thirteen letters from Dr. Butler
to his pupil, which will be sufficiently sampled by the few
which I can alone print.   Copies of all the letters are in
the British Museum.   Dean Scott died so comparatively
recently that the merest outline of his career will be alone
necessary.

He was born January 26th, 1811, and educated first at
St. Bee's and then at Shrewsbury, whence he proceeded
to Christ Church, Oxford, where he gained the Ireland
Scholarship in 1833 and was placed in the first class *in
literis humanioribus* the same year.   Shortly afterwards
he was elected to a fellowship at Balliol.   The first
edition of Liddell and Scott's Lexicon appeared in 1843
—to be followed by six other editions, each more complete and valuable than the last.   What more need be
said about a work that is familiar to all who take the
smallest interest in Greek literature ?   He was elected to
the Mastership of Balliol in 1854, and in 1870 was further
rewarded by Mr. Gladstone, who appointed him to the
Deanery of Rochester as a place of honourable repose.
There he remained till his death, which occurred, after a
lingering illness, December 2nd, 1887.

From the Rev. W. Tournay.

"Wadham College, *December 16th,* 1829.

"My dear Sir,—I have very great pleasure in announcing Herbert Johnson's success in the examination school. He is placed *with the highest commendation* in the first class.

"Massie was not examined. Having been diligent and idle by fits and starts, he overworked himself at the last, and was physically disqualified from appearing. We have advised him to abstain from books and thought for a month, and then employ in moderate continuous exertion the remaining interval between that time and the Easter examination. This he promises to do; but a paternal hint from you may be useful, especially if it arrive about the 15th of January.

"Thomas manifests much talent, and a most ingenious character, but he cannot be either scolded or coaxed into a steady attention to anything. Among other topics which I have employed in talking with him is his large debt of justice and gratitude to you. He remains here during the vacation, vowing great vows of hard study. Can you help to make him keep them?

"From Longueville I expect a regular unbroken progress towards success, and I am glad to see that his health does not fail him."

     *   *   *   *   *

CHAPTER XXII.

Correspondence, January 25th, 1830—March 1st, 1831.

From Dr. Keate, Head-Master of Eton.

"Eton, *January 25th*, 1830.

"DEAR DR. BUTLER,—We were very much gratified by the receipt of your letter on Friday, for we were really uneasy about you when we heard the account of snowdrifts that were brought to us on Thursday. If your friends permitted you to leave Oxford Thursday evening, I trust that the remainder of your journey, though it must have been beset with difficulties, was equally successful. I certainly was not aware, when I saw you leave my door, of the dangers which you and many others would have to encounter on that and the following days. But in some parts of the kingdom the fall, or rather the drifting, of snow seems to have been tremendous, and I must allow that both your boys and mine may make out a good case if they are a little behind their time; not but what they could and would force a passage if the thing was reversed, and their course was directed home-wards—in that case there would be many Hannibals.

"You are very kind to speak with satisfaction of your very short visit to Eton, and under such circumstances with regard to weather. I sincerely hope that you will soon pay us a longer visit and in more genial weather, and you may be assured that Mrs. Keate and myself shall be most happy when we find it in our power to avail ourselves of your very kind invitation to Shrewsbury.

"I should have written to you, if I had not received your kind letter, to say that a cane was left at my house by one of your party, and we rather fancy it is yours. It may be an old friend and a companion of your travels, and you may have the kind of regard for it that I had for one that I used twenty years, and at last left in a hackney coach in London. If it has touched the foot of Mont Blanc while you were gazing at the summit, I am sure you will be glad to recover it, and I beg leave to assure you that I will either keep it till you come to claim it, or will send it to any place which you may wish it to be sent to. Mrs. Keate and all my family beg to join in best compliments to you and Mrs. Butler.

"I am, my dear Sir, yours most faithfully,

"J. KEATE."

TO MR. TOMPKINS, THE LION INN, SHREWSBURY.

"SHREWSBURY, *January 25th*, 1830.

"SIR,—I beg to inform you, and to request you to inform the other proprietors of the Wonder Coach, whose names are unknown to me, that I have made very careful inquiry into the cause of the overturn of the Wonder Coach in Coventry near seven weeks ago, from the effects of which accident I regret to say that two of my boys are still suffering. The result of that inquiry, confirmed by the unanimous opinion of every intelligent person I have seen or heard from who has any means of information on the subject, is, that the son of Mr. Peters is, from his unfortunate lameness, unfit to drive the coach, having no firm seat, and standing up to drive, or at least sitting so lightly as to have no command over his horses in case of a sudden jerk or strain. I feel it therefore a duty to my boys and their parents to represent this to the proprietors, and to say that I cannot think either of travelling myself by the Wonder or suffering my boys to do so, unless the coachman is removed from it. I am aware that Mr. Peters has already been spoken to on the subject without effect, and I hear that the coach has once since been in considerable danger from the same cause. I shall therefore expect an assurance from the proprietors that a more competent coachman is appointed before I again use the coach, as I always have done hitherto; and I think it right to add that I have correspondents in Coventry who will inform me from time to time as to his absolute or only temporary removal. It may also be proper for me to observe that I have no sort of dislike to the individual in question, of whom I know nothing, but that, believing him unfit to drive a fast coach like the Wonder, I feel it my duty in the public station I fill to require his removal."

IN REPLY TO A PARENT WHO HAD WRITTEN DISRESPECTFULLY OF LATIN AND GREEK COMPOSITION AND OF ACADEMIC DISTINCTIONS.

"SHREWSBURY, *January 30th*, 1830.

"SIR,—[I am somewhat at a loss to understand, from your letter with which I am just favoured, whether . . .]"

[This beginning was cancelled.]

"[I make it a constant rule in all my communications with

parents to hold out no expectations to them which are not likely to be fulfilled, and I am therefore induced to trouble you with this letter in consequence of that I lately had the honour to receive from you.] "

[This beginning was cancelled.]

" [The plain-dealing with which I am anxious to act towards all parents who confide their sons to my care induces me to trouble you with a few remarks on the letter I have just received from you.] "

[This beginning was cancelled.]

The following was allowed to stand :—

" You appear to entertain a degree of contempt for composition in Latin prose, and a much greater for Latin verse, together with a low opinion of academic honours. I am not about to enter into a discussion upon the subject further than to say that, if Latin composition either in prose or verse consisted merely in stringing a few words or phrases together, I should not be much disposed to differ from you on the subject. My view of it, however, is very different, and taken on very different grounds ; but it is useless to trespass on your time by discussing a point upon which your mind seems thoroughly made up, and indeed I have not the leisure to do so, had you the patience to hear me. But I conceive it my duty distinctly to tell you that composition both in prose and verse is an essential part of education here, and that University prizes are always considered with us as the most honourable proof of talent combined with industry which a young man can exhibit.

" [If therefore you wish your son not to attend to composition, I should recommend you to place him at some school where it is not taught, and most earnestly and especially do I request that, whatever opinion you may yourself entertain of academic honours, you will not induce him to undervalue them if you wish him to continue under the tuition of one who thinks it a great happiness to have obtained, both in his own person and through his pupils, a competent share of them.] "

[This paragraph was cancelled.]

" While your son therefore remains here he will always be exercised in composition both in prose and verse, and the higher he gets in the school the more he will have of it. Permit me also most earnestly to request that, whatever opinion you may yourself entertain of academic honours, you will not induce him to undervalue them so long as he continues under the tuition of one who thinks it a great happiness to have obtained, both in his own person and through his pupils, a competent share of them."

To the Rev. T. S. Hughes.

(Original in possession of Mr. Hughes's representatives.)

" St. Taffy's Day, 1830.

" Dear Hughes,—I firmly believe the original Greek genitive to have been in ΘΕΝ signifying the *locus a quo*, and the dative in ΘΙ signifying the *locus in quo*—all which I have before stated and given reasons for. I also believe the genitive plural not to have been distinguishable in its primary form from the genitive singular. Any man who is deeply read in the archaisms both of Greek and Latin will concede this—just as you cannot tell whether ΑΘΛΟΝ is ἆθλον or ἄθλων in the inscription before us.

" Furthermore, I believe Σ to have been the second universal antient form of the Greek genitive, being a fragment of the ΘΕΝ which was its primary, and I merely wrote the lunated Ϲ because I wanted to show it sprang from the Θ. I believe the angular form of the Σ to be the most antient, but this is ἐν παρέργῳ.

" I will not venture to say that E stood antiently for AI. I incline to the contrary opinion, because, as you properly observe, it very often stood for EI. I would, however, wish to give my former translation a somewhat more general sense, and translate it 'the prize of the Athenians,' still understanding 'Αθήνηθεν to signify 'those who came from Athens,' not ' from Minerva.' If you take it for Minerva, I think the expression τῶν 'Αθήνης ἄθλων,' from the games of Minerva,' would be the best translation.

" For your Latin question you must invoke higher names than Lempriere. If Smyth is the man whose epitaph in Sardinia I wrote a few years ago, I would not have said such handsome things as I did of him if I had thought he would have plagued me after his death with such an ill-conditioned place as Stampace. I know nothing of it. Stampa*le* is the modern name for the antient Astypalæa, which seems to be out of the question.

" As to the inscription itself, I can give you a glimmering of light. Iolaus, as everybody knows, was the friend and charioteer of Hercules, and, as Pindar tells us, received at Thebes nearly equal honours with Hercules himself. There is a great debate among the learned whether the Iolai, or Iolæenses, or Ilienses, were the most antient inhabitants of Sardinia. Now this seems settled by the inscription, which says civitas iolæ, if that inscription is found in Sardinia, as I suppose from your letter it is. This is all that I can tell you by way of lighting your candle. Look to Diod. Sic., iv. 29, 30, for Iolaus—to Drakenborch's Livy, xl. 19, for the Ilienses—and in the latter you will find further references. The only other place that I know in form approaching to Stampace is Stampæ, now Étampes, between Paris and Orleans ; but Stampace seems to me a modern G[reek ?] name. The inscription itself is not to be found in Gruter or Muratori.

"Tom will be at Cambridge to sit for a fellowship at St. John's in the middle of March, and can bring back anything you have.

"I had only two men to sit at the Classical Tripos—neither good ones—but both would have been high in the first class if they had sat when they first left school. Believe me truly yours,
"S. BUTLER.

"The inscription is a little suspicious to me. I should like to know more about it."

The earlier part of this letter refers to the inscription

TON AΘENEΘN AΘΛON EMI

on the celebrated Burgonian vase now in the British Museum (Second Vase Room, pedestal 4). This vase was brought to England by Mr. Hughes, and given by him to Professor E. D. Clarke, on whose death it passed into other hands and ultimately became the property of the nation.

I see the inscription is now rendered, " I am one of the prizes from Athens," which is right, for later Panathenaic vases have since been found on which the inscription is *TΩN AΘHNHΘEN AΘΛΩN*. For further correspondence on this subject see in the British Museum a letter from Mr. Hughes, dated February 21st, 1830, and Dr. Butler's answer, February 23rd, 1830.

FROM NATHANIEL VYSE, ESQ.

"ALBION COACH OFFICE, BIRMINGHAM, *March 5th,* 1830.

"VERY REVEREND SIR,—In reply to your favour received by guard of Wonder Coach yesterday, I beg to state that the proprietors, finding all remonstrance with Mr. Peters ineffectual as to removing his son from driving the Wonder, they immediately on receipt of your letter to Mr. Tompkins called a meeting at Coventry, and gave Mr. Peters notice to quit the working of the Wonder. This, according to custom or law, takes a month, which will expire this week, when, as soon after as the stock can be valued, such arrangements will be carried into effect, as to drivers and the regularity of the coach, as I trust will retain the liberal patronage and very kind intentions you have so obligingly expressed."

To the Rev. James Tate.

"Shrewsbury, *March 8th*, 1830.

" My dear Friend,—I *did* mean to have paid the postage of my letter, because I did not think it worth the price at which you have rated it. You have taught me better, and I shall profit thereby.

" I cannot conceive any man more unfit to advise you about a bargain with booksellers than myself, who never yet had impudence enough to make a bargain with anybody. My agreement with Longman about my Geography and Praxis is this—he prints, and we share profits : luckily we have no loss to share. This gives the bookseller an interest in selling the work, and I find it answer *extremely well.* Your London bookseller will do this, and must arrange with all other booksellers. You will have nothing to do with Deighton—it will be his concern.

" The book is so scholarlike, so clear, so accurate, and got up in such good style, that it is sure to sell well.

" I cannot remember my observations in the lost, perhaps mislaid, letter.* They were principally on the arsis in Homer, and on that and final cretic in the Tragedians. I had illustrated my positions with real cases. I have not been able to do this now correctly, but any imaginary ones will answer to a scholar like you just as well. The short vowel is lengthened, say some, not by any power on the vowel itself, but because the greater stress on the pronunciation enables you to pronounce the subsequent consonant as if it were long. Thus μᾰ | λᾱ μᾰγᾰ is sounded μαλαμμεγα [and this is indeed for the most part practicable, but not always : for instance, Διᾰ μὲν ἀσπίδος ἦλθε, etc. It may be done when a consonant follows the lengthened vowel, but when a vowel follows it is impracticable. But what are we to do with those terrible cases which are in Thesi ? Ἕως ō, for I cannot submit to εἶὸς ŏ. This is too generally put.] † Before a liquid it holds well :—

καὶ γάρ τε̆ λιται	pronounced	τελλ
μαλα μεγα	"	αμμ
κατᾱ νοον	"	ανν
χωλαι τε ρυσσαι τε	"	τερρ

" Before the smooth and middle mutes tolerably, but examples are not so frequent. π is common in a long compound word, ἀπονέεσθαι ; κ not so common, but I bring to mind ναυλοχον εις λιμενα και ; τ in the famous exhortation Χανθε τε και βαλιε τηλεκλυτα ;

---

* No draft of this letter was found by me. I print the accents and breathings as I find them in the draft.—Ed.

† The passage in brackets is cancelled in the original MS.—Ed.

β unusual—I cannot recollect an instance, unless you insist on writing ἔβαλε for the usually written ἔββαλε, and I think it hardly fair to adduce ωμοισι βαλε, where ν may be inserted; δ unusual, but not so much so, yet we write ἔδδεισεν, not ἔδεισεν. Now why do we do this, and not write ἀππονεεσθαι, διεμμοίρατο, unless that the two latter are so common as to make the representation to the eye unnecessary, while the former are so unusual as to make it requisite? γ you may perhaps find in γενέῃ or some such instances, but I think not very usual. [Of the aspirates some seem to have had much the same fate as their corresponding lenes, only that I must insist upon those who double the consonant not doubling the aspirate. I mean, if αἰολὸν ὄφιν had the consonant doubled at all, I suppose it must have been pronounced. Ἀθάνατος may have been pronounced ἀθθάνατος, but I do not believe it. I would rather imagine it to have been ἀτθανατος, or, still better, ἀθανατος; ὅπφιν or ʽὄφιν, not ὄφφιν—at least the second aspirate must have been, if I may coin a word, sdrucciolated, or slurred exceedingly.] *

"But I conceive that if the second aspirate was pronounced at all, it must have been slurred exceedingly, so as hardly to have been heard, no more so than to give a hardness to the vowel preceding—ἀθάνατος, ὄφιν—where I may call the second aspirate sdrucciolated."

FROM RICHARD SHILLETO, ESQ. (AFTERWARDS REV.)

"TRINITY COLLEGE, *March* 11*th*, 1830.

"MY DEAR SIR,—I am ashamed that your very kind letter should have remained so long without acknowledgement. Not being conscious that I deserved the congratulations you bestowed upon me, I was agreeably surprised to find that I had acquitted myself so much better than my highest expectations. My well-wishing friends have already set me down for the University Scholarship next year—that is in case the Batty, for which Lushington cannot sit, is declared vacant; but I suppose I shall disappoint them all. However, if I am to have one good chance, I am determined to set my shoulder to the wheel, and I may possibly be as lucky in my examination papers as I was the last time. I was very glad to find that Hildyard is at all events determined to keep up the credit of Shrewsbury at Cambridge. Oxford has long ago ensured Payne's success in the next Ireland; Scott, I should imagine, will not come very far behind, and there are hosts of others who will not let our fame die there. I only wish you would send some more deserving men here, as there is but a scant supply."

---

* The passage in brackets was cancelled in the original draft.—ED.

From the Rev. H. Drury.

"Harrow, *March* 15*th*, 1830.

"My dear Butler,—I had told Longley that I should write to you this morning, but have since been so annoyed that, had not yours come, I should have delayed answering your first for a day or two. The real and simple reason I did not do so before was because I expected daily your ' Papers,' * which have not yet come to hand. Many thanks for the invite to Shrewton, and the inquiries about the snowstorm, which was indeed most formidable.

"The annoyance I am under, and which I beg you to communicate to Charles if you have any common opportunity (not otherwise), is that I received an express at eleven this morning, and a letter at one, to say that my son Byron was dangerously ill of a scarlet fever at Portsmouth. I must therefore dispense with aught else than a direct answer to yours. Kennedy comes here to-morrow as examiner. Do send me your Papers."

*　　　*　　　*　　　*　　　*

From Dr. Jenkyns, Master of Balliol.

"Balliol College, *March* 18*th*, 1830.

"My dear Sir,—I am perhaps taking a liberty, but I feel so much pleasure at the event that I cannot refrain from offering you my congratulations on the fresh honours to your school by the election of another of your pupils (Payne) to one of Dean Ireland's Scholarships.

"You may remember that when I had the pleasure of seeing you here, I spoke most highly of the young man's diligence and exemplary conduct. He in every respect richly deserves the very eminent distinction he has obtained, and his success will, I trust, act as an incentive to continued exertion and preparation for other opportunities of honourable emulation and more solid advantage.

"He had on this occasion twenty competitors, and many among them of considerable character and pretension."

From Peter S. Payne, Esq.

"*Friday, March* 19*th*, 1830.

"My dear Sir,—I am sorry that I have suffered one post to pass without writing to inform you of the unlooked-for success which I have obtained in being elected Ireland Scholar. I have not merely to express my gratitude for the kindness and forbearance shown towards me throughout the whole of my career as your pupil, but more immediately for the advice with regard

---

* Examination papers.—Ed.

to Latin which you gave me subsequently to my failure of last year. I read, according to your desire, with attention Cicero *de Oratore*, Terence, and eight books of the *Epistolæ ad Familiares*. You will be delighted to hear that Scott is confidently said to have been second. Everybody exclaims against your monopoly of University scholarships.

" I hope you will not have fears as to the probability of my being intoxicated with my present success. Knowing, as you do, my natural disposition, I cannot expect that such apprehensions will not suggest themselves to you.

      *   *   *   *   *

" Dr. Jenkyns seems warmly to participate in the pleasure I feel, and signified to me his intention of writing to you immediately."

The following letter refers to a complaint made by Mr. Jeudwine to the trustees on the score that Dr. Butler's arrangements were unfair towards the second master. The trustees supported Dr. Butler on every point.

FROM DR. KEATE.

"ETON, *March 24th*, 1830.

" DEAR DR. BUTLER,—I am afraid I must have appeared to you very rude and negligent ; but strange as it may seem, it is yet true, that I have been so occupied since I received your letter that I have not been able to put pen to paper. I have now found something like a leisure half-hour, and I proceed to answer your questions as distinctly as I can, but I must first express my surprise and regret that any one should wish to distrust those arrangements which have raised your school to its present state of prosperity and glory, which is sufficiently proved (in addition to numerous instances in former years) by the Senior Wrangler, the Pitt and Ireland Scholarships of the present year, upon which accumulation of honours I heartily wish you joy.

" I will now answer your questions nearly in the order in which you have put them.

" 1. The second or lower master, as he is called here (and he is the only master under the head-master who is recognised by the Statutes), does not hear the boys of the fifth or sixth or even of the fourth form—indeed no boys who belong to the upper school. His school consists of the first, second, and third forms : the third is the highest form under him. His school is quite distinct from the upper, and he appoints his own assistants, not without communication upon this point with the head-master, nor without the sanction of the provost. The number of the lower school at present is about fifty.

" 2. All the assistant masters of the upper school teach boys in higher classes than those taught by the second or lower master.

" 3. The fifth form is divided into three. I hear the sixth form and the upper division of the fifth. The two senior assistants hear the middle and lower division of the fifth : other assistants also share the duty of hearing the sixth and fifth forms when they say by heart.

" 4. A small salary is paid by the College to the upper and lower masters.

" The example of Eton seems all on your side. If your opponents appeal to that, your system is not likely to be disturbed. You have my sincere wishes that it may not be deranged.

" I send you a bill of the school, according to your request, as it stood in July last : the names of course are not all the same at present, but the numbers are nearly the same. As I know not by what other conveyance to send it, I send it, bulky as it is, by the post. I shall be glad to know the result of these commotions in your kingdom."

From the Rev. R. A. Thorp.

" C. C. C., *June 12th*, 1830.

" My dear Sir,—I have to thank you for having sent one of your pupils to stand here at our late election of a Lancashire Scholar.

" Mr. Bateson * acquitted himself so well as to make it a difficult matter to decide between him and the successful candidate ; his scholarship we were much pleased with, and in everything but composition he was quite equal to Mr. Wilson. I have only to beg you again to accept my best thanks for having sent Mr. Bateson, and to hope, when we have any other vacancy, you will allow me to communicate the circumstance to you."

From Nicholas Carlisle, Esq.

" Somerset Place, *June 19th*, 1830.

" My dear Friend,—
　　*　　　*　　　*　　　*　　　*

" Amidst the rage for novelties in this huge Leviathan, a Geographical Society is projected. I, as I know your taste and

---

* Afterwards Master of St. John's College, Cambridge. What passed between Bateson and Mr. Thorp on this occasion will be found in letters bearing dates February 10th—March 1st, 1831.

skill in that pleasing science, have caused your Name to be put down as a Member, together with my own.   When three hundred names are entered, a special meeting is to be called, and Rules and Contributions to be agreed upon.   At present it is proposed that an admission fee of £3, and an annual payment of £2, shall be the limitation; but if you do not like the company of Croker, and Barrow, and a long train of Scotch intriguers, pray let me know, that I may withdraw your name,—before you are troubled with any of their circular letters.

" If I can get to you in the Autumn, I will,—but the holidays at the Museum are so short, that they do not admit of either extension of journey or rational enjoyment when abroad—it was a woful day to me when the Royal Library was removed from the palace."

*   *   *   *   *

From Dr. Burton.

"Oxford, *June* 19*th*, 1830.

" My dear Sir,—I have the agreeable office of communicating to you another triumph.   We have managed to throw open a Craven Scholarship to the University at large, and Mr. Scott has been this day elected out of fourteen candidates.   I am *ex officio* one of the examiners, and I have no hesitation in saying that he was very decidedly superior to the others.   I will send you a set of the papers by the first opportunity.   I think I sent you those of the last Ireland examination.   In great haste.

" Yours very truly,
" E. Burton."

From Robert Scott, Esq., afterwards Master of Balliol and Dean of Rochester.

" Hutton Hall, Ayton, N.B., *July* 7*th*, 1830.

" Dear Dr. Butler,—As I came here to my grandfather's immediately on the commencement of the vacation, it was only by a circuitous communication that I received the very kind letter which you had written to my father, and for the kindness of which allow me to return my most sincere thanks, and again to assure you of my deep consciousness that anything which I have done is entirely owing to my having been your pupil—' It was not I, but Shrewsbury in my likeness.'   Allow me also to congratulate you upon the other memorabilia of the year. C. Kennedy and Hildyard have more than kept up our credit at Cambridge, so as to counterbalance Grove's losing the Latin verse with us.   The Kennedys are getting prizes by cartloads (' *Dicentur plaustris vexisse poemata* '); and if George keeps it up,

they will give us an admirable example of the classic cyclic poems
'*ad mea perpetuum tempora carmen.*'
"Ch. Ch. is claiming the 'eldest Hope' of that family because
he has taken a mastership under Dr. Longley. All the tutors are
quite envious, and afraid that after such education no one will
think it worth while to go to college at all!"

     *   *   *   *   *

To the Rev. J. P. Potter.

"Barmouth, *July 8th*, 1830.

"Rev. Sir,—I received your essay on the means of discovering
the senses of words, which you have done me the honour of
sending to me, just as I was stepping into my carriage ten days
ago on my way to this place. I beg to thank you for it, and can
assure you that I have read it with very great satisfaction. I am
delighted with the good taste and accuracy of discrimination
which pervade the whole work, and am persuaded it will be of
great use to boys in the higher forms at schools and to young
men at the University. I cannot quite agree with you in thinking that so much of the metaphysics of philology can be attained
by younger boys as you suppose them capable of. More than
thirty years' experience may perhaps give my opinion some weight
on this score, but I am satisfied that for boys in the higher forms
your book will be very useful.

"I have attempted something in the same way, though with
less logical and metaphysical severity, in my Praxis on the Latin
Prepositions, a copy of which I have ordered to be sent to
Messrs. Parkers for your acceptance.

"I shall now venture to throw a few remarks on paper for
your consideration, premising that I have no books or literature
here of any kind, and therefore you must take this αὐτοσχεδίασμα
with due allowance for want of all kinds of references; I suppose
even dictionary, grammar, or lexicon, to say nothing of classical
authors, are not likely to be heard of in the latitude of Barmouth.

"P. 79. I do not observe that you notice the use of *hic*
for 'my client,' because he stands next me, which affords a
peculiarly apt illustration of your explanation of this pronoun.

"P. 84. 'Annum jam audientem, idque Athenis.' You say here
in the translation the *id* might be left out, as it is merely wanted
to recall the *audientem*. I cannot understand this, as *idque* is
particularly emphatic here—a pupil of Cratippus, and that too
at Athens, as we might suppose a man who is pupil to an
eminent professor *in* the University to have more advantages than
out of it. Again, you say the *id* might be left out, but say nothing
about the *que*. But you could not say *Athenisque*—nay, you could
not even, not properly, say *atque Athenis*; *etiam Athenis*, you
might say it, but would not say it well; nor do I know any way

in which you could say what Cicero means to say so well as by *idque*, and therefore cannot see why in translation the emphatic *id* may be omitted, especially as he again refers to this very point of learning at Athens twice in the same sentence, speaking of the *auctoritas urbis et exempla*.

"P. 204. I am very much pleased with the accuracy of your observations on *que*, *et*, and *atque*. They are points which I am accustomed to impress more briefly on my boys by telling them that *que* couples more closely than *et* and *atque*. Your multitude of instances are in my opinion quite necessary to make the distinction clear and intelligible to youthful minds, and you have shown, if I may be allowed to say so, great tact, discrimination, and learning in selecting them.

"P. 217. 'Metaphors derived from weight.' This is a very acute and just observation.

"P. 227. 'We may remark the way that the use of the letter *c* and *q*,' etc. This is a very acute and, as far as I am aware, original observation, on which I have something more to say; but I must first stop to observe that the remainder of this paragraph from 'perhaps the *qu* was selected,' etc., to the end of the sentence '" *Curiosi*" at Rome' pleases me least of anything in the whole book.

"I must now go a little deeper into the metaphysics of philology than you have gone on this head, and I shall be gratified if I find that you approve of the substitution that I have to offer for the *qu* of *quæro*. It seems like a digression to begin by saying that *cum*, p. 67, is not derived from συν, but you will see how this assertion will be brought to bear on the subject.

"I will not assert that *cum* the adverb of time and *cum* the preposition are different words, for the primary notion of union appears in both; but *cum* the preposition cannot possibly be derived from συν. It has not one single element in common with it; *c* is not cognate with σ, υ is not cognate with the Latin *u*, and ν is not cognate with the Latin *m*—except you would refer to the termination of nouns in ον being changed into *um* in Latin, which is the change of a termination, and not of separate letters, and therefore not applicable to the present case.

"Now in my praxis I derive *cum* from ὁμοῦ, in which every element is consistent. *c* is consistent with ', *u* with ο, and *m* is identical. The two last of these assertions I need not prove. The first perhaps requires some illustration.

"The earliest Greek aspirates were (I place them in the order of their roughness):—

" 1. The roughest of all, the guttural χ—or in its very roughest state γ, in its smoother κ—combined with what I may call the middle aspirate, or what we now mark ', and what was formerly written *H*. This I may call the guttural aspirate.

" 2. *H* or '; this I may call the dental aspirate.

" 3. ͷ, the digamma, or what I would call the labial aspirate, which did not amount to so rough a breathing as *H*, but which required some more breathing than the mere *spiritus lenis*. Even of this I conceive there were two kinds, as of the χ: one where it was combined with the dental aspirate, as ͷυιος, which in our English characters might be written *wh*; and the other where the dental aspirate was wanting, as in ͷοινος, which might be written as *w* only.

"I need not go further in the much deeper and more varied guttural aspirations of the Hebrew or Arabic. I cannot even pronounce the Greek χ, and often call upon a Welsh boy (the language of this country has a singular affinity to that of the Greeks and Hebrews) to do it for me, when I want an example of its guttural power for the purposes of grammatical illustration.

"Now to the point. You recollect a line in Catullus, ' Chommoda dicebat, si quando commoda vellet,' *i.e.* he pronounced the *cum* or *com* of *commoda* as though it had been written with a χ. He gave more than the present aspiration of ὁμοῦ to the word, by pronouncing it as if it were χομοῦ. From such a Latin pronunciation as this, attempted to be softened down by persons of ears and organs less delicate than the Greeks, as the Romans certainly were, the guttural κ remained, though the dental aspirate was dropped, and thus I get the connection between the *c* of *cum* and the ' of ὁμοῦ.

"Now you observe, and justly, that *is* answers to *quis?* *ea* to *quæ?* *id* to *quid?* *tantus* to *quantus?* *talis* to *qualis?* etc., and so *tam quam*, *tot quot*, and *tum quum*. You observe again, and very acutely, pp. 228, 229, that the *qu* or *cu* in *quum* or *cum* originally expressed interrogation, and to this answer (as in analogical instances) was made by the similar sound *tum*. [All this is the result of a philosophical and reflecting mind; but I think you will grant, after what I have said, that your *quum*, with its two letters expressing interrogation, is different from my *cum*, with its *c* derived from the aspirate of ὁμοῦ; and though want of accuracy led the Romans to write *c* for *qu*, just as they wrote in a slovenly way *cui* for *quoi*, and *qui* for *quei*, yet I am advocate for preserving this distinction, and for writing *quum* when the adverb of time and *cum* when the preposition of union is meant to be used.] *

"But what is this *qu*? Certainly not the two first letters of *quæro*, which perhaps is derived from this very *qu*, and αἴρω. Not the *Cu* of *Curetes*, who, I suppose, derived their *Cu* from the Sabine word *Qu*-iris, a spear.

"I conceive it to be this. In all countries, but especially in those in which the feelings are warm and the imagination quick, as was, and is, the case in warmer and more Eastern climates,

---

* The part within brackets was cancelled in the draft.—Ed.

there is a greater natural impetuosity than in colder ones, and this would lead men in their ruder state and in the infancy of language to speak their words more vehemently, and to pour them forth, if I may say so, from the bottom of their hearts. This occasioned those deep and by us unutterable gutturals of the Oriental languages and of early Greece. But in asking questions there would be more than usual impetuosity among an eager and inquisitive people. Hence those words which are in general use as interrogatives would be most deeply articulated and would be all strongly aspirated. In process of time as language refined these aspirates would soften, and what is *chol* in Hebrew, and was first χολος in Greek, would become ὁλος ; and what was ὁλος would become still softened among nations of colder climates till it settled into *whole*, with the aspirated digamma.

"Now as ὁμοῦ becomes changed into *chom* or *com* or *cum*, so other words, especially of general interrogation, would be softened down, and the guttural part only of the χ would remain, instead of the guttural and aspirate : hence you would have *quis, quantus, quot, qualis*, etc., in Latin as interrogatives, the *qu* being sufficient to mark the earnestness of the speaker.

"That this is not merely chimerical may be seen by examination into other languages besides the Latin. Thus what in Latin is *qu* is in Greek ' and in English *wh*. The original rough ὁπου of the Greeks was softened into που, ὁποῖος into ποῖος and κοῖος, ὁποσος into ποσσος, ὁποτε into ποτε, and so on ὁπως into πως.

"The deep guttural of the Greeks was diluted by the Saxons (who, I suppose, received it from the Scythians or Sarmatians north of Greece) into the aspirated digamma.

"Hence we have for our general interrogatives *w*ho, *w*hich, *w*hat, *w*hen, *w*hy, *w*here, *w*hence, etc. I need not remark on the close affinity between *qu* and *w*, and how far our who, where, when, whence, etc., is the Scottish quho, quhair, quhen, quhence, etc., thus connecting the Roman and Saxon forms.

"Your observation about the answer to *quum* being made (as in analogical instances) by the similar sound *tum* is very true, and I think affords a strong confirmation of my theory of the origin of these sounds, for it is singular that in almost all instances the answer is made by the thinnest of the cognate mutes : ποσος, τοσος, οιος, τοιος, ποτε, τοτε, etc. ; qualis, talis, quantus, tantus, quum, tum, etc. ; when, then, where, there, which, this, whence, thence, etc. This cannot be chance—there must be a cause for it ; and if I have not assigned the right one, I shall be very thankful to anybody who will give me a better.

"I have to beg your pardon for troubling you with so long a letter. You owe it to the pleasure I have received from your book, and the opportunity I have of a little leisure here ; for had I been at Shrewsbury, I could only have returned you my thanks in a few words. I shall be gratified in knowing that you have received this unmerciful packet, and in any opportunity that may occur of seeing you at Shrewsbury.

"I remain, dear Sir,
"Your obliged and faithful servant,
"S. BUTLER."

To H.R.H. THE DUKE OF SUSSEX.

" August 20th, 1830.

"SIR,—I have the honour to present to your Royal Highness an attempt in my humble capacity of archdeacon to reform and simplify the ecclesiastical laws relating to my office. The inquisitorial *farrago* which I have swept away is really curious as a specimen of the exercise of spiritual authority, especially where it relates to the laity. I venture to hope that I have made what I now substitute plain and intelligible to all parties whom it affects ; and though the labour is confined to an humble subject, I venture to offer it to your Royal Highness, knowing that you despise nothing, however humble, which is likely to be useful.

"I am, Sir,
"Your Royal Highness's most dutiful and faithful servant,
"S. BUTLER."

I found no copy of the scheme above referred to among Dr. Butler's papers, nor any notes or other trace of it.

FROM THE REV. A. C. BROMEHEAD.

"ECKINGTON, October 4th, 1830.

"DEAR SIR,—I have been applied to in a matter wherein I should like to be favoured with your opinion. A man of bad character married into a respectable family in this parish. She (his wife) is dead and buried in the part of the churchyard appropriated to the sepulture of his wife's family, and was buried at their expense. He is desirous of putting up a headstone, and they think with a view of taking possession of a part of their burial-ground. They wish me to prevent him from putting up the headstone ; but I am not quite sure of the power a minister has to prevent the introduction of tombstones, provided the party wishing to put up the stone be willing to pay the usual fee. 'Tis true the claim of 5*s.* for a headstone and 10*s.* for a flat stone seems to imply a power to refuse the introduction of the stone altogether. But *quere*, has not custom sanctioned a right on the part of the parishioners to bring tombs into the churchyard on the parties paying the usual fee ?

"There is a clause in your printed directions to the churchwardens forbidding the introduction of heavy cattle into the churchyard. Is this meant totally to exclude cows or heavy horses? The latter I think very dangerous, on account of stamping on the flat tombstones with iron shoes; but cows put in occasionally can't, I think, do much harm; and indeed I don't see how a country churchyard can be kept decent without either cows or horses being admitted. The grass gets so long that the headstones are half hid, and the long grass is very troublesome in making graves. I believe that (although objectionable) the parson's horse has from time immemorial had the depasturing of the churchyard in country places; but this is a custom much better discontinued. Cows I never knew do any mischief, although I have known them for years in this churchyard. Something must consume the grass, because to mow it is impossible on account of the unevenness of the surface. I shall also esteem your opinion on this subject a favour. The family alluded to are anxious to have your opinion at your earliest convenience. I hope my son conducts himself to your satisfaction."

Cows now are never seen in a churchyard; but when I was young, in my father's parish certain of the cottagers who kept a cow used regularly to turn their cows into the churchyard to eat the coarser grass which sheep would not touch, and this, so far as my recollection serves, was the practice of the neighbouring parishes. In Gunning's reminiscences of Cambridge the following passage (Vol. II., p. 263) bears upon the same practice:—

"During ——'s first year at Gorleston he was very popular with his parishioners, who fully believed his representations of the cruel persecutions he had undergone at Cambridge; but after a time their confidence in him was shaken, and constant contentions were the result, in which he usually came off victorious, as his parishioners had great dread of lawsuits. Among many claims he made was the right of removing from the churchyard all gravestones that chanced to be thrown down by cattle, which he kept there himself. When subsequently building a house these gravestones were used for the pavement of a scullery and also of an oven, out of which it was reported that a huge loaf was drawn 'AGED 73.'

" He died in April 1832, after a long and painful illness, in the sixty-sixth year of his age."

FROM ROBERT SCOTT, ESQ.

"CH. CH., *December 24th*, 1830.

" MY DEAR SIR,—Having had the pleasure of being made a student of Ch. Ch. this day, I think that there are none beyond the circle of my own relations to whom I am more bound to communicate it than to yourself. And certainly next to the Dean who gave me it for what I had done, no one has a better claim to my gratitude than you, under whose auspices I learned everything that procured it for me. I assure you I often try to compare what, thanks to you, I am with what I certainly should have been if I had not been so fortunate as to have been under you ; and I trust I never shall forget how much I owe to Shrewsbury.

"I was much gratified to hear of the success of the play this Christmas, and wished earnestly to have been able to see it. But wishes will not alter the Calendar term, and our tutors would think an English play but a sorry excuse for deserting a Greek one. So here I was obliged to stay past the time of its performance ; and as at collections the Dean was kind enough to offer me the studentship, I was too glad to remain the week intervening before the election. To-night I set off for Ludlow, and am to stay with the Beales for a week ; from thence I must return to commence, before term begins, my direct reading for the Ireland. As to this scholarship I am in a very great perplexity : for I am conscious, on the one hand, that a great deal is expected from me on account of my last year's place, and that it would look very disgraceful if I seemed to relax in my exertions after having received this reward from my College ; while, on the other, I feel that the course of reading, etc., here is so far from making me more fit for the trial than I was last time, that, fresh as I was, I actually had an advantage from my having come newly from school. However, I shall of course do my best, and exert myself to appear at least by my diligence, if not success, grateful to those who have such claims upon me."

To Robert Scott, Esq.

"Emmanuel Lodge, *January* 1st, 1831.

"Dear Scott,—Though I hardly know where a letter will be likely to find you, I think it best to send my congratulations to Oxford, from which place the cause of them is derived. Possibly Mrs. Butler and myself may pass through if we return home from Eton, as I have some thought of doing.

"The Dean has done you an act of kindness not the less valuable for its being just, as well as highly honourable to him and to yourself. Read for the Ireland and fear not ; even should you fail you cannot but acquit yourself with great credit. Accept my best thanks for what you have done already for the credit of Shrewsbury School, and what I trust you will yet do on more than one occasion. My first letter in the new year is this of congratulation—I will only add *multos et felices.*

"Believe me, dear Sir,
"Your very sincere friend,
"S. BUTLER."

FROM THE REV. R. A. THORP.

"C. C. C., *February* 10th, 1831.

"MY DEAR SIR,—I beg to inform you, as I have done on other occasions, that we are about to fill up three scholarships now vacant in our society. Two of them are confined to persons born in the diocese of Exeter, and one to natives of the county of Gloucester. I need not say how glad we shall be to find amongst the candidates any who have had the very great advantage of being pupils of yours.

"Allow me to take this opportunity of mentioning a subject which has given me considerable pain. A pupil of yours, whose name I will not mention, applied through a friend in Oxford to me to know if he could stand here without testimonials from you, inasmuch as he feared he should fail of procuring such, as you felt very indignant at one of your pupils who had been a candidate for a Lancashire Scholarship not having been elected by us to it. I was not the least aware of your considering your pupil aggrieved on that occasion, or that you bore towards us any grudge in consequence, and I freely mention the circumstance to you, because I believe there is either a mistake or misunderstanding respecting it. I thought highly of your pupil, and I expressed myself so to you in a letter afterwards. But I think you yourself, if the whole examination had been laid before you, would have decided as we did. We still, however, thanked you for having sent up so good a scholar as a candidate, and I think I mentioned the feeling of the College on that subject in my letter to you. I trust, however, there is no ground for the story at all, and I am sure, for my part, I never had the slightest suspicion of any displeasure on your part."

TO THE REV. R. A. THORP.

"*February* 14th, 1831.

"DEAR SIR,—Two candidates intend to offer themselves for scholarship at Corpus from this school. Templer, a Devonshire boy, and Waller, of Gloucestershire: of the good conduct and moral character of both I can speak in the highest terms—of their attainments the examiners must judge for themselves.

"As you fairly enter upon the subject of the last examination of one of my pupils, I will be quite candid in my reply. I was dissatisfied, and I had resolved never to volunteer sending another candidate to you, but I never said that I would not give any boy who applied to me a testimonial, and in fact I have been asked for and readily consented to give testimonials to the two boys in question. They are highly deserving boys, and I trust my direct and plain answer to the question you have asked me will be no disadvantage to them in their examination. It becomes me to give you a statement of my reason for dissatisfaction, which I hope you will take in good part, and which I also hope may lead to an explanation satisfactory to all parties.

"With regard to the merits of the respective candidates on the occasion I allude to, I can say nothing, having had no opportunity of judging. I am not foolish enough to suppose that a boy whom I bring forward may not meet with competitors much better qualified than himself, and if the business had been one of mere examination of the candidates I should have concluded that the examiners did their duty between the candidates according to the best of their judgement, and there the matter would have ended.

"The statement which I took down from Bateson on his return here is in substance as follows.

"That he was asked a number of questions by you respecting me which I can hardly conceive a gentleman would feel himself justified in putting to the pupil of any respectable master.

"One of these was, whether I was not in the habit of particularly preparing boys for examinations of this sort (in plain words therefore, whether I did not cram them, as it is called, for a particular purpose, instead of giving them general and scholarlike knowledge): to which he indignantly and truly answered in the negative. Another was, whether I did not give private instructions, and what I charged for doing so—which met with the same answer. A third was, whether I actually attended the school myself—as if I reaped the fruits of a deputy's talents and labours. Surely, sir, the station I hold might exempt me from indignities like these.

"Another question was to give you an accurate account of a week's work here—which he did. He then says that, having learnt that English themes formed no part of this (in fact they are written in a lower part of the school), you particularly asked him if he had done any English themes, and that to this he answered 'No'; that after this the whole composition given in the examination consisted of two English themes and a copy of Latin verses; no Latin theme—no Greek prose—no Greek verse —no Lyrics—all of which he had told you were part of the week's work here—were set. In the course of this examination, he says, you asked him if the examination was as hard as he had expected, and if he had read the parts he was examined in, which I hold to be very unfair and ensnaring questions—though he answered them fairly, which is more than every candidate is likely to do. With regard to the former of these questions, it was asked him on the Wednesday night, when there was yet a day and a half of the examination to come, and to this was added a question whether as much composition had been set as he had expected: to which he replied 'No.'   He was then asked what he expected more: to which he replied, 'Greek composition.'   The next question was, 'Would that have helped you?'   His answer was, 'I think it would.'   No more composition was set, though it was allowed by young B. that the candidates were so nearly equal that it was difficult to decide, and they would probably have made the decision easier.

"These are the points, in a short compass, on which I feel that I have ground of dissatisfaction.   As you have entered on the subject I have fairly stated them.   I hope they may not be prejudicial to the two present candidates from this school, neither of whom are nearly so much versed in composition of any kind as Bateson was—in fact they have scarcely begun to compose in Greek.

"I am, dear Sir, your obedient, faithful servant,

"S. BUTLER."

FROM THE REV. R. A. THORP, CORPUS CHRISTI COLLEGE.

"*February 24th*, 1831.

"MY DEAR SIR,—I have to acknowledge the receipt of your letter of the 14th inst.; and when I add that I read it with unmixed amazement, I feel that the expression will hardly convey a just idea of my utter unconsciousness that the few passing words I exchanged with Mr. Bateson could have been so misinterpreted and abused.   I have hitherto been prevented by a press of other duties from replying, but I take the earliest leisure to give you the very fullest explanation, and shall be truly glad if the causes of your dissatisfaction are removed.

"In the first place let me preface thus much—that your pupil had a sort of a claim on my notice, and I felt desirous as far as I could to notice him, remembering that when I stood myself a word of recognition from any one of the electors would have been a great encouragement to me.   Under such circumstances, where both parties are unexpectedly thrown together, one is often puzzled to find conversation; and what so natural in the case of a boy fresh from school as to ask how he liked school, what he did there, and so forth?   And I say this because I am just as likely as not to make the same or similar remarks to any boy who comes to me from any school direct.   To fancy that every such question has beneath it a deeply concerted meaning or covert indignity is really to make one's words as significant as the celebrated shake of Lord Burleigh's wig.   In fact I spoke to Bateson just what occurred to me at the moment on the occasions when I was

obliged to meet him; and so far from there being anything con-
strained in his replies, he was disposed to speak to me of school
with just as much freedom as he seems to have spoken of college
on his return.

"Having said thus much generally, I proceed to the several
causes of offence enumerated. With regard to the first, I did ask
if he had been reading out of school hours with a view to the
present examination. It would surely have been no discredit to
him to have done so, or to you to have directed him. When an
undergraduate here is about to undergo any important examination—as, for his degree, the Ireland Scholarship, fellowships at
Oriel, Balliol, etc.—he not only has, but expects to have, assistance from his tutor beyond and above the course of ordinary
lectures; nay, from them he is often altogether excused, in order
to be enabled to devote his time exclusively to the special examination before him.

"Masters of some of the highest and best schools have asked
of me beforehand what kind of reading and composing would be
most likely to promote the success of their pupils in our examination, and I have recommended books, and in the case of rejected
candidates who could stand a second time I have particularised
the causes of failure for the very purpose of directing their
master's attention to those deficiencies. All this, both at college
and school, may by you be called 'cramming' (for I never used
the word nor expressed myself in the coarse manner which appears
to have been reported to you); but surely it is of little moment
if a boy can produce the knowledge in his own person from what
wiser head he derived it. Therefore there could be no indignity
meant in my question, inasmuch as I should have thought it very
creditable to all parties if your pupil had been 'particularly prepared.' As to the inference drawn, in which lies the sting, that I
entirely disclaim.

"The two next questions are much distorted; but I will tell
you what I did wish to know, and why that information was
desirable for me. I am often asked to recommend schools, and
on one of these occasions had been urgent with a friend of mine
to send his son to Shrewsbury. The boy was young, and his
father was anxious to know if he would come at all, at first, under
your care and instruction in school or out of it. Every one
knows that at Eton, Westminster, Winchester, and other schools
the head-master does not teach any but the higher forms, and
has under him other masters to take the care of the lower parts
of the school. Therefore I asked when a boy came under you.
I never inquired whether you attended the school yourself, but
I said interrogatively, 'I suppose Dr. Butler does not teach all the
school himself? Is there any system of private tuition?' If you
are acquainted with the practice at Eton, you will see at once
what I meant, where the lessons, though said in school, are learned

under a private tutor at their boarding-houses. There again I am obliged to correct the form of my questions, and again to disclaim altogether your inferences.

"To proceed. I perfectly recollect asking for an account of a week's studies at Shrewsbury. I was comparing, in my own mind, the studies there with those pursued here. Your pupils have lately proved themselves great proficients in scholarship, and I confess I should have been glad to borrow any hint from your system in improvement of our own.

"I think I need not reply to what you insinuate, that there was a disposition to take your pupil at a disadvantage in the progress of the examination. From the indignity of such a suspicion I too, in your words, might be exempted. I simply say this much, that we are by our statutes obliged to require Latin verse, that it has always been our practice to set most store by English composition, but I asked of Bateson if he had been practised in English themes in order to make all allowance in his favour with regard to those exercises, and that the plan of the whole written examination is arranged long before the candidates present themselves, and that all of it is printed which can be so—a practice now generally adopted throughout the University.

"After the examination was over I spoke as kindly as I could to Bateson, and commended his examination. He made a pettish reply (the only time he did so), and appears to have impressed you with very incorrect notions of the treatment he received here. As to the result of the election, our judgement turned more on the *vivâ-voce* separate construings than upon the quality of the exercises.

"I have, in conclusion, to thank you for your candour, and for the power you have given me of endeavouring to satisfy your mind that you have mistaken both me and my words. What I, to adopt the same freedom, have to be sorry for is that you make imputations of motives and design which my words will not bear out, and which I think the station I hold ought to protect me from. Had you, for instance, met any pupil of mine and asked him if he had any extra help from me previous to taking his degree, if he was under the care of the tutors, or only instructed by one, or if the public tutors took private pupils or not, I should not have concluded you had any meaning beyond a passing inquiry in such questions; and if my pupil had told me you had covert design in what you asked, I should have impressed upon him that he must have been mistaken, and that your character protected you from the imputation. But even without any ground you have permitted yourself to think and write unworthily, when you twice say you hope your freedom of remark will not injure the new candidates from your school. However, I will not press this point beyond merely mentioning it. I thank you again for your unreserved statement. I have shown by the length of my reply my wish to satisfy you, and it ought to be satisfactory to you to know that, whilst the questions with some alterations are allowed, the interpretations of them are altogether disclaimed.

"I remain, with undiminished regard, very faithfully,

"R. A. Thorp."

To the Rev. R. A. Thorp.

"Shrewsbury, *March 1st,* 1831.

"My dear Sir,—I must beg leave to inform you that I have only this afternoon received by post your letter dated February 24th, and bearing the Oxford postmark of February 27th. This will I hope satisfactorily account to you for a silence which might otherwise appear the result of premeditated rudeness or delay.

"As you are good enough to disclaim any intention of hurting my feelings by the questions which you put to Bateson, I very readily acquiesce in your disavowal, and beg to thank you for your courtesy in making it; but as you appear to impute to me something like precipitance in taking up the matter too warmly and in listening to a perverted account, I will beg to add a few words in my own justification on that head.

"I took down the account from the boy's lips as he returned. He is a boy whose manners are blunt, but whose word may as safely be relied on as that of any person I know. I have again examined him to-day, and he does not make the slightest difference in his account; and though he may, and indeed must, have been mistaken in one point, I am sure he makes no wilful misrepresentation. He says that he still believes your first question to have been, not whether I taught the upper form (which in fact is all I do teach, though I examine some form every week), but whether I taught at all in the upper school. I should also have placed much less stress on this and all the other questions had he not told me (and he now repeats the declaration) that he inquired of several of the other candidates whether you had asked them similar questions, and that they uniformly answered in the negative. It was this which made them look pointed in his case. Farther, with regard to the arrangement of the examination previously to the candidates coming up, he told me then, and he repeats it now, that so far as the printed papers were concerned he doubts not that the whole was previously arranged, but that the subjects for the English themes were brought in with the ink wet, and that they thus formed an exception to the rest of the examination, which exception, after the questions put to him, did seem to him remarkable, especially as two English themes were set.

"Now though you have kindly explained this, and though I find that your inquiries were dictated by nothing but a blameless curiosity or even a friendly intention towards him or myself, under the circumstances I have stated I cannot but think myself excusable for the view I took of them. I rejoice to find myself mistaken, and I beg in my turn to apologise to you for my error, for such I must now consider it, though I trust you will see by this explanation that it was not taken up on light or captious grounds.

"Hoping that we have now brought this matter to a mutually satisfactory conclusion,

"I remain, dear Sir, yours faithfully,

"S. BUTLER."

END OF VOL. I.